Praise for *The Wish List*

'Feel-good and enormous fun. It's a...'
Sophie Kinsella, *Sunday [Times]*
author of Love...

'I love this author – her writing... root for her characters and won't stop laughing until the end... the perfect rom-com to take on a staycation.'
Daily Mail

'*The Wish List* is packed full of wit, warmth and heart. I loved seeing Flo bloom as she learns to ask herself what she really wants from life.'
Beth O'Leary, *Sunday Times* bestselling author of *The Flatshare*

'Sophia Money-Coutts cements her stance as the new Queen of rom-coms. The perfect holiday read (or just for when you need a pick-me-up). Pacey, laugh-out-loud funny and heart-warming.'
Evening Standard

'Impossibly hilarious yet also so hopeful and heart-warming to boot – I read it in a day!'
Abbie Greaves, author of *The Silent Treatment*

'Smartly written with humour, warmth and some very saucy scenes, it's a modern romance to savour.'
Sunday Mirror

'Funny and biting, I couldn't get enough.'
Laura Jane Williams, author of *The Love Square*

'Equally saucy and heart-warming, *The Wish List* will satisfy all your cravings for a fix of feel-good fiction.'
Red

'Funny, touching and totally addictive. I've got a smile on my face now just thinking about it!'
Zara Stoneley, author of *The First Date*

'Saucy... fizzing comedy meets light-touch feminism in this slice of escapism.'
Metro

Sophia Money-Coutts is a journalist and author who spent five years studying the British aristocracy while working as Features Director at *Tatler*. Prior to that she worked as a writer and an editor for the *Evening Standard* and the *Daily Mail* in London, and *The National* in Abu Dhabi. She's a columnist for the *Sunday Telegraph* and the *Evening Standard* and often appears on radio and television channels talking about important topics such as Prince Harry's wedding and the etiquette of the three-some. *The Wish List* is her third novel.

**Also by
Sophia Money-Coutts**

What Happens Now?
The Plus One

The Wish List

SOPHIA MONEY-COUTTS

ONE PLACE. MANY STORIES

HQ
An imprint of HarperCollins*Publishers* Ltd
1 London Bridge Street
London SE1 9GF

www.harpercollins.co.uk

HarperCollins*Publishers*
1st Floor, Watermarque Building, Ringsend Road
Dublin 4, Ireland

This edition 2021

2
First published in Great Britain by
HQ, an imprint of HarperCollins*Publishers* Ltd 2020

Copyright © Sophia Money-Coutts 2020

Sophia Money-Coutts asserts the moral right to be
identified as the author of this work.
A catalogue record for this book is
available from the British Library.

ISBN: 978-0-00-837057-2

MIX
Paper from
responsible sources
FSC
www.fsc.org
FSC™ C007454

This book is produced from independently certified FSC™ paper
to ensure responsible forest management.

For more information visit: www.harpercollins.co.uk/green

This book is set in 11.5/16 pt. Bembo

Printed and Bound in the UK using 100% Renewable Electricity at
CPI Group (UK) Ltd

For Vix, my brave friend.

'Be careful what you wish for, you may receive it.'

THE SORT OF THING YOUR GRANDMOTHER
SAID BUT, ACTUALLY, IT'S ANONYMOUS.

THE LIST

- LIKES CATS.
- INTERESTING JOB. NOT GOLF-PLAYING INSURANCE BORE LIKE HUGO.
- BOTTOM AND SEXUAL ATHLETICISM OF JAMES BOND.
- NICE MOTHER.
- NO POINTY SHOES.
- NO HAWAIIAN SHIRTS.
- NO UMBRELLAS.
- READS BOOKS. NOT JUST SPORTS BIOGRAPHIES.
- NO REVOLTING BATHROOM HABITS. E.G. SKID MARKS.
- AMBITIOUS.
- ADVENTUROUS.
- GOOD MANNERS. E.G. SAYS THANK YOU IF SOMEONE HOLDS THE DOOR OPEN FOR HIM.
- ISN'T OBSESSED WITH INSTAGRAM OR HIS PHONE.
- FUNNY.
- ACTUALLY TEXTS ME BACK.
- DOESN'T MIND ABOUT MY COUNTING.

CHAPTER ONE

'TWO, FOUR, SIX, EIGHT, ten...' I muttered, taking the steps two at a time. Shit. Eleven steps. An odd number meant that dinner was going to be bad.

That absurd evening at Claridge's was where it started. That was how the list came about. As the quietest member of my loud, combative family, I often dreaded dinner with them. But I suspected this evening would be especially painful, which was why I counted the steps from the Hyde Park underpass into the evening sunlight. It was a game I called Consequences. If there'd been an even number of steps, the dinner would be all right. It would pass without drama and prove my family could behave normally. But no, eleven bastard steps. That dinner was always going to be tricky.

Technically, it was a celebratory evening because Mia had become engaged to Hugo. My half-sister had agreed to marry a man with all the intelligence and sensitivity of a spatula and everyone was meant to be excited. Patricia, my stepmother, had almost spontaneously combusted with joy at the idea of her daughter marrying a man who wore a signet ring, drove a Mercedes, belonged to a Surrey golf club and earned over £200,000 a year working for an insurance firm called Wolf & Partners.

I was less excited. I knew why Mia had said yes. Everyone seemed to say yes these days. They said yes in private, on a beach or up a mountain, then rushed to tell their 652 closest friends on Instagram that they'd said yes, sometimes with the hashtag #ISaidYes to underline the point. A lunatic hashtag since nobody was ever going to put up a photo above the hashtag #ISaidNo, were they?

Mia had posted her picture from the terrace of an expensive Italian restaurant a week ago. The shot was mostly of her left hand in front of her chest so we could all see the diamond as big as an eyeball on her finger. Her nails were fuchsia, her blonde bob was brushed and her face was smooth with make-up designed to look natural but had, in fact, taken Mia over an hour to put on that morning – she'd found the engagement ring a month earlier in Hugo's boxer shorts' drawer and realized he was about to propose.

You could just see Hugo behind Mia in this picture, as if he was trying to photobomb his own engagement shot. Underneath, Mia hadn't just written #ISaidYes, but also #sparkly, #dreamscometrue, #heputaringonit, #shinebright-likeadiamond, #happytears, #togetherforever and, finally, just #love. I'd spent a good deal of time scowling at this picture, trying to decide which hashtag was the worst. Was referencing both Beyoncé and Rihanna in a social-media post designed to alert the world to your engagement something you had to do now? I was thirty-two, but nonsense like this made me feel 900 years old.

I shook my head again at the thought of those hashtags. My half-sisters and I were different. I'd always known that. Mia and Ruby had confidence, hair that did what it was told and an intricate understanding of which Kardashian sister was which. I had none of those things. Still, we'd grown up together and remained living together in our narrow childhood house in south London. They were closer to one another than they were to me, almost their own separate little gang of two. I minded this some days, when I heard them laughing in one another's bedroom, or when they draped their legs over one another on our sofa in front of the TV while I always sat in a separate armchair. On better days, I told myself this was just biology. They were full sisters, I couldn't compete with that. But, while it might not have been fully reciprocated, I loved them as if they were my full sisters and figured it was better to co-exist with their bad habits (wiping mascara on the towels, never putting a mug in the dishwasher, eating my yoghurt) rather than move somewhere else and risk flatmates that were even worse.

I never thought one of them could be so different that she'd decide to marry the most boring man in Britain. And yet here we were, all off to Claridge's to say 'Cheers!' because Mia had declared that was where she wanted the wedding in less than four months' time. It seemed quick, as if she wanted to lock Hugo down as fast as possible, but Mia said winter weddings were more 'chic' than summer weddings.

She would have berries in her flower arrangement and mulled wine at the reception. Her head was full of these intricate details. She'd also already decided that Ruby and I would be her bridesmaids so I gloomily anticipated wearing something the colour of sick.

All of us were going to Claridge's that night, apart from my father, that is, since he was the British ambassador to Argentina and for the past six years had lived in an Edwardian mansion in Buenos Aires. He couldn't fly home for the dinner, he'd apologetically emailed me to explain, because he had a meeting with one of Argentina's biggest soybean exporters.

If Dad was back, I'd be rolling along the pavement with a bounce. Although we emailed every couple of weeks (I'd update him on new history books; he'd send me back brief updates, mostly about the weather), I missed his physical presence and wished he was closer, more in my life. However, the soybean magnate took precedence and so, gathered that night would be me, the happy couple, Patricia and Ruby. So long as she showed up. Ruby – blessed with the cheekbones of Kate Moss and breasts of a Barbie doll – was a model. Or trying to be a model. She'd been signed to an agent for a few years but had only been cast in magazine adverts for washing powder and toothpaste. Recently she'd been asked by Senokot, the constipation brand, to star in a series of posters for the Tube but turned them down. 'You'd never catch Kylie Jenner doing that, Flo,' she'd declared in the kitchen at home.

Still, she thought of herself as a 'creative artist', which meant she seemed to operate on a different timescale to the rest of us, as if time was a bourgeois construct she didn't need to bother with.

One Christmas, Ruby didn't come home until long after we'd finished the turkey, by which point Patricia was halfway down a bottle of Bailey's and demanding that Dad use one of his government contacts to find out where she was. This far-fetched idea was forgotten when Ruby waltzed through the door sometime after five, claiming that her phone battery had died, the buses weren't working and her credit card had been stopped which, in turn, meant that her Uber account was frozen. 'Oh my poor darling,' Patricia had slurred, clasping Ruby to her chest. 'We must get you another credit card. Henry? HENRY! Can you order Ruby another card?'

I shook my head again. Patricia would almost certainly overdo it that night, ordering bottle after bottle of champagne, and the only topic of conversation would be the wedding. At home in Kennington, there'd been little discussion of anything else since Mia returned from Puglia, flicking her engagement ring about the kitchen like a knuckle-duster. It was 'the wedding' this and 'the wedding' that, as if there'd never been a wedding in history before, nor would be after it. Should Ruby or I ever choose to get married ourselves, I imagined that Mia's wedding would still be referred to as 'the wedding' in our family. Not that this was likely, I reminded myself.

Because although I was thirty-two and had two arms, two legs and a face with its features in vaguely the right places (I hated my thin upper lip), I'd never had a boyfriend. Never been in love. True, there'd been a five-week fling at Edinburgh when I'd fallen for a second-year history student called Rich. But I'd ruined this by being too keen. I'd assumed after our first night together that he was my boyfriend, not realizing that Rich thought otherwise. He kept sneaking into my halls at 2, 3 and 4 a.m. during those brief first weeks when I'd found myself bewitched by a man for the first time, but there was a Thursday evening not long afterwards when my friend Sarah said she'd seen him snogging another girl in the Three Witches. I plucked up the courage to text him about it and Rich replied 'What are you, my wife?' The pain was so intense and sharp I felt like a small child who'd stuck their finger into a flame. That was the end of Rich.

I'd had precisely three very short flings since, one-night stands really, although I didn't realize they were one-night stands at the time. You don't, do you? I thought each one might be the start of something. Perhaps this one would finally be my boyfriend? Or the next one? Or the one after that? But they never morphed into boyfriends and I never fell in love because, after sleeping with me, they never texted or called me back. I'd tried to pretend I didn't care after that.

No point in boyfriends, I told myself, when newspapers and magazines were full of women grumbling about relationships. 'Dear Suzy, my boyfriend wants me to talk dirty every time we have sex and I've run out of vocabulary. What do you advise?' Or 'Dear Suzy, my husband always puts the empty milk carton back into the fridge instead of the bin. Should I divorce him?' If I ever wrote a letter like this, I would ask 'Dear Suzy, I'm thirty-two and I've never been in love but I'm pretty happy with life, although I still live with my sisters and I have a couple of weird habits. Sometimes I think not having a boyfriend by my age makes me strange, but can you ever tell in advance if someone's going to hurt you?'

I stopped on the pavement and looked up at the façade of Claridge's for a quick pep talk. Listen up, Florence Fairfax, this is going to be a cheerful evening and you will smile throughout. You will not look as sombre as if you're at your own funeral because your sister is marrying a man who judges others by their golf handicap. You will sound convincing when everyone clinks glasses. You will not count every mouthful. Get it together.

I glanced at my feet and realized I'd forgotten the heels I'd carried into work that morning in a plastic Boots bag and I'd have to wear my work shoes instead. Black, with velcro straps and a thick rubber sole, they were the sort of shoes you see advertised for elderly men in the back of Sunday supplements. I wore them because I spent all day on my feet working in a Chelsea bookshop. Who cared if I looked like an escapee from a retirement home? I was mostly behind the till or a table piled with hardbacks. Except now I had to attend Mia's celebratory dinner at Claridge's looking like someone who'd had a recent bunion operation and been issued a pair of orthopaedic shoes.

Hopefully nobody would notice. I smiled at the doorman standing beside the hotel entrance in his top hat and pushed through the revolving door into the lobby.

★

'Florence darling, what on earth have you got on your feet?' Patricia asked, loudly enough for several other tables to hear. Mia and Hugo were already there.

'Sorry,' I muttered, leaning down to kiss my stepmother on the cheek. 'Left my other shoes in the shop.'

'Well sit down quickly and nobody will see them,' Patricia carried on, nodding at an empty chair. 'I've ordered some champagne.' She was a woman with birdlike features – hooked nose, beady eyes – who minded about the wrong shoes and the right champagne very much. Twenty-five years earlier, she'd joined the civil service as a secretary called Pat and observed that those who progressed quickest seemed to be in a secret club. They wore the same suits and had the same accents. They talked about tennis as if it was a religion, not just a sport. She very much wanted to be part of that club, so she saved up to buy a suit from Caroline Charles, upgraded from 'Pat' to 'Patricia' and stopped saying toilet. She clocked my father as a target. He was a grieving widower whose wife had recently been killed in a car crash and was talked of as a rising star in the department. Patricia moved in quickly. Marrying someone from this club would guarantee entry into it.

Within a year, Dad had proposed and she was living in our Kennington house. I was three and seemed to have observed these changes in my life in bewildered silence. Mia came along another year on, which meant I was bumped from my first-floor bedroom up a flight into a new room which overlooked the street. Ruby was born the year after that, and I ascended into the attic.

'Hi, guys,' I said, standing over Mia and Hugo. Their heads were both bent to the table; Mia was reading a brochure, Hugo was tapping at his phone.

'Oh, I don't know. We could have it in the French saloon but it can only seat 120 people. Hi, Flo,' said Mia, glancing up and waving a hand in the air as if swatting a fly before looking back to her brochure.

I'd never liked 'Flo'. It made me think of Tampax. I'd been christened Florence after my maternal grandmother, a thin, energetic Frenchwoman who lived in an old farmhouse outside Bordeaux surrounded by village cats and apricot trees. I'd spent long stretches of my summer holidays there when I was younger, bribed to pick up fallen fruit. If I collected several baskets a day, Grandmère poured me a glass of watered-down wine that evening. It had been our secret and I adored her for it, for treating me like a grown-up when nobody else seemed to, when nobody else would talk to me about Mum and I was scared that I'd forget her. If anyone had dared called Grandmère 'Flo', she would have sworn at them in French. She'd died when I was fifteen and I'd clung to my proper name ever since, as if it still linked me to those summers, although I'd long since given up correcting my sisters.

'Hugo, say hello to Flo,' added Mia.

'Hullo, Flo,' said Hugo, raising his head from his phone and smiling weakly before lowering his gaze to his screen again. Honestly, I'd met more interesting skirting boards. If he was physically attractive I might have understood, but he looked like a pencil in a suit: tall and gangly, with an overly gelled hairline that had started receding, carving out the shape of a large 'M' on his forehead.

I looked from Hugo's head to the table before sitting down. Five place settings, two candlesticks and one fishbowl of white roses equalled eight, which was fine because that was an even number.

'Where's Ruby?' I asked as a waiter appeared with a bottle of champagne and held it in front of Patricia.

Patricia nodded at him. 'Very good. On her way from a casting, didn't you say, Mia?'

'She said she might be late but we should go ahead.' Mia held up her champagne flute and watched as the waiter poured, then held it up for a toast.

'Everyone ready?' she said. 'Here's to me. And Hugo,' she added quickly. 'Here's to us, and to the best wedding ever.' She squealed and scrunched her face as if on the verge of ecstasy at the thought of herself in a white dress.

'Darling, I couldn't be prouder,' said Patricia.

'So exciting!' I lied as we clinked glasses.

Hugo winced and patted his chest – he had weirdly thin fingers too – as he put his glass down on the table. 'Mia, have you brought any Rennie with you? You know champagne always gives me heartburn.'

Ruby arrived an hour later when we were halfway through the main courses. 'Sorry, they kept us all waiting,' she said, interrupting a debate which had been running for fifteen minutes about whether Mia and Hugo should have a wedding cake made of cheese or a Sicilian lemon sponge by the East End baker who'd designed Prince Harry and Meghan's cake.

'Hi, guys, hi, Flo, hi, Mum,' she added, dutifully circling the table and kissing each of us on the head before throwing herself in the seat next to me. 'I could murder a drink.'

'We were just discussing my cake,' said Mia, a forkful of fish paused in the air.

'Our cake,' corrected Hugo.

'Catch me up, what have I missed?'

'What was your casting for?' asked Patricia, who dreamed of Ruby modelling on the cover of *Vogue* so she could boast to her friends at bridge club.

'A new campaign for cold sore cream.' Ruby glanced up at a hovering waiter. 'Could I have a vodka and tonic please? Slimline tonic.' She turned back to the table. 'And it was crap. I'm not doing it even if they ask me.'

Ruby never seemed to mind missing out on jobs. Castings came and went every week and she shrugged them off, convinced that her big cover moment would come along one day. It helped that she was twenty-six and still had a credit card bankrolled by our father.

'Oh well,' said Patricia. 'What do you want to eat?'

'Er...' Ruby looked at our plates. Hugo was chewing a rib-eye; after a debate of several minutes over whether the fish was cooked in butter or oil, Patricia and Mia had opted for the sea bass with the thyme cream on the side; I was having chicken but had swapped the truffled mash for chips because I thought truffle smelled like the crotch of my gym leggings and why anyone would want to eat that was beyond me. Plus, I could count the chips as I ate them. I couldn't handle very small food like peas or grains of rice because they were too fiddly to count. Chips were fine.

'Whatever Florence is having please,' said Ruby. 'I'm desperate for a fag but...' She gazed around the room, as if anyone else would be smoking.

'Can we get back to the wedding?' demanded Mia.

Ruby sat back in her chair. 'Yes, sorry. What's the plan?'

'We're having it here but I'm worried about numbers. Are you bringing anyone?' Mia narrowed her eyes. 'Do you want to bring Jasper?'

Jasper Montgomery was Ruby's latest boyfriend, a rakish playboy and the son of a duke who was to inherit a castle in Yorkshire and thousands of acres. Patricia was thrilled; Mia had become less pleased about our sister's posh new relationship as the weeks wore on because Jasper kept turning up at home unannounced, late and pissed, leaning on the doorbell until someone answered it, usually Mia, whereupon Jasper would tumble into our hallway.

'How on earth do I know?' Ruby replied. 'The wedding's not until Christmas. That's...' she counted by tapping her fingers on the table, 'four months from now. I can't predict where we'll be then.' She was as relaxed about relationships as she was about timing. And this nonchalance, combined with her freckles and long, chestnut-coloured curls (she'd once been told she resembled a 'young Julia Roberts' in her headshots), meant that men fell about her like skittles.

'Flo, what about you?' said Mia.

'What d'you mean?'

'Are you bringing anyone?'

'To your wedding?'

'Yes, obviously to my wedding. What else would we be talking about?'

'Our wedding,' said Hugo.

The question made me defensive. 'Well I mean, no... I didn't... I don't... I can't imagine who that would be, so...'

'Florence, sweetheart, I've been thinking about this,' interrupted Patricia, and my jaw froze, mid-chew. Patricia's tone had become wheedling, the widow spider seducing her prey before the kill. 'I think it's high time you considered your love life. You're thirty-two, darling. You really should have had a boyfriend by now. What will people think otherwise? Time waits for no man. Or woman, in this case.'

I swallowed. 'Perhaps they'll think I'm a lesbian, Patricia.'

'Gracious me. Are you a les...? Are you one of those?'

I picked up a chip and dunked it in the silver pot of ketchup beside my plate. 'No, sadly.'

Even though I'd spent years pretending I didn't care that I'd never had a boyfriend, years telling myself it wasn't very feminist to worry about such things, privately I did mind. Was it my flat chest? My size eight feet? My pale colouring, or the mole on my forehead that I tried to hide with my hair? Could men tell that I was so inexperienced? Did I emit an off-putting, sexless smell?

Deep down, of course I wanted to fall in love. Doesn't everyone? I'd spent my teenage years ripping through romantic novels and dreamed of being as alluring as Scarlett O'Hara, with the sassy intelligence of Jo March and the porcelain delicacy of Daisy Buchanan. In reality, I was starting to feel more like Miss Havisham. But although I allowed myself to brood about this on dark Sunday nights, I never admitted as much out loud and I didn't want to discuss it with my family. Especially when my sisters' allure was so much greater than my own.

We'd lived as a trio for years. Dad was posted to Pakistan when I was eighteen. Five years later, the Foreign Office moved him to Argentina. That was when Patricia moved into a flat in South Kensington. She'd never liked our house in Kennington because she didn't think the postcode was fashionable enough, so she persuaded Dad to take out another mortgage and buy her one somewhere else. Patricia insisted it was to allow Ruby, Mia and me to remain living at home but the truth was Patricia felt she deserved to live in a posh flat with thick carpets, expensive floral wallpaper and an SW7 postcode. She was the wife of an ambassador, after all, even if she spent most of her time in London. She visited Buenos Aires every couple of months and Dad flew back for the odd meeting, but they spent such long stretches of time apart I used to wonder how their relationship was a success. Over the years, I'd realized it thrived precisely because of the long periods away. If they lived together full-time, one of them would have murdered the other. Patricia was the highly strung neurotic who made everyone take their shoes off when visiting her flat; Dad was the stable rudder. She wanted a husband who could afford her weekly haircuts and dinners in expensive restaurants;

he needed a woman willing to be the diplomatic wife when she did visit. Patricia never minded cutting the ribbon at the opening of a new textile factory or chatting up the wife of the soybean magnate. The South Kensington flat was stuffed with official photographs taken at these events.

Anyway, ever since Patricia moved out, boyfriends had arrived at our house more often than the postman. They were mostly Ruby's but, before Hugo, Mia's hit rate had also been high and I'd often come downstairs in the morning to find men called Rupert or Jeremy hunting for tea bags in the kitchen. The only man who made it into my room was ginger, had four legs and was called Marmalade – my 17-year-old cat.

'But we do worry about you,' breezed on Patricia, 'so what I've decided is that you should go and see this woman I read about in the hairdresser in *Posh!* magazine – she's got a funny name. Gwendolyn something. A love coach. Or guru. Can't remember which. But apparently she's brilliant.'

I squinted across the table. 'A love coach? What do you mean?'

'There's no need to be embarrassed, darling. Think of her like a therapist but for relationships. You go along, talk to her about your situation and what you're looking for, and she helps you work out all your funny little issues.'

'What. Do. You. Mean?' I repeated slowly, enunciating each word.

'I just think it must be a bit lonely at your age, still being on your own when your sisters are getting married. Sort of… unnatural.'

'Mum, hang on,' interjected Ruby. '*I'm* not getting marr—'

Patricia held a hand up in the air, signalling that she wasn't finished. 'Don't you want to meet someone, darling?' she said, leaning towards me. 'Don't you want to find a lovely chap like Hugo and settle down?'

I looked at Hugo, who was repeatedly running his index finger across his plate to mop up his steak juice, then sticking it in his mouth.

'Patricia,' I started, 'it's the twenty-first century. Single women aren't illegal. We can drive cars, we can vote. We can own property. We can play in premiership football teams and...' I paused, trying to think of more, 'we can do whatever we like with our own body hair. We can dress how we like. And we can have sex with ourselves, if we like, no man necessary—'

'Goodness, Florence, let's not descend to vulgarities,' replied Patricia, puckering her lips as if she'd just sucked a battery.

But I was building to a crescendo and enjoying myself: '—basically, we can do whatever the hell we like and we certainly don't have to have a boyfriend just because other people say so.'

I leant back in my chair and glared defiantly at her, but Patricia was like a whack-a-mole you couldn't kill.

'Darling,' she replied, cocking her head to one side. 'Always so resistant. What if this lady can help you?'

'I don't need help!' I replied, although I sounded squeakier than intended, so I swallowed and started again. 'What I mean is that I'm happy as things are and I don't need to see a mad old bat with a pack of tarot cards.'

'It all sounds very above board. She has an office on Harley Street.'

'Oh, Harley Street! That settles it. She's got to be legit if she's on Harley Street.'

'Florence, come on, you're being very silly about this. All I was offering was a session with someone who might be able to help you think about things in a different way.' Patricia paused and reached for her wine glass. 'Your father thinks it's a good idea. He does *so* worry about you.'

I wasn't sure what was more humiliating: being told to go and see a love coach or the thought of Dad discussing my relationship status with Patricia.

I dropped my head and muttered into my chest.

'What's that?' asked Patricia.

'Nothing,' I replied, snapping my head up. 'Fine, if you and Dad think it's a good idea then I will go along for a session. One session, so long as we never have to talk about my relationship status in this family ever again. Deal?'

'That's the spirit,' said my stepmother, one of her claws reaching across the table to pat my hand. 'I'll fix up an appointment. My treat. It'll make your father so happy.'

'I think it's a good idea,' added Mia. 'Come on, Flo, surely you don't want to be on your own for ever?'

'She might be helpful,' echoed Ruby, looking at me sympathetically. It was the way you'd look at someone who'd just been told they had a terminal disease and three days to live.

Hugo was still mopping steak juice with his finger.

God, my family.

'Fine,' I repeated, picking up another chip and jabbing it in the air at them like a knife. 'But if I go, you all have to remember what I said tonight – we're never ever discussing my love life as a group activity again.'

'All right, all right, Germaine Greer,' said Mia, 'keep your hair on. Now, can we chat dates for wedding dress shopping? Since you two are bridesmaids, I want you in the same thing. I was thinking coral?'

So I was right about the bridesmaid dress being sick-coloured.

★

It was bright the next morning, the sun already warming the attic, so I got out of bed and stood in front of my full-length mirror, naked apart from my pants, to gauge how fat I was feeling. I knew I wasn't really fat. Not *fat* fat. But I examined my stomach in the mirror every morning anyway. Bloated? Not bloated? I poked my belly with a finger and slumped so it bulged out beneath my tummy button, then straightened again. I cast my eyes down over my thighs (I wished they were smaller), upwards towards my chest (I wished it was bigger) and then ran a hand through my hair which hung in no discernible style to just below my shoulders. I had to straighten it every time I washed it, otherwise it frizzed out, making me look like a spaniel.

I showered and returned to my bedroom. From the hanging cupboard, I retrieved one of four pairs of identical navy trousers from Uniqlo. From my tops drawer, I took out and unfolded a navy T-shirt. I laid them on my bed and returned to my chest of drawers for a pair of ironed and folded black knickers, peeled from a neat row, plus a bra. I dressed, tied my hair up in its usual ponytail and made my bed.

'Let's go, pal,' I said to Marmalade, scooping him up and counting the stairs in my head as we went down – two, four, six, eight, ten, two, four, six, eight, nine, two, four, six, eight, ten.

I put two slices of bread in the toaster for breakfast: toast with honey, one cup of coffee. After that, I'd make lunch. This, too, was always the same: a cheese and tomato sandwich with butter and pickle, which had always gone pleasantly soggy by 1 p.m., and a piece of flapjack from a batch I made every Sunday afternoon.

I was bad with change. Didn't like it. So I wore the same outfit and ate the same lunch every day because it made me feel safe. It was a form of control; if my daily life remained unvarying, constant, then nothing calamitous could go wrong. I liked uniform days which ended with me lying on the sofa, reading, while a cookery show played on TV. Ideally one with Mary Berry in it. I liked Mary because she was neat and orderly.

Occasionally I worried such a quiet, unambitious life meant I'd be alone for ever, never brave enough to fall in love or go abroad. The furthest I'd ever travelled was to my grandmother's in France, which was ironic considering my parents were keen explorers who met in India. Mum had been an idealistic 23-year-old who taught English at a school in a Mumbai suburb, and lived in a small apartment nearby where she was woken in the morning by monkeys shrieking on her balcony. I'd always held on to the idea of those noisy monkeys, one of the only stories I could remember her telling me.

Dad was living in the city at the same time, a student writing his dissertation on dynastic Indian politics. This topic had apparently acted as an aphrodisiac on Mum, who'd met him one evening when he was invited over to dinner by her flatmate. That was that. They became inseparable, until the car crash in London eight years later. The crash that rocketed into our lives like a comet and changed everything. That was when I realized change was bad. So, the same clothes; the same lunch; every Monday, by and large, the same as the previous Monday, and the Monday before that. If life stayed the same, life was safe.

That morning, I ate my toast while listening to the radio – a Cabinet minister had been forced to apologize for making a joke about vegans – and ushered Marmalade into the garden.

Mia left for work first. She worked for a fashion PR company, quite senior now, and was responsible for telling women that they should wear crochet and tartan this season and that animal print was out. She'd given up on me because I refused to wear anything other than my self-imposed navy uniform to the shop. Ruby would generally lie in bed until midday, depending on whether she had a casting, then leave a trail of mugs and milky cereal bowls around the house which I put in the dishwasher every evening since, by then, she was always out.

I slid lunch into my rucksack, a waterproof navy job bought several years ago from Millets for its many compartments. It fitted my purse, my lip balm, my house keys, a spare hair tie, a packet of paracetamol, my phone, my sandwich, my flapjack and whatever book I was reading. I didn't understand women who left the house with a handbag the size of a matchbox. How could they go about their day looking so self-assured when all they had on them was a debit card and a lipstick? What if they got a headache?

I reached under the hall table for my hideous work shoes, fastened them and set off on foot for the shop. A distance of exactly 2.6 miles, much of it along the Thames.

I walked to most places playing Consequences, another form of control. It had started when I was four, the year after Mum died. That was when I started totting up the number of classmates every morning to make sure they were all there. Only when I reached fourteen could I relax. Everyone present. Some days, it was only thirteen, which would make me anxious until Mrs Garber said it was all right, the absentee's mother had called to say they had a stomach bug and they'd be back in tomorrow.

After my classmates, I counted the chairs in our classroom to make sure there were enough. Then the pencils in my pencil case to check I hadn't lost any; the paintings on the walls; the carrot batons on my plate at lunchtime; the books in my rucksack on the way home again. I counted the stairs when I got back and tried not to let the flight between the bathroom and Mia's room bother me – Mia was just a baby then – because it was an odd number. Only nine stairs on that flight and I preferred even numbers. They felt more secure, more stable. No number was left out because they all had partners. To my 4-year-old brain, not being left out was important.

My obsessive counting slackened its grip as I grew older but it still remained a habit. Dad and Patricia had despatched me to various specialists over the years, but a succession of armchair experts, asking how angry I felt on a scale of 1 to 10, had done little to cure me. I knew the number of keys on the grubby work keyboard (104) and the number of biscuits in the various packets we ate at work for tea (Jaffa Cakes: 10; chocolate Hobnobs: 14; orange Clubs: 8). I knew the number of steps downstairs to the shop basement (13), the number upstairs to the travel section (12) and the number of caffeine-stained mugs that hung from the wooden tree in the office kitchen (7).

Time had been the only real help. That, and the fact that I'd become better at hiding my habit. I wore an old-school watch with little hands so I never had to see an unsettling digital time like 11:11. If I was watching television at home, the volume had to be set at an even number by the remote control. Every other week, I went to an anxiety support group called NOMAD (No More Anxiety Disorders. Blame the founder, Stephen, for its unfortunate name, although luckily most members saw the funny side). But these days, the meetings were more to catch up with my friend Jaz than to actively participate.

This morning, I played Consequences by counting the number of cars I passed. Often, while doing this, a little voice whispered that if a blue car followed a bus then it would be a bad day, but if it was a white car, something good would happen. Logically, I knew this was rubbish and that I was making up rules for myself. But I couldn't help it. If a blue car, or a green car, or a yellow car, or whatever colour car my brain decided was bad that day did follow the bus, I'd feel panicked, alarmed at what might happen. It was relentless, my brain's constant paranoia, but counting gave me a sense of order. I felt guilty if I didn't count things in the same way that others did if they didn't go to the gym.

At first glance, Frisbee Books wouldn't strike anyone as a suitable office for a maniac obsessed with neatness and numbers. Tucked away off a busy Chelsea shopping street, it looked like it belonged on the set of a Dickens film. Its wooden front was painted dark green, with 'Frisbee Books Ltd' in white lettering. Underneath that was a big window with two rows of books on display, lined up for passing shoppers.

Stepping inside was like falling into the library of an extremely untidy recluse. The walls were covered in shelves that supported thousands of books pressing up against one another. Just over 43,000 books. The shop floor was strewn with tables of different sizes loaded with books in bar-graph piles. Military hardbacks on one table (we sold a lot of those in Chelsea); memoirs stacked high on another; cookery books on a table beside that. Fiction and non-fiction was separated in two halves of the shop – non-fiction as you walked in through the door, fiction off to the right.

Norris, my boss, had inherited the shop from his uncle. It had opened in 1967 when London was swinging, but Uncle

Dale thought his bookshop should stand as a cultural sandbag against the likes of Jimi Hendrix and the miniskirt. Norris took over the shop in the early Nineties when Uncle Dale had a hip replacement and could no longer stand all day. Two years on, he died in his sleep leaving Norris the bookshop in his will.

Frisbee Books hadn't changed much since. There was a 12-year-old computer in the basement that Norris used for accounting and ordering. Otherwise the shop ran as it always had done. Loyal customers dropped in to order a new biography of Churchill that they'd read about in *The Spectator*. Middle-aged women browsed for birthday presents. American tourists stood outside in shorts and wraparound sunglasses, taking pictures of the 'cute bookstore' they'd found for friends back in Arkansas.

I'd asked nine independent bookshops across London for a job when I graduated from uni. In my letter, I explained that I fell in love with *A Little Princess* when I was eight, had barely looked up from a book since, and all I wanted to do now was help other people find stories they could lose themselves in. In my last week at Edinburgh, fellow English Literature graduates boasted of internships at publishing houses or acceptance into law school, but I suspected that working in a corporate office would mean making presentations in boardrooms and bitching about your colleagues. Not for me.

I got four replies to my letter; five were ignored. Two replies asked me to get in touch via the official application form on their website, and one said they only accepted employees with retail experience. Norris was my life raft, sending me a postcard suggesting I come along to the shop for a cup of tea.

He was a human bear with tufts of grey hair protruding from both his head and his ears, as if he'd recently stuck his fingers into a plug socket. He didn't ask anything about my retail experience. While giving me a tour of the shop, he simply wanted to know what I was reading (I'd pulled an old Agatha Christie from my bag) and demanded to know whether I owned a Kindle. Norris growled the word 'Kindle' with suspicion and I'd admitted that I used to have one until I dropped it in the bath.

I instantly regretted the bath comment because Norris paused by the 'F' shelf and his eyebrows leapt several inches in surprise. But then he moved on to the authors beginning with 'G' and asked whether I was a morning person because he wasn't much good before he'd finished his thermos of coffee and would I be all right to open the shop. Our chat took fifteen minutes, after which Norris said he'd see me the following Monday.

I'd arrived nervously that first morning, stammering when customers asked where they might find the latest Ian McEwan or if we had an obscure political book by a Scandinavian writer in stock. The first time I ran a transaction through the till I was so afraid of fluffing it that I spoke robotically, like a Dalek: 'That. Will. Be. £12.99. Please,' and had to be prompted for one of our paper bags. But I soon settled into the routine.

Today, it was my turn to unlock, so I arrived just after nine, turned on the computer behind the till and ran a Stanley knife across the boxes from the distributors. New stock to be put out. Although it might not have looked like it, there was an order to the shop that I understood. If a customer came in and asked for a Virginia Woolf or a travel guide to the Galapagos, I could point them to exactly the right spot. I knew the shop as well as I knew my home. Or better, perhaps, since I rarely went into Ruby and Mia's bedrooms (too messy, used cotton pads everywhere).

I knew the customers who came in every day to browse but actually lived on their own and just wanted some company. I recognized the punters who were time-wasters, loitering between appointments, who would finger multiple books before sliding them back into the wrong shelf. And in quiet moments, it also allowed me time to work on my own book, a children's book about a counting-obsessed caterpillar called Curtis who had fifty feet and was late for school every day because it took so long to put on all his shoes. I'd also come to see Norris as a sort of mad uncle and could tolerate his daily habits – sitting on the downstairs loo for twenty minutes after his coffee, ignoring the phone so I always had to pick it up, leaving indecipherable Post-it notes on the counter about customer orders that were often lost.

Then there was my colleague Eugene. He was a middle-aged actor who'd worked at the shop for the past decade to pay his rent since he was rarely cast in anything. He had a bald head that shone like a bed knob, wore a bow tie every day and made me rehearse lines with him behind the counter, which often startled customers. Recently, there'd been a dramatic death scene when Eugene, rehearsing for a minor role in *King Lear*, had ended up lying across the shop floor.

Either he or I opened up before Norris arrived late every morning, his shirt fastened by the wrong buttons, thermos in hand; this was special coffee he ground at home and made in a cafetière before decanting it and solemnly carrying it into work in his satchel. I'd made the mistake of asking what was so wrong with Nescafé not long after I started work there and the cloud that passed his face was so dark I'd wondered if I'd be fired.

Anyway, he'd arrive and there was always grumbling about the traffic or the weather before he went downstairs into his office to drink this coffee from his favourite mug – 'To drink or not to drink?' it said on the outside. Half an hour later, he would reappear on the shop floor in cheerier humour and ask whether any customers had been in yet.

But that morning, I was still standing behind boxes of new stock when Norris arrived early and rapped on the glass.

'You all right?' I asked, unlocking the door to let him in. He looked more dishevelled than usual, shirt and trousers both crumpled, and he was panting, as if 73-year-old Norris had decided to run into work that morning from his house in Wimbledon.

'Let me go downstairs for my mug and I'll be up to explain.' He strode towards the stairs and disappeared. I returned to the boxes and wondered if he'd tried to get on the Tube using his Tesco Clubcard again.

He thumped back up the wooden stairs not long afterwards and put his coffee on the counter with a sigh.

'What?' I asked, frowning. 'What's up?'

'Rent hike.'

'Another one?'

Norris nodded and wiped his fingers across his forehead. There'd been a rent rise last year but we'd expected that. Uncle Dale had had a long lease on generous terms and it had been up for renewal. Also, Chelsea had changed since he died. What was always a wealthy area of the city had become even more saturated with money: oligarchs from the East, American banking dollars from the West, along with the odd African despot who wanted his children to go to British boarding school. This meant the shops changed. Gone were the boutiques and coffee shops. In came curious replacements selling £150 gym leggings and cellulite cures made from gold leaf – shops for oligarchs' wives. But although Norris had grumbled about the new lease for several weeks, he'd said it was fine and I'd believed him. It remained business as usual.

But this was different. Norris was panicked.

'Is it manageable?'

'I don't know. It's a lot,' he replied, his voice uneven. 'I'm going to ring the accountant later to discuss it but I wanted to let you know now. Just in case… Well, we'll see. I'll let you know.' Then, as if he couldn't bear to discuss it any longer, he changed topic. 'Any post this morning?'

'Not really. A few orders overnight but I'll deal with those.'

'All right, I'm going back downstairs. Shout if you need me.'

'OK,' I said, before looking around the shop, trying to imagine it as luxury flats with underfloor heating, marble floors and those hi-tech loos with nozzles that wash and dry your bottom. It was an absurd idea. It couldn't happen. Not on my watch.

★

When I got home that night, I found Hugo and Mia bickering at the kitchen table. He'd moved in about six months before, a temporary measure while they did up a house in Herne Hill ('the new Brixton', Hugo pompously told anyone who asked).

I had mixed feelings about their house being finished. On the one hand, this meant Mia would move out and, for the first time in a decade, she, Ruby and I would be separated. And although my sisters were closer to one another than they were to me, Mia's departure would mean change and I'd miss her. On the other hand, it would also mean that Hugo stopped creeping upstairs to my bathroom to do a poo when I wasn't there. He denied this but I knew he was lying; he left traces on the porcelain and I'd once found a copy of *Golfing Monthly* lying on the floor.

That evening, they were squabbling over their wedding list and Hugo, his shirtsleeves rolled up to his elbows, was stabbing at the list with one of his weird fingers.

'Hi, guys,' I said, making my way to the fridge.

'I'm sorry you don't like him,' went on Hugo, in a high-pitched voice, 'but he's my boss and it's imperative that he's invited. I'm sure he didn't mean to graze your bottom. It was probably an accident.'

Mia sighed and leant back from the table. 'Well he did and

we've already got half your office. Anyone else you need? The receptionist? The window cleaner? Someone from your IT department?'

'Actually, Kevin has always been very helpful with my computer.'

I opened the fridge and stared into it as I wondered, for the ninety billionth time, why Mia had said yes to him. Was a house in Herne Hill with an island in the kitchen, underfloor heating in the bathrooms and Farrow & Ball-coloured walls worth it?

She sighed again behind me. 'Fine. Your boss can come. But that means we still need to lose…' she went quiet for a few seconds, tapping her pen down the list, 'about twenty people.'

I closed the fridge. It would have to be eggs on toast. I didn't have the energy for anything complicated. After Norris's announcement that morning, he'd stayed downstairs for most of the afternoon, leaving Eugene and me on the shop floor.

I'd leant on the counter, writing a list of ways I could try and help. A petition was my first thought. People always seemed to be launching petitions online. Sign this petition if you think our prime minister should be in prison! Sign this petition to make sugar illegal! Sign this petition to make the earthworm a protected species! I could set up a Facebook page for the shop and launch the petition on there, with a hard copy of it by the till for our less computer-friendly customers. I liked the idea of a cause, imagining myself as a modern-day Emmeline Pankhurst. Perhaps I could wear a sash? Or that might be taking it too far. But a petition, anyway. That was the first thing to organize.

The shop needed an Instagram account, too. Norris still refused to have a mobile phone and insisted that Frisbee could do without social media. I'd long protested, saying that it wasn't the 1990s, but it had fallen on Norris's deaf, hairy ears. So, a petition and an Instagram account. Plus, a new website. That was a start.

'How was your day, Flo?' asked Mia.

'Fine. I'm making scrambled eggs. Anyone want some?'

'No thanks. Wed-shred starts now.'

'Eggs do terrible things to my stomach,' added Hugo, but luckily none of us could dwell on this because Mia's phone rang.

'Hi, Mum,' she said, picking it up.

I cracked two eggs into a mug and reached for a fork.

'Yep, yep, no, I know, yep, we're doing it now, yep, no, yep…' she went on while I whisked.

'Yep, she's here, hang on,' said Mia, holding her phone in the air without standing up so I had to cross the kitchen.

I put the mobile to my ear with a sense of dread. 'Hi, Patricia.'

My stepmother went straight in. 'I've spoken to this woman's office and she can see you on Tuesday afternoon at five.'

'Which woman?'

'The love coach. She's called Gwendolyn Glossop. Does five on Tuesday work for you?'

'The shop doesn't close until six, so—'

'Florence, darling, you're selling books, not giving blood transfusions. I'm sure they can spare you for an hour. I've told your father and—'

'All right all right all right. I'll be there.'

'Right, have you got a pen? Here's her address, it's—'

'Hang on,' I said, hunting for a pen on the sideboard. No pens. Why were there never any pens?

'Floor 4, 117 Harley Street,' carried on Patricia.

'OK, I'll just remember it.'

'I'm so glad, darling, I do hope she helps. Now can I have Mia back again, I need to talk to her about vicars.'

I handed Mia her phone just as the toast popped up. Black on both sides, a bit like my mood, I thought, sliding them both into the bin.

*

While Eugene dusted shelves the following morning, I told him about this appointment. He was more enthusiastic than me.

'Darling, how thrilling,' he said, his back to me as he swished the pink feathers back and forth like a windscreen wiper. 'Do you think she'll have a crystal ball? I saw a palm reader after Angus left and she told me that I'd soon meet the third great love of my life.'

'And did you?'

'No.' He lowered the duster and held his palm close to his nose, inspecting it. 'It's this line that runs from your little finger.' He looked up. 'But perhaps I just haven't met him yet? I expect he'll be along any second, waiting for me on the 345 bus.'

THE WISH LIST37

I wasn't sure about that. I'd never seen anyone who looked like a great love on the 345, so I merely nodded and Eugene returned to his dusting.

Angus was Eugene's ex-boyfriend, the second great love of his life after Shakespeare, he always said. They'd met while studying drama at university and had been together for twenty years, but not long after I started working at Frisbee, Angus moved to New York to direct a performance of *Evita* and they'd separated. He'd remained there since and was now considered one of Broadway's top musical directors while, back in London, Eugene constantly auditioned for roles he never got.

Barely a day went by when he didn't mention Angus, as if a proud parent watching his offspring blossom from afar. He kept up with his shows, read his *New York Times* reviews out loud to me in the shop and occasionally emailed him to say congratulations. I was never sure if Angus replied to these, I didn't like to ask. Still, Eugene was one of life's sunbeams, a positive person who remained admirably upbeat in the face of these disappointments, so his enthusiasm towards Gwendolyn Glossop didn't surprise me.

'So you think I should definitely go and see this woman? It isn't a bit… tragic? Or mad?'

Eugene tutted. 'Absolutely not. What have you got to lose?' He turned back to me and held the duster high in the air. 'Boldness be my friend.'

'What's that?'

'*Cymbeline*, act one. And I think you should look upon this as an exciting opportunity.' He spun to face me again. 'Because without meaning one jot of offence, angel, I think my mother gets more action than you.'

'Doesn't your mother live in a retirement home?'

'In Bournemouth, exactly my point.'

I was about to object but heard Norris's heavy footsteps on the stairs.

He glanced from Eugene to me, tufty eyebrows raised. 'You two all right up here?'

'We are indeed,' said Eugene. 'I'm just advising our young colleague on matters of the heart.'

Norris had been married decades ago to a lady called Shirley but now lived alone. On quiet days in the shop, Eugene and I sometimes speculated about his private life. Had Shirley run off with the postman, driven away by Norris's gruffness? Had waking up beside that amount of ear hair become too much to bear? Had Shirley given up life in an untidy Wimbledon flat for a dashing younger man on the Costa Del Sol? Eugene's dramatic nature meant he tended to get quite carried away with these speculations but we remained none the wiser. Norris wasn't the sort to discuss anything emotional.

'I don't want to know,' he said, waving his hands in the air as if protesting. 'I just came up for the post.'

I handed it over to him and mouthed 'Shhhh!' at Eugene. The fewer people who knew about my appointment with Gwendolyn, the better.

★

The following Tuesday, I arrived at 117 Harley Street and was told by a receptionist to take the lift to the fourth floor.

'Are there any stairs?' I hated the jerkiness of lifts in old London buildings like this, clanking and creaking like a dodgy fairground ride.

'Take the fire exit next to the lift,' instructed the receptionist, not looking up from her magazine.

I played Consequences as I walked up. If the steps were even, it would be a helpful hour, which made me feel less freakish for never having had a boyfriend. But what would it be if the stairs were odd? What was the worst outcome of this session? If they were odd numbers, I'd never have a relationship and I'd become one of those little old ladies you see shopping by themselves in the supermarket, hunched over a wheelie trolley and buying tins of fish paste for their solo suppers.

The first flight had thirteen stairs and I felt a spasm of panic. The next two had eleven and the last nine. Disaster.

I walked along a corridor which smelt of instant coffee and stopped at the door with a small sign that said 'Gwendolyn Glossop, MS, Love Coach and Energy Healer.'

I knocked.

'Come i-hin!' came a high-pitched voice.

I pushed it open to find a salmon-pink room. Salmon-pink walls, salmon-pink curtains, salmon-pink sofa and armchair. On the sofa were four cushions – two shaped like red hearts and one which had the letters 'LO' on it beside another that said 'VE'. Grim.

Decorating a wooden dresser behind this sofa were several

statues of naked women. My eyes slid along them. Nineteen in total, with rounded bottoms and pert breasts. Wooden statues, bronze statues, statues carved from stone, even a purple wax statue, although that one had started melting and was headless. On the opposite wall was a mural of clouds and classical figures in togas. It was as if I'd stumbled through the back of a wardrobe, from the clinical starkness of Harley Street into a deranged computer game.

'Welcome, Florence,' said Gwendolyn, pushing herself up from the armchair. She was a large woman wearing purple dungarees that fastened with buttons shaped like daisies. Silver earrings dangled from her ears and she had the sort of cropped haircut you get when you join the army. The tips of her eyelashes were coated with blue mascara and the look was completed with a pair of green Crocs.

She pointed at a woman in the mural, a brunette whose toga had slipped off one bosom but not the other. 'That's Aphrodite, the goddess of sexual pleasure. Are you familiar with her?'

'No, I don't know her, er, work.'

'Ah, never mind.' We shook hands, a row of bangles dancing up and down Gwendolyn's forearm, and she gestured at the sofa. 'Please have a seat.'

She reached for a pad of paper and a pen from a coffee table while I leant back against the cushions and tried to relax. All the pink made me feel like I was sitting in someone's intestines.

'And how are we today?' Gwendolyn asked, glancing up from her pad with a smile.

'All right.'

'Not nervous?'

'No,' I fibbed. This was mad. This room was mad. This woman was mad. Patricia was mad. I pretended to scratch my wrist so I could push up the cuff of my jumper and look at my watch: fifty-eight minutes to go.

'I'm going to ask a few preliminary questions before we get stuck into the real work,' said Gwendolyn, raising her chin and cackling before dropping it and becoming serious again. 'Can you tell me why you're here?'

'Because I have a socially ambitious stepmother who thought it would be helpful, so I said I'd try this out so long as she never interrogated me about my love life again,' I replied. I might as well be honest.

Gwendolyn cackled again and scribbled a note. 'And can you tell me about your relationship history?'

'Not much to tell. There was someone briefly at university ten years ago. Very briefly. But that's pretty much it.'

'Nobody else?' said Gwendolyn, her forehead rippling with concern.

I picked at a scrap of cuticle on my thumb then met her gaze. 'A few one-night things. But nothing more than that. I'd like to fall in love,' I said, trying to sound casual, as if I'd just said I'd like a cup of tea. 'Course I would. But the right person hasn't come along.'

'Mmm,' murmured Gwendolyn, looking from me to her pad. She shifted in her armchair and crossed her right ankle over her left knee so a Croc dangled from her foot. She looked up and squinted, as if she was trying to see inside me, then back at the list. 'Mmm, yes, what I think we need to do is clear your love blocks out. I can sense them. Your subconscious is very powerful. You're stuck. Hurting. Lonely. Do you want to stay lonely, Florence?'

But before I had a chance to reply and say I wasn't lonely and, actually, I quite liked going to bed at whatever time I wanted, Gwendolyn ordered me to lie back on the sofa and close my eyes.

'Across the whole thing?'

'Yes, yes, stick your legs over the end. That's it. Put a cushion under your head. There we go.'

Resting my head on a heart-shaped cushion, I noticed a cherub painted on the ceiling. I closed my eyes to banish it, wondering how many minutes were left now.

'I'll light a candle to dispel the forces of darkness and then we'll get going,' she said. 'Eyes closed.'

I shut them as she started asking questions in a velvety voice. 'What grievances are you hanging on to, Florence? What can you let go?'

I thought about replying 'trapped wind' but suspected Gwendolyn wouldn't find this funny. Then I smelt herbs so opened one eye again; she was circling her hands around my face without touching it, as if my head was a crystal ball.

'What's that smell?'

'It's sage and frankincense oil for emotional healing. But forget the herbs. Close your eyes and think, who are you holding on to in your heart? Can you let them go?'

The questions continued while Gwendolyn wafted her oily fingers above my face.

'Set an intention for your healing. Ask yourself: what do I need right now to open my heart to the love I deserve?'

I wondered what to have for supper when I got home. I was starving. Soup? The thought of ending a day with soup was depressing.

'We need to break down the wall around your heart,' she went on. 'Imagine a bulldozer smashing that wall, Florence, opening the path to true intimacy.'

A baked potato? No, it would take too long and I hated it when they weren't cooked in the middle.

'Now open your eyes and sit up, and we can make a start,' said Gwendolyn. 'I've cleared those blocks and you should be feeling clearer and calmer. Less defensive.'

I opened my eyes feeling exactly as I had nine minutes earlier.

Wiping her hands with a tissue, Gwendolyn explained that she wanted me to write a list.

'A list? Like a shopping list?'

Gwendolyn nodded, the silver teardrops swinging in her earlobes. 'Exactly, my precious. Like a shopping list, except for what you want from a man, not Asda. Ha ha!' Her mouth opened wide at her own joke before she was serious again. 'What do you want in a man, Florence?'

'Er...'

'Because you need to ask the universe for it,' she said solemnly. 'These things don't just fall into our laps. You need to manifest your desires and attract the right vibrations into your life, summon them to you.' Gwendolyn stretched her arms in front of her and pulled them back as if playing a tug of war with these vibrations.

'OK,' I replied. I was going to play along with this mad hippie. Play along for the session then leave and tell Patricia that she was never, ever to interfere with my love life again.

Gwendolyn tore a piece of paper from her pad and handed it to me. 'Use a book to lean on.'

I reached underneath the glass table for the nearest book, which had a silhouette of a cat on the front. *The Power of the Pussy: How To Tame Your Man*, said the title. I covered it quickly with my piece of paper. The power of the pussy indeed. Marmalade would be horrified.

'Help yourself to a pen,' went on Gwendolyn, 'and I want you to write down the characteristics that are important to you so the universe can recognize them and deliver what you're looking for.'

'How many characteristics does the universe need?'

'As many as you like, poppet,' she replied, flourishing a hand in the air like a flamenco dancer. 'But the more specific the better. Don't just say "handsome". The universe needs clear instructions. Write down "has all his own hair". Don't say "athletic". Say "goes to the gym once or twice a week". Remember, it's your list. Your wish list for the universe to answer.'

I wished she'd stop talking about the universe. I went quiet and blinked at my piece of paper. What to write? I couldn't possibly take this seriously, but on the other hand, I had to write something to convince this nutter that I'd at least thought about it.

After twenty minutes of sighing, chewing the biro, nearly swallowing the little blue stopper at the end of the biro, laughing to myself, closing my eyes and shaking my head before sighing again, I'd come up with a few suggestions. I totted them up and felt uneasy. That was fifteen. I needed one more to make it even. I gnawed the end of the biro once more and thought of a final addition.

THE LIST
- LIKES CATS.
- INTERESTING JOB. NOT GOLF-PLAYING INSURANCE BORE LIKE HUGO.
- BOTTOM AND SEXUAL ATHLETICISM OF JAMES BOND.
- NICE MOTHER.
- NO POINTY SHOES.
- NO HAWAIIAN SHIRTS.
- NO UMBRELLAS.
- READS BOOKS. NOT JUST SPORTS BIOGRAPHIES.
- NO REVOLTING BATHROOM HABITS. E.G. SKID MARKS.
- AMBITIOUS.
- ADVENTUROUS.
- GOOD MANNERS. E.G. SAYS THANK YOU IF SOMEONE HOLDS THE DOOR OPEN FOR HIM.

- *ISN'T OBSESSED WITH INSTAGRAM OR HIS PHONE.*
- *FUNNY.*
- *ACTUALLY TEXTS ME BACK.*
- *DOESN'T MIND ABOUT MY COUNTING.*

I handed the piece of paper to Gwendolyn who inspected it while I checked my watch. In twelve minutes, I could go home for supper, whatever it was. Eggs again? Could one overdose on eggs?

'Well,' said Gwendolyn, looking up. 'You clearly listened to what I said about being specific. This line about James Bond, for instance…'

I spread my hands in mock innocence. 'You said it was a wish list. So I thought, why not? If I can truly put down any bottom I wanted, why not go for his?'

The corners of Gwendolyn's mouth tightened as she glanced back at the list. 'What's wrong with umbrellas?'

'Not very manly,' I said. I had a thing about this. Hugo never left the house without his umbrella. It seemed fussy and faint-hearted; you'd never catch Mr Rochester or Rhett Butler faffing about with an umbrella.

'And you want someone who's both ambitious and adventurous?'

I nodded. Ambition was to guard against the sort of man whose dreams stopped at 'golf club membership' and someone with a spirit of adventure might encourage me to be braver, to venture further afield than south London.

'Fine,' she went on, 'but you could jot down a few more

personality characteristics. What about kindness, or generosity? And does he want children?'

'I don't know,' I replied, because I didn't know. I had to find a boyfriend first and that seemed hard enough.

'And what's this about your counting?'

'Nothing,' I said quickly. 'Just a... weird thing I do. Like a tick. I count things. In my head.'

'Hmmmm,' mused Gwendolyn, narrowing her eyes at me as if I was the oddball in the room. 'Well, what I'd like you to do is some deeper work over the next week or so. Really think about this list and finesse it.' She held the piece of paper back out.

'All right,' I replied, taking it from her. 'And then what? Do I need to find some sort of cauldron and burn it?'

'You are naughty!' said Gwendolyn, grinning and clapping her hands to her thighs. 'No, darling, just leave it somewhere safe so you can come back to it at our next appointment.'

'What next appointment?'

'Your stepmother booked a package. Did she not tell you? We have another three to go.'

I exhaled. Three more sessions in this Pepto-Bismol room. Three more interrogations with this giant fairy. But how to reply? I could hardly say, 'Absolutely not, I'd rather skip naked through the streets of London.'

She reached into her dungaree pocket and pulled out her phone. 'Let's see... I always think it best to allow at least a week between the first and second appointment, to allow you enough time to think about your list. So what about two weeks' today? Same time? There's a new moon that night so it's wonderful timing.'

I smiled back, my lips pressed in a straight line because otherwise I thought I might scream.

And then, once I was standing back on the Harley Street pavement, I folded the list and slid it into the side pocket of my rucksack. The manifesting power of the universe indeed. What a load of absolute, Grade-A nonsense.

CHAPTER TWO

LATER THAT WEEK, I was dealing with Mrs Delaney and didn't notice the blond man loitering in the biography section. It was raining, which drove more people into the shop since it was a peaceful place to pass time until the clouds moved. Unhurried. Relaxed. No assistant ever approached you in a bookshop and said, 'Would you like to try a pair of heels with that?' Customers could browse undisturbed while their coats dripped quietly on the Turkish rugs.

Mrs Delaney had been visiting Frisbee Books for decades. She lived in a big house overlooking St Luke's Church, a short wobble away on her walking stick, and liked to come in every week to discuss new gardening books. She was exceptionally keen on gardening (although she didn't do it herself, she had a man called Cliff who did that), and Eugene and I took it in turns to deal with her. This morning it was my turn, so I was leafing Mrs Delaney through a new book about rewilded gardens. It wasn't going well because she declared every photo of daisies and cow parsley 'a disgrace'.

'That's even messier than the last!' she said, as I reached the final page, a picture of a butterfly on a clump of grass. 'Not for me,' she said. 'I'll be off.'

Mrs Delaney waved her stick in the air as a goodbye before tottering out into the rain. I stepped under the wooden beam separating fiction and non-fiction to slide the rewilding book back onto its shelf.

'I'm so sorry to trouble you,' said the man.

I turned to help him, my automatic smile in place.

'It's only that I'm here to pick up a book my mother ordered.'

My mouth fell open like a trapdoor but no words came out. It was his old-fashioned clothes that struck me at first. Over a white shirt he was wearing a pair of blue braces which fastened with little buttons to the top of his trousers. Then I stared at his face and wondered whether his pale blue eyes and almost invisible blond eyelashes meant he was Scandinavian.

'She said she got a message saying it's in,' he persisted. 'If you wouldn't mind…'

'Yes, sure, sorry,' I said, shaking my head as if to wake myself up. He didn't sound Scandinavian. He sounded very English. 'What's she called?'

'Elizabeth Dundee.'

'OK, give me a second.'

I stepped behind the till into a small side room that led off from it and ran my finger up and down the shelves until I found the order slip that said Dundee.

'Here you go,' I said, carrying the book round to the front of the shop again. I held it out and only then saw what it was called: *The Art of Arousal: A Celebration of Erotic Art Throughout*

History. There was a painting of a woman having sex with a swan on the cover.

'Oh,' I said.

'Ah,' said the man, in a low, clipped tone. 'Yes. I might have known. It's Zeus. He transformed himself into a swan and seduced Leda. Quite odd, those gods.'

'Looks like it,' I replied, and we both gazed at the book in silence for a few moments before he spoke again.

'I'm also looking for something else.'

'What is it?' I asked, keen to alleviate the awkwardness of discussing bestiality with this handsome blond man.

'A book called *The Struggle*. You don't happen to have it, do you?'

'Should have, but it's a novel so it'll be back through here.'

I waved him into the fiction area after me. *The Struggle* was a book as fat as a brick, one of the summer's biggest sellers, partly because the Irish author had given a series of interviews in which he denounced anyone he was asked about. The Prime Minister? A gobshite. The English in general? A load of gobshites. The Queen? A rich gobshite.

I leant over to scan the table of hardback fiction to find a copy, suddenly very aware that the handsome man was behind me and I was wearing my biggest knickers, the ones with an elasticated waist that pulled up to my belly button and gave me a very obvious VPL. Mia had once insisted that I needed 'to give thongs a chance' and left a couple at the bottom of my stairs from one of her fashion clients. But when I'd carried them to the safety of my bedroom for further inspection,

I couldn't work out which bit to put my legs through, and when I finally got them on and glanced over my shoulder in the mirror, my bottom looked so exposed, so vast and white and wobbly, that I wondered why anyone wanted that effect anyway. I'd stashed them at the back of my underwear drawer where they'd remained ever since.

I found the book's gold spine on the edge of the table. 'Here you go,' I said, sliding it free and handing it to him. 'Have you read any of his others?' I wanted to distract him from my enormous pants.

'No,' he replied. 'Should I?'

'I've only read his first one. This is better, but that was good too. A coming-of-age tale. Growing up in Dublin in the Seventies, trying to escape family politics, actual politics and then he…' I stopped. 'Well, I won't give it away. But it's good, yes,' I said, blushing as he held my eye.

He turned the book over where, on the back cover, the author, Dermot Dooley, glared up at us.

'Looks pretty angry with life, doesn't he?'

I snickered. 'True.'

Up close, he smelt fresh, of a lemony aftershave. Without moving my head, I raised my eyes from the book to his face. It was as if part of me recognized him. He felt familiar. But if he'd been in here before I would remember it, surely? Eugene and I would have fought to serve him and Eugene was normally quicker than me with the hot ones.

His eyes met mine and I blushed again. Busted.

'Thanks for finding it. And my mother's book. You're brilliant, er…'

'Florence,' I said, smiling back at him, 'and not at all. It's my job.'

'Thank you all the same.'

'You're into contemporary fiction then?' I ventured, stepping back behind the till and taking the books from him.

'Absolutely, when I get the time. Why?'

'Sorry, nosy of me. Just…' I stopped. 'Well, I shouldn't really say it but most men come in here looking for Wayne Rooney's autobiography.'

'Oh Christ,' he said, clapping a hand to his forehead. 'That was the other one I was supposed to pick up. Don't suppose you've got a copy?'

I looked up from the till and laughed.

'What about you?' he asked.

'What d'you mean?'

'What do you read? I suppose I've never really thought about it before, but does someone who works in a bookshop have to read all of these?' He gestured at the shelves.

'No! Luckily not. We share it. I'm novels. Eugene, that's my colleague, he takes on non-fiction and plays. There's a system so that if someone comes in we can help them, er, find a book they fall in love with.'

I felt embarrassed for describing it like that but he didn't seem to hear because he was concentrating on the cards in front of the till. 'Sorry, can I chuck these in too?' He handed me a pack of cards with Vermeer's *Girl in a Pearl Earring* on the front, except the woman's face had been replaced with a cat. It was part of a series of greetings cards that I'd insisted to

Norris we should stock. And I'd been right. There had been *Mona Lisa* as a cat, a Van Gogh self-portrait as a cat and a cat dressed as Holbein's *Henry VIII*, but they'd all sold out.

'You like cats?' He looked more of a dog person. Wellington boots on the weekend, three Labradors, a tweed hat.

'I do. My mother has three Persians.'

'Cute. And altogether that'll be £36.45 please. Do you want a bag?'

He shook his head. 'No, not to worry.'

'But it's raining,' I said, nodding towards the windows. Outside, people scuttled under umbrellas like giant black beetles.

He grinned again. 'A bit of rain won't hurt.' He tucked the books and his cards under his arm. 'Not sure I'm going to fall in love, though,' he said.

'Huh?' I said. I'd been gazing at his chest – at a small triangle of blond hair exposed at the top of his shirt – and misheard.

'With him,' the man said, flashing Dooley's headshot at me again. 'You said you find books for people to fall in love with.'

'Right,' I replied, laughing too loudly. He meant Dooley. Obviously he wasn't talking about me. Come on, Florence. People don't go about their lives falling in love with others they meet in bookshops. That only happened once in *Notting Hill*.

'Thanks so much for all your help,' he said.

'You're welcome,' I replied as he made for the door. 'I hope you enjoy it.'

He held his fingers to his temple, saluting. Then he was gone into the drizzle.

I felt a pang of disappointment at his disappearance but heard Norris coming upstairs, so tried to rearrange my face.

'Pass us the order book,' he said, standing on the other side of the counter. I handed it over in silence.

'You all right?' he added.

'Yeah, fine. Why?'

'Just look a bit flustered. Where's Eugene?'

'Upstairs, restocking travel.'

Norris opened the book and reached for a pen.

'You missed Mrs Delaney,' I went on.

'My lucky day. She buy anything?'

'No. But someone came in to collect an order and I sold another copy of *The Struggle*.'

Norris blew out heavily through his nostrils. 'I'm not sure one hardback a day's going to keep us open. Ah, we'll see,' he said, closing the book and handing it back to me.

'I've been thinking about this and I've got a plan,' I said, straightening up and deciding to broach my ideas.

Norris's eyebrows waggled with suspicion.

'We need to sort out the website. And I thought about a petition. Online and in here. I'll get everyone who comes in to sign it.'

He didn't reply.

'And we really should have Instagram by now, Norris. I can run it, it's easy. And Twitter.'

'Twitter?' Norris barked it as if it was a dirty word.

'It's free marketing, quite literally.'

'No, no, no,' he replied, shaking his head as he made for

the stairs. 'Can't think about all this now. I've got enough on as it is.'

I stuck my tongue out at his back. 'Didn't want to think about it now' was always his excuse. It was maddening. And irresponsible.

Then came the noise of Eugene clattering downstairs. He dropped an armful of empty boxes on the floor in front of the till.

'They can't stay there,' I said.

'Calm down, bossy boots,' he replied, leaning on the counter and panting. 'I'm famished. Do you mind if I have first lunch? Not sure I'm going to make it to second.' Lunches in the shop were divided into first (an hour at twelve thirty) and second (an hour at one thirty), decided between us every day.

'Nope, you go.'

'Thanks,' replied Eugene, yawning and stretching his arms over his head. 'See you in a bit,' he said, already halfway through the door before I could shout at him about the boxes.

'Men,' I muttered to myself. At home, I lived with two sisters who never put a mug in the dishwasher; in the shop, I worked alongside men who only thought of their stomachs. I wondered which was more trying. Not that long ago, Mrs Delaney had told me that gladioli plants were asexual. Sounded a much easier life, being a gladioli.

As I bent to slide my fingers under the boxes, the doorbell tinkled behind me so I stood up quickly, aware that another customer was being subjected to my bottom. 'Sorry,' I said spinning around, 'I'm just tidy— Oh, hello.'

It was the man in the braces.

'Hello again,' he said, grinning. His hair was damp and there were dark spots on his shirt front from the rain. 'I only… Well, I hope you don't mind… The thing is I don't go around London asking women I meet in shops this, but I wondered if you might be free, or might be interested, in perhaps having a coffee with me?'

'A coffee?' I repeated, as if I didn't know what coffee was.

'Or a drink,' he said. 'Whatever you like. I'd just like to talk to you more about books, if you wanted?' He ran a hand through the wet strands of his hair and looked expectantly at me.

'Er…' I was so surprised by his reappearance that, as if witness to a baffling magic trick, I went mute.

'If you can't, or don't want to, or if you're taken and don't for some reason wear a wedding ring – it's often very hard to tell these days – then forget I ever asked and I'll never come in here again. Although that would be a shame since it's a splendid bookshop. But if none of those things apply then I would like very much to buy you some sort of beverage – hot or cold, it's entirely up to you.'

'Er…' I started again, willing my brain into action. 'Yes, lovely,' I said, over the top of the boxes. It was only two feeble words but it was better than no words.

'Good. I was hoping you'd say that. What's your number?' He reached into his trousers and pulled out his phone.

Number, I told myself, you can do this. I duly read it out to him.

'Marvellous,' he said, pocketing his phone. 'I'll text you. Maybe this weekend?'

'Lovely,' I said again, feeling dazed.

'It's a date,' he said. 'See you soon.'

'See you soon,' I repeated, although he was already gone. I dropped the boxes on top of the fiction table and exhaled slowly, then squinted at my reflection in the window pane. Did I look different today? Was my hair less like a spaniel's?

'Florence, duck, you know those shouldn't be there,' said Norris, appearing on the stairs again and pointing at the boxes. 'Put them out the back, please.'

I didn't even protest that, actually, it was Eugene's fault for abandoning the boxes and I was moving them for him. I just did it.

And it was only while flattening them with my feet in the stockroom that I realized two things: firstly, I didn't even know the man's name. And secondly, Gwendolyn's list! I froze and my hands flew to my cheeks as I remembered what I'd written. He was a tall, absurdly attractive and seemingly funny man who read books, liked cats and clearly didn't think a drop of rain was going to kill him. But that had to be a coincidence?

Course it was. I laughed and shook my head as I started stamping down the boxes again. As if the universe had anything to do with it. Obviously it was a coincidence. There was no way that lunatic in her daisy dungarees had sent that beautiful man in here.

★

I had a NOMAD meeting that evening so I left Eugene to lock up and walked to the primary school where they were held, a few streets from the shop. Peering through the classroom porthole, I saw my friend Jaz already sitting in one of the child-sized plastic seats. A man I didn't recognize had folded himself into a front-row seat and was scowling at the finger paintings. We were a small group, normally about eight or nine, and we sat in rows surrounded by colourful finger paintings and art made from pasta. At the front, under a large whiteboard, our leader Stephen would try and encourage a sensible group discussion while we ate custard creams. It was always custard creams. Stephen brought them himself, along with a travel kettle, several mugs and tea supplies.

I pushed open the door. 'Hi, Stephen,' I said, waving at him.

He spun around from his plate of biscuits and beamed at me. 'Good evening, Florence. All well?'

'All pretty brilliant, actually,' I said, dropping my bag on the small red seat next to Jaz. Her 4-year-old, Duncan, was sitting cross-legged on the floor in his sweatshirt and school trousers, earplugs in, watching a video on her phone. 'How come Dunc's here?'

Jaz sighed. 'Because his dad's a premier league asshole who didn't make pick-up.'

She said this loudly enough to make Stephen's shoulders twitch. Dunc, fortunately, was too engrossed with his phone to overhear. I ruffled his hair and he looked up and grinned happily before dropping his gaze back to the screen.

Jaz's ex, Dunc's father, was a plumber called Leon. He and

Jaz had been together for a few months when she got pregnant. She'd presented him with the happy news only for Leon to admit that, actually, Jaz wasn't the only woman whose pipes he was seeing to. They'd split and Leon had been a sporadic father ever since. Occasionally he'd take him to the Battersea zoo to see the rabbits and the frogs (Dunc, very into animals, wanted to be a vet when he grew up), but he and Jaz were generally on bad terms.

Dunc was the reason she'd started coming to these meetings. Jaz was a hairdresser who worked in a Chelsea salon but, when he was a baby, she'd started obsessing about his food: his food and her food. She panicked that he'd eat or swallow something — a crisp or a grape — that had been contaminated by her own hands with chemicals from the salon. She began to only eat food with a knife and fork, and nothing could touch her fingers at any stage of the cooking process, which had drastically shrunk her diet.

By the time she started coming to the meetings on the advice of her GP, she was only eating ready meals since she could just peel off the cellophane. Ready meals for breakfast, ready meals for lunch, ready meals for supper. It was the same for Dunc — a 2-year-old reared almost exclusively on Bird's Eye. When I joined the group a few months on, Jaz (and Dunc) had graduated from just ready meals to ready meals along with pasta and vegetables so long as they came in a frozen bag and she didn't have to touch them before cooking. Now, she let them eat most things, apart from fruit by hand, but she still came along every other week so we could whisper in the back row. We made an unlikely pair – me, the bookish 32-year-old in ugly shoes and Jaz, the forty-something hairdresser always wearing animal print – but we'd become close. Although outwardly very different, we both knew what it was like to feel as if we'd lost control of our own brains, as if we were being operated by an internal puppeteer constantly giving us pointless and exhausting tasks.

'You all right?' I checked, looking from Dunc on the floor to Jaz. Today she was wearing a white T-shirt over a pair of snakeskin leggings.

She sighed again. 'Yeah, just dead as a dingo.' Jaz often confused her expressions. A couple of weeks ago she'd complained to Stephen of feeling as if she was between 'a sock and a hard place'.

'Dodo,' I corrected.

'One full colour and three perms today. Three! Honestly, these women. What were they thinking? And then I had to rush to school to get this one.' She nodded at Dunc and I glanced at the phone screen to see he was watching some sort of nature documentary, a lioness tearing into the hind leg of an unlucky zebra.

'What's going on with you though?' she added. 'Why the good mood?'

I didn't immediately answer. I just smiled at her.

Jaz leant forward in her small seat. 'Why you looking like that?'

'Got asked out today.' I'd been bursting to tell Eugene all afternoon but every time I nearly did, the door would ring and someone else came in to escape the rain.

'What d'you mean? By a guy?'

'Yes! Thank you very much for looking so astonished.'

Jaz whooped and jumped up, clapping with delight. 'Serious? You going?'

'Everything all right, Jasmine?' Stephen looked up from his custard creams. He was a man almost as round as he was tall who could have been mistaken for an IT teacher – short grey hair, black glasses, always wore short-sleeved shirts with a tie. Nerdy but kind. He saw himself as a south London shepherd, trying to help his flock every other week with a ninety-minute discussion and biscuits.

'All fine, Stephen, don't you worry,' said Jaz. 'Just found out that your woman here's got a date.'

I hissed as I sat. 'Shhhhhh, not everyone needs to know.'

'My congratulations to Florence,' said Stephen. 'And, Jasmine, as you're clearly so full of beans, you can be today's tea monitor.'

Jaz winked at me and headed for Stephen's kettle, plugged in in the corner behind the classroom sandpit. I fished my phone from my bag. No message yet but it was probably too soon.

I put my phone face down in my lap and looked around as the others started arriving. Notable members of our group included Mary, a middle-aged accountant who had a phobia of buttons; Elijah, who ran a nearby dry cleaners and was obsessed with conspiracy theories; Lenka, a nurse who suffered hypo-chondria, and Seamus, a Dubliner who'd been diagnosed as a compulsive hoarder and lived in a Pimlico flat full of newspapers that dated back to the Sixties. The council was trying to kick him out but Seamus kept coming up with legal reasons to stop them.

The meeting started as soon as Jaz had poured the right number of teas into the right number of mugs and handed them out. To the background noise of slurping, Stephen introduced the newcomer, a man called Paul, before asking how everyone was.

Lenka immediately jumped in. She was often suffering from something new she'd read about on the Internet.

'Not so good today, Stephen,' she said. 'I am not sleeping so well at the moment.'

Stephen tutted. 'Oh, Lenka, I am sorry. Would you like one of these while you tell us about it?' He held out the plate of custard creams.

'I am not sure why all of a sudden I am having these troubles,' she went on, taking a biscuit. 'I think perhaps it is my bad neck, and then I wondered if it was maybe too much coffee when I am at work, so I have stopped drinking the coffee. But then I read on my mobile that if you cannot sleep it might be a sign that you maybe have that disease where you forget things, what is it called, it is named after that man who used to be on the telly?' She bit into her custard cream and looked around at the rest of us.

'Alzheimer's?' volunteered Mary.

Lenka shook her head. 'No, no, the other one. You see? I am forgetting these things already.' She had another mouthful of biscuit.

'Parkinson's?' said Stephen.

Lenka's eyes widened and her head went up and down like a nodding dog.

'All right, Lenka,' said Stephen, who was careful never to rubbish any suggestion in this classroom. 'I think what we should perhaps do is look at other factors which might be preventing you from sleep. For instance, are yo—'

'You mustn't use your phone so much, Lenka,' interrupted Elijah. 'The government can see everything you can, they know what you're searching for, they know what you're rea—'

'Yes, thank you, Elijah,' said Stephen, wrestling back control. He had to do this quite often. In a session last month, Elijah insisted that Prince Philip had ordered Princess Diana's death, which made Seamus, a staunch monarchist, threaten to leave the room. The situation was only resolved when Stephen changed the subject by asking me how I was getting on with my Curtis the counting caterpillar story, a project which had been his idea in the first place. Knowing I loved books, he'd suggested that I give story-writing a go. He'd been right. With the encouragement of the other NOMAD members, I'd come up with the idea and slowly – very slowly – started writing it. I found the process soothing. On bad days my brain would play Consequences with everything I saw (if the next car is red, today will be bad. If there are an uneven number of biscuits in the tin, today will be bad. Three pigeons in the square not four? Bad). Finding a spare hour to write helped calm my mind down, but I guess Stephen had known that.

'How did this date come about then?' Jaz asked from the corner of her mouth.

'Came into the shop,' I whispered. 'Although he suggested a coffee. Is a coffee definitely a date?'

'A coffee with a man you don't know is a date.'

'What if it's a job interview?'

'Give me strength. Then it would be a job interview. Is he interviewing you for a job?'

'I don't think so.' I explained the episode in more detail: his mother's book. His intriguing clothes. His return twenty minutes later to ask me for the coffee.

'There we go,' said Jaz, folding her arms. 'It's a date. A coffee can be a date. They do it in America all the time. What's he called?'

'I don't know.'

'You don't *know*?' she replied, so loudly that it attracted Stephen's attention.

'Jasmine and Florence, are we OK?'

'Yeah, all good,' said Jaz. 'And top story, Mary. Really compelling. Carry on.' Jaz stuck her thumbs up at the front.

Mary, who'd turned her head to look towards us, glanced back at Stephen. 'Er...' she faltered.

'Go on, Mary,' said Stephen, staring at Jaz with a pointed expression. 'You were telling us how you feel on the sad anniversary of Humphrey's death.'

'Oh no,' whispered Jaz, slumping forward on her desk. Humphrey was Mary's parrot. Late parrot. He'd died last year and been the main topic of discussion at these sessions for months afterwards.

We sat in respectful silence for a few minutes while Mary continued, but I knew Jaz wouldn't be able to zip it for long.

'So when you going to see him?'

'Not sure,' I said, between my teeth.

'So you don't know his name, you don't know anything about him and he dresses like a Victorian undertaker.' She paused. 'I dunno about this.'

'What do you mean?' I said. I felt as if she'd pricked the bubble in my stomach with a pin.

'Just be careful. Could be a weirdo.'

'OK, but there's one more thing I need to tell you about.'

'What?' she hissed.

As quietly and succinctly as I could, I explained about Gwendolyn and the list. 'Is that weird?' I whispered when I'd finished. 'I don't believe in that stuff but it seems a weird coincidence, no?'

'You got this list?' she said. I nodded and reached under my chair to pull the piece of paper from my rucksack.

Jaz smoothed it across her thigh with the side of her hand and read it.

I counted them off on my fingers. 'One, he dressed well. Two, he was into books. Three, his mother collects cats. And he made me laugh, so he's funny too.'

'What was his bum like?'

'I didn't see. He looked like he was in pretty good shape. But what if it's like that Tom Hanks film?'

Jaz snapped her head up and frowned. 'Which one?'

'The one where he makes a wish and it comes true, and he's an adult when he wakes up in the morning. What if this is like that?'

'You think you've written a list describing your perfect man and now it's come true?' Jaz looked at me sideways. It was the sort of look you'd give an adult who'd just announced they'd believed in fairies. 'Girl, you need to get laid.'

'Yes, all right, so everyone keeps telling me,' I said, remembering Eugene's joke about his mum as I snatched the piece of paper back. I felt a flash of bad temper. Yes, I was unpractised when it came to dating, but it wasn't as if Jaz was the relationship oracle. After Leon, there'd been a succession of boyfriends and the last one, who she insisted was 'the one', turned out to have a wife and kids in Solihull.

'Just be careful, babe,' she went on, making me feel guilty for such mean thoughts. 'Listen, why don't you tell me where you have this coffee, and I'll come along too? I can sit at a different table like a bodyguard? You won't even notice me. I'll be totally incoherent.'

'Incognito.'

'Exactly.'

Luckily, Stephen called out Jaz's name and asked if there was anything she wanted to share, to show Paul how it was done 'as a valued and long-standing member of the group'. Jaz, inflated with pride, stood up and started explaining her story, beginning with how she knew she had to get help when she was eating Bird's Eye chicken jalfrezi for breakfast. I sat in my small chair thinking. Should I be worried? He didn't seem like a psychopath. But maybe that's what psychopaths wanted you to think? I folded the list before shifting in my tiny chair. Jaz was just being overprotective. I'd meet him in a public place and all would be fine. I just had to remember not to wear my work shoes.

*

The shop was already unlocked when I arrived the next day. I dropped the keys in my bag and pushed open the door.

'Hello?'

I expected to hear Norris's voice from downstairs but no reply. Then I noticed the counter. Usually it was tidy. Order book in place, the previous day's Post-it notes thrown away, pens in the pot, any paperwork that needed to be looked at by Norris in the in-tray. But the till drawer was open and loose papers covered the counter, held down by a motorbike helmet.

I glanced at the rest of the shop. Books had been moved, too. The biography table was a mess and a pile of hardbacks had cascaded to the floor. I stepped towards it and noticed a mug rolled on its side, its contents making a dark pool on the floorboards. 'Oh my God,' I murmured. A burglary! This was a crime scene!

I froze as I heard steps behind me.

'Hello,' said a male voice.

I spun round to see a stranger looming over me, a mop in one hand and a bucket in the other.

'Are you a burglar or a new cleaner?' I asked, confused. He was huge and, in my defence, dressed like someone who operated mostly at night: black T-shirt that stretched across his broad shoulders, black jeans and black Doc Martens boots. He also had wild, curly black hair and black tattoos that snaked down both arms.

'Neither, as it happens,' he went on, brushing past me with his cleaning equipment and stepping down into the non-fiction section. 'But I dropped my coffee while checking this place out so thought I'd better clean it up before Norris gets in.'

How did this giant know Norris?

'I'm Zach, by the way, nice to meet you.' He put down the bucket and held out a large hand, forcing me to step towards him and shake it. I felt annoyed at his casual manner. What was this man doing in here throwing coffee?

'How do you know Norris?'

He started mopping but he was an inefficient mop wringer who transported more water from the bucket to the floor than vice versa, moving it around the floorboards, before dunking the mop back into the bucket and repeating the process. I couldn't bear it.

'Give it to me,' I said, holding my hand out.

'OK,' he said, handing the mop over. More dripping on the floorboards. 'I'm going to make another coffee. Want one?'

'No thanks. And I hope you don't think me rude but who are you exactly?'

'I'm Zach.'

'Yes, you said. But what do you mean? There isn't a Zach who works here.'

'Norris's nephew,' he said. 'Did he not mention me? I'm coming in for a bit. To help with the website. And the social side of things. I'm a photographer but between jobs at the moment and he needed help so, here I am.' He flung his arms wide as if to demonstrate his physical presence even further.

'Right,' I said, as I bent over and tried to get the water from the floorboards back into the bucket. 'Did you need help with the till?' I nodded at the counter.

'Yeah, sorry,' he said. 'I was trying to find Norris's password.'

'Password?'

'For his computer, downstairs.'

'Oh. It's bottom123.'

'Bottom?'

I looked up from the mop. 'It's the donkey in *A Midsummer Night's Dream*, my colleague's idea of a joke.'

'You guys sound wild. I'll be in his office if you need me.'

He headed for the stairs before I could reply and left me mopping with the fury of a woman who'd just found an alien pair of knickers in my marital bed. Such an air of entitlement! And how typical of Norris not to have mentioned him. Improving the shop's website and social media had been my idea. If this tattooed nephew couldn't even wield a mop, how was he going to improve our financial situation?

Eugene came through the door minutes later. 'Good morning, fair colleague,' he said, sweeping an arm out in front of him. Then he stopped and frowned. 'What are you doing?'

I wrung out the mop for the last time. 'Cleaning up after our new colleague.'

'What new colleague?'

'Norris's nephew. Called Zach.'

'I didn't know he had a nephew,' said Eugene, rotating his arm around his neck to unpeel his silk scarf. Then he snapped his fingers at me to get my attention. 'Maybe he's related to Shirley?' he whispered.

'No idea. Didn't ask him.'

'Where is he?'

'Downstairs.'

'I might go and say hello.'

I followed him downstairs to stash the mop and bucket back into the cupboard. Zach was hunched over Norris's computer in his cramped office, muttering at the keyboard.

'Zach, this is Eugene, Eugene, this is Zach,' I said, pausing in the office doorway before carrying on towards the windowless basement room that served as both stockroom and staff dining room. On one side of it were boxes and shelves of pristine books, spines uncracked, waiting to go out to customers or replace sold books upstairs. On the other, a rickety wooden table decorated with coffee stains. The loo and cleaning cupboard led off from another door behind the table.

'Are you joining us full time?' I heard Eugene say to Zach as I tipped the water into the loo.

'Not sure, to be honest, mate,' Zach replied. 'You don't happen to know the password into this thing, do you? That girl upstairs said it was to do with a donkey?'

I slammed the cupboard door closed on the bucket and mop while Eugene helped him.

'Yes, it's Bottom123 but you need an uppercase "B".'

'Ah, thanks, mate, you're a genius.'

Eugene, the traitor, laughed with pleasure. 'Not at all. Do you need anything else?'

'Nah, don't worry. I'll wait for my uncle to get here.'

On my way back to the counter, I paused at the office door. 'I'm going to man the till. Eugene, can you deal with the deliveries?' Then I looked at Zach. 'Is that motorbike helmet on the till yours?'

'Ah, that's where I left it. Yeah. I'll come grab it.'

'You ride a motorbike? That's very manly,' said Eugene, in an awed tone.

Oh good, I thought as I climbed the stairs, more testosterone. Just what this place needed.

Norris arrived an hour later as Eugene was telling me about his latest audition for a cross-dressing role as the nurse in *Romeo and Juliet*.

Eugene opened the door for him. 'We've met Zach.'

Norris looked blank, as if he'd never heard of a Zach.

'Your nephew,' I clarified.

'Oh him,' Norris replied, unbuttoning his duffel coat. 'Yes, Zachary. Did I not mention him?'

'No,' I replied coolly.

'He's very good with computers and all that sort of thing so I asked if he'd help out here. We can all work together on it, of course, but Zach's a photographer and seemed to have a few ideas so I thought, why not?'

Childishly, I refused to smile back at him as I held out a few envelopes. 'He's downstairs having hacked your computer and here's the post.'

'Thank you. Everything all right up here?'

'Absolutely,' said Eugene, quickly.

'Grand. Shout if you need me.'

Norris went downstairs and I made a noise of disgust from the back of my throat.

'I don't get what's so bad about him?' said Eugene, picking up his copy of *Romeo and Juliet*. 'He seems nice.'

'I'm sure he is. It's just that I've been banging on to Norris about the same ideas for months. It's irritating to have someone else swoop in and take over.'

'OK, but do you know what I think will help?'

'A personality transplant?'

'Maybe, but my suggestion is more immediate.'

'What?'

'More rehearsing. We're about to get to the bit where Shakespeare makes a bawdy penis joke. Come on. It'll cheer you up.'

'Go on then.'

We recited lines all morning, breaking off to help the odd customer before getting back into character, then I took first lunch and went downstairs with my Tupperware.

'Florence?' shouted Norris, as I tried to scurry past his office to the stockroom unnoticed.

I stopped, briefly closed my eyes and retreated two steps.

I tried never to go into Norris's office. It was too claustrophobic and untidy: dusty books and yellowing manuscripts were piled on the shelves, ketchup sachets and little salt packets lay scattered across his desk like confetti, pens and dirty forks protruded from an old mug. There should have been health and safety tape criss-crossing the doorway: Enter At Your Own Risk.

Zach, I noticed, had already carved out a small space for himself and a laptop at the end of the desk.

'Yes?'

Norris cleared his throat. 'I've told Zachary that he can take photographs of the shop floor later.'

'Content, for the website and Instagram,' added Zach, turning from the laptop screen to look at me.

'Oh I see, we're allowed Instagram now, are we?' I raised my eyebrows at Norris.

He flapped a hand at me as if I was being hysterical. 'Yes, yes, well, Zachary's explained it and it seems like a sensible idea, so could you and Eugene have a tidy up?'

'After lunch is fine,' said Zach, his eyes dropping to my Tupperware.

'Good of you,' I muttered.

'What?'

'Nothing, nothing. Anything else? Can I get anyone a cup of tea? Coffee? A foot massage?'

'A coffee would be amazing if you're making one,' Zach replied.

'I'm not but the kettle's in the kitchen.' I gave him my best fake smile before heading to the stockroom.

One, two, three, four, five, six, seven, eight. I didn't even realize I'd counted each mouthful of my sandwich until I'd finished. The arrogance! What did a photographer know about running a bookshop? I'd been here for nearly ten years and suddenly this smug nephew was bossing me about. I tried to read my book but I couldn't concentrate, so I went back upstairs, told Eugene he could go for lunch and straightened the tables of books in silent fury.

Zach appeared upstairs an hour later, by which point I was back behind the till discussing the previous night's *Masterchef* with Eugene.

'Do you mind if I leave these here?' He put his laptop and camera on the counter and strolled around the shop floor, squatting every few minutes and narrowing his eyes across the floorboards as if he was on safari and trying to spot a lion in the distance.

'This all seems very professional,' Eugene said admiringly, so I kicked him in the ankle.

'Ow! What was that for?' he grumbled, bending to rub his leg. Such a baby. It wasn't even that hard.

'Trying to work out the best angles,' Zach said, stepping back towards us and leaning over the counter to look down at Eugene. 'You all right?'

'He's fine,' I said. 'And can you not leave your coffee there, please, because it'll stain the wood.'

Zach picked up his mug and grinned at me. 'Sorry, madam. Won't happen again.'

'Hand it over,' said Eugene. 'I'm going downstairs to make tea. Anyone want one?'

'I'll do tea,' I said, intercepting the mug just as Eugene reached for it. I suddenly very much wanted to be in a different room.

'Thanks. And I'd love another coffee,' said Zach. 'If that's not too much trouble?'

'No trouble. Milk? Sugar?'

'Just milk, please.'

'Sweet enough already,' joked Eugene as I headed for the stairs, which made me want to kick him again.

Downstairs, I flicked the kettle on and decided to take much longer than I normally would with the tea run. I could probably stretch it out to twenty minutes or so if I really tried, but my thoughts about tea-making vanished when I felt my phone vibrate in my pocket and pulled it out to see a message from a strange number.

Hello! It's Rory, who bought the books from you yesterday. Might you be free for a spin round the Royal Academy and a coffee on Sunday afternoon?

I stared at the screen. Rory seemed the right name for him. Posh, unquestionably, but that was fine so long as he wasn't the sort of man who still talked about what school he went to and that he wanted to marry a rugby ball. Putting my phone down, I held my breath as I opened the fridge (it always smelled like a very old mouse had died in there) and thought about what to reply. Should I wait a bit? I couldn't. I was too excited.

That would be lovely! I typed. Was an exclamation mark immature? But the words looked too severe without, as if I was texting a grandparent. *That would be lovely! Let me know what time works for you*, I decided, adding an 'F' and a small 'x' before clicking send.

I'd often scrutinized couples in restaurants or in the parks

I walked through, watching them laugh together. How had they got to that point? What was their secret? Maybe now it was my turn. Maybe Rory would hold my hand on Sunday and other people would look at us and think, 'What a nice couple.' Then I told myself to calm down. This was exactly what had happened in the past: I'd been too eager about someone, wondered how many children we'd have after the first drink and then they'd vanished. But not this time. No, no, no. This time I would get it right.

★

Before I could hold hands with Rory at the Royal Academy, however, there was a hurdle to clear: dress shopping with Mia, Ruby and Patricia on Saturday afternoon. Mia had made a wedding dress spreadsheet and emailed it to us all so we were 'prepared'. There were dictators who'd put less effort into military coups than Mia had put into this spreadsheet. It was colour-coded with multiple columns for each dress and space for a final mark out of ten. Who was it by? Was it strapless? A-line? Did it have a fishtail? What kind of silk was it? Where was the lace from? My favourite column on this spreadsheet was the one that asked, 'Have any celebrities worn this dress?' I wasn't sure whether Mia deemed this a good or a bad thing but guessed it depended on the celebrity. Meghan Markle would presumably score higher than Kerry Katona.

Mia, Ruby and I took the Tube from Kennington together. Mia and Ruby discussed dresses while I brooded on what to wear for my date the next day. I hadn't mentioned this to them.

Half of me wanted to scream about it. More of me knew that talking about it would invite unwanted speculation.

We walked down Bond Street towards the boutique. As Mia pushed open the door, I heard Patricia bullying the receptionist.

'I don't want too much chest on show,' she was telling her. 'Can't bear these modern brides with their bosoms racing down the aisle before them.'

'Morning, Pat,' Ruby said loudly. Calling their mother this was a long-running joke between her and Mia.

Patricia turned round. 'Ruby, please. You know I hate that. And Mia, I was just saying we're after something demure. Not too much…' she flapped her hand around her own chest and then lowered her voice, 'cleavage.'

'Mum, it's my wedding. I could go down the aisle in French knickers if I wanted,' she replied, as Patricia kissed us all in turn. Her lips left a damp patch on my cheeks.

'You could but your father and I might not pay for it.'

Mia pulled her laptop from her bag and waved it at her mother. 'I've done a mood board.'

I could already detect the roots of a headache from the candles burning in the boutique. I picked one up and squinted at the label. Meringue-scented. Candles were getting sillier.

'This is Hilda,' said the receptionist, as a middle-aged lady with blonde hair pulled into a neat doughnut appeared in front of us. 'She'll show you to your changing room.'

Hilda ushered us into a large, well-lit room with one cubicle in it. Cream walls, cream carpets, cream sofa. More meringue candles. An array of bridal magazines fanned on a coffee table.

I flung myself on the end of the sofa and picked up a magazine as Mia opened her laptop.

'OK, so I'm thinking along these lines,' she said. 'Grace Kelly, but with a contemporary twist. Big skirt but structured body.' She swivelled the screen at Patricia and Hilda.

'Oh yes,' said Hilda, smiling approvingly at Mia, 'a classic.'

I looked back to my magazine. On the front was a model in a strapless dress holding a bunch of white roses. '**White hot!**' said the cover line beside her. Underneath that, another line read: '**Cake crazy! The most fashionable flavours this summer.**' How could a cake flavour be fashionable?

'**What his mother REALLY thinks of you,**' screamed another headline.

Our kitchen table had become increasingly weighed down with these magazines in the past two weeks, Mia's neon Post-it notes sticking up from the pages. Fourteen days. That was all it had taken for her to transform from semi-normal person into a bridebot, incapable of having a conversation unless it was about the thickness of an invitation card.

She stepped into the cubicle but didn't bother to pull the cream curtain closed as she stripped. For someone so uptight, Mia had a curiously relaxed attitude towards her own nudity. I'd rather have eaten spiders than stand in front of my family in a bra and thong. It made me wonder whether I had to dig out one of Mia's lacy thongs from the back of my pants drawer for my date. Surely my underwear didn't matter much for a trot round an art gallery?

While Hilda helped Mia into something that looked more like a marquee than a dress, Patricia's attention shifted.

'Florence, darling, how was your session with Gwendolyn? Was it helpful?'

I held my breath, debating how much to share. 'It was fine,' I replied carefully.

'Shit, the love coach!' said Ruby, dropping her phone in her lap. 'Sorry, Flo, I forgot to ask.'

'What did she say?' my stepmother went on.

'You guys ever heard of patient confidentiality?'

'Oh, come on, darling, it's only us. And Hilda. And we won't tell anybody, will we?'

Hilda, unsure what she was agreeing to, shook her head at Patricia.

'She made me write a list,' I said resignedly.

'What kind of list?' asked Mia from the cubicle.

I leant my head against the back of the sofa, eyes closed. 'A list of whatever I'm looking for in a man. Must be tall and have all his own hair, that sort of thing.'

'What was on your list?' asked Patricia.

'I've read about this online,' piped up Hilda. 'It's like a sort of… wish list?'

'For God's sake,' I muttered, opening my eyes. 'Yes, it's like a wish list. You write a list of traits; mine included likes reading, is adventurous, has an interesting job and, er, is into cats. And then you put it out to the universe and supposedly the universe will deliver him.'

'Sounds mad,' said Mia.

'Agreed,' said Ruby. 'Where did you find this woman again, Mum?'

'In *Posh!* magazine. She's very well respected,' said Patricia. 'When's your next session, Florence? I think you need to take it more seriously. What have cats got to do with anything?'

I placed my palms on my knees for strength. 'In a couple of weeks, unfortunately. You said I only had to go to one session and then I find out you've booked a package of them. I'd rather enter a convent than go back to that room.'

'You might have to enter a convent at this rate.'

'Actually, I've got a date tomorrow.' I hadn't meant to let it slip out but I wanted to silence her.

Needless to say, she was the first to reply, 'Darling! How exciting.'

'With who?' said Mia.

'So it's worked?' added Ruby.

I shook my head. 'It's nothing to do with the list. He came into the shop and we chatted, not for very long, but then he asked me for a coffee. So I'm meeting him tomorrow.'

'What time tomorrow? Can I do your make-up?' said Mia.

'Afternoon. And yes, but can you not make me look mad? Nothing too over-the-top. You know I don't wear much make-up.'

'Oh, Flo, stop fussing. A bit of eyeshadow never killed anyone.'

'Who is he though, darling?' persisted Patricia. 'Do you know anything about him? Is he safe?'

'I can't tell you anything else,' I said, shrugging. 'Only that he's called Rory and he likes books.'

'Rory, what an excellent name!'

'Just remember we're dressing you for it,' said Mia sternly, before looking at herself in the mirror. The dress was sleeveless with a skirt that billowed to the floor and was covered in little crystals. 'Fuck no, not this one. I look like I'm going to my prom.'

CHAPTER THREE

ON THE TUBE TO Green Park, my stomach writhed like a sack of snakes. Mia and Ruby had forbidden me from walking because they said it would make me sweaty. Or sweatier, I thought in my seat, peering underneath my jacket to see dark damp patches already spreading across my armpits. I was wearing a knee-length green dress of Ruby's which belted at the waist. 'Emphasizes your tits,' Ruby had said.

I'd replied that I didn't have any but she said that was rubbish and I needed to stop hiding them in 'boring old work shirts'.

While sitting on a stool in front of her bathroom mirror, Mia had set to with a bewildering array of make-up brushes. Foundation, concealer, highlighter. Dab, dab, dab. A light dusting of eyeshadow. 'Just to make your eyelids less purple,' she'd explained. 'And you need to sort out your brows.'

'What's wrong with them?'

'They need their own stylist. Hold still.'

A waggle with an eyelash curler. Multiple coats of mascara. Eyebrow gel. Bronzer smoothed across my forehead and down my nose. The flick of a blusher brush along my cheekbones.

'Lipstick,' mused Mia, scrabbling through her make-up bag.

'No,' I insisted. 'I've got some Carmex in my bag.' Thinking of it on the Tube, I reached for the small pot and unscrewed the lid before running my finger along my mouth. I exhaled into my hand to check my breath. Better have a Smint.

When the doors opened at the station, I was so nervous I didn't want to get out. Then, while the escalator rolled upwards towards daylight, I rechecked my armpits and reminded myself to keep my jacket on at all times.

As I walked under the archway into the academy's cobbled courtyard, I slipped my fingers underneath my sleeve to feel my pulse. Should it be beating that fast or was I seconds away from a medical emergency? I looked up at the pale stone of the academy walls and started counting the windows as a distraction: 'One, two, three, four…'

'Florence! Over here!' said a voice, and I squinted in the corner to see Rory waving. He was leaning casually against the stone wall in a pale blue suit and a brown trilby and didn't look nervous at all, but if you'd asked me my own name and what year it was, I couldn't have told you. To me, he seemed as intimidatingly handsome and composed as a male model.

'Hello,' he said, when I neared him. He took off his hat and leant forward to kiss me on the cheeks. That citrus smell again.

'Hi,' I managed back, already blushing. I could hardly look at him but when he caught my gaze, I saw his eyes matched the colour of his suit.

'Shall we go in?' he added. 'It's had terrific reviews. Have you read any?'

I shook my head. I didn't know much about art – art books were Eugene's territory.

Rory rattled on as he held open the main door and led us towards the staircase. 'I'm not a huge fan of their religious work. Too flowery and idealized. But the *Telegraph* called this "a sexy riot of flesh" and I thought, well, we can't miss that, can we?' He laughed and stepped up to a desk at the top of the stairs. 'Two, please.'

I looked up at a huge poster on the wall in front of us. 'Sex, Power and Violence in the Renaissance Nude,' it said, above a painting of a naked woman, asleep. One hand was draped over her head, the other was rootling between her legs.

'Medieval masturbation,' said Rory, nodding at it.

I laughed and blushed again. Was it possible to die from blushing?

'Come on,' he said, and I felt his hand on my back as he ushered me through the door into the first gallery. I edged my way around a large woman in a fur coat to read an introduction on the wall but the text was too small.

'Let's not bother with that,' said Rory, waving a hand at the wall. 'I'll tell you about them as we go.'

It was excruciating to begin with. The first painting we stood before was by Titian, a naked Venus washing her hair in the sea, nipples as bold as raspberries. 'See that?' said Rory, pointing at a shell floating beside her thigh. 'She was born and carried ashore on it.'

Next were a naked Adam and Eve, Eve rubbing an apple forlornly against her cheek. Then a picture of a fat and completely hideous baby Jesus by a Flemish painter. With each one, Rory explained its backstory and my embarrassment at being surrounded by so much nakedness dissolved. As did my claustrophobia from the packed galleries because it meant I could lean into Rory to listen to him.

'How do you know about all this?' I asked him.

'My mother. She's always loved art and I'm an only child so I got the full education. The full monty. No beach holidays. It was Rome, Florence, Venice... Off to see whatever exhibition she could find. Oh look, this Titian is exquisite,' he said, reaching for my hand and pulling me in front of another reclining woman. Although one of her hands was also resting in her groin, she was staring at us with a bored expression.

'Isn't it extraordinary?' said Rory, his eyes scanning the canvas. 'It's one of his most famous, painted for an Italian nobleman of his new wife. Do you see the dog and the maids?' He pointed at a small spaniel curled on the sheets and two women in the background.

I nodded.

'It's supposed to serve as a reminder to his wife, with all the drudgery of marriage, not to forget about the bedroom.'

He turned and winked at me and I burst out laughing, before clapping a hand over my mouth. The atmosphere in the galleries was too hushed for hoots of laughter.

'Shall we get a coffee?' he said, grinning back.

'Yes, good plan,' I said gratefully. I felt that imbued sense of cultural improvement at having drifted through a set of galleries, but the naked ladies – all rounded hips, hair tumbling

artfully over their shoulders, and breasts as round as rock
cakes – were starting to blend into one another.

Rory told me to bag a seat by the café's windows while
he queued. I glanced at the other tables as I sat and wondered
whether we looked like two people on a date or two friends
catching up. Surrounded by tourists and tables covered in
empty sugar packets, this suddenly didn't feel much like a date.
More an interview, like Jaz had said. Perhaps Rory would
come back to the table and ask me what my strengths and
weaknesses were and where I saw myself in five years' time?
I looked at my phone.

Ruby: **Update please!**

Mia: **Is he coming to the wedding?**

I slid it back into my bag as Rory twisted his way between
the tables towards me with a tray.

'Here we go,' he said, lifting off the coffees and a plate of
shortbread, before sliding the tray on to a spare chair so it
was hidden underneath the table. 'Otherwise it's like we're at
school. Urgh,' he shuddered.

'How's your book?' I asked, having thought of the question
while he was queueing. Good to have something prepped and
avoid awkward silences.

Rory frowned.

'*The Struggle.*'

He screwed his eyes shut. 'I have a confession.'

'What?'

'I'd read it before.'

'What d'you mean?'

'Before I came into the shop. And Dooley's first book, *In the Middle of the Night*. You were right. It is terrific.'

'But how come you…'

'Bought it? Because I wanted to keep talking to this charming woman who worked in the shop. She's called Florence, and her surname is…?'

'Fairfax,' I replied, blushing again. I'd have to see a doctor.

'Called Florence Fairfax, exactly. I wanted to keep talking to her. And to gloss over the fact my mother had just bought a book about eroticism.'

I laughed then leant backwards, fearful that I'd just wafted coffee breath all over him. 'Oh I see,' I said. 'So it was an evil ploy?'

'For it to be evil, there'd have to be evil intentions, wouldn't there?'

'And you don't have evil intentions?' I asked, trying to replicate his coolness when it was the sort of question on which so much depended. The sort of question some of us take to heart, rolling the answer about in our heads like a marble in case any intelligence can be gleaned from it.

Rory shook his head. 'Not in the least. I am a thoroughly upstanding sort.' He leant back and hooked his thumbs through his braces.

'What do you do?' I asked. I couldn't imagine him in an office sweating over a spreadsheet.

'I work in the Foreign Office.' He announced this as casually as if it was the post office.

'Blimey. Doing what?'

'I'm a spad. It's a nickname; it means a special advisor.'

'To who?'

'To the minister, but I'm hoping, at the next election, to run as a candidate.'

'As an MP?' I tried not to sound incredulous.

He nodded. 'My grandfather was one and since I was a teenager I've thought, well, why not?'

'Conservative?' I was guessing as much from his Radio 4 accent as well as his clothes.

Rory twisted one side of his mouth into a grimace before answering. 'If I said yes, would you hate me?'

I smiled. 'No, I think it's… amazing to want to go into it at all. I can't imagine it. All those speeches.' It was my turn to shudder.

'But let's not talk politics,' said Rory, crumbling the short-bread and holding a piece out. 'I spend my life talking about politics. What about you? How is it that Florence Fairfax comes to be working in a Chelsea bookshop? What's her story?'

'Just always have,' I said, fiddling with the handle on my coffee cup. 'Studied English at uni and wasn't sure what to do with it. But I loved reading. So ended up there.'

'You think you'll stay?'

'At the shop?'

He nodded.

'Yes. Although…' I paused and sighed, 'the rent's going up and Norris, he's the owner, is in a flap about it. So who knows. But I write children's books on the side. Well, not books. Book, singular. About a caterpillar called Curtis. So I'm hoping that I can do something with that.'

'Sweet, and what about your family?'

'About them?' I asked, momentarily confused. He'd rattled off a number of questions so quickly, almost as if it was an interview, and I was worried that I'd answer the wrong thing.

'What are they like? Do you get on with them?'

'Oh I see. Yes, mostly. I live with my two sisters in Kennington. Well, technically they're my half-sisters. And my dad, actually, hang on, you might have come across him, he's called Henry Fairfax, the ambassador to Argentina?'

'You're joking?'

I shook my head.

'No, I haven't met him but I know who you mean. What a coincidence that he's your father. Wasn't he in Pakistan, before?'

'Exactly. Good knowledge!'

Rory grinned. 'Part of the job description. Do you go out there much?'

'Argentina?' I shook my head again. 'Never have. He comes back every now and then, although usually it's pretty brief and just for meetings.'

'Is your mother with him?'

'Nope. She died when I was three.' I'd become so used to explaining this that I forgot the effect it had on other people, their stammery awkwardness.

'Oh Christ, there I go with my big feet. I'm sorry.'

'It's OK. It was years ago.'

'What happened?' he asked, his eyes remaining on mine.

'Car crash. Not her fault. Just… one of those accidents.'

He winced. 'I'm so sorry.'

'It's all right. I'm pretty lucky in many ways; I've still got family around me.' I reminded myself of this whenever I woke in the sort of mood where I wished I could swap lives with somebody else I saw on Instagram. I was lucky; I had a good job and I still lived in my childhood home. I'd fall in love eventually. Had to. Even Hitler had a girlfriend. I couldn't be the only person who'd never have a proper relationship.

'I think that's a bit harsh on yourself, isn't it?'

I frowned. 'How come?'

'Well,' Rory started, leaning across the table, 'I think if you grew up without your mother, you don't have to tell yourself that it's all right because you've still got a couple of sisters and a father. It doesn't work like that.'

'I've also got a very involved stepmum,' I added, grinning at him.

'In that case I take it all back. What are you grumbling for?' he said, which made me laugh, and nobody had ever made me laugh when it came to conversations that skirted around my mother. Normally I tried to avoid the subject altogether.

We sat at the table for another hour chatting, finding our way around one another. He'd grown up in Norfolk and now lived in Pimlico. I told him about my French grandmother and my half-sister developing a wedding fetish.

'You don't want to get married?' Rory asked and I instantly felt like I was about to trigger a tripwire. What was the right, casual, unstudied answer to this in front of a man you already liked?

'Er, yeah, I think so,' I started. 'I just… can't imagine losing my mind over it.'

'I can't wait.'

'To get married?' I checked, surprised.

'Indeed. The whole shebang: wedding, family, dog.'

'Oh right,' I replied, unsure what else to say. It seemed unfair that men could admit this, could declare they were desperate for domestic harmony but women were supposed to keep any such aspirations hidden. 'I thought you liked cats?' I asked, mindful of both my list and Marmalade, who was probably, at that moment, cleaning his bottom on my bed.

'Ideally we'll have both.'

I tried not to give it away but I felt like my whole face lifted into a smile at the 'we' in that sentence.

'Right,' he said, reaching under the table for the tray. 'This has been splendid but I'd better get back. Various bits and pieces to read before tomorrow morning.'

'Cool,' I replied, wishing the afternoon hadn't sped by so quickly. But if this was it and I never saw him again like all the others, it had been nice. Better than nice. It had been great. I hadn't done anything embarrassing, apart from sweat continually for three hours, and all I needed to do now was get home and have a large glass of water.

'What are you up to this evening?' he asked.

I usually spent Sunday evenings making my flapjacks and obsessively refolding my knicker drawer. 'Not much.' I shrugged. 'A book in the bath, probably. Early night.'

He slid the tray into a metal stand and we walked out

silently, my heart thumping in time with our steps back down into the courtyard.

'So,' Rory said, stopping just before the stone arch on to Piccadilly and turning towards me. 'How are you getting home?'

'Walking.'

'All the way to Kennington?'

I smiled. 'I like walking. It's not that far.'

'Okey-dokes, I'm going to jump on the Tube. But that was lovely, thank you.'

'Yeah, me too. Shit. I mean, not me too, but thank you, too. If that makes sense?' I blushed again.

'I know what you mean,' Rory said, before kissing me lightly on the mouth. 'See you soon, Florence Fairfax.'

I watched his back as he walked towards the station. If he turns round in the next six seconds, I told myself, then this is really something and he won't disappear on me. I counted in my head, feeling a creeping sense of panic. Please could he turn? Please could he look back at me? My excitement would turn to gloom if he didn't.

He spun when I got to four and grinned, saluting at me as he had in the door of the bookshop. I smiled back then started my walk home. It was astonishing how quickly it could happen. In the space of an afternoon, my brain had pushed out all other thoughts so now there was only room for Rory. I didn't even notice the colour of the cars passing me.

★

He messaged the next morning. I realize this is pathetically keen, but I'd like to see you again soon. Are you available for dinner tomorrow?

If it had been my own funeral the following night, I would have leapt up and insisted that, actually, I was feeling much better.

I replied saying I was free and he sent another back saying could I 'present' myself at a restaurant in Battersea called Ratatouille at 8 p.m. He messaged like he talked, as if Mr Bingley had got hold of a mobile. It impressed me; it seemed more sophisticated than other men. On the Ambergate Road WhatsApp group that consisted of me, Ruby, Mia and Hugo, Hugo sent messages like 'Mia, what time ru home?' and 'Cn sum1 buy bog roll?' as if he couldn't spell really quite basic words.

'Eugene, do you mind if I take first lunch?' I asked on Tuesday morning. 'I've just got a few, er, errands.' I'd rediscovered an old black dress from Whistles in my cupboard but it had a low-cut neckline which needed a new bra that winched everything up a couple of inches.

'No, absolutely fine, my darling. You go,' Eugene replied. 'Good morning, Adrian,' he added, as one of our regulars stepped through the door. 'How are we today?'

'Capital, capital,' Adrian replied. He was a retired general who liked our history books.

'Do you need a hand or are you happy left to it?'

'Not to worry,' said Adrian as he staggered towards the biographies.

'If you don't mind me saying,' Eugene said, as I returned my attention to the non-fiction table in front of me, 'you seem unusually cheerful today.'

'That's probably because I've got a date tonight.'

Eugene clapped his hands to his cheeks. 'Sound the trumpets! How has this come about?'

'He came in here, and we had a coffee on Sunday. And now it's dinner tonight.'

'Where?'

'Ratatouille? In Battersea?'

He nodded approvingly. 'Very good choice.' Then he frowned at me. 'What are you wearing?'

'Not this, don't worry,' I said, brushing my hands down my navy T-shirt and sensible trousers. 'I've found an old black dress.'

'With which shoes?'

'With heels and a pair of tights.'

He nodded again. 'All right, I will allow it. And I do hope you've booked yourself a waxing appointment.'

'What, why?'

Eugene sighed and shook his head at me. 'Darling, you mustn't go into battle unprepared.'

'I'm not sleeping with him yet,' I replied primly, looking back down to the table of books and straightening a pile of Napoleon biographies. I'd thought about it, obviously. Last night, I'd tried to imagine swinging one leg over Rory's hips before unbuttoning his shirt but the fantasy was interrupted by Marmalade kneading the pillow beside me.

'You remember what I said about my very old mother in her retirement home?'

'Yes, yes, yes.'

'All right,' said Eugene, holding his hands in the air, 'just a friendly reminder. But tell me, who is this lucky man?'

'He's called Rory. And he seems charming and clever. And he works for the Foreign Office. He wants to be a politician and—'

A bark of laughter interrupted us from the stairs and Zach appeared with his camera around his neck. He was still taking photographs for the new website and seemed to be taking a long time about it, but I told myself that the trail of devastation he left behind him – cold coffee cups abandoned on bookshelves, his motorbike kit cluttering up the wrapping area – was for the greater good of the shop.

'What's so funny?' I asked.

'Sorry,' said Zach, stepping towards us, 'but you're going on a date with a politician called Rory. A Tory, right? Got to be with a name like that. Rory the Tory. Ha!'

I didn't reply.

Zach looked from me to Eugene and back again. 'It's just, oh come on, he sounds like something from an Evelyn Waugh novel.'

'You've read many of his, have you?' I couldn't imagine Zach – black T-shirt and black jeans again today, black hair falling over his forehead – sitting down with a copy of *Brideshead Revisited*. He looked more like a lumberjack than a reader.

'I have,' said Zach, crouching down to take a picture. 'Most of his, anyway, but *Scoop*'s my favourite because it's about war journalism and that's what I've always wanted to do.' He looked up from his camera. 'How about you?'

I had to hurry the conversation on because I hadn't actually read much Waugh and I'd only seen the film version of *Brideshead*.

'Rory's not like one of his characters,' I said, defensively. 'He's clever. And funny. And...' I was about to go into detail about his wardrobe, mostly for Eugene's benefit as I knew he'd appreciate the braces, but I stopped myself. Zach would only laugh. 'And he's not a politician yet anyway.'

'But he is a Tory, right?' needled Zach.

'So what?'

'Nothing,' he said, squinting back into his camera. 'I'm sure he's lovely. I'm sure he doesn't eat babies for breakfast or want to run the NHS into the ground.'

I felt a flash of anger. 'That's so predictable.'

'What is?'

'Making assumptions about people based on their name. Assuming he's some sort of monster when you don't know anything about him. How can you pigeonhole someone like that. It's just...' I paused, mentally groping for the right word.

Zach looked at me expectantly.

'It's just...' I went on. 'It's just... very boring!'

'Children, children,' interrupted Eugene, 'let's not ruin poor Adrian's morning by shouting about politics over him.'

'I'm quite all right,' croaked Adrian, flapping one hand from the corner.

'I'm going for lunch,' I snapped, reaching under the till for my rucksack. I couldn't slam the shop door because it had a guard on its hinges, but I would have done otherwise. Arrogant, rude computer geek, I thought, while I stood half naked in an Intimissimi changing cubicle and shortened a black bra strap. I'd pity whoever had to date him, frankly.

★

I waited until the others had left that night before changing in the cramped loo downstairs. Squinting in the mirror above the basin, I tried to do my eyeshadow like Mia had demonstrated. Light brown over the eyelid. Dark brown just beneath the eyebrow. Blend. I leant back to inspect it and almost screamed. What was a racoon doing in this bathroom? I took it all off again with a wipe, glanced at my phone and realized I needed to get to the restaurant in half an hour. Shit. Forget the eyeshadow. I reapplied wobbly eyeliner and mascara to eyelids that had turned pink from the rubbing and dabbed blusher into my cheeks.

Next, bus along the King's Road and over Battersea Bridge as I counted the number of cars we passed. I was sweating, obviously, when I pushed through the restaurant door. How did normal people do it? I wondered, wiping a bead off my upper lip with a finger. How did normal people go on dates and manage to survive it all without dying of shame and embarrassment (and dehydration)? How did the human race manage to reproduce when even sitting across from someone in a restaurant was such a horrifying obstacle course?

I handed my bag and coat to a waiter when I heard him behind me, his voice alone causing a clap of adrenalin to surge through me.

'Hello.'

'Hi,' I replied, spinning round. The greeting! What sort of greeting did you go for if you'd already kissed on the mouth? Did you revert to two kisses on the cheek? Or another peck on the mouth? One kiss with that awkward half hug? I wished that I was more experienced in such matters as Rory leant towards me, kissing me on the cheek and squeezing the top of my arm. Not an option I'd even considered.

A waiter showed us to a dimly lit table in the corner – one candlestick and a small bunch of primroses in a jam jar – and pulled my chair out.

''ere you go, sir, madam, thees are thee menus and 'ere is thee wine leest,' he said, with such a thick French accent I thought he might be faking it.

'Thank you very much. Glass of champagne?' Rory asked me across the table, hanging his dark suit jacket on the back of his chair and revealing a pair of red braces.

'Amazing. Yes please.'

'Two glasses of Billecart, please, and I'll keep this,' he said to the comedic French waiter, tapping his fingers on the wine list.

'So,' he said, leaning forwards on the table. 'How was your day, dear?'

'Fine,' I replied, smiling shyly. I'd ignored Zach all afternoon while he took more photos, trailing cables along the floor and moving books from the right place to the wrong place on the basis 'they looked better' where he put them. But he forgot to slot them into place again afterwards so I tidied after him while Zach loitered by the counter, talking Eugene through his camera settings. 'It was fine,' I repeated. 'How about you?'

'Bloody marvellous and we're celebrating!'

'How come?'

'Because today I got the phone call from the party saying I'm on their list.'

'List?'

'For becoming a candidate at the next election. There are various hurdles to clear before you can fight a seat and have to get on an official list before you can apply to any constituency. But today I was approved for that list.'

'Congratulations! How exciting. So what next?'

He exhaled. 'You have to wait, basically, for a seat to come up. And they have to approve you, and you have to fight an election. And normally first-timers are given marginal seats and it's a long slog. But I'm hopeful.'

He dropped his voice and boomed across the table, 'This is not the end. It is not even the beginning of the end. But it is, perhaps, the end of the beginning.'

'See? You're made to be a politician,' I replied, laughing at his performance.

'It's actually Churchill who said that.'

'Right,' I replied, 'I knew that.' I didn't, so I glanced down at the menu to hide my cheeks for a few moments before the waiter reappeared. He placed two glasses of champagne on the table and took our order.

'I think we should have a dozen oysters,' Rory said. 'You eat oysters, yes? They're excellent here.'

'I've never actually had one.'

'Good God! We must correct that instantly. So a dozen oysters, and then, Florence, what would you like?'

'Could I have the cod, please?' I said, automatically picking the dish which didn't come with anything too fiddly and tiny to count.

'And I'll have the bourguignon,' said Rory. *Pomme purée* and… some carrots, I think. Ah, hang on, the wine.' He ran a finger down the wine list and hummed to himself for a few moments. 'And a bottle of the Côte du Rhone, please.'

'Absolument, monsieur.'

'Ah no, sorry, hang on,' Rory said, and the waiter turned back to him again. 'We're having oysters to start so what Sancerre do you have?'

'We only 'ave one,' he replied. 'A very nice 2016.'

'Fine,' said Rory. 'A bottle of that and then the Côte du Rhone, please.'

My head was swimming with oysters and wine as Rory turned his attention back to me and rubbed his hands together. 'I love the moment when you've just ordered and it's all ahead of you, don't you?'

I burst out laughing. I wasn't sure I'd ever met anyone so sure of himself.

He cocked his head at me. 'What?'

'You! Your self-confidence. I wish I could be more like it.'

'Really? You seem a cheerful sort.'

'Do I? Good. I can be, sometimes.'

'But not others?'

I thought about the days that my brain seemed locked in battle against me, a small but angry voice telling me the exact opposite of what I wanted to hear. 'If only you were a stone lighter,' or 'Why is your hair so crap?'

'No, not always.'

'Everyone has their moments but look at us now.' He sat back in his seat and stretched out his arms. 'Here I am in one of my favourite restaurants, opposite a very beautiful and intelligent woman, having just ordered oysters. Nothing much wrong with that, is there?'

I laughed again. 'Have you always been this positive?'

He nodded. 'Think so. Why not? It's why I want to go into politics. More people should be like this. Could be like this, instead of moaning all the time. "Oh, the schools, the housing crisis, the health service." Well, come on, if we all stopped being so downbeat, things could be better. Don't you think?' He leant forward, his elbows on the tablecloth, his blue eyes locked on mine.

'Yeah, maybe. But I'm not sure it's as easy for some people.' Then I paused, and to indicate I was teasing, smiled across at him. 'What's the ultimate goal then – Prime Minister?'

'Ideally,' he said, as the waiter poured him a thimble of white wine to taste.

'Seriously?'

He nodded.

'Marvellous,' said Rory to the waiter, before grinning at

me and leaning forward on the table again. 'Why not? You have to dream big.'

'Right, yeah, I guess,' I replied, remembering that 'ambitious' was also on my list. I had a large mouthful of wine and was still mulling this over when another waiter staggered to the table with a large silver bowl.

'Oh great stuff, the oysters,' cried Rory. 'Let's make space.' He moved the salt and pepper as the waiter lowered the bowl full of ice, lemon quarters and the oysters, wet and shiny in their shells like the contents of a sneeze in your palm.

I reached for the smallest one and a slice of lemon.

'Bottoms up,' said Rory, as he lifted a shell to his own mouth and threw it back.

I let mine slide down my throat without chewing. Was it supposed to be that creamy?

'Mmm.' I tried to sound appreciative.

'What about you?' he asked. 'Do you think you'll always be in London?'

'Not sure. It's always been home but it doesn't seem very adventurous, staying in the same place all your life.'

'What about the country?'

'Maybe. How come?'

'I'm a country person,' said Rory, seeing off another oyster. 'I spend my life on a plane now, but ideally I'll end up with a seat in Norfolk, near home. Do you like Norfolk?'

'I've never been,' I replied, poking at a shell with a teaspoon.

'It's wonderful. The sea, the beaches. The fish! The most outrageously delicious fish. And did you know that it's the only British county without a motorway in it? Isn't that a good fact?'

I laughed again and nodded. And as he talked, I relaxed. I even thought I might be enjoying myself instead of worrying about the next thing that could go wrong. Lifting my glass, I finished it and felt suddenly high on the novelty of being in this restaurant and sitting across from him. A real-life date.

'I think I could be very happy doing all sorts of constituency business up there,' he went on. 'There's an excellent bookshop in a town called Holt. So you could just take over that.'

'What?'

'When you come and live with me in North Norfolk,' he said happily, before draining the last oyster. 'Goodness, they were smashing. Weren't they smashing?'

I was so taken aback by this casual mention of a future in Norfolk that I couldn't focus on the oysters. It was quite the statement for a second date but I could sense that part of me found his certainty comforting. I often couldn't decide whether I was going to have a good or a bad day until a certain number of blue or silver cars had passed me on the way to work, and yet here was a man who seemed to know that his entire life would pan out just as he wanted it.

By the time the cheese trolley rolled up to the table after our main courses, I was drunk. We'd spent most of dinner having an increasingly impassioned debate about our favourite and least favourite writers. Rory declared he hated American novels. I'd always held romantic ideas about American writers and defended them. Then I bet that he liked the Scottish writer George MacDonald Fraser. There was a certain type of public school-educated man who loved the sexually depraved escapades of his hero, Harry Flashman. Rory replied that he did indeed and, just as the cheese trolley came to a halt beside our table, he leapt in the air to pull an imaginary sword from its scabbard, neatly smacking the cheese-pushing waiter in the face with his fist. The waiter staggered backwards clutching his nose; Rory started apologizing.

'*Ai*! *Quel imbecile*!' the waiter mumbled through his fist.

'Look, I'm so sorry,' followed up Rory, 'it was an accident. I was trying to show my friend a scene from a book. Are you all right? Oh dear, I think you might need some tissues. Have you got any tissues?' he shouted in the direction of the kitchen. 'Or a drying-up cloth?'

Other diners in the restaurant paused to watch this spectacle.

'I think we'd better leave,' said Rory, sitting down at the table minutes later, once the waiter had been helped off the restaurant floor with a fistful of kitchen roll held to his face.

He asked for the bill and paid, silencing my offer to pay my half with a fierce stare.

In return, emboldened by the wine and Rory's own confidence, I asked if he wanted to come back to mine. It felt right. He'd made me feel secure enough to be brave and I couldn't imagine that he'd vanish the following day without even a text message. I'll admit, there was a small, buried piece of me that wanted to prove my family, Eugene and even Jaz wrong, to show that their jokes about my lack of love life were unfair. But it wasn't just that. I wanted to do this. I wanted to remain in Rory's hypnotic company.

'I'd love to,' he replied, so I ordered an Uber and collected my tote bag and coat. Rory apologized to the staff again and we stood on the pavement outside waiting for our Toyota Prius.

'Good evening, my dear fellow,' Rory said, falling into the car after I'd shuffled across the back seat. 'We're off to Kennington, I believe.'

'He knows, it's all right,' I said, before letting out an enormous hiccup which made both the driver and Rory stare at me.

'Sorry,' I said, but then came another one, loud as a frog's croak.

'Look at me, I've got a brilliant cure for this,' Rory said as the car pulled out.

I turned my head.

'Bit closer,' he said, so I slid towards him on the seat. Another hiccup. Practically a burp. But the champagne, and red wine on top of white wine, had left me too drunk to be embarrassed.

He stretched out his hands and cupped his fingers around my forehead, one thumb on each cheek, as if he was investing me with magical powers.

'What the he—'

'Shhhh,' he commanded. 'Concentrate. Look at me.'

'I don't understand. What's this do?'

'Shhhh, just stay quiet for two minutes.'

He carried on staring into my eyes, his fingertips pressing into my head. It felt like a playground blinking competition, just more intense, and I wondered briefly what it would be like to have his face looking down on mine in bed.

'Why are you blushing?' he asked, fingers still in place.

'I'm not!'

'I think you're cured,' he said, dropping his hands. 'See?'

I sat back and waited for a hiccup. None came.

'Hang on though, I'd better just check,' said Rory, so I turned again and he raised his hand, only to scoop it round the back of my head and pull me into him for a kiss. A longer kiss than before, and no tongues because a Toyota Prius is an intimate space and we were only inches away from Aaron the Uber driver. But it made me feel as if I was floating all the same. I just prayed that my sisters would be in bed when we got back.

★

They were, fortunately, and the house was black.

'I'm right at the top,' I whispered to Rory, closing the front door quietly. I didn't want to risk making a noise and Mia or Ruby, or even Hugo, poking their head from their bedroom doors, so I led him straight upstairs.

'Stay here,' I whispered, once we'd reached my room. 'Two minutes.' I shut myself in my bathroom to pee and brush my teeth. I suspected my tongue tasted of garlic.

I peed and wiped with extreme care, then kicked my tights off on the bathroom floor and went back bare-legged to find Rory stretched out on my bed.

He extended an arm for me to lie down on his chest, on top of the duvet. We lay still for a few minutes before he rolled on to his side and looked at me.

'Hello,' he said, and then came a proper kiss, his mouth pressed hard against mine. His fingers dropped slowly from my face, down my neck, skimmed over my chest and down the length of my dress.

He reached its hem and tugged. This panicked me. I was trying to concentrate on my kissing technique but, equally, how to get my dress over my head without flapping around like a trout on the deck of a trawler.

'Stand up and take it off for me,' he whispered, which made my stomach fizz. At least, I hoped it was fizzing because of Rory and not one of the oysters.

I stood unsteadily and reached behind my neck for the zip while maintaining eye contact with him. This was hard to do alluringly; I felt like someone had just dared me to lick my elbow. The thought made me snicker.

'What's funny?' Rory asked from the bed. His face – serious, intense – made something flare inside me again. Please could it not be an oyster.

'Nothing,' I said quickly, undoing the zip as far as I could before pulling it down my back with my other hand. Twirl it around my hand like a showgirl? I couldn't. It seemed too silly. I laid the dress carefully on my bedroom chair.

'Now those,' Rory instructed, his eyes dropping to my knickers.

I hooked my thumbs into the elastic either side of my hips and inched them down my legs. Was this seductive? It didn't feel very seductive. My bottom stuck out behind me as I bent to slip them over my ankles and I decided I felt more like an elderly user of a public swimming pool, trying to maintain her balance while she peeled off her wet bathing costume.

I dropped the knickers on the floor. Would worry about the mess later. But now I was standing on my bedroom carpet in front of him wearing only my bra. That felt weird. What sort of psychopath walks around their bedroom with just a bra on?

Rory left me standing uncertainly in front of him as he pulled his braces off his shoulders and, with one hand, tugged his shirt over his head.

'Come here,' he said, so I knelt on the bed. But the bra was still worrying me. When should the bra come off? Should I do it?

He slid a hand between my thighs and pulled one of them across his hips so I was straddling him, then he leant forward and expertly undid the bra with one hand. Dropping it to the carpet, he lowered his hands to cup my bottom, pulling me towards him so he could suck each nipple in turn.

I sighed at this, closing my eyes and leaning into him, resting one hand over his shoulder on my bedroom wall. Rory's tongue flicked my right nipple, then my left and made me want to howl with pleasure. What was I thinking, forgoing this for so long? Masturbating was all very well, and I had an alarmingly purple vibrator that I kept neatly tucked in a drawer under my bed, alongside a pack of wipes to clean it afterwards, but it wasn't anything like this. If masturbating was a boring old piano scale, this already felt like a Chopin sonata.

Rory pulled back his head to kiss me again and I felt an electric thrill at the warm sensation of his skin against mine.

I ran a hand down the line of hair that spanned his chest, aching for him to do the same, for his hands to map every inch of my own body.

Some years ago, I'd watched a Josh Hartnett film and snorted with disbelief at a scene where Josh made a woman orgasm simply by wafting an orchid across her body. It seemed unlikely. Wishful thinking, Josh. But now I understood. If Rory carried on kissing me while his hands skimmed my bare back, I was going to scream so loudly I might wake my sisters.

Stop thinking about your sisters, Florence.

His hands ran down my ribcage giving me goosebumps, but then he lifted me off him and stood up. I watched as he unbuckled his trousers and pulled them down with his boxers. My eyes flicked from his face to his penis, looming out at a pleasing angle towards me. Although I'd never been sent any dick pics, I'd always found the concept strange. Why would sending a picture of something that looked like a Cumberland sausage do it for anyone? But Rory's penis didn't look like a Cumberland sausage. It looked as well-groomed as the rest of him.

'Lie down,' he instructed.

I lowered myself from my headboard, legs bent, and he knelt between them.

'Please touch me,' I said, surprising myself. I hadn't planned that. It just came out.

He grinned back and shook his head. 'Not yet.' Pushing my knees further apart with his hands, he knelt between them before gently kissing up each inner thigh in turn, his stubble tickling the softest, most sensitive parts of my legs.

'Oh my God, oh my God, oh my GOD,' I panted. The ache in between my legs had turned to throbbing. He had to touch me. Please could he touch me. Please could he just reach up and—

'JesuSSSSSSS,' I sighed, as I felt his mouth over my clitoris and his tongue flicking just below it and back up again. He'd repeated the pattern all of three times when I realized I was going to come. I couldn't hold it. A heat spread from the arches of my feet and flooded my lower body until it reached the spot where Rory's tongue was pushing harder and harder and harder and...

'I'm going to come, I'm going to come, I'm going to come, I THINK I'M COMING,' I gasped, grinding my hips into his mouth and gulping for another breath.

Imagine actually choosing to be a nun and giving this up.

'Don't move,' he said, raising himself up on his knees before falling forward, pinning his arms around my shoulders. Moving one hand so it held my chin, he stared seriously into my eyes and pushed into me. I gasped again and again while he slid in and out, kissing me on the neck, across my collarbones and then my mouth. His lips pressed against mine and his tongue thrust into my mouth with more urgency. And when he started groaning, I felt a deep, primeval pleasure that I was making him do this. He was making these sounds because of me. After such a period of abstinence, it made me feel more like a normal person, a normal functioning person who could have sex without panicking about the subsequent drama and heartache that it might create. Except this was much better than normal. It felt sublime, up there with my fifteenth birthday when I was given Marmalade.

Stop thinking about your cat, Florence.

I banished him from my mind as I ran my fingers up and down Rory's back and he sped up. Back and forth, back and forth, while I congratulated myself on the perfect night, the perfect date, where we talked and talked and I didn't say anything premature like 'Where shall we go for our honeymoon?' or 'I can't wait to meet your mum'.

And now this: pretty perfect sex. No embarrassing fart noises. No awkward fumbling. No moment where he strayed near my bottom because I wasn't into that.

And it was just as I was daring to hope that there might be a second time, praying that he wouldn't ghost me, that he thrust for the final time, froze on top of me and shouted 'COWABUNGA!' as he came.

Oh, OK. So it was nearly perfect.

★

I woke the next morning feeling polite again. 'Morning,' I said to Rory, in much the same way that I said it to Eugene every day.

Rory reached over and kissed me on the head. 'Morning, my little *chou-fleur*.'

'You sleep all right?' I asked, wondering how I was going to get out of bed without flashing my bottom. I'd slept on the wall side of the bed, which either meant climbing over Rory or shuffling down the mattress and walking around the foot of it.

'Yes, this bed is outstanding,' he replied, yawning and stretching his arms out, deliberately draping his forearm over my eyes.

'Get off, you weirdo. I need a shower.' I pushed his arm away and decided on the end of the bed route, wiggling down it with as much dignity as I could (not much) before heading to the bathroom. But he caught my wrist as I passed his side of the bed and pulled me in for a kiss. I held my breath but he held open his side of the duvet and pulled me down on top of him.

'I've got to get in the shower,' I said, trying to direct my breath away from his face.

'Ten minutes? Come on, you have ten minutes,' he insisted, before running his hand down my body. I sucked my stomach in and realized I needed to pee. But Rory was kissing down my neck and along my shoulder and I didn't want to fight him. His hand pushed open my legs and I sighed through the corner of my mouth, directing my breath at the wall instead of his face. Nobody would die if they arrived at the bookshop and had to wait ten minutes for the new Stalin biography.

It was only ten minutes. That was all it took for him to make me groan before he shouted 'Cow-a-bung-aaaaa!' again in my ear, his body pressing mine down. I gave it a minute or so before sliding out from underneath him and shutting myself in the bathroom.

I really needed the loo now. I could feel my stomach… moving. Those oysters, I remembered, turning on the shower to try and disguise any noises.

I sat on the loo and decided I couldn't go. Not with his head on the other side of the wall. Too close. So I held it in and climbed over the side of the bath into the shower. Cowabunga, I kept thinking. Quite strange? But he hadn't mentioned anything afterwards so neither had I.

'Hey, Rory, the sex is great but can I just ask why you keep shouting like a cartoon character at the end of it?'

I wasn't bold enough. Maybe it was one of his weird jokes? I liked him. I *really* liked him. I didn't want to find a fault with something so small. It wasn't as if it was an ex-girlfriend's name. I rinsed my hair and turned the shower off, rough-drying it while standing on the bath mat. I wanted to saunter back into my bedroom like a bikini model, tendrils of damp hanging loose over my shoulders, instead of hair so wet and flattened I looked like Dougal from the *Magic Roundabout*.

But when I opened the door, he was gone. His clothes had been picked up from the bedroom floor and the bed was made. Not as perfect as I would have liked because the pillows were in the wrong place. But not bad. I went to my bedroom door and listened. From the kitchen, I could hear Mia and Ruby's voices, so I dressed as if the attic was on fire and rubbed in some tinted moisturizer while taking the stairs down two at a time. Two, four, six, eight, repeat, before rounding the banisters and skidding towards the kitchen.

'Morning, all,' I said, panting. 'This is Rory. Rory, this is Mia and Ruby.' I put a hand on the kitchen table and leant on it to try and steady my breathing.

'You all right?' asked Rory.

'Yes, all good. Just, er, a very hot shower.' I glanced at Ruby, sitting beside the sink in her dressing gown. 'You're up early?'

'I heard Mia chatting to Rory and I couldn't miss that, could I?'

'We've just been chatting about his job,' added Mia, 'and it sounds very *interesting*.'

She said this with a sly smile, which made my heart speed up. She mustn't mention the list. On no account could Rory find out about the list. There was no sensible way of explaining that, shortly before meeting him, I'd visited a witch doctor on Harley Street and asked the universe to find me a boyfriend.

'And all that *adventurous* travelling he does!' said Ruby. 'Plus, you probably have a lot of time for reading, Rory, with all that time on a plane?'

Rory looked from one sister to the other, momentarily confused. 'Er, yes, yes, I have to say I do. That's how I met Florence, did she tell you? I was in the bookshop.'

'She did. It seems quite the coincidence.' Ruby's eyes, alight with mischief, danced from him to me and then back.

'Mmm, anyway, Rory, do you want a coffee?' I said, reaching for the kettle.

'No, no, I'd best be off.'

'To the office and your interesting job?' asked Mia.

Rory laughed. 'Yes, exactly.' He stepped forward to kiss me on the cheek. 'But thank you for a magnificent evening.'

I nodded up at him, briefly awed that there was a handsome man in the kitchen because of me and not one of my sisters.

'Wonderful to meet you both,' he said, waving a hand at them.

'You too,' they shouted, as I led Rory through the hall and opened the front door.

'See you soon, I hope?' he asked, turning back to kiss me again.

'Sure,' I said, smiling, which was a casual way to put it when every cell in my body was screaming 'YES, YES, WHAT ABOUT TOMORROW? ARE YOU FREE TOMORROW, OR THE NEXT DAY, OR THE DAY AFTER THAT? OR HOW ABOUT FOR EVER? ARE YOU FREE FOR EVER?'

He left, his jacket slung over his shoulder, and I went back to the kitchen.

'A magnificent evening, hey?' said Ruby, still sitting on the counter. 'You need to tell us everything right now.'

They got the edited version while I drank my coffee and made my lunch. 'Nice dinner, no awkward silences, home,' then, 'yes, OK, we slept together.' It felt strange talking to them about sex when I never had before.

'And?' pushed Mia. 'Come on, I need more than that. Hugo and I normally only do it on Sunday mornings before golf and even then it's quite quick because he never wants to miss the first tee.'

'And nothing. It was nice,' I said, wrapping my sandwich in clingfilm while trying to banish the mental image of Hugo having sex in his Pringle golf socks.

'Nice?' said Mia. 'Just nice? Flo, a cup of tea and a piece of cake is nice. You can do better than that.'

I slid my lunch into my bag and headed for the hall, but

shouted back at them over my shoulder. 'All right, it was amazing, he spun me about like an Olympic gymnast *and* we did it again this morning. OK, got to go, see you guys later, bye!'

'I'm going to tell Pat!' Ruby shouted as I closed the door behind me.

I walked to work, thoughts rolling around my head like lottery balls.

Good things about Rory: he was hot, funny, clever, ambitious.

Bad things: 'COWABUNGA!'

I could still hear him shouting it. But I had very little to compare last night's performance to. Maybe that's what everyone was doing these days? Maybe it was a thing?

I pushed open the shop door just as I remembered what I'd written on my list: 'Oh my God, James Bond!' I'd written 'Bottom and sexual athleticism of James Bond' on my list and admittedly I had fairly limited experience, but Rory had definitely put in an energetic performance. Twice.

'I'm flattered but it's Zach,' said Zach, lowering his camera from his face.

I shook my head. 'Sorry, ignore me, I was just thinking about… something.'

'About James Bond?'

'Sort of. Long story. Why are you in so early?'

'Better light at this time of morning,' he said. 'Plus, I'm not in anybody's way. You all right?'

'Yes,' I snapped. 'How come?'

'You look terrible.'

'Thanks.'

'Sorry,' he replied. 'Just a bit pale,' he added, circling a finger around his own face.

'I'm hungover,' I said, dropping my bag behind the till.

Zach swivelled to face me. 'Of course! The big date! How was it?'

'Good, thank you.'

'Sorry,' he said again, sensing my coolness. 'Being nosy. And sorry about yesterday too. I didn't mean to be flippant.' He held his hands up in the air as if surrendering. 'It's none of my business.'

'That's all right,' I said, because it was the simplest answer and I didn't want to talk to him. I needed a coffee.

The door jangled as the day's deliveries arrived. Five boxes of books.

'Can I have a chat to you about something?' Zach asked once I'd signed for them.

'Now?'

'Or later if you'd prefer. Nothing urgent.'

'Can we do it closer to lunch? I need to set this lot out,' I said, gesturing at the boxes.

'Sure. I'll get out your way,' said Zach. He went downstairs and I opened the drawer under the till for the Stanley knife. I ran it across the first box, pulled out as many books as I could with one hand and started scanning them into the system. I arranged them in even piles in front of me before reaching back into each box. Hardback fiction, non-fiction, paperback fiction, non-fiction. 'Two, four, six, eight,' I mumbled, double-checking each pile.

'Why d'you do that?' said Zach, reappearing on the stairs a few minutes later.

'What?'

'Count everything.'

I shrugged. 'Just a habit.'

He put a mug down in front of me. It was coffee. 'I heard you doing it while I was taking pictures yesterday and I was wondering if it was some sort of system you have. Anyway, here you go. Thought you could do with it.'

'Thanks,' I said simply.

Eugene was at his *Romeo and Juliet* audition so I busied myself with putting the books out all morning in silence. Zach appeared again just before lunch to ask if it was a 'good moment' for our chat.

'Are you firing me?' I asked, following him downstairs to the office.

He laughed. 'I don't think my powers extend that far.'

Norris had gone out but it still felt an awkwardly cosy space for Zach and me to squeeze into. I hovered in the doorway as Zach lowered himself into one chair, then pulled Norris's desk chair towards him and motioned for me to sit.

'I've written a plan for the shop. I'm sorting out the website. Instagram, Twitter and all that,' he said, scrolling down a Word document on his laptop. 'But what I was also thinking is events.'

'Events?'

'Yeah, like talks. Readings. Q&As. That sort of thing. That's what I wanted to talk to you about. Have you ever done them here?'

'No. Can you make much money from them though? Realistically?' A small, ungenerous part of me wanted to pour scorn on his idea.

'It's not just about cash. Well, it's partly about cash. But it also means more people through the door, more sales. And we could even record them and put them out as a podcast. It's pretty easy, I could do it on this.' Leaning forward in his seat to gesture at his screen, his knee touched mine and I pulled it away as if he'd given me an electric shock.

'Sorry.'

'Have you mentioned it to Norris?'

Zach shook his head. 'Nah, wanted to see what you reckoned first.'

'It might work,' I said, trying not to sound too enthusiastic although I knew it was a good idea. When I was a teenager, I'd been considered nerdy for my excessive reading. Reading on the bus into school, reading at break, reading on the bus home again. Reading had always been the only way I could stop myself from counting. But nowadays, books had become cool and nobody was called a nerd for being into them. It was fashionable to post pictures of whatever you'd just finished reading on Instagram, to listen to podcasts about books and to buy tickets for readings by the latest millennial poet. Millennial poets! I had an idea.

'Actually,' I said, 'there's a new anthology out by Fumi next month.'

Zach frowned.

'She's an Instagram poet,' I explained. 'Posts haikus. Has

a pug called Percy. People are obsessed with her, and the dog. She sold about a zillion copies of her debut last year. We could try and get her for a reading. I'm not sure she'd do it but we could ask?'

'Yeah, that's the kind of thing,' said Zach, pulling his phone from his jeans pocket. 'Fuck me, she's got nearly a million followers.' He moved the phone closer to his face. 'What's she doing with that dog?'

I peered at his screen. Fumi's latest picture was a bathroom selfie with her pug tucked under her arm. She was pouting at the camera in a purple bomber jacket. Both she and the dog were wearing sunglasses. '**Have a #beautiful day my babies**,' said the caption, followed by a string of purple hearts.

'Yeah, that's her. Might be worth trying to get them for Norris's reaction alone.'

Zach laughed. 'Right. So do you want to check with him or shall I?'

'You do it,' I said, still smarting that Norris had ignored my suggestions.

The bell rang upstairs as the door opened so I stood, keen to get out of the claustrophobic space. 'I'd better get back.'

'OK, cool, but you think events are a good idea?' he asked as I was halfway through the door. 'You know this place better than me.'

I turned back, feeling a pang of guilt that I hadn't been supportive enough. 'Yes, all right, very good, nice work.'

'Just call me James Bond,' he replied with a wink.

'Don't push it,' I shouted behind me.

The rest of the afternoon dragged. I ate pink wafers surreptitiously behind the till while Eugene quizzed me about
my date, although I had to pause my story every time the door
jangled and another customer came in. I didn't want to give
our more elderly customers a stroke.

'I take it all back about my mother and I hereby award you
nine out of ten,' he declared, holding an imaginary paddle up
at me when I'd finished my update – Eugene was a big *Strictly
Come Dancing* fan and had recently pinned up a calendar in the
stockroom so he could cross off the days until it started again.

'Why don't I get ten?' I asked, reaching for another wafer.

'Because it's early yet and I want to see how you progress.'
He picked his phone up from the counter. 'What's his surname
again? I'm going to google him.'

'Dundee.'

Eugene tapped at his phone. 'Oooh, he is handsome. Lovely
eyes. But there's only this one picture. Can't find much else
about him.' He frowned at me.

'No I know, he doesn't have social media.' Rory had
explained this over dinner. No social media meant no dodgy
photos or tweets that could come back to haunt him when he
became a politician. He had it all mapped out.

'Oh but look,' Eugene said, excitedly. 'He's a "rising star"
on this list.'

He put on a serious voice and read from the screen.
'"Rory Dundee, thirty-seven, went to Harrow, then landed
a First in Politics, Philosophy and Economics at Cambridge.
Currently works as a special advisor in the Foreign Office but

has ambitions for high office. The grandson of former Tory agriculture minister Edward Dundee, Rory has impressed civil servants with his can-do attitude and ruthlessness. Whispers say that he's headed for the top.'"

He put down his phone and clapped his hands together. 'Ruthless, I love it! When you're living at Downing Street, can you have me round for drinks?'

'Eugene, do not mention drinks,' I said, lying my head on my arms, unused to having a hangover on a weekday.

'If you get married, you could be the First Lady,' he went on.

'Eugene…'

'Can I be your dresser? You'll need a dresser.'

'Eugene…'

'Can I come on your private jet?'

I lifted my head up, unable to bear it any longer. 'Eugene, let's not get carried away after two dates. And the prime minister doesn't have a private jet. That's in America.'

He pinched his finger and thumb together and ran them across his mouth. 'All right, I'll zip it. But I'm excited. I have a good feeling about this one.'

I got a message from Patricia that afternoon too. She'd obviously spoken to Mia. 'Darling, he sounds PERFECT. A politician in the family! Your father will be thrilled. Keep us posted!'

'In the family'? Patricia was deranged. Although annoyingly, I could already sense a tiny, giddy bit of me – a very, *very* small bit – daring to imagine what that would be like.

CHAPTER FOUR

I SAW HIM TWICE in the next two weeks. Dinner both times: once at a pizza place in Borough Market, the next at a Japanese restaurant the size of a shoebox in a Knightsbridge basement. There, we sat at a counter while the chefs passed dainty plates of sushi straight to us from the kitchen and I was so happy to be on a fourth date that I didn't even mind eating rice, which I normally avoided on the basis it was too fiddly to count. But here, I just did it. No fuss.

I'd started noticing that people looked inquisitive when I was out with Rory. First they studied him; drawn by his accent, they'd next take in the old-fashioned trousers and the braces.

Then they'd look at me, but only briefly before their eyes flicked back to him. This applied particularly to other women but I didn't mind. I was just proud to be there, sitting, talking, laughing in his company.

There were only a couple of things that worried me. Firstly, I often felt quiet in his presence, as if I wasn't dazzling or captivating enough while he talked about politics, about art and about the dozens of exotic cities he'd visited across the world. He seemed so much more worldly, especially when it came to his exes. He often mentioned them and there seemed to be dozens; it was 'Tallulah this' or 'Sophia that'. I imagined the sort of women you see smiling from society magazines – wearing hairbands and showing off their perfect dentistry. Rory's obvious romantic experience made me feel a tiny niggle of insecurity about my own.

Secondly, the 'cowabunga!' thing. It kept happening. After the Japanese, he'd slammed his hand so hard against my bedroom wall at the critical moment I worried that he'd punched through the plaster. But I didn't want to spoil anything by asking him about it. Wimpy, I know, but what if I ruined everything?

I hurried along the pavement to my second session with Gwendolyn, keen to discuss the situation. You see very few people skipping along Harley Street. Mostly they amble along fearing the needle or a poke in the prostate. But I had questions to ask. I wasn't sure quite how to phrase these – did you send a handsome blond man into the shop on purpose? Are you a real witch? – but I'd figure it out.

Rory had flown to Nigeria over the weekend with the Foreign Minister but WhatsApped me every day. I felt a tragic little thrill every time I saw his name pop up on my phone. He'd texted me back! And again! Byron might have written great love letters but, from Rory, even a message about what he was having for dinner or a photo of his hotel room gave me a buzz.

I counted myself upstairs to the fourth floor of the Harley Street building and knocked on Gwendolyn's door. On her command – another shrill 'Come i-hinnnnnn!' – I pushed it open and winced, having forgotten the pinkness of the room.

'Florence, poppet, wonderful to see you, have a seat,' she said. She was dressed as if she'd just returned from her gap year in Thailand: baggy cotton trousers, white T-shirt, flip-flops, a purple bandana wrapped around her head.

I sat. She cocked her head and smiled. 'How are you?'

I wondered when I should mention Rory. I was torn between wanting to announce that I'd met someone who shared several items on my list, and being unable, or unwilling, to admit it to her, lest she claim all the credit. 'Good. I've, er, actually been on a couple of dates since we last met.'

Gwendolyn closed her eyes and smiled serenely. 'Ah yes. I thought as much. I could tell it the moment you stepped into the room. Since I removed those love blocks, your energy is quite different.' She opened her eyes. 'Tell me about him.'

'He's, well, he's got a few of the qualities on my list. That's what I want to talk to you about,' I said, reaching for the folded piece of paper in my bag. 'Because it seems a coincidence—'

'Is it a coincidence or is it the universe granting you your wish?' she interrupted, with the same, wide smile. Maybe she was on drugs. Maybe you could only talk like this if you took heavy-duty medication?

'It can't be the universe,' I said, smoothing the list on my lap. I ran my eyes down it. 'I mean, it can't be. It doesn't make sense. You can't have made this hap—'

Gwendolyn interrupted again by reaching towards me. Her hand, decorated with gold rings, looked like that of a medieval king.

I gave her the list and she frowned down at it. 'Does he like cats?'

'He says he does.'

She nodded as if that was to be expected.

'Does he have an interesting job?'

'Yes. He works for the Foreign Office but wants to be an MP beca—'

'Does he have an impressive bottom?'

I blushed. Now I'd seen him naked, I knew he did. No spots. No hair. Not too insubstantial and bony but not too chunky either. That looked weird on men. At uni, there'd been a geography student with a curved, womanly bottom and he always wore jeans that emphasized it. Big Bum Bert we'd called him. Poor Bert.

'Yes,' I replied.

'And how is his...' her voice dropped here to a whisper, 'performance?'

My face turned as pink as the room as I heard the echo of 'COWABUNGA!' in my head. 'It's... impressive.'

'Has he got a nice mother?'

'Not sure.'

'And his clothes?'

'Definitely no pointy shoes or Hawaiian shirts.'

She continued running down the list and I agreed that Rory ticked all of them. I wasn't sure about the bathroom habits yet, admittedly, and I hadn't told him about my counting. But otherwise it was a perfect match.

'It sounds as if the universe has delivered, darling,' said Gwendolyn, folding the list and handing it back to me. 'He seems very promising. You said you wanted someone with the sexual energy of Sean Connery...'

'James Bond,' I clarified. 'I didn't actually specify which one. And if we're picking, Sean wouldn't actually be my first choice. I'd rath—'

Gwendolyn silenced me by holding up a hand. 'Florence, you're getting distracted. Let's stick to the point; what's worrying you about all this?'

'I'm not worried. I'm just not sure I can believe it, that writing this list has made it come about.'

She spread her hands in front of her. 'Why should it matter if you believe it? It's happened. You've met someone.'

'But what if it's too good to be true? What if it all goes away again?'

'Ah,' said Gwendolyn, waggling a finger at me. 'That is something entirely different. That is your own self-belief. But I can do something about that.'

'What?' I was instantly suspicious.

She glanced at my hands, first right, then left, and then flicked her eyes upwards. 'Are you wearing any jewellery?'

I reached under my jumper for the gold chain I always wore with the capital letters 'A' and 'F' hanging from it. Dad had given it to Mum after I'd been born. She was called Amélie, so the necklace represented the first letters of our names mingling together. 'This,' I said, tugging the necklace towards her. 'Why?'

'Remove it and we shall enact a short ritual.'

'What kind of ritual?'

'A little ritual to help with your self-confidence, nothing to worry about. Hand me the necklace.'

I removed the chain and Gwendolyn laid it on the coffee table between us. 'Now we need Venus,' she said, standing to reach for the shelf. She picked up one of the naked statues, the purple wax one whose head had already been melted, and placed it beside the necklace. Next, she reached into a drawer under the table for a box of matches and lit the candle. 'Close your eyes and imagine you're sitting in a circle of pure light.'

'What?'

She batted a hand at me. 'Eyes closed, please. Imagine the circle. Are you doing that?'

I nodded, except I wasn't imagining a circle of pure light. Instead, I was imagining how embarrassing it would be if anyone I knew could see me acting out the instructions of a sorceress in flip-flops.

'Come to me now, the love and the energy of the four archangels.'

I held my breath to prevent a snigger.

'I call upon Archangel Raphael in the east,' she said, 'I call upon Archangel Michael in the south, I call upon Archangel Gabriel in the west and I call upon Archangel Uriel in the north.'

Her voice became louder. 'Venus, the power of love, please come to our little ritual!'

I wondered how long this would go on for. I wanted to be home in time for *Masterchef*.

'I call on Venus and the archangels to bless this amulet,' she continued, almost shouting by this point, 'to charge it with love, with passion, with stability and with protection. Help the physical and spiritual qualities of Florence, er...' she paused.

'Fairfax,' I muttered, eyes still closed. She might be a witch but she was terrible with names.

'That's the one! Florence Fairfax, to help her physical and spiritual qualities shine out into the world from now and for ever onwards.'

'Amen,' I said, thinking it sounded right in the circumstances.

'No need for an amen. But you may now open your eyes.'

I opened them to see her blow out the candle and scrape the chain off the table. 'Here,' she said, handing it to me. 'Wear this and you will be imbued with more positivity about life.'

I doubted this very much but fastened the necklace. 'What's the ritual supposed to do?'

'It will encourage a powerful energy to develop within you, helping you to vibrate at a much higher frequency and draw people towards you. And it will encourage your new friend Roger...'

'Rory.'

'It will encourage your new friend Rory to fall magnetically in love with you,' said Gwendolyn, clenching her fist and thumping it against her chest. 'Now, we have two sessions left,' she went on, 'so shall we schedule them now or do you want—'

'I'll call you,' I said quickly, standing up. 'I'll have a look at my diary and let you know.'

'I look forward to it,' she shouted behind me as I opened the door.

As I walked home, I tried to detect a growing magnetic field within me. My stomach rumbled as I crossed Lambeth Bridge but I think it was just hunger.

★

Later that evening, I was refolding my T-shirts when Rory rang. Seeing his name on my phone screen made my stomach somersault.

'Hello, how's Nigeria?' I asked, smiling down the phone.

'Hot,' he said. 'But listen I can't be long as we've got an official dinner about to kick off. I just wanted to see if you were free on Thursday?'

'I think so, how come?'

'I'm having drinks with a few friends at the House of Commons. On the terrace. Would you do me the very great honour of being my date?'

'Course,' I said, still smiling. 'Do I need to wear anything special?'

'Absolutely not,' he replied, 'but bring some ID. They'll make you go through security. And that's marvellous news! I feel better about being away from you now. Got to dash. I'll see you then.'

'Great,' I said, although he'd already hung up. I dropped my phone on my bed just as there was a knock on my door.

'Can I come in?' It was Ruby.

'Sure,' I said, surprised. Mia and Ruby were constantly in and out of each other's bedrooms, borrowing shoes and stealing hair ties, but they rarely came upstairs into mine. I'd become used to this and pretended not to mind, even though it was another small but significant demarcation underlining that I was different to them, that I wasn't quite in their gang. And to be fair, my room was more spartan than theirs. No cushions on my bed. Grey blinds on my skylight windows instead of curtains. The only photo was on my bedside table, taken on my third birthday in the kitchen downstairs. I was wearing a party hat, the elastic digging into my chubby chin, and beaming at my cake. It was shaped like a '3' and covered in Smarties. My mother was crouched protectively around me, also wearing a party hat over an abysmal perm. It was the last photo taken of us together.

'Hey,' I said, as Ruby appeared from behind the door. 'What's up?'

'Can I sit?' She nodded at my bed.

'Course. You all right?'

She pinched her lips together and inhaled. 'I'm fine,' she said, 'but I was wondering if I could borrow some money?'

'Money?'

'You know the papery stuff that buys things?'

'What for?'

She didn't reply.

'Ruby?'

'It's kind of embarrassing,' she said finally.

'Try me.'

'A personal thing.'

'How personal?'

Ruby pressed her hands to her face and spoke through her fingers. 'I think there's something wrong down there.'

'What do you mean?'

'An STD,' she mumbled through her fingers. 'I think Jasper might have given me something.'

'OK, what are the symptoms?'

She dropped her hands and scrunched her nose. 'Burning. Like a really bad burning. And itching.'

'What about discharge?'

'Gross! Can you not use that word?'

'Sorry,' I said, 'that's just a thing sometimes, isn't it? Cottage cheese or whatever. But hang on, I'm not saying I won't lend you money, but can't you get a free test for this kind of thing?'

'I can't get an appointment until the end of the week and also…' She paused. 'OK, this is going to sound stupid, but what if I'm spotted?'

I pinched my lips together to stop myself from smiling. Ruby had been on television once in an advert for Andrex but, sure, she was going to get asked for her autograph in an STD clinic.

'There's a place off Harley Street that can do all the tests for £300 tomorrow and it's same day results. Blood tests, swabs, the lot. But I'm broke and I don't want to put it on my credit card in case Dad sees. I don't want to ask Mia because it will go straight back to Mum. And I don't want to ask Jasper because if he has given me something, I want to cut his blue-blooded penis into very small pieces and feed it to the birds. So I thought of you.' Ruby looked up at me hopefully.

'Flattered, thanks.'

'Oh, go on, Flo, pleeeeeease. I can't tell you the pain. It's like I've chopped a chilli and had a good rummage down there.'

'All right, all right.'

She leapt up from the bed and hugged me. Her hair smelt of cigarettes. 'Thank you. You're the best. Can you transfer it now and then I'll book it first thing?'

'Yes,' I replied wearily.

'Amazing, thank you, thank you,' said Ruby, releasing me and heading for the door.

She vanished downstairs again leaving me standing in my bedroom, shaking my head. Was it OK to feel strangely proud that she'd asked me for this kind of help over anyone else? I decided it was, especially because Ruby didn't seem that emotionally traumatized by her fiery private parts.

★

I was on the phone to a customer the next morning when Zach appeared by the counter and loitered.

'I'll wait,' he mouthed, when I pointed at the phone to underline the fact that I was busy. It was off-putting, Zach hovering in front of me while I tried to concentrate on the demanding American who wanted me to find a book about the history of the tractor which was printed in 1942.

'What is it?' I asked, when I finally hung up.

'Your Instagram poet has said yes.'

'What? I thought she'd never go for it. And the dog?'

'Yeah. The publishers are keen. Just spoke to them. I think they see it as a credible place for her. A grown-up bookshop instead of, well, reciting that dross to a million 16-year-olds from her bedroom. But they've suggested Thursday next week. Is that too soon?'

'WHAT?' I repeated, more loudly. 'It's way too soon. Have you told Norris?'

'I have and he says we're in charge of the whole thing. Come on, we can do it, you and me. Do you want to grab lunch and make a plan?'

I thought about the sandwich and apple in my bag. Having a different lunch to the one I had planned meant a change in routine and a change in routine, even if it was giving up my cheese and tomato sandwich, made me feel uneasy. Plus, I didn't want to have an awkward, stilted lunch with Zach. I tried to think of an excuse.

Eugene shouted over a pile of books he was shuttling around the shop floor.

'Go on, you big jessy,' he urged, before looking at Zach. 'She's going to tell you she's brought her lunch, which means she can't possibly have anything else.'

Having worked alongside one another for five years, Eugene and I had learned each other's tics and habits. He always left the Stanley knife out on the counter and he told every customer to 'have a magnificent day', which made me want to beat him over the head with a very thick hardback. He knew my lunch routine. But because we'd become friends over the years, he was one of the rare people who was allowed to rib me for my neuroses.

'It's wasteful to throw it away,' I insisted.

'Fine,' said Zach. 'Bring your lunch and I'll grab a sandwich from somewhere. Then we'll go sit in the square.'

An hour later, I unwrapped my sandwich and kicked my foot at an approaching pigeon, while Zach sat on the arm of the bench, his Doc Martens on the seat, already halfway through his baguette.

'I've got a mate we can get chairs from, that's easy,' he said, his mouth full. 'And the recording's a doddle on my computer. Do you think we need to offer drinks?'

We were interrupted by the ping of my phone. It was Ruby. 'Sorry, hang on,' I said. 'It's my sister.'

Zach waved a hand as if to say no problem and I opened the WhatsApp.

IT'S GONORRHOEA! Can you BELIEVE it? I'm going to knee that asshole in the goolies so hard he'll never be able to have sex again. But thanks for lending me the $$$! See you later! Xxxx

Yikes I'm sorry, I typed back. *Antibiotics?*

I put my phone down. 'Sorry, family stuff.'

'All OK?'

'Kind of. Love-life stuff.'

'Yours?'

'No!' I answered quickly. Zach had such a direct manner he made me feel exposed, as if I might say more than I intended, and I was uncomfortable at the idea of discussing Rory with him again, risking his scorn. 'My sister's love life.'

He opened his mouth to ask something else but I jumped in first. 'OK, this event, if you really think we can pull it off, what are we asking a ticket?'

'Twenty quid? I reckon that makes sense, and we could get seventy chairs in upstairs, which means £1,400.'

I nodded slowly and then squinted at him. 'I think we need to give them a drink if we're charging that.'

Zach ripped another hunk from his baguette – so big it could barely fit into his mouth. It was like eating next to a marauding Viking. 'Fine,' he said after a few chews. 'Chuck in a few bottles of wine, some paper cups. Crisps if we're feeling generous. Now all we need to think about is who's going to interview her.'

'Nobody needs to interview her. It's a reading.'

'Yeah, about that...' he started.

'What?'

'I agreed with the publishers that we'd interview her. Do a quick chat, more like an introduction. She's shy, apparently.'

'Shy? She can't be that shy. She tells a million people every day what she's wearing and takes selfies in bed.'

He wiped his mouth with the back of his hand. 'I guess it's different if it's a phone screen. So what I was thinking is, why don't you do it? Intro, few haikus, quick Q&A, done.'

'ME? No way, uh-uh, sorry.' I'd rather have eaten the one-legged pigeon pecking at crumbs underneath the bench than talk in front of an audience.

'But it was your brilliant idea,' he said, his tone more cajoling. 'And you know about her. It's got to be you.'

'Zach, I can't talk in public. I really can't. Why can't Eugene do it?' I stared at the paving stones in front of the bench and instinctively started counting them in my head.

'No way. He'll start acting out one of her poems and nobody will ever come to an event again. And I can't do it because I'm in charge of photos and recording.'

I stopped counting when my gaze reached the black railings on the edge of the square, and I brushed the crumbs off my trousers. Under the bench, the pigeon was now dragging itself towards a cigarette butt. The idea of speaking in front of an audience made me wish I could shape-shift into a bird and fly away. When I started going to NOMAD and Stephen invited me to share my story, I was so nervous that I stood up and said, 'Hello, my name's Stephen' and everyone had laughed. My confidence had grown since then and I could usually remember my name but, still, a big audience of paying punters, Fumi next to me, Zach recording it. The cheese sandwich spun inside me.

But it wouldn't help the shop if I said no, and perhaps I could invite Rory? He might be impressed to see me standing up in front of a crowd interviewing an Instagram poet. Confident, capable Florence making everyone laugh instead of nervous, sweating Florence worried about saying the wrong thing.

'OK, I'll think about it.'

'You're my hero,' said Zach, holding a hand in the air.

Reluctantly, I high-fived him back.

*

Later that night, Rory called me from Nigeria again to retract
what he'd said about not having to wear anything special
for drinks at the House of Commons. Apparently there was
a dress code, women had to wear dresses, and would I mind
very much wearing one?

'I *have* to wear a dress?' I said, down the phone. 'Are we
going to a drinks party in 1929?'

Rory apologized and said it was ridiculous, that he didn't
mind what I wore at all and I could come naked, as far as he
was concerned, although it would make him furiously jealous
of all the men who would stare at me. 'And indeed of all the
women.'

'Hang on, I thought it was drinks with friends?'

'It is.'

'Who are all these people? And how come there's a dress
code?'

'It's work friends,' Rory told me, before reiterating that it
was all 'terribly absurd' but he didn't want me to feel out of
place.

The result of this conversation was that I arrived at
Westminster tube station that Thursday evening in a yellow
dress and pair of block heels I'd panic-bought from Zara.
Yellow seemed a cheerful idea at lunchtime, but now I felt like
Homer Simpson and the shoes were already rubbing my heels.

I crossed the road and walked through a set of black gates,
then down a slope to the entrance Rory had told me about.

After showing my driving licence to a surly policeman, I found him waiting at the end of the security belt.

'You look like a daffodil!' he said, kissing me on the cheek.

It wasn't clear if this was a compliment or not. 'I hope it's all right,' I replied, wriggling my right foot to relieve the pressure of the new blister. 'But how are you? How was your trip?'

'Oh fine, fine, official business,' he said, ushering me into a vast stone hall with a vaulted ceiling like a cathedral.

'Wow, look at this place!' I wanted to stop and gawp but Rory was hurrying us along the paved flooring.

'So what's the deal tonight?' I asked, trying not to hobble. Hobbling isn't alluring, Florence; ignore the throbbing on your heel and keep up.

'Deal?' he said over his shoulder.

'You said work friends, so who exactly?'

'There'll be various of us, I expect, I won't know everyone.' He led me up nine steps (an uneven number, bad) and through a door into a corridor which smelt like school, a powerful combination of Pledge and stew.

'OK, but who will you know?' I persisted.

'Just a couple of people from the office, a chap called Noddy and another colleague called Octavia. It's a networking thing.'

'Networking? Rory, I thought you said it was drinks with friends?'

He stopped in front of a door, through which I could hear bar noise, and put his hands on my shoulders. 'It's various friends, a few of them, just at a work event. OK?' He kissed me on the forehead and took my hand. 'Come on, I can't wait for you to meet them.'

It was as he led me through the door that I noticed a sign outside it which said, 'A Conservative Future wine reception'.

A political drinks party! He hadn't said anything about that. What if I said something dim? What if I met someone who asked me to tell them the philosophical differences between Labour and the Conservatives and I had to admit I wasn't sure? Who was the current home secretary, the one with the loud handbags, or the man who looked like a frog?

He pulled me through the stifling room, past people chatting and laughing in huddles. 'Hello, hello, lovely to see you,' he said, smiling broadly at them all as we passed, before tapping a tall man on the back.

'Noddy, there you are.'

The giant swung round and grinned. 'Hello, old bean, how are we?'

'Tremendously well,' Rory replied, releasing my hand to shake his. 'Noddy, I'd like you to meet Florence. Florence, this is Noddy, one of my oldest school friends.'

'Hi,' I said, and tried not to wince when this man – Noddy? Could I really call him that? – crushed my palm with the strength of a Trojan. He had a square face and the bleached teeth of an American film star.

'Florence, good to meet you.'

'You too.' I couldn't call him 'Noddy'. It was too ridiculous. I retrieved my hand and let it fall by my side, limp as a washing-up glove.

'Who's here?' Rory asked. 'Have we missed anything?' He reached for two glasses of white wine from a passing waiter and handed me one.

'No. Nothing to report. The PM might look in later. Didn't you say that, Octavia?' Noddy turned to a blonde woman beside him.

I felt immediately intimidated by Octavia because, quite apart from her very short black dress and cascading hair, she was wearing Ferrari-red lipstick. Every now and then, inspired by a celebrity photo, I tried a red lipstick in Boots but they all made my teeth look yellow, which was why I stuck to Carmex.

As if she could sense my wariness, she smiled at me with her red mouth but not her eyes. 'Octavia Battenberg, how do you do?' she said, extending a hand. She also had scarlet nails.

'I'm good, thanks,' I said, smiling back, hoping that my eyeliner hadn't started running. What kind of name was Octavia Battenberg? Where were all the normal people?

'Hi, darling,' Octavia said, leaning into Rory and kissing him on both cheeks.

'Hello, Tav, how are you?'

'Extremely well. And yes, apparently we might be graced with the PM later but nobody's entirely sure.' She spoke in a posh drawl, as if ejecting every word was an effort.

'Do you all work in the same office?' I asked.

Octavia looked from Noddy to Rory, then me. 'Sort of. We're all fighting for the same team, if you know what I mean?'

I didn't, but I didn't want to let her know that, so I nodded. 'Yes, totally.'

'Do you work in politics?' she asked.

'No, for a bookshop in Chelsea.'

'A bookshop! How adorable.'

'How can bookshops possibly survive these days?' interjected Noddy. 'I buy all mine from Amazon.'

'It's where we met,' said Rory, sliding his arm around my waist and pulling me into him. 'I went in to collect something for my mother and there she was.'

'Darling Elizabeth, how is she?' asked Octavia, placing one hand on Rory's arm.

'She's terrific. I'm off down there next weekend, as it happens. I'll send your best wishes.'

'Please do. And to your father,' said Octavia, before switching her attention to me again. 'Have you met Rory's parents? They're divine.'

'No, er, no I haven't.' My blister was getting worse and I could feel a bead of sweat running down my stomach. This situation was intolerable.

'Oh look, there's Jacob,' Octavia suddenly said to Noddy. 'We must go and talk to him. Lovely to meet you,' she said unconvincingly to me before blowing Rory a kiss and snaking her way through the room with Noddy behind her.

'How do you know her?' I asked, trying to sound light, as if I didn't care about the answer.

'Our parents live near one another so we grew up together. Isn't this fun?' He grinned at me as he said this, his eyes alight as if he actually meant it. 'Come on, let's have another glass of wine and I'll introduce you to more people.'

He led me through the room, stopping every now and then to say hello to someone. Several congratulated him on being approved for the party list. One man, whose capillaried face was so maroon it matched his tie, clapped Rory on the back and said he was looking forward to working with him. I swallowed another glass of wine, ate several cheese straws and pretended to laugh at their obscure political jokes.

Just as Rory whispered that we could 'run away', a man I vaguely recognized stepped in front of us. He had wavy white hair and a pair of tortoiseshell spectacles perched on the end of a bulbous nose. 'Rory Dundee, I believe?'

'Absolutely, Secretary of State, a privilege to meet you,' replied Rory. More hand-shaking.

'And who's this?' asked the man.

'This is my girlfriend, Florence,' Rory replied.

'Ah, good man. We all need a Florence in our lives.' He leant towards me and winked.

But I was too stunned at being called a girlfriend to care about the pervy old dinosaur. He blathered on to Rory that the party was very lucky to have him and expecting great things while I stood there mute. In my head, there was a big neon light flashing: 'GIRLFRIEND, GIRLFRIEND, GIRLFRIEND.' Rory had called me his girlfriend, which meant I, Florence Fairfax, had a boyfriend. Other women seemed to bang on about their boyfriends all the time and now I could be one of them, although obviously I'd try to be less irritating about it.

I practised various lines in my head: 'My boyfriend Rory works in politics' or 'My boyfriend and I went to the cinema last night.' It sounded weird. Good weird, not bad weird. It had all just been very quick. A few weeks ago, the only man in my life had been Marmalade. Maybe Eugene, on a good day. Now I had Rory.

'You know when you know,' Jaz had told me at a NOMAD session some months before. Although that was just after she'd started dating the cheat who had a family in Solihull so she'd been wrong. Did I know about Rory? I glanced up at his face as if I could measure my feelings by examining him.

'That goes without saying, Secretary of State,' he said, nodding enthusiastically at the dinosaur. 'Anything the party needs, I'm your man.'

I wasn't sure I did know quite yet, but I had a good feeling about him. I just needed to pluck up the courage to tackle the 'Cowabunga!' thing.

★

We went back to his place in a cab, which meant I could slide my horrible shoes off in the back as we slid through dark London towards Pimlico. I hadn't been to his flat yet and was intrigued. I wondered what his bedroom was like. Neat, I presumed. I couldn't imagine Rory had a bedroom with bad linen and thin pillows.

'Did you enjoy that?' he asked, as he traced his fingers up my thigh. That alone was enough to set me off. Even if his bedroom wasn't tidy, I told myself, I was about to have sex and should be too excited to worry about shirts on the floor.

'Yeah, it was… interesting.'

'Sorry,' he said, pulling a guilty face. 'I know it was probably more work than you'd imagined. But I'm glad you were with me.'

'No, no, it was fun, seeing behind scenes. And girlfriend, huh?' I said it while smiling coyly at him. I didn't want to scare Rory out of it, to take it back.

He grinned. 'I blurted it in the moment but I wanted to say it. I thought about you all trip.' Then he leant over and pulled my face towards his, his fingers under my chin. 'Will you be my girlfriend?'

I almost laughed at the corny absurdity of it but reined myself in. It would ruin the moment. Instead, I nodded very slightly and he closed his mouth on mine. Every nerve in my body danced at this, and my irritation about Octavia and her perfect lipstick vanished.

When the cab pulled up a few minutes later, I opened the door and tiptoed across the pavement in my tights.

'What are you doing?' he said, climbing out after me.

'Sore feet,' I said, sensing that blisters were on the list of Bodily Things That Aren't Very Sexy To Discuss, like moles and ingrown hairs.

He led me up a short path to his front door and reached into his suit pocket for the keys. 'After you, madam,' he said, pushing it open.

I wiped my damp feet on the doormat and blinked in the dark as Rory closed the door behind me. It was a house, not a flat, and I seemed to be standing in a hall with a chequered stone floor which led to a flight of stairs.

He dropped his post on a table beside us and stepped more closely behind me. 'Hi,' he whispered into my neck.

'Hi,' I whispered back, shivering as Rory ran his hands down the side of my body. I tried to turn around but he held me in place.

'Don't even think about it, stay right there, please, hands on the table.'

I laid my palms on it as he crouched down behind me, his hands running up my legs, and I suddenly wished I'd worn stockings instead of an 80-denier pair of opaques from M&S. Mia always wore stockings, claiming that they were more comfortable. I found this a dubious excuse and suspected it was simply another maxim that women told themselves because they thought men preferred stockings to tights. Stockings seemed unpractical – what if one fell down? Say what you like about a thick pair of opaques but at least they kept your bits warm.

Rory didn't seem to mind the tights. He peeled them down with my knickers and I lifted each foot in turn so he could remove them. At the warm sensation of his hands on my bare skin, I dropped my head back and sighed. Then he stood, running his hands back up my legs as he did, one thumb brushing between them when they reached the top.

Next, pressing his erection into me, he reached around my waist and tugged the drawstring of my Homer Simpson dress.

'Shall we go upstairs?' I whispered. There was a mirror above the table decorated with wedding invitations and a new-born baby card which announced that Araminta had been born three weeks earlier. I couldn't concentrate on sex while looking at a photograph of little Araminta in a woolly hat.

Plus, now my dress was untied at the waist it hung around my body like a Victorian nightie. I wanted to pull it over my head and feel Rory's skin against me again. I wanted his hands and his mouth over every bit of my body. And I wanted to touch him. I felt lazy standing there, my feet on the cold floor, my hands on the table, as if I wasn't pulling my weight.

'We're staying here,' Rory replied, pulling the skirt of my dress up again so his hands could feel underneath it, running over my hips and up to my bra. He yanked the cups aside and pinched my nipples hard, making me gasp. As he pinched, I instinctively pushed my bottom out into his groin. OK, maybe the hall was all right for a moment. I just wouldn't look at Araminta.

Rory dropped one hand back down to between my legs, lightly brushing the tips of his fingers back and forth along the skin there. I groaned, desperate for him to rub me harder and for this to be more of a joint activity. I reached behind to the crotch of his trousers and tried to undo the button at the top but, one-handed, facing away from him, it was impossible. Luckily, his hand found mine and he undid his flies so I could take hold of his penis. Making a circle with my fist, I lightly traced my fingers up and down it.

'Harder,' he moaned into my hair.

How hard? I was uncertain. It seemed a delicate thing, a penis. I didn't want to pull on it as if I was ringing a church bell. I tightened the grip of my thumb and forefinger and Rory sighed again into my hair, which I took as a good sign.

'Harder,' he urged so I made the circle of my fingers smaller yet again. Could one break a penis? Please can I not break this, I thought, as I moved my hand up and down. It would be just my luck to get a boyfriend and then immediately snap his most precious part.

After a few moments, Rory moved my hand off him, lifted up my dress and pushed into me. It felt rough at first, so I shifted slightly, leaning further forwards on the table, his hands on my hips, the folds of my dress halfway up my back. This angle was better, and Rory sped up, back and forth, back and forth until the table was banging on the wall in front of it in time with his thrusts and my necklace was swinging from my neck like a pendulum.

'Oh my God, oh my God,' he started repeating, faster and faster until his body froze, glued to mine, suspended in the moment. 'COWABUNGAAAAA!' he groaned into my shoulder as we both remained rooted in place, my body bent at a right angle so my head was resting on my arms.

The trouble was, there never seemed to be a good moment to broach this.

★

Ruby, Mia and I were all at home the following night. This was rare for a Friday. Normally, it was just me lolling on the sofa with a book and they stayed out until late, returning home at two or three in the morning when the mingled fragrance of frying bacon and cigarette smoke wafted upstairs to the attic and woke me. But as Ruby had dumped Jasper, and Mia wanted to discuss her hen party, we were staying in. Ruby, in an astonishing first, had offered to cook but changed her mind later that evening and said why didn't we get a Deliveroo instead.

'I haven't got my phone on me,' she said, looking from Mia to me as we sat around the kitchen table. It was a cunning ploy she'd pulled before since it meant one of us had to order via our phone, thereby paying for the delivery.

'I'll get mine,' said Mia. She went back into the hall to find her bag.

'How was it?' I quickly asked Ruby.

She frowned back.

'Ending things with Jasper?'

'Done,' she replied, flicking a hand in the air. 'Although do you know what he said?'

I shook my head.

'How did I know I hadn't given it to him? Ha! As if *I'm* the one who's been shagging everybody between the age of eighteen and eighty in London.'

'How are you feeling?'

'Fine. Amazing. I didn't even cry.'

'I mean down there.'

'Oh. Better. On these very strong antibiotics which mean I can't drink so—'

'Why aren't you drinking?' asked Mia, breezing back into the kitchen.

'Having a night off,' Ruby replied, putting a finger to her lips at me.

'Seriously?' Mia said, opening the fridge. 'I've brought back a bottle of champagne to try. Although not champagne, technically. Sparkling English wine. Hugo says we should think about it for the wedding.'

'Go on then,' said Ruby.

'That was difficult. Flo?'

'Yep, please.'

Mia reached into the back of the glass cupboard for the champagne flutes which had been my parents' wedding present. They were almost never used. Drinking from glasses that Mum would have unwrapped at the start of her marriage gave me a pang of wistfulness but Mia soon interrupted that.

'Christ, these are dusty,' she said, blowing into one.

'Can we have Thai?' said Ruby, re-establishing control over dinner now that she didn't have to pay for it.

There followed a fifteen-minute discussion on which Thai we would order from, which nearby Thai had the best ratings, whether it was the Thai we ordered from last time which did the prawns that gave Ruby a dodgy stomach, and whether we should order one coconut rice or two. Thai menus – long on noodles and rice – were a problem for me, so I ended up ordering a soup and some vegetable spring rolls.

Dinner sorted, we carried our glasses to the TV room and took our usual seats: Mia and Ruby spread across the sofa, me in the armchair by the window. Tonight I barely noticed the divide because I needed to reply to Rory's latest message without interference.

Earlier that day, I'd texted him saying we were preparing

for a big event next week with Fumi, hoping that he might be impressed with the coup of landing such a star. He replied but didn't mention this. Instead, he asked if I was free the following weekend to stay with his parents in Norfolk. But then Zach had appeared upstairs and bossily said could I order the wine for the event because he only drank beer, so Eugene and I spent an hour on the Majestic website sniggering at the pretentious reviews. And while we were doing that, Jaz dropped in after school with Dunc in order to show off his new reading badge and I'd completely forgotten to reply to Rory.

Mia picked up the remote control; I stared down at my phone.

'I'm thinking London,' she said, flicking through channels.

'For what?' replied Ruby.

'My hen. I don't want to go away. I don't want us to do the walk of shame through Luton wearing sombreros. I want it to be chic. Drinks and dinner somewhere and then a bar afterwards. No penis straws. No penis anything. If I see a penis on my hen I'll scream.'

Ruby rolled her eyes. 'What's the point in a hen party if the bride isn't neck-deep in penises? I'm going to buy you one of those giant penis outfits! Owwww,' she said loudly, as Mia thwacked her on the leg with the remote control.

'I mean it, Rubes. None of that. And absolutely no stripper. If I get even a whisper that you've paid some greasy waiter to grind his bottom into me I'll demote you from maid of honour. I'll make it Fl—' Mia looked across the room and caught my eye. 'I'll make it someone else instead. And no Mr and Mrs either. None of my friends need to know what my favourite position is. Or Hugo's, for that matter.' She pretended to shudder. 'Unedifying.'

'What's Hugo doing for his stag?' I asked.

'Prague.'

'The same weekend as the hen? The one before the wedding?'

'Mmm.'

'Isn't that risky?' said Ruby.

'Why?'

'What if he gets in a fight and has a black eye or someone shaves his eyebrows off?'

'Have you met Hugo?' said Mia, glancing at each of us in turn. 'Come on, even paintballing's been deemed too dangerous. They're going to play crazy golf and have a few beers.'

'Sure,' snorted Ruby.

'And anyway, it's tradition.'

'What is?'

'Having the stag and hen parties closer to the wedding. I read about it in *Be More Bride* magazine. Traditionally, it was known as the last night of freedom and always held the night before the wedding. The ancient Greeks used to do it, apparently.'

'Yeah, but the ancient Greeks probably just overdid it on wine and threw a few javelins,' said Ruby. 'I'm not sure they travelled abroad in matching T-shirts to drink thirty-eight pints and pay a tenner to watch some poor local woman strip.'

'Is that all they do it for? A tenner?'

'I don't know, do I! I'm just saying that's what stag dos are. Beer and strippers. And drama. Always a drama.'

'It'll be fine,' insisted Mia. 'Who needs a top-up?' She held the bottle up from the sofa. 'Flo? You're very quiet.'

'Sorry. I'm trying to write a message to Rory.'

She squealed as she stood to top up our glasses. 'How is your boyfriend?'

'Er, good. Officially my boyfriend, actually.' I wondered when saying that would stop feeling so weird. Ever?

The bottle froze in Mia's hand. 'Oh my God, when did that happen?'

'Last night. I met some friends of his, well, it was more of a work thing. But he introduced me as his girlfriend and then actually asked me on the way home.'

'Sweet! But you don't sound very excited.'

'No, no, I am. And I really like him. I'm just a bit dazed. It's all happened so fast.' My mind briefly flitted back to the night before: one moment as single and sexless as one of Mrs Delaney's gladioli; the next bent over a hallway table while my new boyfriend went at me like a Black & Decker power tool.

Mia shrugged and lowered herself back down on the sofa. 'When you know, you know.'

There it was, that saying again. 'But what if I don't know?'

'That's fine too.'

'Then how are you ever supposed to know? If you know when you know but, also, you don't have to know when you know?' I wasn't sure I was making sense. Maybe it was the champagne.

'All I know is that I never want to have sex again,' interjected Ruby.

'What?' said Mia, turning from me to her sister.

'I broke up with Jasper yesterday.'

'What? Why? You all right?'

'Various reasons,' said Ruby. 'And I'm fine. But I'm off men for the time being.'

'I give that all of three minutes,' replied Mia, before looking back to me. 'Flo, listen. I didn't know with Hugo for ages. Months. He was perfectly nice but not that exciting and his morning breath could have killed a horse.'

'But you're marrying him?' I said, feeling a sense of relief at asking the question. I glanced at Ruby who widened her eyes at me and shook her head, indicating that she didn't want to get involved.

'Yes,' went on Mia, with an exaggerated nod. 'Because one day I woke up and decided that this was what I wanted. I'd had enough of dating. I wanted to be married, a family, all that stuff. So I bought him some dental floss and a bottle of industrial strength mouthwash and that was that.'

Briefly, I thought back through the great romances I'd read. In none of them did the heroine buy her hero a bottle of Listerine. But who was I to judge another person's relationship? If this was what Mia really wanted, then I had to stop worrying about it. I must have still looked concerned, though, because she arranged her face into a sympathetic expression. 'Don't worry,' she said. 'A few doubts at the start of something is totally normal, Flo. Especially when, no offence, you haven't got anything to compare this with.'

'It's not doubts. It's kind of the opposite. I'm worried that

I'll do something wrong and it's all going to disappear again. I suppose I'm worried that it's too good to be true.'

'I get it,' she replied. 'But you're overthinking it. He likes you, clearly. He's asked you to be his girlfriend.'

'He's invited me to meet his family next weekend too,' I added. 'Is it not just a bit quick?'

Mia narrowed her eyes at me. 'How old is he?'

'Thirty-seven.'

'So he just knows what he wants,' she said, with another shrug.

'Also,' added Ruby, 'if he wasn't messaging you and inviting you to stay with his family, you'd be sitting here complaining that he'd gone silent.'

'True,' I said, thinking back to the few flings I'd had where they'd done just that.

'And what's the sex like?' Ruby went on. 'If I'm never having sex ever again I need to get my kicks where I can.'

I wondered if I should ask them. Encouraged by the champagne, I decided I should. It was comforting, talking like this. I couldn't remember a time when we'd had such a frank joint conversation. 'OK, so the sex is amazing. He just sort of… knows exactly what to do. But there is one thing.'

'What?' they both chorused together.

'He does this thing…' Then I stopped again, unsure how to explain it.

'Cough up,' ordered Ruby.

'OK, but it's got to stay between us, promise?'

'Obviously,' said Ruby, waggling her fingers at me to indicate more speed was required. 'Come on, what is it?'

'OK, so he does the thing,' I repeated, 'like, at the end…'

'When you've finished shagging?'

'Rubes, can you let her speak?' said Mia.

'I am! Flo, continue. He does this thing…'

I sighed. 'It's not afterwards. It's right before. Or actually right when he…' I stopped again. I didn't want to say the word 'comes' out loud but what else was there? 'Orgasms' seemed too sex therapist and 'ejaculates' too biology teacher. 'It's when he comes,' I said quickly. 'He says something. He always says "Cowabunga!"'

Ruby laughed and then clapped a hand over her mouth. Mia pressed her lips together and frowned as if thinking over a challenging crossword puzzle.

'OK,' she said, after a few beats of silence. 'It's not *that* bad.'

'Isn't it?'

'No! Hugo likes talking dirty but he's really bad at it.'

'Not him too?' said Ruby, her mouth and eyes wide with mirth. 'This is too good. What does he say?'

Now it was Mia's turn to look embarrassed. 'Just stuff like "Has someone been a naughty girl?" or "Who's a hungry girl, then?"'

'Hugo! Jesus Christ,' said Ruby, laughing so hard I thought she might choke, which made me laugh harder, and eventually even Mia joined in, so all three of us were almost crying, shoulders shaking, faces creased.

'Blimey. I wouldn't have thought he had it in him,' I said, a few moments later when I'd regained control of myself.

Mia smiled and nodded slowly. 'Yes, every now and then he can surprise me in that department.'

'On Sundays before golf?'

'Exactly,' she drawled.

'You cannot possibly marry someone who says "Who's a hungry girl, then?"' Ruby told her, wiping her cheeks with her thumb. 'Imagine being ninety and still having to listen to that.'

'I won't be having sex when I'm ninety,' said Mia.

'What? I will be.'

'I thought you weren't having sex ever again?'

'I'm not. Not for a bit anyway.'

'So it's not that bad?' I said, still wanting reassurance. 'The "cowabunga!" thing?'

'Noooooo,' Mia insisted again, shaking her head. 'In the grand scheme of things, it's really not.'

'Not compared to "Who's a hungry girl then?"' said Ruby, still laughing. 'Honestly, I'm never going to forget this.' She nudged Mia with her foot. 'Hey, what time's he home tonight? I'm going to ask if he's hungry and wants any leftover takeaway.'

'If you dare,' said Mia, kicking her back.

'OK,' I said, trying to distract them before a fight broke out. 'So I should forget about it and not say anything? Not even a joke?'

'No! Definitely not a joke,' said Mia. 'Men aren't into jokes about their performance.'

I made a mental note of this. 'And I should say yes to the weekend with his parents?'

'Yes, go.'

'I agree,' said Ruby. 'And I don't think you should be put off by it either. He's showing his appreciation, if anything. In fact...' She paused.

'What?'

'I think you should raise him.'

'What d'you mean?'

'Why not send a little nude, just to show you're thinking about him?'

'Rubes,' warned Mia.

'What?' said Ruby. 'Flo is new to all this, I'm trying to help.' She looked from Mia to me. 'Just a flash of nipple or something to encourage him. But keep your face out of it.'

'Thanks,' I replied, deadpan.

She shook her head. 'No, only because then you can't be recognized by anyone else.'

I grimaced at the idea of trying to take a photo of my own nipple. And just a nipple on its own, a singular nipple. Was that sexy? Wouldn't it look like a lone flesh tag? 'I'm not sure it's my kind of thing, a nude. But thank you, both, for the advice.'

'You're welcome,' said Ruby, happily, before turning back to Mia. 'How far away's the Deliveroo man? I'm *hungry*.'

CHAPTER FIVE

SO I SAID YES to staying with his parents and Rory replied that he was 'ecstatic!'. He was in Belgium for a few days accompanying the minister on a trip to Brussels, which meant, after sinking two more bottles on the sofa with Mia and Ruby on Friday evening, I spent my weekend with Marmalade. Sitting cross-legged on my bed on Saturday afternoon, I wrote another few pages about Curtis the counting caterpillar until I got bored and my eye fell on my phone.

A nude? I tugged at the neckline of my T-shirt and looked down. Braless, my boobs were resting on the stomach roll underneath them. Would that sight turn anyone on? It seemed unlikely. Best not scare him away, so instead of taking a photo, I picked up my phone and texted him to see if he was free on Thursday evening to watch me interview Fumi.

On Sunday, I did my Fumi homework. Her new anthology was called *Bad Fairy* and it made me feel like a voyeur, as if I was reading a teenage diary. The poems were sad lamentations about a date not texting her back, about the planet burning up, about Fumi hating her knees. Her knees! I'd never thought about whether I hated my knees or not. They were just my knees.

And yet on Instagram, there was a more confident Fumi beaming at the camera, showing off a new pair of sunglasses, a new haircut, a restaurant in San Francisco where she'd fed Percy the pug prawn dim sum for dinner, and a selfie in her first-class cabin on a flight to Tokyo. Each post had thousands of comments underneath; fans declaring they loved her, that they loved her hair, her jacket, her shoes and her eye make-up, fans declaring that they wanted to marry her, others pleading for her to message them back. Underneath a picture of Fumi with her arms wrapped around Percy, one fan had written, 'I wish you could hold me like that' with a sad emoji. It seemed a big world for a 19-year-old to live in. No wonder she took Percy everywhere with her; he was the equivalent of a childhood toy, a comfort blanket.

'I'm not sure you'd appreciate a first-class seat,' I said, looking down at Marmalade, who slept almost anywhere – along the back of a radiator, occasionally in my bathroom sink – but mostly on my pillow. 'Come on, you need to go out,' I said, scooping him up and heading downstairs to make a cup of tea.

Ruby was still asleep even though it was 2 p.m., and Mia and Hugo were busy putting Le Creuset pots and bath towels on their wedding list at John Lewis. So I sat at the kitchen table with my tea, writing a list of questions. Fumi's publisher had asked for them in advance so they could be approved. She'd said no questions about her love life, even though dozens of her poems talked of just that, and no questions from the audience.

But she was happy to talk about 'her work, her personal sense of style, her important role as an international influencer, and her beloved writing partner, Percy'.

After I'd read for another hour, Marmalade slunk back through the cat flap and weaved around my legs.

'It's impossible to concentrate if you're doing that,' I told him, but stood and opened the cupboard for a tin of condensed milk. His weekend treat.

Ruby appeared in the kitchen as I sat back down.

'Hiya, Flo,' she said, sleepily. 'What you doing?'

I stretched in my seat. 'Just work. We've got an event at the shop this week. An Instagram poet doing a reading and I've got to interview her.'

'Cool,' said Ruby, taking my yoghurt from the fridge. She sat on the kitchen table, feet on a chair, and ate it straight from the pot with a spoon. 'Who's the poet?'

I'd have to buy another pot. I hated sharing with anyone, whether yoghurt, water bottles or soup spoons. Who were those weirdos who let another person lick their ice cream? The idea of another person's tongue running across my scoop of ice cream made me want to scrub my mouth with bleach.

'She's called Fumi.'

Ruby's eyes widened. 'I know her! I follow her on Instagram. I'm obsessed with that dog. Have you seen it? She took him shopping in Gucci the other day.'

'I know,' I replied, grimly. She'd bought Percy a gold dog collar decorated with little 'G's around it.

'How come you're doing that? Doesn't sound very Frisbee to me.'

'New strategy; we're trying to get customers who aren't 500 years old and almost dead into the place.'

'When is it? Can I come? Pleeeeeease can I come? I'm not 500 years old.'

'It's Thursday evening and sure, if you really want to. I'll reserve you a ticket.'

'Do I have to pay?'

'Yes.'

Ruby wrinkled her nose.

'All right, I'll get you a free one but only if you tweet or post about it. And you can keep Rory company.'

He'd replied saying he 'wouldn't miss it for the world'.

'I get to hang with Cowabunga! Even better.'

'Ruby...'

She waved the spoon in the air. 'I promise, I promise, it's our secret. But thanks, Flo, you're the best. Right, I'm going to have a bath.' She stood up from the table, left the spoon sticking out from the yoghurt and went back upstairs. As a test, I willed myself to sit behind my laptop as long as I could, ignoring the pot. Leave the mess, I told myself. Nothing bad will happen. But it wasn't even two minutes before I stood and threw it away, then washed up the spoon and wiped the table down again. Pathetic.

The following morning, I stuck my head into the downstairs office and asked Zach if I could reserve two tickets. One for my sister. One for Rory.

'Ha! Rory the Tory's coming, is he?' Zach said, spinning in his chair. 'Can't wait to meet him. But yes, course.'

'Thank you,' I replied over my shoulder, making my way back to the till. I couldn't face getting into an argument with Zach today. Or any day that week, in fact, as I became increasingly nervous about Thursday evening.

He'd launched the shop's Instagram account – @Frisbeebooks – on Monday afternoon with a photo of Fumi and an announcement that she'd be speaking at the bookshop. She duly reposted it to her 973k followers which meant that, by the time we closed that evening, we'd sold all seventy tickets.

By Tuesday lunchtime there was a waiting list of over two hundred people and, as I walked home that evening, all I could hear in my head was the shriek of the shop phone over and over again as Fumi fans rang to beg for a space. 'Sorry, sold out,' I apologized, even when one girl cried and insisted that she needed to be there because Fumi was her 'religion'.

The calls continued until Wednesday afternoon when Norris declared he'd had enough and unplugged the phone. 'I'm SICK of all this technology,' he bellowed across the shop floor, making a customer drop a cookery book on her foot.

'The telephone was invented in 1876, it's hardly modern,' muttered Eugene, as Norris thumped downstairs to his office again. But we were all grateful for the peace that followed.

On Thursday morning, I dressed more carefully than usual. Same outfit (navy T-shirt, navy trousers) and same face (tinted moisturizer, mascara), but I took more care. I made sure I wasn't wearing my biggest knickers so I wouldn't have a VPL. I dried my hair properly, running a brush through it instead of my fingers. I rummaged in the drawer of my bedside table for a pair of gold hoop earrings I rarely wore.

'Get you, Liz Taylor,' said Eugene, clocking the earrings as soon I arrived.

'Don't. I'm feeling sick already.'

'You're going to be fabulous,' he replied just as Zach shunted the door open with his shoulder because his arms were full of snacks. He staggered to the counter and dropped the various packets. Bags of Haribo, ready salted crisps, boxes of herbal tea, apples and small bottles of fizzy water.

'What's this for?' I asked.

'Her rider,' Zach replied.

'Huh?'

'Oooh, it's what celebrities have in their dressing rooms,' explained Eugene, picking up a pink box of tea. 'Like, if you're Mick Jagger, it's what you need to have before you go on stage.'

'I'm pretty sure Mick Jagger doesn't demand Fangtastics before going on stage,' said Zach, 'but this is what her publisher emailed me last night. Oh, I nearly forgot these.' He reached into his back pocket, pulled out a box and held it up for us to see. 'Organic chicken biscuits for the dog.'

I gave a snort. 'She's not Madonna.'

'Not yet.'

'Can you put it away somewhere other than here? We've got to open up.' I'd spent that week obsessively tidying, putting books back into their rightful places. Running my fingers along the shelves, I'd played Consequences. If there was an even number on a certain shelf, Thursday evening would go without a hitch. Odd? I'd do something awful like fart on stage.

Zach gathered the shopping up. 'Your wish is my command. The publisher also asked about a dressing room. Where shall we put Her Majesty?'

'Stockroom?' suggested Eugene.

'That'll do,' said Zach, heading downstairs.

By lunchtime, I felt so ill I couldn't eat my cheese and tomato sandwich.

By teatime, I wondered whether I could fake my own death to get out of it. Fake my own death and disappear to live in Africa like Lord Lucan, although I'd find it very hard to leave Marmalade behind. Why had I let Zach force me into this? Why wasn't he doing it? I raised my eyes to the ceiling above me. Zach was the one in charge, after all, thundering about the shop like a matador ordering Eugene to move chairs and tables.

I tried to distract myself by writing my questions on Frisbee notecards, before unpacking four boxes of Fumi's book and arranging them in even piles on a signing table beside the till. The door jangled and I looked up to see a gaggle of teenage girls come in and glance nervously around them.

''Scuse me,' one of them asked. 'Is this the right place for the Fumi talk?'

I looked at my watch. It was only 4.28. 'Yep,' I replied. 'But it's not for another couple of hours. Do you have tickets?'

They nodded simultaneously. 'We just want to make sure we have good seats,' said the ringleader.

'The chairs aren't out yet,' I replied, just as there was

a thump on the floorboards above my head and another shout from Zach. 'Come back closer to six?'

They nodded again and left. But the door kept swinging open. Ring ring. Ring ring. Ring ring. Every few minutes another herd of fans would appear to check that they were in the right place, to see if there were any spare tickets or cancellations, to plead with me for a space.

Norris appeared upstairs from his office at one point to see what the 'commotion' was.

'Close it early,' he said, his face darkening at the sight of the crowd outside the shop windows. 'Put up a sign. Too much noise.'

I pulled a sheet of paper from the printer and wrote in neat black capitals: 'Please queue here for the Fumi event. Doors will open at 6 p.m.' I stuck it to the door-pane, flicked the lock and texted Rory – *Have locked door so if you get here early, ring and will let you in xxx.*

Upstairs, Eugene was unfolding chairs in lines across the Turkish rugs. Zach was sitting on the floor, leaning up against the shelves, phone clamped to one ear, hands flying over his laptop keyboard.

'OK,' he said, 'OK, great. Yes, all fine here. That's perfect. Looking forward to it.'

'That was Fumi's agent,' he said, lowering his phone. 'They're on their way. Can I just get you to do a sound check?' He pointed to two chairs at the front of the room, a microphone stand between them.

I felt a wave of adrenalin soak my insides but said nothing.

Mustn't show fear in front of Zach. Instead, I walked forward and perched on one of the two seats, then positioned my mouth over the microphone. 'Er, testing, testing, one two three.'

'Bit more,' shouted Zach, not looking up from his screen.

I couldn't think of what else to say. And if I was this tongue-tied now, in front of a room which contained just Eugene and Zach, what would I be like in front of seventy people?

'Tell me your deepest, darkest secret,' said Zach.

'What?' I squeaked.

'It's only for sound. But never mind. Just tell me what you had for lunch.'

'Nothing,' I snapped, 'because I'm so nervous I couldn't eat.'

He grinned at me from behind his laptop. 'You're going to be fine.' Then he shook his head. 'Scrap that, not just fine. You're going to be great.'

'You sure?'

'I am,' he said, head back down, tapping at his laptop. 'But that's all good to record.' He looked up expectantly. 'Ready?'

'Think so,' I replied but my voice gave me away. It was like a vole had swallowed a helium balloon.

*

Fumi arrived with her agent and a bodyguard the size of a mobile home. He had a Russian accent as thick as his neck and was called Igor. Against a backdrop of shrieks outside, where the queue now snaked down the street, Zach introduced everyone. Fumi was wearing a short pink dress under a furry coat, spotted black and white like a Dalmatian. Her feet were laced in a pair of black ankle boots, her nails were long and silver and her hair was bubble-gum pink. The dog was asleep in her arms. Norris's mouth fell open and he gasped as if seeing the Pyramids or the Coliseum for the first time.

'This is Percy,' Fumi said, holding one of the pug's paws out for Norris to shake. She had a girlish American accent and didn't seem like the sort of diva who'd demand fizzy water and apples in her dressing room. Standing between the twin pillars of Igor and Norris, she seemed more like a schoolgirl.

Norris extended a hand and shook the paw. Zach lifted his camera from the strap around his neck and quickly took a picture. 'Hello and welcome,' said Norris. 'We're delighted to have you here.'

'The pleasure's ours,' said the agent. She was an American called Jennifer who looked like she'd never eaten a carbohydrate in her life. 'Where can we put ourselves?'

'Downstairs,' said Zach, 'follow me. Watch your head there, Igor.'

Norris told me to open the door and let the ticket-holders in; Eugene directed them to their seats, mostly gangs of teenage girls.

I smiled at snippets of chat I overheard as they filed past.

'I saw her hair!'

'I saw Percy!'

'Do you think she'll do selfies?'

'I need that coat in my life!'

Ruby was hovering at the back. 'Hi, Flo, I was waiting for Rory but I can't see him.'

'Don't worry. He's not here yet. Will you just save a seat? And I'll text him your number.'

She nodded. 'How you feeling?'

'All right.' This was a fib. I was now so nervous I thought I might throw up on my shoes.

I apologized to the dozen or so fans left outside without tickets, locked the door and texted Rory with Ruby's details in case he needed to be let in. Upstairs came the scraping of chairs and murmur of excited voices; downstairs I could only hear Jennifer's undulating American murmur. I picked up my notecards and headed for the stockroom.

'Everyone ready?' I said, sticking my head inside it. Igor was holding Percy, a ludicrous sight in his tree-trunk arms. Fumi was sitting on a chair, busy with her phone. Jennifer turned and smiled brightly at me.

'I think so. Shall we do this?'

Feeling as if a strange, autonomous power had overtaken my legs, I led them upstairs and gestured at a couple of reserved seats for Jennifer and Igor, who handed the dog to Fumi. As she, Percy and I made our way to the front, the room went quiet. We sat and I squinted at the back to see Zach holding his thumb up. I glanced at Fumi, who was clutching a copy of her own book. Percy had settled on her lap and closed his eyes.

That was when I realized I could hear my own heart beating. It seemed unfeasibly loud.

'Hello, er, everyone,' I said, leaning forward into the

microphone. 'And welcome to Frisbee Books for an evening with a special guest who needs very little introduction, the supremely talented poet Fumi and her dog, Percy!'

I glanced at Percy as the claps and cheering filled the room. His eyes remained closed. Presumably he was used to this.

'Thank you. Thank you all, thank you so much for coming,' Fumi said, her voice hushing the applause. 'I'm delighted to be here in London with you all to celebrate my new book, *Bad Fairy*' – a few whoops in the audience at this – 'so I'd like to read a few extracts if I may.'

She read to silence in the room while I tried to stop my notecards from wilting in my clammy hands. There was another rowdy burst of clapping when Fumi finished the final haiku. Called 'Apocalypse', it was about the time she broke a nail.

'Thank you, Fumi, that was brilliant,' I said when the room had fallen quiet again. 'And as you said, this is your new book, your second anthology by the age of twenty-one, following on from your debut last year. When and why did you start writing in haikus?'

Just as Fumi opened her mouth to respond, Percy woke and sneezed in her lap.

The audience laughed.

'Please excuse him, I think he's got jet lag,' she said, to more laughter. 'So, I started writing when I was very young, my father taught English in Kyoto and...'

As she talked, Percy jumped down from her lap and sniffed my feet. I tried to continue listening but found it hard to concentrate while he snuffled around my ankles.

'I'm so sorry, is he bothering you?' Fumi asked, breaking off from her answer and looking down at my feet.

'No, no, not at all!' I said. 'Please go on. He's fine.'

But as she started talking again, Percy reared up on his hind legs, his front feet on my knee, and started humping my ankle.

Nervous laughter rippled across the seats in front of us.

'Oh, goodness, Percy! I'm so sorry,' said Fumi, her silver nails flying to her cheeks. The laughter grew as Percy continued to shag my trainer.

'No, no, it's OK,' I hissed, recrossing my legs, shaking Percy off in the process. I sat back and smiled at Fumi, encouraging her to continue. But that didn't fool the nymphomaniac dog for long. Within seconds, he'd wrapped his paws around my calf and was at it again, his bottom pumping back and forth, dry humping my foot.

The audience had now fully lost it and the room echoed with their howls as I tried to swivel my legs away, only for Percy to leap right back on my ankle and redouble his efforts. What was wrong with this dog? Why was it so obsessed with my hideous shoes? It was going at my leg like a teenage boy.

'Get off,' I growled, leaning over to try and pull him away with my hands. I looked up at the audience and smiled, as if to reassure them that this was all fine, but all I could see was phones. A bank of phones. Everyone was taking pictures of me, gurning at the camera, while Percy the pug made love to my foot. How could I stop it? How does one stop a sex-crazed dog? I couldn't kick him, could I? Christ, the laughter was getting louder.

Suddenly, a meaty pair of arms appeared in front of me and Igor picked Percy up by his collar. I felt my panic subside as he carried him back to his seat. My cheeks were on fire, I'd started sweating (obviously) and my trouser legs were covered with fine, pale, pug hairs.

'Well,' I said, a few moments later when the laughter had finally stopped. 'I'm very flattered. But, sorry, Fumi, shall we pick up where we left off? You were talking about why you began writing haikus?'

Unruffled, Fumi carried on while I sat back in my seat, arms clamped to my sides, waiting for the heat in my cheeks to subside.

★

The only good thing about the foot-shagging debacle was that Rory didn't see it because he hadn't arrived. I realized this downstairs as I stood behind the till. Fumi was sitting at the table beside me, signing books for the long queue of fans who wanted selfies with her and Percy. He'd returned to her lap and was sitting proudly as an emperor. I narrowed my eyes at him. Say what you like about cats but they'd never do anything so impolite.

'Where's Rory?' I mouthed at Ruby, who was hovering by the door.

She shrugged and shouted back, 'Not sure. But I'll wait for you.'

It took over an hour for the shop to empty. Fumi, with

another wave of Percy's paw, said goodbye and thanked us before carrying him to a black people-carrier parked outside. Jennifer climbed in after her. Zach and I watched from the shop door as Igor heaved himself into the front of the car and they drove off.

'Well, that was a disaster,' I said, turning to him.

'Rubbish! You were great!'

'Zach, that animal was out of control. I've never been so mortified in all my life.'

'You were amazing, Flo,' said Ruby, behind us. 'I'm Ruby, by the way,' she said to Zach, grinning at him.

'I'm Zach, hi. I work with your sister.'

'I guessed. It's very rude of her not to mention you before.'

'She can be pretty rude,' he replied, before leaning in closer to Ruby, 'but don't tell her I said that. I'm quite scared of her when she's angry. You should see her with a mop.'

The exchange made me want to kick them both in the shins. Oh Ruby, surely not? She couldn't be into Zach. He dressed like a teenage gamer and needed a haircut. His arms were more tattoo than human being. He was arrogant and bossy. He ate food like a hungry Labrador. He was... I stopped running through my list of the things I least liked about Zach as he and Ruby carried on chatting in front of me.

'A model! I can see that about you,' he said, which made Ruby laugh and flick her hair to the other side of her face.

Urgh, flirting was disgusting.

'Drink!' shouted Norris, appearing on the shop floor with a tray bearing a bottle of champagne and several mugs. 'You were all brilliant, especially Florence, and I want to say thank you.'

He balanced the tray on the non-fiction table, covering up the faces of Cromwell and Queen Victoria, and opened the bottle with a pop.

'I got a selfie with the pug!' said Eugene, handing the mugs around.

'Don't mention that dog,' I said, peering into the mug he'd given me. Its sides were dark brown with tea stains. Could I drink champagne from this?

'Cheers!' said Norris, holding his mug in the air. 'We've sold 126 copies of that daft poetry book, on top of the tickets.'

'I got some great photos,' said Zach, lifting the camera from around his neck and scrolling through them. 'I'll post them online tomorrow.'

'I don't want to see them,' I said.

'I do!' purred Ruby, stepping closer to Zach to look at his camera screen.

So much for that self-imposed period of abstinence, I thought. If I came downstairs in the morning to find Zach in our kitchen looking for tea bags, I would move out. What if I bumped into him in a towel? Gross. Or what if I had to watch telly while they snogged on the sofa? Nope. Oh my God, what if he and Ruby ended up getting married and we all had to spend Christmases together? The thought was unbearable.

'Where's your man, Florence?' Zach asked suddenly, looking up from his camera. 'I thought he was coming?'

'Yep, he is. I mean, he was, but I think he's been held up in the office.' I didn't know this for sure, since Rory still hadn't messaged, but I didn't want to admit to as much. I felt a strange sense of conflict, annoyed at Rory and yet keen to defend him against Zach.

'Maybe he's been held up by the Prime Minister,' suggested Eugene, before gasping, 'What if it's a matter of national importance?'

'All right, let's not exaggerate,' I said, jumping at a rap on the shop window behind me. 'See? There he is.'

I put my mug on the tray and hurried to open the door.

'I'm so sorry,' Rory said, wincing at me. 'I got caught in the office with a crisis and missed your big moment. I'm a terrible, terrible boyfriend so… here are these.' He pulled a bouquet of blue peonies from behind his back and leant forward to kiss me on the side of my head. 'Forgive me?'

'Don't worry,' I replied, not wanting to seem difficult. 'Come in, come say hi to everyone.' I took the flowers and pulled him into the shop with my other hand. 'Everyone, this is Rory. Rory, this is Eugene, Norris, you've already met my sister Ruby, and Zach.'

'Hello,' Eugene said instantly, pushing in front of the others to shake his hand. Even after a long day in the office, Rory looked impressive, a day's stubble darkening his jaw.

'Hello again,' said Ruby, waving at him. 'I think you might have a small hairy rival for your girlfriend's affections.'

'Norris,' said Norris, holding out a huge hand.

Which left Zach.

'Rory Dundee, how do you do?' said Rory, extending his arm towards him.

Zach shook his hand but I could feel disdain radiating from where I stood. 'You missed her big moment.'

'Argh, I know,' Rory groaned, letting go of Zach's hand and clapping it to his chest. 'We just have this developing crisis in Oman.'

Zach failed to look impressed. Eugene made a strange sort of cooing noise.

'Drink, Rory?' Norris said, nodding at the tray of champagne.

'Yes please, thank you. Although I hardly feel I deserve it, being this abominably late. What's this about a rival?' He reached around my waist and kissed my head again.

I sighed. 'Fumi's dog tried to have sex with my leg. On stage. In front of everyone.'

'Sensible dog,' Rory replied, which at least made me smile.

'Florence was brilliant,' went on Zach. 'You should have seen her.'

Rory screwed up his face, 'Ah, damn Oman. I wish I'd been here.'

'Yes, tell us about your job, Rory,' said Eugene, before lowering his voice conspiratorially. 'It sounds ever so important, but only if you're allowed; you don't have to tell us any state secrets or anything.'

'No, no, not important,' Rory replied, dazzling Eugene with his widest smile, 'a mere cog in the wheels of government.'

Zach made a snorting noise which he turned into a cough. 'And you want to be a Conservative MP, Florence says?'

'I do,' replied Rory. 'Or at least I hope to be.'

'I'd vote for you,' interjected Eugene.

'Zach…' I warned.

'What?' he replied, all innocence. 'Just asking.'

'Not a fan?' said Rory. He was still smiling but I saw a muscle in his cheek flex.

Zach shrugged. 'My mum's a teacher, so not really.'

'In that case she should be grateful.'

'Grateful?'

'Absolutely. We've invested billions in the school system and increased teachers' pay.' Rory sounded cool, but I could still see that tiny muscle pulsing.

'"We?" Rory, you're not an MP yet,' I joked, trying to lighten the atmosphere.

'And what do you do?' Rory asked, his eyes remaining on Zach. 'Florence hasn't mentioned you.'

'I'm a photographer, just working here to help out for a bit,' he replied. Zach, too, was trying to sound unruffled, but his stance – as upright as a candlestick, shoulders back – gave him away. It was like watching the gorilla enclosure at London Zoo. 'But I'm also just a decent human being so I care about those less fortunate than us.'

'As do I,' said Rory, flashing another smile at him.

'Enough,' interrupted Norris, crossing his hands in the air in front of him. 'No bickering. Come on, this is a celebration.' He poured the remainder of the champagne into our mugs. Norris and Rory then talked politics while I watched Ruby flick her hair all over Zach as he showed her more of his photos.

'Right, I'm off home,' announced Norris, not long afterwards, draining his mug.

'Pub?' said Eugene hopefully, looking at the rest of us.

'Sure,' replied Zach.

'I'm in,' added Ruby.

I looked up at Rory. 'Fancy it?'

He grimaced. 'I'd love to but this situation in the Gulf is ongoing and I'll need to be in early. You stay. You don't have to come back with me.'

I weighed up my options. Go to the pub where Eugene would make us drink shots (tequila, it was always tequila) and watch Ruby flirt with Zach, or go back to Rory's and sleep next to him.

'Let's go back to yours,' I said. 'Just hang on a second while I get my bag from downstairs?'

'Course.'

I skipped downstairs and up again in less than a minute, not wanting to leave Zach and Rory unattended.

'Come on, you,' Rory said, reaching his hand out for me when I reappeared.

I took it and looked back at Zach. 'You all right to lock up?'

He nodded and we were almost through the door, Rory holding it open for me, when Zach shouted behind us, 'Best of luck with solving the Middle East.'

Rory hailed us a cab and I seethed the whole way to Pimlico, trying to work out who I disliked more: Percy or Zach. But once in Rory's bedroom, he pushed me back on his bed and went down on me with such thorough focus and precise attention that I forgot about both of them and almost yelled 'Cowabunga!' myself.

★

'FLORENCE, MY DARLING,' shouted Eugene when I arrived at work the following morning. 'HAVE YOU SEEN YOU'RE A ME ME?'

'Eugene, what are you going on about?'

'You're a me me, LOOK!' he said, thrusting his phone at me.

I looked and felt my stomach cartwheel. There was meme after meme on Twitter of Percy shagging my foot. **'Was it good for you too, Percy?'** said one of the memes, on a shot of Percy wrapped around my calf while I snarled, red-faced, at the audience.

Eugene scrolled down his phone. Dozens of pictures and in every one I looked desperate, my mouth turned upwards in despair and my panicked expression suggesting I was being attacked by a lion instead of a small pug.

'Leg humping, it's what I do,' said another meme.

'Look at this one, it's brilliant, and it's been retweeted nearly three thousand times!' said Eugene. This was a particularly bad shot of me, taken when I was trying to pull Percy away, bearing my teeth at him like an angry gargoyle. **'Happy hump day!'** said the caption.

'And there are videos,' said Eugene, delightedly, showing me a GIF of Percy's bottom thrusting at my trainer, his tail quivering in excitement.

'Enough,' I said, swiping his phone away from me. 'I can't bear it.'

'But you're an internet star!'

'Eugene, I do not wish to be an internet star because a dog fancied my shoe. I don't want to be an internet star anyway, but I definitely don't want to be one for this.'

The door jingled as Zach swept through it.

'Morning, you viral sensation, what a triumph! The Instagram account has been tagged about a million times, look...' He walked towards us and held his phone out.

'I don't want to see,' I said primly, opening the drawer for the Stanley knife.

'Oh come on, it's funny!' said Zach. 'Eugene, back me up.'

'Not interested,' I replied, running the blade across the packing tape. 'I knew interviewing her would be a disaster and now look what's happened.'

'It's not a disaster,' insisted Zach. 'We couldn't have paid for this kind of publicity. It's amazing! And it's all thanks to you. You and a horny pug, anyway.'

'I don't want to hear another word about it,' I said. I could feel my cheeks burning again. It was all Zach's fault. If he hadn't started working here, there wouldn't have been the event, and if there wasn't the event, I wouldn't be all over the internet being violated by a dog.

He changed the subject. 'I like your sister!'

'I don't want to hear about that, either.'

I felt Zach and Eugene exchange looks behind my back and carried on lifting books out of the box.

'OK, if anyone needs me, I'm going to sift through my photos from last night,' Zach announced. He thudded downstairs and I glared over my shoulder at Eugene, who was still looking at his phone with a grin.

'Do you want to help me with these?' I snapped, gesturing at the boxes.

He looked up from his screen of memes as if I'd just caught him sneaking a tenner from the till and slid his phone into his pocket.

'How was the pub?' I asked a few minutes later, trying to sound carefree while running the knife along another strip of brown tape with the intensity of a murderer.

'Fine. Had a few shots and went home again.'

'Nothing I should know about? No gossip?'

Eugene looked up at me blankly. 'What sort of gossip?'

'Never mind,' I replied, reflecting how fortunate it was that he worked for a bookshop and not the security services.

By lunchtime, the situation hadn't improved. Nor had my mood. If anything, both had worsened. As the memes had spread on Twitter, the shop front had come under siege from Fumi and Percy fans taking pictures outside. They posed individually and in groups, making the peace sign with their fingers underneath the Frisbee Books Ltd sign. A few of them dared come into the shop and ask if I'd be in their photo with them. The fifth time I was asked this, by a lanky boy in a Superdry T-shirt, I stomped downstairs. Zach was sitting at his laptop editing photos.

'This is a nightmare and it needs to stop,' I said.

He spun in his chair and stretched his hands back behind his head. 'Listen, I'm sorry you're upset but it's great for the shop and it'll all blow over in a couple of days.'

'That's it, is it? That's your answer to me being harassed all morning? I'm a national laughing stock, Zach!'

He sighed and puffed out his cheeks. 'Why don't you go home early? Eugene and I can manage. Go home and have a drink tonight. By tomorrow it'll be old news.'

'Fine,' I said. Normally my sense of duty would make me feel guilty about sloping off early but today I couldn't give a fig. I marched back upstairs.

'I'm off,' I said to Eugene, reaching for my bag from behind the till. 'See you Monday.'

I opened the door feeling like a celebrity who has to leave their hotel and face banks of waiting paparazzi and fans outside. Except there were only two girls standing there, giggling as one extended her arm to take a selfie of them both, and they didn't notice me. Still, as I started walking home, I was livid. And I blamed Zach entirely.

CHAPTER SIX

RORY HAD EMAILED ME a list of items to bring for our country weekend with his parents. It included wellington boots, a waterproof coat and something 'smart' for the evening. This panicked me into borrowing a strapless red dress from Mia.

'Is it not a bit... red?' I said, looking doubtfully in her full-length mirror that night. The waistband of the dress was so tight I felt like a ketchup bottle. Would I explode if I sat down? Perhaps I simply wouldn't be able to sit all evening.

'I know what I'm doing, Flo,' Mia replied. 'They'll be the sort of people who wear black tie on the weekends and you don't want to feel out of place, do you?'

Still, at least the red dress distracted me from the Percy debacle.

That evening, I packed it along with an old pair of wellies and a dusty Barbour that I found buried on the coat stand in the hall. Plus six pairs of knickers, two bras, one pair of pyjamas, two pairs of jeans, four different types of top that ranged from casual T-shirt to frilly peasant shirt, two jumpers, my plain black dress from Whistles (what if they went to church on

Sunday?), and three pairs of shoes. Converse, black pumps and red heels to go with the dress.

These provisions meant that I arrived at King's Cross on Saturday morning dragging a large suitcase behind me as if I was off to the South Pole for several months instead of Norfolk for one night. Still, better to be prepared. You never want to run out of knickers.

Rory laughed when he spotted me under the departures board. 'Let me take that,' he said, reaching for the bag.

'Where's your stuff?' I asked. He had nothing with him. Just his satchel hanging over one shoulder.

'Keep various bits and pieces at home. Christ, this is heavy.'

'Sorry.'

'Anything for you. Right, come on, platform eleven. Let's go before the plebs get all the seats.'

He set off for the ticket barriers, booming 'Excuse me, sorry, sorry, excuse me!' at other travellers before I could tell him off for being a snob. He stowed my bag and we found a table nearby. I sat by the window while Rory took off his tweed jacket, folded it and slid it carefully on top of his satchel in the overhead rack. He sat with a book on Margaret Thatcher he'd retrieved from the satchel and rubbed a hand up and down my thigh.

'You all right?' he asked.

'Yep, all good.'

'I mean about the dog situation.'

'Oh, that,' I said. We'd texted about it the previous night but I'd tried to play it down. 'Yeah, fine. I mean, there are now ninety bajillion photos of me grimacing like a gargoyle on the internet but hopefully people forget these things.'

'I blame that character you work with. What's he called? Jack?'

'Zach.'

Rory scowled. 'How did he allow the situation to get so out of control?'

'Well, he was at the back of the room, so he cou—'

'And did you see the way he looked at me?' he interrupted. 'When I mentioned what I did? I suppose he's some sort of communist.'

'I think Ruby's quite keen on him.'

'Surely your sister has more taste than that?'

I opened my mouth to reply and then looked out of the window, unsure who I should defend.

'Anyway,' Rory went on, his voice more conciliatory, 'I just wanted to make sure you weren't too humiliated. But let's forget it all and have a decent weekend. I'm thrilled you're here.'

'Me too,' I replied, although I was nervous about meeting his parents, especially his artistic mother. 'Has nice mother,' I'd written on my list. 'What's your mum like?'

'Like? What do you mean?'

'You know, what's her deal? Are you close?'

Rory scratched his chin. 'She's quite eccentric. Her father, my grandfather, was a reasonably famous portraitist so they had a bohemian upbringing – illegitimate siblings, wine at breakfast, affairs with the nannies and so on. But I adore her. As will you,' he said, squeezing my leg, 'don't worry.'

'I'm not worrying,' I lied. 'And what about your dad?'

'He's also mad. Very English. Practically stitched into his red corduroys.'

'Ah, so that's where you get it from?' I teased. Rory looked like a posh chimney sweep today, in a navy wool waistcoat over a light blue herringbone shirt, with navy trousers and a pair of suede ankle boots.

'Maybe,' Rory conceded, sliding his hand down my leg and pinching me around my knee.

'Ouch!' I said, and dived for his leg to do the same but he caught my wrist.

'Nice try but you're not that strong.'

'Oww, all right, time out,' I said, and he released my wrist. I settled back against my seat again. 'What did your dad do?'

'He was in the army, then left and went into the City, and now is mostly concerned with killing things. Pheasants, fish, our neighbours.'

'Is that why they live in the country?'

He shook his head. 'No, it's my mother's childhood house. She was the favourite child so it was left to her, which caused an almighty row in the family and now nobody speaks to one another.'

'Families, huh?' I said, leaning my head against his arm. Hearing that his were as barking mad as mine was strangely comforting.

'Mmm.' Then he tapped his book. 'You happy if I read this?'

'Oh, sure.' Although I felt a slight pang of disappointment at this. I'd imagined my first minibreak weekend with a man would be a glorious, exhilarating adventure where nobody else in the world mattered (especially not Margaret Thatcher), and in between bouts of euphoric sex where I came every time, we'd discuss the big issues in life: religion, potential children's names, our favourite flavour of crisps. I know I'd written 'must like reading' on my list but I didn't mean he had to do it all the time.

I turned away to watch through the window as London slid by, counting the carriages of an old train as we passed it. If there were an even number, his parents would like me and I wouldn't embarrass myself. 'One, two, three, four, five…'

'What are you doing?' Rory asked, head lifting from his book.

'Nothing,' I replied quickly, glancing across the aisle through the other window where there were no old trains and nothing to count. No counting this weekend, Florence Fairfax. Keep that madness locked down.

Almost two hours later, we caught a cab that smelt of fried onions from Norwich station.

'It's about twenty minutes,' Rory told me, before talking to the driver for the entire journey. About the weather, about the football, about the local MP who neither of them liked.

'He talks a load of old squit,' said the driver, before catching my eye in his mirror. 'Excuse my language,' he said.

I shook my head and smiled at his reflection as Rory rattled on. You could put him down on the moon and he'd find someone to chat to. He'd charmed everyone in the shop on Thursday night. Well, nearly everyone. But Zach hadn't even

given him a chance. He'd just assumed the worst about Rory
and stubbornly refused to change his mind. And then he'd been
busy flirting with my sister. I wondered, yet again, whether
anything would happen between them and glanced at my
phone. I hadn't heard a peep from her since Thursday evening
and she'd been out last night. Maybe with Zach? Maybe, right
now, Zach was waking up in my house and playing hunt the
tea bag in my kitchen? I narrowed my eyes at the thought as
we slowed down and the taxi pulled through an old metal gate
with a sign on the front of it: Rollmop Manor.

We crunched along a gravel drive, flanked by lawn, before
the driver stopped. All I could see through the window was
a front door surrounded by stone pillars.

'That'll be £18.50 please,' he said and I tried to pay since
Rory had bought our train tickets.

'Definitely not,' he said, passing a twenty to the front.
'You're on my tab.'

'I'm always on your tab,' I said. I felt guilty. Our bill was
constantly uneven because Rory paid for everything: for coffees, for dinner. For taxis. For bottles of wine and bunches
of peonies.

'I hope so,' he replied, kissing me briefly before opening his
side of the car. 'Chop chop, let's find the matriarch.'

I climbed out, grateful for fresh air after the onions, and
was about to stretch when a grey blur hurtled across the lawn
and jumped at me so I staggered, nearly falling to the gravel.
'JESUS CHRIST IT'S A WOLF.'

Its paws were on my shoulders so I skipped back a couple

of steps to try and free myself. 'Help, Rory! Help me. How do I get it off?' I shrieked.

'Merlin, get down!' Rory said, but he was laughing. 'It's not a wolf, you big wimp. It's my mother's greyhound. Merlin, here, boy.'

Merlin dropped his paws and trotted to Rory. My heart was thumping against my chestbone and I felt stupid. Why had I become some sort of dog magnet? I eyed Merlin warily as he thrust his head under Rory's hand. He was the size of a small pony. How much did that thing eat?

I brushed the dog hair off my chest and glanced up at the house. It looked old, built from pale yellow stone with two storeys of sash windows running across it. In the middle, around the front door, was a circular porch with pillars either side, ivy knotted around them. An old-fashioned pram with a large hood and silver wheels was parked to one side.

The door opened. 'Welcome, my darlings,' cried a woman in a purple kaftan. Her white hair was plaited over one shoulder and she was barefoot. Eccentric dressing clearly ran in the family, I thought, suddenly feeling very urban in my jeans and ankle boots.

Rory stepped forward first. 'Hi, Mummy,' he said, kissing her on both cheeks, before looking over his shoulder. 'This is Florence.'

I smiled and walked around the other side of Rory to greet his mother, trying to avoid Merlin and ignore the fact that my boyfriend had just called his mother 'Mummy'.

'Good to meet you, Mrs Dundee.'

She waggled a finger at me. 'I can't bear being called that. It makes me feel so old. Elizabeth, please.'

'Sure,' I replied, awed by her elegance. Up close, Rory's mother looked like an old Hollywood star. The corners of her blue eyes crinkled when she smiled but her skin still shone like butter.

'Come in, come in,' she said, ushering us through the door. 'Are you hungry? Lunch is ready. Goodness, what a big bag. Are you staying all month?'

'No, sorry, I just wasn't sure what to bring so OH MY GOD...' I jumped as the door swung closed behind us, revealing a looming polar bear standing on its hind legs.

'Ah yes, that's our bear. Bi-polar, we call him. My great-great grandfather shot him on an expedition he made to the Arctic in 1894. Rory, take Florence's bag upstairs and we'll go and see about drinks.'

'Right-o,' said Rory, making for a curved staircase which ran up from where we were standing. I gazed around me. The hallway looked like a posh junk shop. Under the curved staircase was a dusty grand piano. Against the opposite wall was a grandfather clock, ticking but telling the wrong time. And in between, facing us, was a large fireplace puffing clouds of grey smoke. It made me feel cold. If possible, it was colder inside than it had been outside.

'This way,' Elizabeth beckoned me. 'The kitchen's warmer.' She moved like a ghost, gliding through a doorway into a large kitchen which looked out on to the lawn behind the house. Her three cats were lying on the kitchen table in a patch of sun.

'Your cats!' I said. 'What are they called?'

'Pablo, Claude and Frida. After the artists. We give everything very silly names here, I'm afraid. There's a peacock stalking around the garden called Salvador. What would you like to drink? I'm making a jug of Bloody Mary.'

'Lovely.' The kitchen was warmer but it was also an Aladdin's cave of crap. Beside an Aga was a laundry basket exploding with socks and shirtsleeves. Silver dog bowls and saucepans dotted every surface as if catching leaks. I glanced upwards. There was a brown watermark shaped like France on the ceiling. On one side of the sink was a stack of newspapers piled so high it looked in danger of cascading to the floor at any second. On the other was a fruit bowl which contained only brown fruits. Brown apples, brown pears, withered grapes and bananas that seemed to have passed the brown stage and gone black. I sniffed. Above the smell of overripe bananas and dog, I could also smell burning.

'Right, what can I do?' said Rory, coming through the doorway. 'Where's Daddy?'

Daddy? Oh no.

'Shooting,' replied his mother. 'And you can fetch the sherry for me, then take the partridge out of the Aga. Killed only last weekend!'

'Lovely!' I said again, trying to sound enthusiastic.

★

An hour later, I was still hungry. Rory had been right about the eccentricity. Having served us each a tiny, charred bird on a plate with nothing else, no vegetables, Elizabeth fetched a lump of cheese from the fridge. Next, she'd retrieved two bottles of red wine 'from the cellar', blew the dust off them and set them down on the table.

As a result, I felt that discombobulating sense of being drunk while it was still light outside.

'I'm going to walk the cats,' she announced, standing up.

'Florence, my darling, feel like a stroll?' said Rory.

'You don't want to walk with me,' replied Elizabeth. 'Why don't you show her round the garden?'

The mystery of the pram was revealed while I stood under the porch minutes later, trying to slide my feet into the wellingtons. It was a challenge after four glasses of wine.

Elizabeth, wearing a khaki mackintosh over her kaftan and a silk headscarf tied under her chin like the Queen, appeared from inside carrying all three cats and dropped them gently into the pram, before lowering the hood as a new mother might to protect her baby. 'See you in a bit,' she said over her shoulder. 'The Battenbergs are coming for dinner so drinks in the drawing room at six!'

'I did warn you,' said Rory, as Elizabeth pushed the pram down the drive.

'I like her. She's different.' I wasn't just being polite. Her whimsical, devil-may-care attitude was refreshing. As she trudged through the metal gate at the end of the drive, it looked like she was taking a new granddaughter out for a spin. If anyone peered under the hood they'd get a heck of a shock, although presumably they were used to the sight round here.

I looked at Rory and laughed, before clapping a hand over my mouth. He'd put on a tweed coat and tweedy hat which made him look like Sherlock Holmes. Tufts of blond hair poked out from under the ear flaps.

'What?'

'Nothing,' I mumbled, still laughing from behind my fingers. 'I just didn't know I'd be playing Watson while you solved a mysterious crime on this walk.'

'Florence Fairfax, you are going to pay for that,' he said coolly.

'What do you mean?'

In less than a second, Rory had wrapped his arms around me and reached inside my coat to tickle me. I hated being tickled.

'Oh my God, stop!' I screamed, wriggling free and running down the path around the house towards the lawn. The wine made me clumsy but I staggered through a narrow gap in a hedge before he caught the hem of my coat and pulled me to the grass.

'Nice try,' he said, his arms pinning mine.

'That hat is ridiculous.'

'You have red-wine teeth,' he replied.

Our noses were almost touching and we were being drunk and absurd. But I liked it. This felt more like the romantic weekend I'd envisaged. Two people locked in their own bubble, laughing together as if life in that moment was entirely perfect, nothing else necessary.

He kissed me and put his hand back inside my coat, then reached under my jumper and wrapped his cold fingers around my ribcage.

'Fancy it?' he asked, grinning at me.

'What? Out *here*?'

He nodded and I could see from the intensity of his stare that he meant it. Also, I could feel his erection against my leg.

'What about your parents?' I craned my neck to look back at the house but it was hidden by the hedge. I'd unwittingly run into an enclosed section of the garden, surrounded by the hedge, where herbs were growing in pots and in neat clumps along a flowerbed.

'They're not here,' Rory whispered, lowering his head to kiss me again. 'Don't you want to?'

'Yes, I do. I really do. But it's just…'

'What?'

'I've got a wet bottom from the grass.'

'I can solve that.' He rolled over, pulling me with him, so that his back was on the ground and I was on top of him. I reached back to feel my jeans.

'Yeah, knew it. I've got a wet bum.'

'So take them off,' he said, before he put his hand to the back of my head and pulled me in for another kiss. I wanted to, I could feel myself yielding. But, still, we were outside, lying next to his parents' hedge and it was four in the afternoon. I thought they had scones in the country at teatime, not sex in the herb garden. And Merlin the giant dog would presumably lumber along any minute and try to join in.

'Come on,' he coaxed, 'do it. Take them off for me. Nobody's here.'

So, not wanting to seem uptight, I stood and leant to peer

through the gap in the hedge at the house. No sign of human or dog. I unzipped my jeans and peeled them down as Rory undid his flies.

'I'm not doing it with that hat on,' I said, as I tugged my jeans over my ankles and dropped my knickers on top of them. Rory removed his hat and flicked it like a frisbee over the hedge.

I lifted one leg over him and knelt down, sniggering as I felt the damp grass against my skin. 'This is a very bad idea,' I said, as I reached between my thighs and held his erection, before slowly guiding him into me.

'No, it's not. It's a fucking exceptional idea,' Rory groaned, as I started rocking on top of him. It felt pretty strange at first, given I was still wearing my waterproof coat. From the waist up, I looked like a countryside rambler; under that, well, I was probably blue and pimply given that it was a cold October afternoon and the sun had dropped behind the hedge. But my initial fears subsided after a few moments and disappeared completely when Rory licked his thumb and reached forward to rub me with it.

'Oh my God, oh my God, oh my God,' I repeated, as he circled it again and again around my clitoris.

'Look at me,' he instructed whenever I threw my head back at the intense heat of the pleasure, so I'd drop my chin again and look straight at him.

Moments later, I felt myself start to contract around him as he moved inside me, faster and faster, his hand speeding up simultaneously, pushing harder between my legs.

'Oh my God, oh my God, oh my God,' I gasped, so the words became one. 'OhmygodohmygodohmygodOHMYGOD.'

'Oh my God, COWABUNGAAAAAAAAA!' said Rory, thrusting his head back into the grass as we came together.

'Oh my gosh!' came a different, more surprised voice, as a man's head poked through the gap in the hedge. 'Sorry, old bean, I heard voices and thought you might have lost this.' The man tossed Rory's hat towards us and vanished again.

'Ah,' said Rory, glancing at the hat, which had landed next to my bare knee. 'Florence, you've now met my father.'

★

I was embarrassed for various reasons when I came downstairs with Rory for drinks later that evening. Largely because I'd been caught rolling around on top of him in the herb garden. But also because Mia had got it wrong about the strapless red dress. Everyone else in the drawing room looked liked they were off to a Quaker meeting: men in corduroy trousers, women in muted dresses with long sleeves. I looked like I was going to the opera. Plus, the hourglass cut of the dress pushed my chest so high my cleavage practically started at my chin. I felt wretched. And cold. According to Rory, his father only put the heating on if the garden pond had frozen over.

'Daddy, meet Florence, Florence meet Daddy,' Rory said, introducing us as soon as we walked in.

'Hello, Florence. Mortimer Dundee, how do you do? I hardly recognize you with your clothes on!'

'I think the less said about that the better,' Rory said quickly. 'How was shooting?'

'Bloody good fun. Now what are you both having to drink?'

Pulling open a cupboard door behind him, Mortimer revealed a mirrored drinks cupboard with bottles of jewel-coloured spirits.

'Gin and tonic, I think,' said Rory. 'Florence?'

'Could I start with a water?' I felt as if I'd only just sobered up from lunch.

'A water?' boomed Mortimer. 'Are you feeling all right?' He leant in so close that I could see tiny red spider veins spreading either side of his nose like a road map. 'Perhaps you need to rehydrate after earlier, eh?'

He roared at his own joke before turning back to the drinks cupboard. I breathed as deeply as I could in my dress and wished I'd written 'nice parents' on my list, instead of focusing on the mother.

'And you remember Octavia?' Rory said, one hand on my back as I turned to see the blonde from the House of Commons.

'Course, hello, I didn't know you'd be here!'

'I wasn't going to be, but then my parents said they were coming for dinner so I've abandoned London to join the party,' Octavia said. The red lipstick was back on and she was wearing a pair of black jeans and a black silk shirt which made me feel even more out of place – a painted Russian doll.

'I saw the pictures of you and that dog, so funny!' she added, smirking at me like Cruella de Vil. 'Quite the celebrity.'

'What's this?' asked Mortimer, handing me a tumbler of water and Rory his gin and tonic.

'Oh, Morty, it's hilarious. You must see. Florence is an internet sensation.'

'Is she now?' he said, leering at me from behind his eyebrows.

'No, I promise I'm not, it was just a silly mistake. A dog wh—'

'Rory, sweetheart, hold this for me,' interrupted Octavia. She handed her glass to him and pulled her phone from her jeans pocket.

'Look, Morty, isn't it brilliant?' she said, holding it up so we could all see the screen, my gurning face and Percy wrapped around my leg like a baby koala. 'He's a famous Instagram dog and Florence was interviewing him last week...'

'I was actually interviewing his owner,' I said, trying to regain control of the situation. 'She's a Japanese poet, very successful, her second book's just coming out and she—'

'And Florence was up on stage,' went on Octavia, 'and he started rogering her leg. Isn't that hysterical? The pictures went everywhere. My whole office were crying with laughter about it.'

'Oh, I'm so glad,' I said, with a tight smile.

'What's this?' asked Elizabeth's tinkly voice behind us.

Octavia turned to another gaggle of people standing beside the fireplace: Elizabeth, along with two others I assumed were Octavia's parents. He was wearing a sleeveless maroon jersey over a pink shirt and had the jowls of a middle-aged

UKIP supporter; she looked like Patricia, a helmet of perfectly brushed brunette hair sitting on top of a taut, joyless face.

'Oh, Mummy, Daddy! You must see. This is Florence, Florence, these are my parents, Lord and Lady Belmarsh.' She held up her phone for them and explained the story all over again to hoots of genteel laughter.

I looked to Rory for support but he just grinned and rolled his eyes at me, as if Octavia was a small and unruly child. I felt like someone had forced a poker down my throat and was stoking the embers of last week's humiliation.

'Well, well, well, Florence, you do seem irresistible!' said Mortimer, still looking at me as if I was a rib of beef.

Luckily, there then came the sound of a gong and Elizabeth announced dinner. I drained my water and put the glass back down in the mirrored drinks cupboard with such a noise I worried the shelf had cracked. Luckily not.

*

The dining room was dim, the only light coming from several candles strung along the mahogany table. The candlesticks were made from deer antlers and, on the wall, several foxes' heads with sharp incisors snarled down at us. I looked from the heads to an oil portrait hung from the wall behind Mortimer (alas, I'd been placed next to him). The portrait was a nude, a pale-skinned woman sitting on a rock beside a pool of water, leaning forwards to wash her hair in it. You could see the crease of her bottom.

Mortimer followed my glance. 'That's Elizabeth, you know.'

'What?' I flicked from him back to the white bottom on the rock.

'Done years ago,' he said, as he stuck his finger and thumb into his mouth to retrieve a piece of gristle. 'It was her wedding present to me.'

Dinner wasn't much better than lunch. Elizabeth, tonight in a red kaftan with jewelled slippers that curled at the toes, had carried a large porcelain dish through from the kitchen and announced that we were having game pie. She'd passed plates of this around the table and we'd helped ourselves to vegetables from bowls in front of us.

I managed two mouthfuls of the pie but it was stringy, tasting much as I imagine rat might. In the dark, I looked down at my plate again and tried to hunt for my next mouthful. Something small and spongy rolled under my fork. An eyeball?

'And what do you do with your time,' Morty asked, 'apart from terrorize poor dogs, ha ha!'

'I work in a bookshop,' I replied, giving up on the pie and lifting a forkful of mashed potato to my mouth. Couldn't go wrong with mashed potato. 'That's why I was interviewing this Japanese poet. Because she's pretty well known and has got her sec—'

He didn't let me finish. 'Oh, a bookshop. So you're in trade?' I might as well have told him I worked in a brothel.

The potato was cold.

'You know the one, Daddy. Frisbee in Chelsea?' interrupted Rory from the other end of the table.

'Oh, I simply adore Frisbee,' Elizabeth interrupted, clapping her hands together. 'How wonderful. I'd love to work in a bookshop.'

'I know it,' barked Lord Belmarsh. 'Looks like a charity shop from the outside.'

'It's actually a very special place,' I replied, spearing a small piece of cabbage on my plate in the hope that it was edible. I'd eaten almost nothing at lunch and was now well into my third glass of red wine. If I couldn't eat this cabbage I feared an embarrassing accident. 'It's been there since 1967.'

'But she's not going to work there for ever because she's writing her own book, aren't you, darling?' said Rory.

The cabbage disintegrated in my mouth. 'I don't know how long I'll be there, to be honest,' I replied. 'I really love it.'

'But you want to be a writer instead of selling other people's books,' he urged, and it seemed, briefly, as if Rory was a pushy parent, encouraging me to say the right thing in front of everyone else; that he too was ashamed I worked in a shop.

'Both, if I'm lucky,' I replied with a smile around the table. I felt like a performing seal.

'When are you going back tomorrow, darling?' Elizabeth asked him.

'After lunch?'

'Oh good. I thought we could all go for a ride in the morning. Do you ride, Florence?'

Mortimer leant towards me. 'She means horses, my dear.'

'I used to, yes,' I said. 'But not for years. My French grandmother had a very small, very obstinate pony called Winston that I used to ride into the village and back to get croissants in the morning.'

'Wonderful! We'll go out for a canter after breakfast in that case. Oh dear, Morty, look, there's a vole,' she added, pointing to the skirting board where a small dark object scuttled along the carpet.

'A vole!' shrieked Lady Belmarsh.

'Oh, Mummy, stop fussing, it's not going to bite you,' said Octavia.

I wondered if I could trap it and eat it.

'Morty, go and get Pablo, he'll catch it,' said Elizabeth, putting her napkin on the table. 'And if everyone's finished, shall we go through and sit soft?'

We went back to the drawing room for coffee served in thimble-sized cups. I drank three, mostly to warm up and quieten my hunger pangs, but also to dilute the red wine. There was a box of After Eights on the coffee tray so I had several of those too, scrunching the black paper sleeves in my fist to hide how many I ate.

'Rory tells me you and he grew up together,' I said to Octavia, who was sitting next to me on the sofa.

'Yes! He was my first proper kiss when we were thirteen,' she replied, before turning and pointing towards the windows. 'It was here, actually, during a party one summer. He whisked me into the herb garden and had his wicked way.'

'Ha! The herb garden, that's funny,' I murmured, glancing across the room to where Rory was in discussion with Lord Belmarsh. It wasn't funny, obviously, but I didn't want to let her know that. 'And you're going out with Noddy?'

Octavia's head fell back against the sofa and she laughed. 'Noddy! God no. I love him but not like that.' She paused and glanced at Rory. 'No,' she said lightly. 'No boyfriend at the moment. I'm all free.'

Then she lowered her voice, almost to a whisper, and leant in closer. 'But don't worry, Rory and I wouldn't work.'

'Really? How come?' I squeaked, unable to think of a sharper reply.

'I'm too challenging for him,' she said, with a flick of her red nails. 'He needs someone more docile. Someone who's not going to outshine or threaten him. Someone who'd make a good political wife. Someone, perhaps, a bit like you.' A smirk danced on her lips as I groped for a reply. Why did other people often seem to have such quick retorts at moments like these while my own mouth flapped like a guppy fish? I was too stunned to come up with anything clever.

'I, er, I mean, er, I think it's bit, er, early for that,' I stuttered eventually. 'I mean, we've only been on a few dates and I'm actually not that do—'

'Oh, I wouldn't be so sure,' she carried on, glancing back at Rory. 'I can tell he likes you. And he's been told he needs to find a wife before being given a seat so you could easily end up married, living in this house.' She settled back against the sofa and spread her arms out across it.

I tried to process what she'd just said. I felt like a tiny alarm bell had just gone off inside my skull. 'Sorry, he's been told he needs to find a *wife*?'

Her red mouth formed a perfect circle in surprise. 'Oh,

didn't you know? You mustn't worry too much. It's all political shenanigans. But the party does tend to prefer candidates who can demonstrate family values so Rory's been unofficially instructed to get married.' She paused and smirked again. 'Aren't you the lucky one?'

'Right,' I murmured, gazing at the fireplace in front of us. 'No, no, he hasn't mentioned anything.'

'Hector, darling, I think we should go home and let the dogs out,' said Lady Belmarsh.

'Quite right,' replied Lord Belmarsh, standing up. 'We should be orf, but thank you, Dundees, for a terrific dinner.'

I stood with Octavia and murmured goodbyes like a robot.

'So lovely to see you again, Florence, and see you in London, I'm sure,' she said, with another smile. Unbelievable. The woman would take gold in every category of the Smirking Olympics.

Rory, his parents and I stood in the porch to wave them down the drive.

'That was bloody marvellous, and delicious pie, darling,' Mortimer told his wife as we went back inside.

Suddenly, I felt so tired I could barely stand.

'Rory, take poor Florence upstairs, she looks exhausted,' instructed Elizabeth.

'Knackered, I'll bet,' added Mortimer.

'Yes, Mummy,' said Rory, 'but are you all right, darling? You look awfully pale.'

'Mmm, fine,' I said faintly.

'I'll run you a bath,' he said. 'How about that?'

I nodded silently before we said goodnight to his parents and walked up the curved staircase. What to say? How to say it? Was that what I was? A box marked 'wife' for him to tick? A project?

I decided I'd have a bath and broach the subject in the morning. I was too shattered now. The combination of red wine and coffee was making me both drowsy and jittery. Obviously there was almost no hot water in this arctic house so I lay in the tepid, avocado-coloured bath and counted the flowers up and down the curtains. And by the time I tiptoed back down the corridor in a scratchy towel to our bedroom, Rory was already asleep.

★

I woke the next morning with a cold nose. Our bedroom was freezing. At around 3 a.m., when I wondered if I'd survive the night, I'd scrabbled in the dark for two jumpers and a pair of socks. I'd considered putting several pairs of knickers over my head as a hat before deciding that it might alarm Rory. I exhaled with my mouth open and saw my breath hang in the air, then pinched my thumb and my forefinger around my nose to try and warm it.

'What are you doing?' said Rory, opening his eyes.

'By dose is cold,' I said.

'What?'

I removed my hand. 'My nose is cold.' Then I sniffed and smelled fish. 'What's that?' I asked, fearing that I might have to eat whatever Elizabeth had murdered in the kitchen.

'Kippers. Daddy always has kippers on a Sunday morning,' he said, leaping out of bed, flashing his bottom at me. But not even that could cheer me up. The conversation with Octavia had been the first thought that wormed its way into my brain when I woke, making me feel deflated before I'd even opened my eyes.

He'd already pulled on a pair of trousers and was buttoning a shirt at the foot of the bed. I couldn't bear to extend an inch of bare flesh from under the blanket.

'Come on, lazybones,' he said, pulling the bottom corner of the blanket and whipping it off. The sudden cold made me shriek and curl into a ball on the mattress. 'RORY! I hate you, that's so mean.'

He laughed as he headed for the door. 'As if you could hate me. I'm heading to the kitchen but come down whenever you're ready.'

I sat up and looked around the bedroom for my bag. My mouth still tasted of baked rat. I needed to brush my teeth, get dressed, go down to the kitchen and forage for a piece of toast. They must have toast. You couldn't screw up toast.

Twenty minutes later, I followed the fishy stench back down the long corridor, the stairs and into the kitchen.

'Morning!' cried Elizabeth, standing over the Aga. Rory and his father were sitting at one end of the kitchen table, the cats stretched across the other.

'Morning, Florence, I trust you slept well?' asked Mortimer. He was clearly an advanced-level pervert since even this sounded like an innuendo.

'Yes, thank you,' I fibbed.

'Have a seat,' said Elizabeth. 'Would you like a kipper? I've saved you one.'

I waved my hands quickly at her. 'No! I mean, no thank you. Just a piece of toast would be great.' I pulled out the chair next to Rory, sat and felt Merlin's wet nose push at my forearm. I patted him lightly on the head in case the others were watching, then twisted my body away.

'I'm afraid I've received a boring email from the office,' said Rory, putting a hand on my leg. 'There's a developing situation in Algeria which means I need to go back up after breakfast. Do you mind?'

'Oh no! That means no riding,' said Elizabeth. 'What a pity.'

'That is a pity,' I said, trying to sound sad.

'You'll have to come back for a gallop another time, eh?' said Mortimer, over the top of his paper.

I smiled thinly at him as Elizabeth dropped a piece of toast on my plate. 'There you go, butter and jam on the table.'

'Thanks,' I said, reaching for the butter dish. Oh. It was covered in dog hair. I peered more closely. Or cat hairs, plus a couple of human hairs for good measure. I scraped around the hairs, looked at the jam jars in front of me and decided to stick with butter.

Rory continued tapping at his phone, Mortimer read his newspaper and Elizabeth hummed while shuffling pots around the kitchen so I sat eating my toast and stared through the French windows. I'd talk to Rory on the train. I wasn't sure how to start the conversation but I'd think of something.

This, I decided, with another crunch of hairy toast, was why life without boyfriends was easier. I'd been all right on my own and now I was in a pickle. I liked Rory. I felt a small kick of pleasure inside me every time I remembered that I had a boyfriend, every time I mentioned him to someone. Sure, not very feminist, but it made me feel more normal, less alone. And yet here I was, weakened by him because his behaviour had influenced my own mood. Or maybe that was just what a relationship looked like? I pulled a hair from between my lips and flicked it from my finger to the floor. If I got back to London without dysentery it would be a miracle.

★

Luckily, because it was a Sunday morning, the train was almost empty. We sat at a table and Rory optimistically slid his book on Margaret Thatcher out from his satchel.

'Can I talk to you about something?' I asked, forcing myself to get the sentence out. I knew, once I'd said those words, that other words had to follow them, although I still wasn't exactly sure what those words would be.

'Hmm?' he said, not taking his eyes off the page.

'Do you want to marry me?'

He turned towards me with a grin. 'Florence Fairfax, are you proposing to me on the 11.03 to London King's Cross?'

'No, sorry, that's not what I meant, I'm not proposing.'

'I think you are,' he said in a mocking tone. 'That sounded very much like a proposal to me.'

'I'm not proposing! Listen, I'm being serious – it was something Octavia said to me last night.'

A ripple of alarm passed over his forehead. 'What did she say?'

'She said that you were only going out with me because you'd been told you need to get married for your career, for a seat,' I said, as quickly as I could, as if getting the words out faster made them less painful. 'That someone had told you to find a wife, and that's why you'd picked me.'

Rory closed his book and put it on the table so Margaret Thatcher glared back at me. 'I'm sorry she said that.'

'It's true?'

He sighed, turned, looked away from me through the window and I felt a black surge of anguish. OK, never mind. We'd break up, and that was sad, but Marmalade would be waiting for me at home. And it had been a diverting few weeks. And at least I could say now that I'd had a boyfriend, even if it was only for three seconds. That would shut Patricia up. And I'd probably cry for several months but I'd finally get over it, maybe when I was in my mid-forties. And then I might seriously think about signing up for a nunnery. Were nunneries listed on Google? I'd look when I got home.

'Course it's not true,' he said, turning back a few moments later, just as I was wondering if I had the right shaped face for a wimple.

'So why did she say it?'

'Because she's jealous and always thought she and I would end up together,' he said, with a sigh. He took both my hands in his. 'And yes, it's true the party used to prefer that candidates were married. Solid family men, that sort of thing. But not any more. Come on, Florence, you're better than this, it's not 1919.'

I rolled my lower lip through my teeth. 'So she made it up?' I asked, frowning.

He shrugged. 'That's the only thing I can think of.' He glanced away from me, down the aisle at an approaching rattling. 'Look, here comes the man with the trolley. Do you want anything? Can I buy you a restorative cup of coffee? I think I might have one.'

I wasn't sure I could concentrate on coffee while my brain was still whirring.

'Hello, my good man,' Rory said to the short man in a regulation waistcoat pushing the trolley through the train. 'Could I please have a cappuccino, hold the chocolate.'

'Don't do them,' he replied in a surly tone. 'We do white coffee or black coffee.'

'Ah, of course, what a terrific choice. Well, in that case a white coffee please. Florence?'

'Er...' I looked at the man in the waistcoat as if he'd help me out and sell me the secret to a straightforward relationship instead of a coffee that tasted like puddle. 'No, I'm good, thanks.'

Rory tapped the card machine and took his coffee – 'Magnificent, thank you so much' – before putting his free hand over mine.

'Ignore Octavia,' he said. 'She's a troublemaker sometimes.'

'I will, I just wanted to ask,' I replied.

'Don't be absurd, of course you should ask,' he said, kissing my head before releasing my hand and immediately opening Margaret Thatcher.

★

When we arrived at King's Cross, Rory caught a cab to his office. I took the Northern Line home, inconveniencing every other person on the Tube with my suitcase.

I found Mia and Hugo on the sofa discussing wedding canapés. Mia was cross-legged with her laptop balanced on her knees, Hugo was lying flat along the rest of it, his gangly legs dangling over the sofa arm like a cadaver.

'What do you think, Flo, if you had a choice between the venison carpaccio with fig compote or partridge tart with horseradish cream?' she asked.

'Please, no more partridge,' I said, releasing my suitcase. 'Rory's mother murdered several of them for our lunch yesterday.'

'Course, his parents!' shrieked Mia, shutting her laptop screen and dropping it on Hugo's torso.

'Owwww, Mia, that really hurt,' said Hugo, clutching his stomach.

She ignored him. 'How were they? I've been tits deep in crab cake and scallop goujons since yesterday; tell me everything.'

'It was kind of hilarious,' I replied. I needed a quiet afternoon to go over it in my head. The house. His parents. Nearly being ravaged by a wolf. Actually being ravaged by Rory in the herb garden. The food. Octavia's conversation and my talk to Rory on the train. I looked down as I heard a 'mewl' to see Marmalade sitting patiently at my feet.

'Hi, pal,' I said, scooping him up and scratching under his ear, never more grateful to see him.

'Hilarious how?'

'Mad,' I replied, as Marmalade buried his face in my neck. 'Eccentric. Like, they live in this huge posh house with dogs and chickens, even a peacock, but it looked like a squat inside. Well, maybe not a squat. But it was pretty old and run-down. Curtains that looked like they'd been put up 900 years ago, an extremely casual attitude towards voles and a whole room for boots. Boots! And no heating.'

'That's posh people for you, they spend all their money on horses.'

'They do have horses.'

'Exactly. But you liked them? His parents?'

'Yessssss,' I said slowly. 'They were just quite… different.'

'Don't worry. I loathed Hugo's mother when I first met her.'

'What?' interjected Hugo, pressing his head back into the sofa to glance up at Mia. 'I thought you liked them?'

'I do now,' she replied, running a soothing hand over his forehead before looking at me and mouthing 'No, I don't.'

'All I'm saying to Florence,' she went on, 'is that it doesn't matter if you don't love the parents straight away. There's all this pressure about meeting them for the first time but sometimes other people's families are even worse than one's own.'

'Where's Ruby?' I asked.

'Dunno. Haven't seen her all weekend. Have you invited Rory to the wedding yet?'

I shook my head. 'I'm sort of waiting for the right moment. I just... didn't want it to seem too much.'

Mia rolled her eyes. 'You're fine, you've just been to stay with his parents.'

'He must come,' added Hugo, 'it'll be like having the abominable snowman or the Loch Ness Monster there.'

'What d'you mean?'

'Only that they're also exceptionally rare beasts, a bit like your boyfriends, ha ha!'

Mia punched Hugo in the arm and made him whine again.

'Oh hey, would your friend Jaz be up for doing our hair?' she went on. 'I've booked a make-up artist called Mel so that's sorted. She's amazing, she did the Royal wedding. But I still need someone to do hair.'

'For you?'

'You, Ruby, Mum and me. I've got a mood board. Look.' She reached for her laptop so I quickly picked up my suitcase again. Couldn't face looking at 742 different hairstyles right now.

'I've got to go unpack all my knickers,' I said, 'but I'll text her and ask.'

CHAPTER SEVEN

'A WORD, PLEASE, EVERYONE!' shouted Norris a few days later, as he stood in the middle of the shop just before opening.

I looked over my shoulder and caught Eugene's eye. He frowned at me; I shrugged back. Zach appeared at the top of the stairs and yawned, stretching his tattooed arms. A bird with unfurled wings flew up his right bicep, so delicately inked you could see every feather.

'Morning, madam,' said Zach mid-yawn, his arms still lifted. 'What are you staring at?'

'Put your hand over your mouth,' I replied, walking past him towards the others.

'Is everything OK, Norris?' said Eugene. He was wearing his silliest bow tie, pink with yellow spots. It made him look like the host of a children's game show.

'Eugene, Eugene, calm down,' said Norris, waving a hand in the air as if he was trying to slow traffic. 'It's only to say thank you, again, for the evening last week and any more ideas would be gratefully received since the landlord's not budging on the rent. So we need more. More money, more support.'

'More readings?' suggested Eugene. 'I've been looking at the catalogues and there's a new cookery book by Marigold Shute coming out in the next couple of weeks called *How to Have a Very Merry Vegan Christmas*.'

'Christ on a bike, not the nut-munchers,' muttered Norris.

'I'm not interviewing anybody,' I warned.

'And there's a new Hitler biography by Simon Friedman,' added Eugene.

'Another one?' I asked. 'How is there anything left to say that the last 592 books about him haven't?'

'Hitler's a crowd-puller,' insisted Eugene.

'Steady on,' said Norris, waving his hand at him again. 'But he does sell tickets so can you look into it?'

'I've been thinking about children's events,' said Zach, leaning back against the shelves. 'Hallowe'en is in a couple of weeks, then Christmas.'

'Zachary, why would I want a stampede of kids dribbling from every orifice in this shop?' asked Norris.

'Because if you get the kids, you get the parents. Look, say we do a Hallowe'en party, a tenner a ticket per kid, string up fake cobwebs downstairs in the children's section, do a couple of spooky readings, get a face painter. Job done. Meanwhile, the adults are stuck here for an hour or so. They're going to buy books.'

'You'll probably just get a load of nannies.'

Zach rolled his eyes at me. 'Don't be a grinch. It's what we should be doing. More community stuff, local stuff. And it's good for our social channels. We get tagged in pictures, word spreads. Every little helps.'

'If you want to do local stuff, what about my petition?' I said, looking at Norris. 'A proper campaign against the rent hike. And posters in the windows. That's got to be more helpful than some fake cobwebs.'

'Spoilsport,' muttered Zach.

'Don't worry, I love fancy dress,' said Eugene, patting his arm. 'I'll be there in my pumpkin outfit.'

'Alternatively you could go as a toad,' I suggested, peeved by Eugene's open act of disloyalty.

'We can do both,' said Norris, adopting the tone of a UN peacekeeper. 'Zachary, you can be in charge of events. Let's see how Hallowe'en goes before committing to any others. But I do not want to see a drop of fake blood anywhere. If I see a drop of fake blood there could be a very real accident, all right?'

Zach nodded.

'Florence, you may start your petition, but can you run it past me before you get any placards made up?'

'I wasn't going to get plac—'

'It was a little joke,' said Norris. 'And Eugene, can you please approach Hitler and the cabbage brigade about readings?'

'Yes, Norris, right away.'

'Good, thank you. Can someone open up? I'm going back downstairs if anyone needs me.'

*

There was a NOMAD meeting that night, so I locked up and walked round the corner. 'Hi, Stephen,' I said, pushing the classroom door open. He waved from the teacher's desk at the front where he was fanning out his custard creams. Mary was already in her seat at the front. Seamus, the hoarder, was making tea in the corner. I was always nervous about Seamus being on tea duty because he didn't inspire much confidence on the hygiene front; today he was wearing a coat fastened with orange twine.

'How you doing, babe?' Jaz asked, as I took my usual seat next to her. 'Saw those pictures of you with the dog.'

'Don't,' I replied. 'It was a complete disaster. All Zach's fault.'

'Is Zach the good-looking one?'

'Not you as well?'

'What?'

'Ruby was all over him last week too.'

'I wouldn't mind him climbing all over me,' said Jaz, with a wheezy laugh that attracted Stephen's attention.

'Jasmine and Florence, I wonder if you two would like to sit at the front this week?'

'No, ta, Stephen. We're all right here.'

'If you say so,' he replied, before turning back to his biscuits.

'No Dunc?' I asked.

'Nah. Leon picked him up for once.'

'All fine there?'

Jaz shrugged. 'I handed over Dunc and his school bag, we didn't say much.' She paused and chewed a nail. 'I dunno what he'll give him for his tea.'

'He'll be OK, it's one night.' It felt feeble reassurance but

I didn't know what else to add. And to be fair to Leon, Dunc had only eaten from sterile jars of baby mush for the first two years of his life. One night of nuggets wasn't going to hurt.

'Anyway,' Jaz went on, her face brightening, 'how's it going with that fancy boyfriend of yours?'

'Fancy?'

She turned in her seat and squinted at me. 'I thought you said he wears posh clothes?'

'Oh, right, yes, and good, thanks. Stayed with his parents this weekend. Got caught shagging in the vegetable garden by his dad. The usual.'

'What?' she said, loudly enough for Stephen to glance over his shoulder at us.

'Yeah, he's quite keen on sex,' I whispered.

'You had that on that mad list of yours.'

'What?'

'Something about James Bond. And now you've got yourself a right pervert.' She laughed loudly at this.

'Shhhhhh.'

'Have you been back to see that old witch?' she asked, at the same volume.

'Mmm.'

'And what did she say about it?'

I winced, already embarrassed by what I was about to admit. 'She put a spell on my necklace.'

'For what?'

'A spell for attraction, to transform my energy and make Rory fall in love with me. Or something like that.'

Jaz's head dropped back and she cackled at the ceiling.

'Jasmine!' said Stephen. 'As we'll be starting in a few moments, are you sure I can't persuade you to sit up here?' He gestured at the front row, where Lenka had now joined Mary and was coughing into a handkerchief.

'No, no, we're all right,' Jaz insisted, before looking at me. 'I'm sorry, Floz, I shouldn't laugh. But it is funny, all this. Forget your caterpillar book. Are you writing all this down?'

'Isn't it weird though? That everything's happened like she said?'

She pursed her lips and shook her head. 'Nah, not really. It's what you want to believe, innit?'

'What do you mean?'

Seamus shuffled in front of us, holding two mugs of tea so dark it looked like coffee.

'Thanks, Seamus,' I said, reaching for one handle, trying not to look at his dirty fingernails.

'You're the man,' said Jaz, taking the other mug before breezing on. 'Look, Floz, it's like your counting and me thinking all my food was dangerous. And you thinking you've met Rory because of this list. It's our brains persuading us that it must be true. It's how them fortune tellers work.'

I frowned at her.

'By winkling out people's weak spots and convincing them that only they know the truth.'

'When it isn't true?'

She shrugged. 'Could eating an apple really hurt Dunc? Nah, course not. But I had a little whispery voice telling me it might. And same with you, right? Did you meet Rory because you wrote a list of things you were looking for?'

I didn't reply. I wasn't sure what I believed now.

Jaz shook her head. 'Nah. But you wanted a boyfriend and he happened to come into the shop one day, so you've persuaded yourself that it's because of this list. It's clever, man. It's easy to believe, just be careful.'

'With Rory?'

'With everything. Don't let anyone push you in the wrong direction. You've got to think for yourself.'

I sighed and decided to change the subject. I could feel Jaz's advice acting like a depressant, deflating the excitement I felt about even being in a relationship.

'Talking of the shop,' I said, 'can I talk to you about making a petition?' Jaz had organized one a couple of years before when the council tried to demolish the red-brick block she lived in at the end of the King's Road.

'Petition?'

'For Frisbee. To make the landlord back down on the rent. He only put it up last year and now he's trying to do it again.'

'You should do what we did.'

'What was that?'

'We put up a table on the street one weekend and got nearly two thousand signatures. And the local MP came and took photos. And we had stickers...'

'Stickers!' I hadn't thought of stickers. 'Did it help?'

She shrugged. 'I'm still living there, aren't I? I'll help if you want. I quite like all that. A cause. In the olden times I could have been Joan of the Ark.'

'Joan of Arc.'

'Yeah, her.'

'Mmm,' I murmured. 'We could have a table outside the shop and I'll get a banner made up. I just need to beat Zach.'

'Beat him?'

'He's doing a Hallowe'en party to raise money.'

'Top idea! Can I bring Dunc?'

I tutted. 'Yeah, all right.' Then I remembered Mia's hair request. 'Oh, also, you up for doing our hair on my sister's wedding day?'

'Sure. When is it?'

'First Saturday in December. It'll be me and Ruby who are the bridesmaids. Plus my stepmum and the—'

'JASMINE AND FLORENCE,' shouted Stephen from the front. 'As we're about to start, I'm going to insist today that you both sit here.' He gestured at the seats directly in front of his desk.

'All right, Steve, keep your hair on,' said Jaz, peeling her bottom out of the chair and picking up her bag. 'Come on, Floz. You got us in trouble with Stephen.'

*

The following morning, I downloaded a petition template and personalized it at the till computer while Eugene tidied the customer orders in the cupboard behind me, singing hymns as he went.

'Save our local bookshop!' I typed in big red letters at the top of the document, followed by a short paragraph explaining that we needed support to force our landlord to back down on the rent increase. Initially, I wrote 'evil landlord' but deleted it on the basis that it was a petty barb that made the petition sound less professional.

Zach had come upstairs looking for the stapler earlier and peered over my shoulder before offering to help with the design, but I had primly refused him. The petition was my job. And it looked very official; neat little rectangular boxes for printed names, signatures and email addresses. I felt proud. The suffragettes might have handcuffed themselves to the Downing Street railings but I'd mastered Excel. Both were impressive in their own way.

'How many sheets do you think we need?' I asked Eugene over my shoulder.

He paused from a verse of 'Guide Me, O Thou Great Redeemer'.

'How many signatures can you get on each one?'

'Mmm… about thirty,' I said, scrolling down the computer.

His head popped out from the cupboard like a mole. 'Maybe a hundred?'

'A hundred sheets? Norris will go mad.' The printer was downstairs in his office. Eugene used to print his lines from it until Norris appeared on the shop floor one morning, eyes like a dragon and clutching fistfuls of paper, demanding to know which of us had printed the entire text of *Othello*.

'Just do it when he goes for lunch,' Eugene said with a shrug, before returning to the cupboard and resuming his singing.

I hit print just after Norris left for The Duck and Sausage (he had lunch at the nearby pub every day: a pint of ale and a pickled egg sandwich), and I left it a few minutes before going downstairs to the office.

Zach spun from his laptop and gestured at the printer where dozens of pages had fluttered to the floor and more were spilling out of it, page after page. 'You aiming for the whole of London to sign this?'

'I don't want to run out of sheets on Saturday,' I said, sucking my stomach in and stepping into the tight space between the printer and the back of his chair. I had decided, and Norris had grunted his assent, that this weekend was a good time to erect a table outside the shop and start bagging signatures. The forecast was clear and it was half-term, so I figured families might be out shopping.

'How many did you print?'

'A hundred.'

Zach swivelled round, the back of his chair pressing my bottom into the filing cabinet, and picked up a few sheets from the floor. 'You must have done more than that, look.' He held up a sheet which had the number '178' in the top right-hand corner.

I checked the next sheet out of the printer: 241. And the sheets didn't look like they were supposed to. The table was the wrong way round and the signatures boxes had pushed the spaces for email addresses off the page. How had I done this?

Fucking Excel. Norris would explode. He was always telling us that ink cartridges were more expensive than gold.

'Shit,' I muttered, biting my lip at Zach. 'I don't know. Stop it, can we stop it?' I hit the printer's red button multiple times but the printer kept churning them out, the pages now spooling out and covering my feet. 'Shit, Zach! And the layout's all messed up, there's no space on each one for email addresses. The whole lot's useless. Shit, what a waste. How do I make it stop? Zach, don't just laugh, help!'

'Calm down,' he said, standing up. 'And budge up.'

I bent myself underneath the sloped ceiling as Zach tapped at a few buttons on the machine and it stopped instantly.

'What's going on?' barked Norris, appearing in the doorway.

'Thought you'd gone for lunch,' I said quickly.

'Forgot something I needed to post.' He glared at the floor, a sea of A4. 'What's all this paper?'

'It's the petition which Florence has very kindly spent all morning working on to help you,' said Zach, in the calming tone that you'd use on a child. 'Is that OK?'

Norris reached for an envelope from his desk. 'Yes, yes, fine.' He stuck out his chin to peer at one of the sheets.

'Go and have lunch, we'll show you when you're back,' Zach said, ushering him out. Then he turned back to me, scrabbling around in his Doc Martens, picking up the wasted sheets. 'Email me the document. I'll print it.'

'Thanks,' I said meekly, standing up and feeling child-like myself. Hateful, hateful Excel.

★

The printer wasn't my only challenge that week. On Friday evening, I traipsed along Harley Street, walked up four floors and knocked on Gwendolyn's door.

I waited for her summoning.

Nothing.

I knocked again.

Nothing.

I knocked for a third time and cracked the door open. I didn't want to interrupt any poor, embarrassed soul lying on the sofa while they had a spell put on them.

But instead of anybody lying on the sofa, I was greeted by the sight of Gwendolyn dancing around the room in a pair of large pink headphones, wafting a bunch of burning twigs over her head. I wrinkled my nose at the smell of very strong sweet tea.

'Gwendolyn?'

She didn't hear me.

'Gwendolyn?'

'Oh girls, they wanna have fu-hunnnnn...' she sang, still with her back to me. She side-stepped into the corner, her bottom swinging side to side as she waved the twigs like a rhythmic gymnast twirling a ribbon in the air.

'GWENDOLYN!'

The bottom froze and she frowned over her shoulder, then tugged her headphones off.

'Florence, hello, you're very early.'

I looked at my watch. It was 6.32 p.m., which meant I was two minutes late.

'No, it's, er, gone six thirty.'

'Has it?' Gwendolyn squinted at her watch as if I was lying to her. 'Goodness me, so it has. Right, let me just sort myself out and we'll get cracking.'

She unclipped an old Walkman from the waistband of her patchwork trousers, then dropped the twigs into a small ceramic bowl on the coffee table.

'What is that?' I asked. The room smelled like a hippie's armpit.

'Sage. I had a very troubled client before you, poor man's wife has just left him, so I needed to purify the room, to dispel all the negative energy.' Gwendolyn sat down on the armchair opposite me and briefly closed her eyes. 'Mmm, it's helped.' She opened her eyes. 'Did you know, Florence, that the Latin for sage, *salvia*, means to heal?'

'Er, no, I didn't.'

'So when you burn it, it releases negative ions which neutralize the space around us. But let's not dwell on poor Mr Nicopoulous and his runaway wife. How are you? Is your romance still blossoming like a cherry tree in April? I do hope so.'

'It is,' I said slowly. 'I think so. I went to stay with his parents at the weekend.'

She clapped her hands with delight. 'You did? And how was his mother? You wanted someone with a nice mother, did you not?'

I nodded. 'Yes, and she was nice. Although his fath—'

Gwendolyn interrupted by clicking her finger and thumb several times and shaking her head.

'What?'

'Always this negativity, Florence. Have you noticed it? It's a very pernicious habit of yours, almost as if you can't allow anything to be going well.'

'No, it is going well, it's just that his father was a bit weird. And he's got this old friend called Octavia who told me something strange.'

She sighed as if I was making this up. 'What was it? Tell me.'

I twisted my mouth into a tight knot before answering. 'She just said he was looking for a wife. She basically implied that's all he wanted, and that it could have been anyone, but that I was docile enough to fit the bill.'

'Oh goodness me, Florence, what's wrong with that?' Gwendolyn looked at me with wide-eyed astonishment. 'Don't you want to get married?'

'Yes. But no, not like that. I mean, I don't know. I don't know if I want to marry Rory, not yet. Why do I have to know now? And why is everyone so frigging obsessed with getting married? What is so bad about not being married?'

'Florence…'

But I ignored her and carried on. 'I mean, we've invented driverless cars and vegan cheese but the marker of civilization is still putting on a white dress and staggering twenty metres down an aisle. What canapés to have. What cake to have. A fishtail dress or halterneck? Roses or lilies? DJ or a band? Should our invitations be white or blue? What should our wedding hashtag be? Jesus Christ, a wedding hashtag! That's when you need more going on in your life, if you're busy worrying about your wedding hashtag.'

'Florence, have you quite finished?'

I leant back against the sofa. 'Yes.'

'Well I think there's only one thing for it,' she said. 'We need to do a sage ritual with you too.'

'Why?' I asked wearily, but she was already leaning forward to pick up the small bundle of twigs from the bowl.

'Because it will balance you out. Help clear all this toxic negativity. Now sit there and hold this.'

'Hold what?'

Gwendolyn stood, opened a drawer of the dresser behind her and turned back to me with a pale grey feather. 'This. It's from a very rare type of white-bellied forest owl found only in the Ural Mountains.'

'What am I supposed to do with it?'

'Just wave it slowly in front of you while I perform the smudging ceremony.'

'The *what*?'

'Florence, no more questions, close your eyes.'

I wriggled myself further back on the sofa, dragged the feather back and forth in front of me as if it was a sparkler and listened to Gwendolyn light the bundle of sage.

Inevitably, there was also a mad prayer.

'May your hands be cleansed, that they create beautiful things,' she said, as the first pungent whiff of smoke caught my nostrils. 'And may your feet be cleansed, that they might take you where you most need to be.'

She continued for several minutes, listing pretty much each and every body part. Even my reproductive organs got a shout-out. And the smell! The smell made me want to retch.

'May this person be washed clean by the smoke of this fragrant plant. And may that same smoke carry these prayers, spiralling, to the heavens,' she said finally, before telling me to open my eyes and hand back the feather. 'There, I expect you'll sleep very well tonight. You can report back in our next session.'

One more to go, I thought, as I left her room a few minutes later and headed back downstairs to Harley Street. While strolling home through St James's Park, I glanced down and saw a feather which looked suspiciously like that of the white-bellied forest owl. I picked it up as I heard a cooing above my head in a tree. It was a pigeon, so I'm not entirely convinced that Gwendolyn's feather was from a rare owl at all.

*

When I got back to Kennington, an unexpected situation was unfolding in the kitchen: Mia, Hugo *and* Rory were all sitting at the kitchen table wearing sleep masks over their eyes while Ruby poured red wine into glasses in front of them. Mia had a pink silky sleep mask on; Rory's was lilac and Hugo's was white and fluffy, shaped like a unicorn with closed eyes on the front of it and a small horn protruding from the middle. The table was covered with further wine bottles and used glasses, and from the speaker behind the sink came the sound of aggressive hip-hop. Ruby loved hip-hop.

'Hello,' I said, dropping my rucksack on the floor. 'Rory, how come you're here so early?'

He lifted up one end of his mask and then stood and came round the table to kiss me. 'I finished work before I thought I would. Where've you been? Did you not see my message?'

'No, sorry.' I'd been too busy contemplating pigeon feathers and the effects of sage to look at my phone on the walk home. 'I was working late on my petition,' I added quickly, before Mia and Ruby could remember that I'd had my third session with Gwendolyn.

'Want a glass, Flo?' said Ruby, waggling the bottle at me.

'Yep, thanks,' I replied as Rory sat back down.

He and I had planned to meet here and order a takeaway on the sofa since, when Mia had mentioned the wine tasting a couple of days ago, I'd assumed that she meant they were doing it at Claridge's, not in our kitchen. I wondered how long Rory had been here and totted up the number of open bottles on the table. Eight. There was a relaxed, end-of-dinner-party vibe to the room; the glasses were smeary with fingerprints, there was a bowl of half-eaten crisps on the table and Hugo and Rory had pulled their tie knots loose. But the thought of him hanging with my sisters and Hugo without me made me anxious. Or maybe that was the screaming hip-hop. Just please could they not have mentioned the list.

'What petition? Were you with Zach?' asked Ruby, handing me a glass.

'I do hope not,' said Rory.

'Has he said anything about me?' Ruby added. 'I've started following him on Insta but he hasn't followed me back.'

'No, sorry. And it's just something I'm doing at the shop tomorrow. To try and raise local support and so on and so on. But why the blindfolds?' I pushed on, keen to get off the subject of Zach.

Mia pushed her sleep mask back so her blonde hair stuck out behind it like straw from a scarecrow and explained, 'We thought we'd make it a blind tasting, more fun.'

I watched as Hugo, mask still on, fumbled in front of him for a plastic bowl on the table, then picked it up and spat into it.

Ruby wrinkled her nose. 'Just swallow it, Hugo, everyone else is.'

'A spittoon is how the professionals do it. And I'm not sure about that one at all. The first red was better.'

Ruby sighed and picked up a bottle from the table before squinting at the label. 'That was the Merlot.' She looked back to me. 'I'll come and sign the petition if Zach's going to be there. Dad's back this weekend too, did you know?'

'What? No, I didn't.'

'We're having lunch tomorrow, and then dropping into Claridge's to show him the ballroom,' Mia added. 'Wanna join?'

'Can't. I've got this petition. How long's he back for?'

'Think just the weekend, it's a very last-minute thing. Mum organized it. But listen, why don't we all swing by the shop on the way?' said Mia, presumably noticing the hurt I could feel rippling across my face.

Hugo pulled his unicorn mask down around his neck. 'We've got to be at Claridge's at midday, Mia, I'm not sure we'll have time to fit in a trip to Chel—'

'Yes, we will,' she replied, swatting his arm.

I nodded while straining my eyes wide to stop the kitchen from going blurry. This sense of isolation took me straight back to being small again, to being shunted upstairs and feeling like the odd one out. We were supposed to be a family of five but at moments like this, it felt like a unit of four with an awkward add-on. The difficult daughter, the weirdo who played strange mind games and thought she'd have a bad day if she woke up at 7.13 a.m. instead of 7.14 a.m.

'Great,' said Mia, before turning to Rory with a wide smile. 'You up for meeting the parents?'

'Absolutely, although…' he glanced at me with a wince, 'I might have to go to the office afterwards to do some work.'

'And the best news of all,' went on Mia, clearly still in cheering-up mode, 'is that Rory's coming to my wedding.'

'Our wedding,' sighed Hugo. 'Mia, how many times do I have to say it?'

I looked at Rory in surprise. 'Actually?'

He nodded. 'Absolutely. I'm very honoured to be asked.'

'And to my stag,' added Hugo.

'WHAT?'

'Well, since Mr Popular here only has about three friends…' said Mia, elbowing Hugo.

'That's not true!' he protested.

'Oh, come on, you do.' Her gaze slid back to me. 'Since

he's only got three friends, and Rory's free, he's said he's up for going too. Isn't that nice?'

'Um, yep, if you're sure?' I said, looking sideways at Rory, trying to gauge how keen he actually was.

'Course,' he said. 'I love Prague. Terrific city. Did you know there's more beer drunk there per head than any other country in the world?'

'Great,' I said, before taking a big mouthful of wine and counting to six before swallowing because I felt very out of control at the speed with which everything was moving around me. I don't believe Gwendolyn's sage had done anything to lower my stress levels.

I brooded silently about all this while the others chatted. Dad had presumably been very busy, I told myself. Important meetings all week with beef farmers and Malbec producers. I was thirty-two, not twelve; I needed to stop being so sensitive. I'd see him tomorrow. It would all be fine.

Beside me, Mia was telling Rory about their honeymoon to Sicily. 'I wanted to go to Zanzibar but Hugo was worried about the mosquitos.'

'Mia, they've had very bad dengue fever there.'

'So we're staying in a hotel with not one but two golf courses instead. But it's got an infinity pool and a spa so I'll be fine.'

'His and hers activities. How romantic,' drawled Ruby, rolling her eyes at me.

'You'll have to keep an eye out for the Mafia in Sicily, of course,' Rory added.

'Really?' Hugo said quickly. 'I thought that sort of thing was all over?'

Rory shook his head and looked solemn. 'No, no. It's still very much alive. Just don't carve anyone up on the golf course.'

'Or he'll find a horse's head on his pillow?' suggested Ruby.

'Exactly,' Rory replied, and they both laughed.

'They're joking, sweetheart, relax,' said Mia, as Hugo's brows knitted in panic.

The wine was finished so everyone started murmuring about bed. I stood to clear the glasses from the table but Mia told me off.

'Leave it, Flo, we can do it in the morning. You guys go to bed.'

'Sure?'

'I'm sure.'

I counted the stairs in my head as we went upstairs. Bed, delicious bed. I felt strangely woozy. The sage? The wine? My jumbled emotions on hearing that Dad was back? Hard to pinpoint but I wanted to go straight to sleep and be fresh for a day manning my trestle table.

Rory had other ideas. Once he'd closed my bedroom door, he pulled the lilac blindfold from his pocket and dangled it from his fingers.

'You thief!' I said, trying to snatch it. But he was too quick and sidestepped so I fell forwards on to my duvet.

'Put it on,' he instructed, tossing the blindfold at me.

'What, now? Like this?' I gestured at my clothes and stifled a yawn. Not sexy to yawn in your boyfriend's face when he wants to play a sex game, Florence. It might not be that long, I told myself. If you go to sleep in half an hour, you'll still get six hours at least.

Rory nodded so I tugged it over my head. And when my eyes were covered, he pushed me back on my bed, unbuttoned my shirt and pulled off my trousers. Then he unhooked my bra, peeled down my knickers and started kissing my body, but as his stubble grazed my skin, I kept sniggering.

'Shhhhhhh,' he instructed, as his mouth moved down the hollow of my chest.

'Sorry,' I snorted. 'I'm trying to be serious, it's just…' I cracked up again and lost it, 'funny. And it tickles.'

Rory stopped and I heard him stand up. Then came a noise that sounded like him rummaging through my make-up bag. 'What are you doing?'

'Nothing. Lie down. No looking.'

He came back to the bed and I felt the mattress dip as he knelt on it and kissed me.

'Put your hands above your head.'

I did as instructed and felt him tie them together.

'What is tha—'

'Shhhhh,' he ordered.

Something feathery and light ran up my inner thigh. 'What is THAT?'

'Sssssshhhhhhh,' he said, as the mysterious downy instrument trailed up my stomach, over my nipple, across my neck and down my body. He was kissing me at the same time, brushing my cheeks, my ears, my neck and the top of my chest with his mouth. As the kisses became harder, my laughter subsided and I started writhing at the sensation of being under Rory's mouth – and whatever he was running over me.

'I want to see you,' I said.

'Uh-uh,' he replied, and continued for a few minutes until I was arching my back against the mattress.

It stopped very suddenly and I listened to him stand up and unzip his trousers, leaving me tied and blindfolded on the bed.

'Hang on,' he told me, and I groaned in frustration before I felt the feathery sensation start running down the side of my body again, flicking along the soles of my feet. As the heat increased between my legs, I pressed my chest into the air. 'Seriously, that's too much, PLEASE can we have sex?'

He laughed from behind my head.

Huh? What was he doing there? Something was still tickling my feet and his arms couldn't reach that far. Could they? I twisted my wrists together to see if I could release them but the strap was too tight.

'Rory? Rory? What's going on? Rory?' The dark was now freaking me out.

He knelt on the bed and untied my wrists; I instantly pulled the blindfold off.

Oh no.

Really, really no.

No, no, no.

No.

It was Marmalade lying at my feet, flexing his tail back and forth against them. I felt sick. I felt like one of those perverts you read about in weird magazines who marry their pets. I felt like Catherine the Great who died shagging her horse. I felt furious.

'RORY? Are you kidding me?'

He realized what I meant and shook his head quickly. 'Oh no! It was your make-up brush, I promise, I wasn't using him. It was your make-up brush, and then I got up to strip, and by the time I'd done that he was rubbing himself against your feet. Look.' He reached to the carpet and picked up my bronzer brush, then leant forward and ran it up my chest. I was suddenly a lot less into it.

'Stop, no more,' I said grumpily, pushing him off. I was done with today. I wanted to go to sleep.

Rory dropped the brush on the floor and scooped up Marmalade. 'Come on, boy,' he said, taking him to my bedroom door and shutting him out.

He came back to bed and although I still felt silly, it took him all of three minutes before he'd seduced me all over again. He was insatiable. But also extremely inventive. I didn't recall James Bond ever using a bronzer brush as a sex toy.

*

What time was it? What year was it? What was my name? I woke the next morning with a start, confused by the bright light running around the edges of my window blind. I rolled on to my side and looked at my clock. Shit. It was nearly nine. I'd overslept, and I needed to be in the shop in less than half an hour to put up my trestle table.

I stepped out of bed, saw the blindfold on the carpet and winced. Poor Marmalade. As the needles of hot water hit my neck, I stood with my head hanging, wishing it could purify my soul. I buried my face in my hands and groaned.

I got out of the shower and dressed while Rory lay flat on his stomach, still asleep. Lucky, I thought, because I didn't have the strength for a morning session. Back in the bathroom, I rubbed my face with moisturizer and slicked on a coat of mascara. I needed a coffee but I'd have to get one on the way. I didn't have time to dally in the kitchen.

I arrived at the shop fifteen minutes before opening.

'MORNING, I'M HERE,' I said, bursting in.

Jaz was sitting on the counter in a huge leopard print coat, her purple ankle boots dangling beneath her. 'Hi, how did you get in?' I asked, panting.

She frowned. 'Did you get the Tube like that?'

'Why?'

She reached into her bag and handed me a compact mirror. Ah. Beneath my eyebrows were thick black smudges of mascara. 'Shit,' I said, licking my index finger and rubbing at them. 'Jaz, they won't come off. Help! Why won't they come off?'

She reached into her bag again and brought out a packet of wipes. 'Stand still,' she said, dabbing at my face with one. 'Why so late? It's unlike you.'

I sighed and Jaz winced, turning her face away at my breath.

'Sorry, had some red wine. And then Rory made me have sex with my bronzer brush.'

'WHAT?' she shouted.

'WHAT?' said Zach, appearing at the top of the stairs.

I closed my eyes. This morning was bad. So bad.

'Florence Fairfax?' said Jaz.

'Yes?' I squeaked, opening my eyes.

'What are you talking about?'

I glanced at the clock over the till. 'OK, Jaz, I'll tell you while we put the table up outside. Zach, you didn't hear that.'

'I certainly did hear that,' he said. 'And nice of you to join us. Luckily, I got here early and found poor Jaz loitering outside the door with Dunc.'

'Dunc! Where's he?'

'Downstairs in the kids' section,' said Zach.

As Jaz and I carried the trestle table upstairs, I explained the previous night in more detail, although I left the part about the blindfold and the bronzer brush until we were outside so Zach couldn't eavesdrop. At least the forecast had been right; it was the perfect October day, a clear sky and the sun already high enough to dazzle us as we fought with the table legs.

'What did I say? The guy's a pervert,' Jaz said, once I'd finished explaining.

'He's coming later today so you can tell him yourself,' I said, as I unfurled a banner I'd made that week. 'As are my entire family, including my dad.'

'Your old man?' said Jaz, squinting at me in the sunshine. 'It'd be nice to meet him.'

'Mmm,' I murmured back, realizing that, although I'd mentioned Dad many times in NOMAD meetings, I'd always kept him – and the rest of my family – very separate. But today, everyone would collide. Not just Jaz and my family, but Rory, too, along with Eugene and Norris. And Zach! The thought made me dizzy.

'You all right?' said Jaz.

'Mmm,' I said again. 'Come on, help me with this.' I handed her one end of the banner and picked up the Sellotape from the table.

'Chuck us that,' Jaz said after I'd secured my side.

She taped her corner and we stood back to survey our handiwork.

A BOOKSHOP'S FOR LIFE, NOT JUST FOR CHRISTMAS, said the banner, in wobbly red letters since I'd decided to paint it rather than risk the printer again.

'That? That's the slogan you went with?' said Jaz, her hands on her hips.

Zach opened the door and came out, hand in hand with Dunc.

I squatted down. 'Hello, you've got so big!'

He buried himself between Zach's legs.

'You've got a mate,' said Jaz. 'What are your babysitting rates like?'

'Free to this one,' Zach replied, putting a hand on Dunc's head. 'We've been looking at dinosaur books, haven't we?'

Dunc nodded. 'Yes, and my favourite is the, er...' His small face contorted with concentration before he frowned up at Zach.

'The diplodocus,' said Zach.

Dunc nodded authoritatively.

'You're my hero,' Jaz told him.

'Not at all. But nice work, you two. You all right if I open up?'

I nodded. 'I might make a coffee quickly. Jaz, want one?'

'Yeah, babe. Milk, three sugars please.'

★

The sunshine meant shoppers flocked to the King's Road in their cashmere overcoats and sunglasses. By lunchtime, we had over three hundred signatures and Jaz had gone hoarse from shouting like a town crier.

'Save our local bookshop,' she croaked for a final time before I told her to quit. I could feel the tentacles of a headache twitching behind my forehead.

Zach ferried us tea and biscuits while Eugene manned the till inside, helped by Dunc sitting on the counter, sliding new books into paper bags.

It was around eleven when I spotted a familiar head of silver hair coming towards us.

'Dad!' I cried, one hand shielding my eyes from the sun, the other waving like a small child who'd just spotted her father at the school gates.

He grinned and, behind his spectacles, his eyes crinkled into lines. Time spent in hot countries meant his face had darkened over the years as his hair turned paler.

'Ah, my Florence, hello,' he cried, as I hurried out from behind the table and he wrapped his arms around me.

'Hi,' I mumbled into his overcoat before stepping back and squinting at him. 'How are you? Tired? How was the flight? When do you go back? Where are the others?' I glanced over his shoulder to gauge how long I had him before they arrived.

Dad laughed. 'Which question do you want me to answer first?'

'All of them. Oh no, actually, meet my friend Jaz. Jaz, this is my dad, Henry.'

'Henry Fairfax, hello, very good to meet you.' He held a tanned hand out towards her.

'Henry, my man, you too. I've heard a lot about you.'

Dad pretended to grimace. 'Not all terrible, I hope?' Ever a diplomat, he was always ready to charm strangers.

'Mostly terrible, yeah, but some good,' she replied, with a grin.

He turned back to me. 'Your stepmother and sisters have stopped in a shop down there...' He turned and pointed along the King's Road. 'Patricia wanted to look at hats. And I'm extremely well, only sorry that this trip is so brief.'

'You're flying back tomorrow?'

''Fraid so. Got to be back in the *embajada* on Monday.'

This meant the embassy. Dad was good with languages. He'd picked up Urdu in Pakistan and was now fluent in Spanish. Mum had been the same – born in France, she could natter in French and English as a child and learned Hindi while teaching in Mumbai. Apparently she'd called me 'baby *bandar*' when I was tiny, a Hindi term of affection meaning 'little monkey'. I didn't remember this but Dad had told me once and I'd held on to the phrase ever since, an oral talisman that reminded me of her.

'How is it?' I asked again. 'How are the soybean magnates?'

'Oh fine, fine,' he replied. It was always his answer. There could have been another war brewing in the Falklands and he would have shrugged it off. It was an unflappable calm which explained both why he'd been successful in diplomacy and his marriage to Patricia worked.

'But forget about me,' Dad went on. 'Look at all this!' He waved at my banner. 'I'm impressed.'

'Thanks.'

'How's it going?'

'All right. Got a few hundred names, I reckon. Will you sign?'

'Try and stop me,' he said, picking up a pen.

As Dad leant over the table, I heard Patricia's voice floating towards us. Not the words, just the shrill tone. I watched her approach, flanked by Mia and Ruby. Hugo was lagging at the back, phone clutched to his ear.

'Morning, darling,' said Patricia, proffering her cheek.

'Morning, did you find a hat?'

Patricia made a noise of disgust. 'No, they were all hopeless.'

'I took some photos though, look,' said Ruby, grinning. She pulled out her phone. They were ludicrous: Patricia with what looked like a turquoise bath puff attached to her head; Patricia wearing a pink boomerang; Patricia in a red beret.

'No sniggering please, girls.'

'Oh, Pat, come on, we're only joking,' Ruby replied, slipping her phone into her pocket.

Before Patricia could complain about the nickname I turned back to the table and introduced them all to Jaz, then told everyone to add their signatures to the petition.

'But what exactly am I signing for?' demanded Hugo. 'I don't like signing things I'm not fully informed about.'

Mia tutted. 'Sweetheart, it's to save the shop, and Flo's job. It's not a pyramid scheme.' She held out a pen which Hugo looked at suspiciously before leaning over the sheet and adding his name.

'Is Zach here?' asked Ruby, peering through the shop window.

'He's probably downstairs.'

'Who?' asked Dad.

'My colleague Zach.'

'I'm with you, Rubes, he's a honey,' said Jaz, winking at her.

'Where does he come from? And who are his parents?' demanded Patricia, who was mourning the departure of Jasper from Ruby's life and, with it, the idea of her daughter becoming a duchess who lived in a castle.

'He's Norris's nephew. A photographer.'

Patricia's lip curled. A photographer didn't sound at all like someone who might own a castle.

'He's hot and he rides a motorbike, and he teases Flo, which is very good for her,' said Ruby, grinning. Then she turned from her mother to me. 'I saw Rory in the kitchen this morning, had a cup of tea with him. He said you two were up *very* late last night.'

'Can we not talk about last night,' I said, at a flashback of the bronzer brush. This absolutely was not a topic I wanted to discuss in front of Dad and Patricia.

Jaz cackled.

'I don't want to know,' said Dad. 'I might just go into the shop and have a browse.'

'Me too,' said Ruby, hurrying in after him.

The others hovered in front of the table and Hugo's face flinched as if in pain.

'You all right?' I asked.

'Worried about time,' he muttered, glancing at his wrist. 'Mia, we really should be going if we're going to get to Claridge's.'

'But where's this boyfriend of yours, Florence?' interjected my stepmother. 'I thought he was going to be here? Your father and I are longing to meet him.'

Right on cue, Rory's face appeared behind them.

'Hello, hello,' he boomed, so everyone spun to face him. He was wearing a beige overcoat, Raybans and a pair of leather gloves. 'How's my little campaigner?' he asked, leaning over the table and kissing the top of my head.

'Bit tired,' I said, 'but Rory, meet my friend Jaz and my stepmum Patricia.'

Patricia beamed so widely her eyes formed little slits. 'Rory, hello, I can't tell you how thrilled I am to meet you. We were starting to worry because poor Florence here has never had a bo—'

'BOLOGNAISE!' I shouted. I couldn't think of anything else. I'd panicked and belted out the first word that came to mind.

'Are you feeling all right, darling?' asked Patricia.

'Mmm, fine, I was just thinking about my lunch. And I've never had a proper bolognaise before. Some people make it with cream and others say you should never put mushrooms in it. What do you all think?' I was gabbling, as if speaking faster would alleviate the social tension I felt. This gathering of people, the colliding of several parts of my life, felt like a complicated Venn diagram – and I was right in the middle trying to hold it all together.

'I think we should be leaving for our own lunch,' said Hugo, looking at his watch again. For once, I was grateful to him.

'Stop fussing,' said Mia, 'I need to talk to Jaz about my wedding hair.'

She and Jaz started discussing the merits of loose hair versus bridal up-dos, while Rory peered at the sheets lying on the table.

'How many signatures?'

'Over three hundred, we reckon.'

'Is that all?'

'Oi! I'm quite proud of that.'

'No, of course,' he replied quickly. 'You should be.' Then he glanced up at me. 'Where's your dad?'

'Inside with Ruby, who's chasing after Zach.'

'Not the communist?' said Rory, wrinkling his nose as if someone had just farted.

Patricia gasped. 'He's a communist?'

Rory leant towards her, smirking. 'I don't think officially, but he might as well be. A terrible left-winger.'

'Oh dear, we can't have that,' said Patricia, straining her neck to look inside the shop.

I handed Rory a pen. 'Sign please.'

He added his name at the bottom of a sheet. 'Three hundred and one,' he said, handing the pen back to me. 'And I should probably be getting on to my office.'

'Hang on, you need to meet Dad,' I said, feeling a pang of disappointment that Rory might disappear so quickly when I'd spent the previous weekend sweating with anxiety, hoping I didn't say anything wrong in front of his parents.

'Yes, Rory, I gather you work in politics, like my husband,' Patricia said, placing a hand on his forearm, as if to stop him from physically leaving.

'Indeed I do.'

Patricia patted his arm approvingly. 'I do so love a man with ambition.' Then she glanced at me. 'Wasn't ambition one of the things on your list, Florence?'

'MAGICIAN,' I shouted, cursing Patricia in my head. She seemed completely oblivious to the idea that Gwendolyn had to remain a secret.

'What list?' said Rory.

'A list of jobs,' I lied. 'I wrote it when I was little. They were the jobs I wanted to do when I grew up.'

You wanted to be a magician?' said Rory, with a frown.

'Yup. I loved, er, Paul Daniels. And then I wanted to be a, er, cook. And then I read *The Secret Garden* and decided on books. Isn't life funny?' I laughed too loudly at this, my eyes sliding from Rory to Patricia, then Mia and Hugo and finally Jaz.

They all stood blinking at me, as if they were silently weighing up whether I should be committed to some sort of asylum.

I felt relief flood my body as the shop door opened again and Dad stepped out, followed by Ruby. A distraction. But then Zach appeared behind them with Dunc on his shoulders and the relief was swept away by a spike of anxiety at the thought that he'd say something snarky to Rory.

Christ, this morning was an emotional assault course and the table felt crowded. I wanted to sit down but we didn't have any chairs.

'Dad!' I said weakly. 'This is Rory, Rory, this is my dad.'

'Rory, excellent to meet you.'

'Not at all, sir,' said Rory, pushing his sunglasses on to his head before shaking his hand. 'The pleasure is all mine.'

'No, no, none of that please. And I'm delighted to hear you're joining us for Mia's wedding?'

'It's also my wedding,' chipped in Hugo.

'I am,' Rory replied. 'Very much looking forward to it.'

As Dad and Rory grinned at one another there was a lull in conversation.

'And this is Zach,' I said, for the benefit of those outside who hadn't met him.

Rory spun to face him. 'Oh it's you. Hello,' he drawled.

'Hi, everyone.' Zach released one of Dunc's legs to wave at the semicircle before his eyes reached Rory. He took in his sunglasses and gloves. 'Nice to see you again,' he added. 'Are you off to a *Goodfellas* convention?'

'Ha, no, no,' said Rory, with a short bark of fake laughter.

'Actually I really must be getting to the office, so much paper-work to get through.'

'The Middle East's not going to solve itself,' Zach replied, with a wide smile.

I ground my teeth. I'd been desperate for my family to meet an actual, real-life man I was dating but now I wanted everyone to clear off. This was exhausting. I felt like a very small country, more an island, really, whose threat level had been raised to critical by the presence of various competing factions. I needed peace and space for my jangling loyalties and emotions to calm down.

'We really must go too, Mia,' said Hugo.

'All right, all right,' she said, flapping a hand at him. 'But Jaz, I'll ring you.'

'Sure, babe. Any time.'

Patricia declared they'd catch a taxi to Claridge's from the King's Road and everyone murmured their goodbyes.

'I'm walking that way so I'll come with you,' replied Rory, before leaning over to kiss me. 'Bye, sweetheart, call me when you finish here?'

'Sure.'

Dad hung back as the others headed down the little street towards the King's Road.

'Florence, darling, it's such a coincidence, but I've just discovered that Zach's about to go travelling across South America.'

'Are you?' I said, frowning at Zach. 'I didn't know that.'

'Yeah. When I'm done here. I've been wanting to go to Patagonia for years to take pictures.'

'Lunch, lunch, lunch,' demanded Dunc, his little heels kicking against Zach's chest.

He laughed. 'All right, buddy, we're off.'

'Zach, do get my email address from Florence to look me up,' said Dad.

'I will, thanks.'

A high-pitched shout came from down the street. 'Henry!' It was Patricia, gesticulating at a dawdling taxi.

Dad nodded at her, then looked back to me. 'Bye, darling, sorry this was so brief.'

'That's all right,' I said, stepping out from the table for another hug. 'When are you next home?'

'Probably the wedding,' he said, releasing me.

'Not till then?'

'It's only a month or so away.'

'True.' I nodded at him and told myself that, at least outwardly, I had to act like a grown-up, even though I wanted to hold on to Dad's ankles and refuse to let him leave.

'Be good,' he replied with a grin. 'Great to meet you both,' he added, waving at Jaz and Zach before hurrying towards the taxi.

'And we're going to get some food, aren't we, Dunc?' said Zach, before glancing at Jaz. 'Anything he can't eat?'

Jaz opened her mouth as if she was about to issue a stream of mad rules but then closed it. 'Nah, whatever you like. But let me give you some cash.'

Zach waved a hand at her. 'I've got it.'

They sauntered off and I let myself fall back against the shop's windows with a big sigh.

'Careful,' warned Jaz. 'You all right?'

'Mmm, just tired.'

'Families, eh?' she said, with a sympathetic grin.

'Yeah. Something like that. But listen, you don't have to stay. Take Dunc home when they get back. I can manage on my own.'

'Are you kidding? Getting to shout at all these posh people? Not a chance! Save our local bookshop!' she croaked.

'All right, I'll go and get sandwiches. Any preferences?'

'Not a sandwich. Can you get me the falafel salad from Pret? And a fork. And a handful of napkins?'

'Your wish is my command,' I said, as I checked my phone and saw a message from Ruby asking for Zach's number. I ignored it and slid it back into my pocket. She'd have to wait until I'd eaten forty million calories for lunch.

★

Fortunately, that afternoon was less eventful. I bleated at a few more shoppers. 'Could you sign our petition? No more rent rises! Save Frisbee Books!' Some refused to meet my eye and slid past as if we were buskers on the Tube, rattling a bucket at them. 'Just a name! All we need is a signature to save our bookshop! Just a name!' I persisted. Older people were better than youth. At one point, Mrs Delaney wobbled towards us on her stick and stopped to sign, but she wanted to use her fountain pen and upended her handbag on the table before she found it. She scrawled her signature in spidery letters as Zach appeared outside and offered yet another round of tea.

'Is this your husband?' Mrs Delaney asked Jaz, peering up at Zach from behind her spectacles.

Jaz shook her head. 'No, sadly not. But that is my son.'

This confused Mrs Delaney so she announced she was going inside to have a look at the books.

That was just before a small girl in a pink anorak ran up to the table.

'Hello,' said Jaz. 'What's your name?'

'I'm Maya and I'll be seven soon,' she said proudly.

'Seven! Goodness gracious me. You'll be driving a car next.'

A harassed man appeared behind her. 'Maya, you can't run off like that. Sorry,' he added, looking apologetically at Jaz.

'That's all right,' she replied. 'D'you want to sign the petition? It's for saving the bookshop.'

'Er, yes, go on then,' he said, picking up a pen with a shy smile.

He had a completely smooth face, as if he'd never had to shave, and sandy-coloured hair that stuck up in tufts. But as he bent to sign, I noticed Jaz gazing at him with the tenderness of a doughnut addict walking past a bakery.

'Here you go,' he said, straightening up and holding out the pen.

'No wife around to sign it?' Jaz asked.

He looked embarrassed. 'No, er, no wife.'

'Or girlfriend?' she persisted, which made me want to spontaneously combust with embarrassment and laugh at the same time. Jaz's boldness was one of the reasons I loved her; I just couldn't imagine being like it myself.

'Nope, er, no girlfriend either,' he replied, with a nervous chuckle.

'He needs a girlfriend,' came a small voice beside him, and we all looked down at Maya.

'Shhh, Maya, that's quite enough. Come on, better go home.' His hairless cheeks had turned quite pink.

'But you do,' she persisted. 'Mum said if you had a girlfriend it would make life much easier.'

The man's eyes widened in surprise. 'Oh, did she now? When did she tell you that?'

Maya looked down at her trainers. 'I just heard her say that on the phone,' she mumbled.

'Sorry about this,' he said, grimacing at us before taking his small daughter's hand. 'Right, Maya, we're going to catch the bus and discuss your habit of eavesdropping on adult conversations. Good luck with the shop,' he said over his shoulder as he led her back down the street.

'George Spencer,' Jaz said dreamily, once they were out of sight.

'Huh?'

'He's called George Spencer, look.'

She pointed at the last scrawl on the list of signatures and ran her finger along the box to where he'd printed his email address in neat capital letters. 'Do you think I can email him?'

'What about?'

Jaz tutted. 'Florence Fairfax, this is why you were single for so long. To ask him out! Didn't you think he was cute?'

'Him?' I exclaimed loudly. 'That guy? The human seal?'

She tutted again. 'Don't be horrid about my future husband.'

I frowned at her. 'I think it might be illegal, taking someone's email address from a petition and asking them out. Data protection or something.'

'Rubbish. What's that thing they say? Fortune favours the old.'

'Bold.'

'Oh, I always thought it was an age thing. Like, we all get luckier as we get older because, like, we know more?'

I shook my head. 'Nope, definitely bold.'

She shrugged. 'I'm going to email him. I thought he looked nice.'

'What about her mother?'

She frowned at me.

'Maya's mother. Sounded a bit complicated.'

'Oh that,' Jaz said airily. 'I think it sounded over. Don't worry, Floz, leave it to me.'

I stayed silent, just hoping that this wouldn't end up like the Solihull situation a few months earlier.

An hour later, having taken a photograph of George's email address on her phone, she and Dunc went home. I folded up the table as the sun dropped, taking the shoppers with it.

'How many names do you think you got?' asked Zach, helping me downstairs.

'Nearly a thousand,' I said as I tried to manoeuvre the table round the banisters. 'How many do you reckon we need for the landlord to take any notice?'

'Well, the petition to stay in Europe got six million.'

'I feel like that's ambitious.'

He laughed as we dropped the table in the stockroom and went back upstairs where Eugene was cashing up.

'Fancy a drink?' said Zach. 'I thought we might need one after today so I shoved a few beers in the fridge.'

Eugene tutted. 'I've got an audition in the morning so I need to get home and practise.'

'Florence, you up for it?'

'Yeah,' I said, although I felt nervous. Just me and Zach was weird; I didn't have the energy to bicker for an hour but I couldn't back out now. I looked at my watch. It had just gone six. I'd stay for one beer and ring Rory to see where he was.

'Great, I'll grab 'em, hang on.'

'What's this audition for?' I asked Eugene, as Zach thumped downstairs again.

'*Hamlet.* I won't get it.'

'Don't be so down on yourself. What part you auditioning for?'

'Hamlet.'

'Oh.'

'Thanks for the vote of confidence, my darling, but have fun. See you Monday.'

He rushed out and, since Zach still hadn't reappeared with the beers, I stood at the top of the stairs and shouted for him.

'Let's have them down here,' he shouted back.

I found him standing by the fridge. 'Here you go,' he said, handing me a bottle. 'Shall we sit?' He nodded towards the beanbags in the kids' section.

'There?'

'Yeah, I can't stand up any more today. Come on.' He led me through and fell back on a beanbag, groaning, before reaching up to knock his bottle against mine. 'Cheers, partner.'

'Cheers.' I sat down beside him and took a slug.

Zach sighed. 'That might be the best beer I've ever had.'

'It's good,' I agreed, wishing I could think of something else to say. This was an odd situation. We were sitting on red beanbags, surrounded by children's books, a life-size cut-out of Wally in his red and white top, and Hallowe'en decorations, which Zach had put up ahead of the party. Fake cobwebs, pumpkin bunting, fake spiders.

'So,' I said, unable to bear the silence for another second. 'Patagonia?'

He raised his eyebrows at me.

'You want to go to Patagonia?'

'Oh, yeah. Wanted to for ages.'

'Why there?'

'To photograph the mountains, mostly, but the animals too. You get orcas at the right time of year. And you ever heard of a commerson's dolphin?'

I shook my head.

'It's like a penguin shagged a dolphin. They're black and white. I'd love to see them. And you get amazing eagles. The biggest eagle in the world was from there. Six-metre wings.' He paused and stretched his arms out, the beer bottle dangling from his fingers. 'Six metres. Can you imagine? It's extinct now but, still, I want to go.' Another slug of his bottle. 'You travelled much?'

'Nope, I'd like to. I've just… always been working.' It was an easy excuse. I didn't want to admit to him of all people that the furthest I'd travelled was to a small French village full of apricot trees, that I was too nervous about exploring anywhere else.

'What's your plan?'

'Plan?'

'Yeah. You know, what do you want to do, where do you want to go? Or will you stay here forever?'

'What I really want to do…' I started, before pausing, afraid of admitting it out loud.

He frowned at me. 'What?'

'I'd really like to get my children's book published.'

'You write kids' stuff?'

I looked down and pushed my thumbnail under the label of the bottle. 'I'm trying to. Why? Is that surprising?'

'No, you've just never mentioned it. What's it about?'

I raised my eyes and winced at him. 'I'll tell you but you can't laugh.'

Zach smiled and swigged at his beer.

'Look! You're laughing already and I haven't even told you!'

He shook his head and wiped his mouth with the back of his hand before replying. 'I'm not laughing. It's excitement at hearing about your magnum opus. Come on, tell me.'

I took a breath. 'OK, it's called *The Caterpillar Who Couldn't Stop Counting.*'

He grinned again.

'No laughing!'

'I'm not. What's the storyline? Hit me with it.'

'It's…' Then I stopped.

'What?'

'OK, it's about a caterpillar who has twenty feet, and he's late to school every day because he has to count all his shoes. Every day he has to count all his shoes on and count them off again, and every day it takes him ages and it makes him late, which means he's in trouble with his teacher. And once he's at school he has to count everything else – his pencils, the number of chairs in the classroom, all the rucksacks. And everybody else in his class thinks he's a weirdo so nobody plays with him. But Curtis, he's the caterpillar, is too embarrassed to admit that he just has this… thing about counting. It just makes him feel better. And then one day, his teacher, who's a butterfly called Mrs Flutterby, overhears him counting in the playground and asks him about it, and he tells her that he can't help it, he just has to count everything he sees. And Mrs Flutterby asks if he wants to know a secret. And Curtis nods because obviously everyone wants to know a secret. So she tells him that he has obviously been born with a special superpower for counting, and it's nothing to feel ashamed of or worry about. That he should be proud of it. And suddenly Curtis is the hero of his class for having this superpower and then once he tells everyone he…' I paused. Zach hadn't said a word during this speech.

'Go on,' he urged.

'He realizes that once it's out in the open he doesn't feel like he needs to count so much. I mean, I've still got a few bits to work out, but that's the gist,' I said, flicking the label with my nail again, embarrassed at having spluttered it all out. The story sounded better in my head.

'So it's you.'

'Huh?' I said, looking up from the bottle as if this idea had never occurred to me.

'Curtis is you.'

I wrinkled my nose. 'Is it obvious?'

He nodded. 'Yeah. I hear you sometimes, putting away books or coming downstairs. I quite like it. "Oh, here comes Florence in her enormous work shoes…"'

'Stop it! You can't laugh at my mental habit and my shoes!'

'Sorry, but those shoes are the ugliest things I've ever seen.' Then his face turned serious. 'Why the counting?'

I inhaled and held the air in my chest before replying. 'Because I always have done. Ever since I was little. It's a comfort blanket.'

'For how long?'

'Since I was four. When I could count. My mum died and my stepmother arrived and… it just started.'

He nodded slowly and grinned again. 'Do you do anything else weird?'

It made me laugh. 'No! Just that. What about you?'

'What about me?'

'Do you have any weird habits?'

He gestured at his arms. 'Do tattoos count?'

From here, I could see the bird flying up his right arm, and, on the left, the muscled legs of a man in winged sandals sticking out from underneath his T-shirt sleeve. 'What's the bird?' I asked, pointing at it.

He glanced down and rubbed his fingers across its feathers. 'An owl.' He raised his eyes to mine. 'It was Athene's.'

I frowned, unsure about whether this Athene woman was a family member or perhaps even an ex. The thought of that was weird; Zach hadn't ever talked about his personal life.

'She was the Greek goddess of wisdom and war,' he explained. 'And an owl was her bird...'

'Like Hedwig in Harry Potter?' I said quickly, wanting to cover up the fact I'd assumed Athene was an ex-girlfriend.

Zach grinned. 'Kind of. Her owl symbolizes wisdom, and sat on Athene's right shoulder, her blind side, so she could see the whole truth. So that's why she's here, on my right arm.'

I nodded slowly, ashamed that my classics knowledge was so feeble.

'What about that one?' I asked, nodding at the legs of the man in winged sandals.

'This is Perseus,' said Zach, smoothing his hand over his other arm.

I winced at him, uncertain about the name again.

'The Greek hero who killed Medusa. You know, the gorgon who had snakes for hair?'

'Kind of,' I replied, recalling a childhood book of Greek myths and a woman with a green face and serpents twisting around her head.

'Perseus killed her and then a sea monster called Cetus,' went on Zach.

'Why?'

'Why did he kill them?'

I nodded.

'Why do you think? For the love of a beautiful woman.'

He grinned as I blushed. 'But why did you pick him?' I said quickly, trying to cover my coyness.

'It was my favourite story when I was younger. Mum's a teacher. I told you that, right?'

I nodded. 'Yeah, but that's kind of all I know. What's your deal? All I really know is that you're Norris's mysterious nephew.'

Zach sucked in a breath. 'Another beer first?'

I nodded and, as he took the empties to the kitchen, I realized I was enjoying myself. I'd never spoken this openly about my writing or my counting with Rory. We hadn't bickered. No awkward silences either. The only weirdness was being overlooked by the cardboard cut-out of Wally.

He brought back another two bottles and handed me one before sitting. I took it and waited for him to speak.

'So I'm Norris's nephew but I don't actually know my dad, his brother.'

'Huh?'

'Never knew him. He walked out when I was born, moved to Australia. Mum brought me up by herself. Well, with help from Norris. I don't know if you've noticed but he's pretty useless with money?'

I smiled and nodded.

'He paid for a lot of stuff which I don't think he could

really afford. Mum's car. Holidays. And he gave me my first camera when I was thirteen.'

'It's weird, I've worked with him for five years and never knew any of this.'

Zach shrugged. 'He's private about it. I think he's ashamed of his own brother and felt like he had to make up for him.'

'And now you're paying it back?'

'Trying to, if we can keep this place going,' he said, looking around us.

'But hang on, why the tattoo? You said your mum's a teacher?'

'Right.' He nodded. 'She's an English teacher and used to read me the classics when I was younger. Perseus was always my favourite because he has a happy ending, unlike most of the others who are killed by a ten-headed lion or murdered by their own family. And he ends up in the sky, the Perseus constellation.'

'You know your Greeks,' I said, smiling. I felt guilty at making so many assumptions about Zach – dishevelled, coffee-throwing Zach – that were unfair.

'I've forgotten a lot of them. But I like your story. The caterpillar. I can see it. Can imagine it on the page, all those little shoes.'

'Can you actually? It's no Greek tragedy but I think it's kind of sweet.'

'You shown it to anyone?'

'What d'you mean?'

'Like an agent?'

I shook my head quickly. 'Uh-uh. No way. It's not good enough.'

'I can ask mine if you like? He's a photography agent but they have a literary department.'

I screwed my eyes shut at the very idea.

'Come on, you big wimp. What's the point in hiding it if you want to get it published? I can just ask if anyone wants to have a look at it. No pressure.'

'What if they hate it?' I asked, opening one eye to squint at him.

'Then you show someone else. J.K. Rowling sent Harry Potter and Hedwig to loads of agents before someone accepted it.'

'I'm not sure Curtis the counting caterpillar has as much appeal as Harry.'

Zach spread his hands in front of him. 'How do you know if you don't put it out there?'

'All right. Maybe, thank you.'

'You're very welcome.'

'What do you want to do with photography then?'

He shrugged. 'Travel, let it take me places. Do a trip, sell a few pictures, fund another trip.'

'Where's the best place you've been?'

Zach lifted his bottle to his mouth as he thought. 'There's a town in northern India called Leh. Right up in the Himalayas. One of the most dangerous airports to fly into in the world.'

'How come?'

'Imagine landing in a salad bowl...' He raised his hand flat in the air and swooped it in front of him. 'There are mountains all around so the pilot has to dive and stop quickly because the runway's so short, and the wind gets up every afternoon so you can only land in the morning. It feels like you're riding a leaf.'

'Wow.'

'Yeah, pretty terrifying. My girlfriend hated it. But once you're there it's worth it. The views, the monasteries, the people. The tea! You'd love it. They give you clay cups the size of thimbles which you drink very sweet milky tea from. It tastes like earth. And ginger.'

'I didn't know you had a girlfriend,' I said, instantly wishing I could cram the words back in my mouth. Turns out he would talk about his personal life if pushed.

'Ex-girlfriend.'

Zach said this so quietly it was as if I'd stepped on a ghost. 'Sorry,' I muttered.

'All good,' he said, before draining his bottle. 'It was a mutual thing. We'd been together for so long so I forget sometimes.'

I nodded but didn't reply. The atmosphere felt tighter than it had a moment ago.

'Has Ruby texted you?' I'd given in and texted her Zach's number that afternoon, knowing that once Ruby went after something, she usually ended up getting it.

He looked as if I'd asked whether the Pope had been in touch. 'Ruby? No. How come?'

'Nothing,' I said, feeling nosy again. 'Forget it.'

'Right,' he said, stretching his arms towards the ceiling. 'I'm going to head home. Want a lift?'

'On the bike?'

He grinned and nodded. 'Got a spare helmet.'

'Noooooo, I'll walk.'

He stood and held out his hand to heave me up.

'Thanks though,' I said, 'that was nice.'

'It was. And I mean it, send me your book and I can pass it on.'

'OK, deal,' I said, and then let go of his hand, embarrassed that I was still holding it.

CHAPTER EIGHT

THAT EVENING CHANGED SOMETHING between Zach and me. For the following week, I felt strange around him. Almost embarrassed. It was like we'd both shared too much and he was trying to avoid me as a result. 'Morning!' he'd say with a polite half-smile when he arrived, before disappearing into the basement. There were no Rory the Tory jibes and no abandoned coffee cups or motorbike boots behind the till. He remained downstairs in the office, tinkering with the website and helping Norris with the accounts while I rehearsed with Eugene. His *Hamlet* audition hadn't gone as badly as they usually did, he'd got a part at least, but it was for the role of gravedigger instead of the lead and he only had three lines. Undeterred, Eugene was approaching the role as if it would win him his first Oscar.

Kneeling behind the hardback table one morning during rehearsals, he lobbed a pen pot over it (the table was supposed to represent the grave, the pen pot a skull), then stood up and dusted off his knees.

'Brilliant,' I said from behind the till, adding a few claps for good measure.

Eugene did a little bow but stood up looking troubled.

'You've got nothing to worry about,' I reassured him. 'That was the most convincing gravedigging performance I've ever seen.' It was also the only gravedigging performance I'd ever seen, but he didn't need to know that.

'I'm not worried about my performance. That's in the bag. It's Zach, he's very quiet.'

I hadn't told Eugene anything about my evening drinking beers downstairs. I wasn't sure why exactly; it was as if I wanted to keep it a secret. Zach's furtive behaviour only seemed to confirm this, but if I mentioned it now, Eugene would pick away at me, an amateur sleuth in a bow tie, making me regurgitate our conversation in full. It was easier to play dumb.

'What d'you mean?' I replied.

'Does he seem troubled to you?'

'Troubled?'

'Mmm. Sort of… distant. Not hanging out with us. It's odd that he's not even being rude to you. I might ask him if he's OK.'

'No, don't,' I said quickly. 'I'm sure it's fine.'

Eugene had all the subtlety of a French horn and what if Zach's aloofness *was* to do with me? Had he decided I was too weird? He wouldn't be the first person to avoid me because of my counting. I'd become used to that as a teenager. Or had I upset him by asking about his girlfriend? Or Ruby? His coolness bothered me because the truth was that I'd grown used to Zach's teasing and looked forward to the days when he was in the shop more than the days when he wasn't.

I watched him read to the children gathered downstairs on the afternoon of the Hallowe'en party. He was dressed as the Beast: blue velvet tailcoat that could have come from Rory's wardrobe, a white cravat, a pair of furry slippers that looked like monster's feet. His curls were backbrushed around his head in a black, tangled mess and, through a pair of pointy plastic teeth, he was telling them a ghost story.

He was good at it. He could do multiple accents and swept his arms around him making eerie noises while his young audience rocked from side to side, giggling with fear. To them, Zach seemed to have a magnetic appeal. It had been the same with Dunc.

He caught my eye at one stage but looked down to his book again, carrying on with the story. I slipped back upstairs where several of the Chelsea mothers – blonde highlights, foreheads as smooth as balloons, very white trainers – were browsing the diet books.

Once the kids had been marshalled out, I went back downstairs and poked my head around the office door.

'Knock knock,' I said in a falsely jovial way, instantly hating myself for it.

Zach spun in his seat. He was still wearing the blue tailcoat.

'You smashed it,' I said, with an encouraging smile.

He rested his head back against his seat. 'Thanks. You sell many books?'

'Yeah, a few. Norris's cashing up.'

He nodded but didn't offer anything else and I felt unwelcome.

'I just wanted to ask if it would be all right if I sent you my Curtis the caterpillar story?' I'd been practising that line upstairs because it seemed like a good excuse to talk to him. He'd been so positive about it before.

'Sure,' he said, turning back to his computer.

'You sure? I don't have to if it's difficult or it's—'

'Really, it's no problem,' he said, looking at me again, hands poised over his keyboard.

'OK, thanks. I'll email it to you tomorrow,' I said, but I slunk away feeling stung, as if I'd been a nuisance.

Later, I sighed while crossing the river on the way home from work and told myself to stop obsessing about it. I had plenty to worry about that week already. Chiefly, the Conservatives' Black and White Ball. Rory had dropped this bombshell on me on Sunday evening as we lay in bed. It was a big deal, apparently; the party's annual fundraiser. The Prime Minister went. The Cabinet went. As did their biggest donors – celebrities, finance bosses and Indian telecom billionaires among them. Rory had explained this and then rolled me on to my side, trailing his fingers over my shoulder and across my chest as if just talking about politics had given him an erection. Would I be his date, he'd whispered into my ear, and I would have made a joke about the fact that people normally had a fetish for rubber or leather instead of the prime minister, but by that stage he'd slipped his hand between my legs and I could only groan in reply.

It was the following night and I was carrying home four Asos dresses that had been delivered to Frisbee. I knew Eugene was desperate to give his verdict like a *Project Runway* judge but I hadn't wanted to try them on in the shop and risk bumping into Zach. Plus, the bathroom was cramped and I suspected Asos didn't accept returns which had been trailed in loo water.

Please could one of the dresses look decent? This was the most grown-up party I'd ever been invited to. Please could they transform me into a sophisticated woman who looked like she knew what the home secretary did (something to do with homes?) and not into a gawky teenager who'd rummaged through her mother's wardrobe and circled lipstick on her cheeks.

Once I got back, Mia helped. Sort of. Dress one was declared 'too cheap and shiny'. Dress two apparently made me look like 'an old woman who teaches ballroom dancing on a cruise', and dress three was simply 'disgusting'. But she smiled like a proud mother when I came out from her bathroom in dress four. It was a dark red velvet and off the shoulder.

'Flo, you look like Jessica Rabbit!'

I blinked at myself in her full-length mirror. It was as if the dress was a disguise; normal, sensible Florence with her hair tied back in a ponytail had been usurped by this glamorous pretender. Mia was exaggerating. I didn't have the proportions of Jessica Rabbit. But with make-up and heels, I would look like someone else entirely, someone who could be friends with the glossy Octavia Battenberg. I stood on tiptoes and narrowed my eyes, trying to imagine it.

'What shoes?' she asked.

'My black heels,' I said, still squinting in the mirror.

'No,' she said, waggling a finger at me. 'You're not wearing those shoes with that dress.'

'What's wrong with them?'

'They're the sort of clumpy courts the Queen wears. You can't wear a dress like that with those heels, it's like wearing couture with wellington boots. Hang on...' She jumped off her bed and opened her wardrobe, then crouched to inspect dozens of stacked shoeboxes. 'Not these, not these. Definitely not those but these might work.' She pulled out a box marked 'Jimmy Choo'.

'Uh-uh,' I said, backing away from the box as if it contained a tarantula. 'They'll be too small.'

'Just try them,' replied Mia, lifting the lid off. 'You're not running the marathon, it's only for the night.'

She pulled out a pair which matched the blood red of the dress, with thin straps that tied round the ankle. The heels looked like knitting needles. They were the sort of shoes I'd never even tried on before because they were too delicate – and I never wanted to draw attention to the size of the canoes at the end of my ankles.

Mia knelt and held one out. Wobbling, I lifted my foot and pushed it in. Bigfoot getting ready for his first party.

'And this one.'

I clutched Mia's bedpost so I didn't fall over as she fastened the strap around my ankles, then, unsteady as a newborn foal, turned round to look in the mirror.

'Perfect. Although you need a pedicure. Even Hugo has more attractive feet than you.'

'Thanks. But I can't wear these, they're too tight and I can't walk in them.' My calves were already shaking.

'Just practise tonight. Up and down in the kitchen. I'll teach you.'

It took ten minutes to get downstairs and then Mia shouted at me – 'head back, chin up' – while I tottered along the kitchen tiles. But half an hour later I'd improved. I wouldn't be able to walk very far at the party and dancing would be impossible – I'd have to remain rooted on the spot and wave my hands in the air like a tree in a thunderstorm. But Mia was right: these were the sort of heels that should be worn with a dress like that.

'Cinderella shall go to the ball,' she said, as I sat on a kitchen chair and undid the straps.

'Thanks for your help.'

'Please,' replied Mia, with a wave of her hand. 'I'm good at this shit.'

I pulled off the shoes and wriggled my toes gratefully. 'Where's Ruby?'

'Getting her hair done. She's seeing that guy you work with tomorrow.'

'Zach?'

I said his name so loudly Mia looked up from the hob and frowned.

'Yeah, him. Why? Is that bad?'

I paused for a couple of beats before replying. 'No. Not bad. Just weird. He hasn't said anything.'

But that explained his weirdness. Zach was going on a date

with Ruby and felt awkward about it. The knowledge that this was happening, that I might indeed find him in my kitchen, made me wince. What was I supposed to say in the shop the next day: 'Morning, Zach, have fun trying to shag my sister tonight!'

'Why the face? What's he like?'

'He's all right.' I paused. 'No, he's cool. More intelligent than you might think when you see him because he's always quite scruffy and covered in tattoos. But it turns out the tattoos are actually from Greek myths and not just a skull and crossbones. And he's basically single-handedly saving the bookshop, and he's one of those people who's nice to everyone. Well, everyone apart from Rory. He doesn't like him much. And he's amazing with kids. We did this Hallowe'en party last week and they all loved him.' I paused again. 'So... yeah, he's cool.'

Mia raised her eyebrows at me. 'Sounds like you should be going out with him.'

I retched and stuck my tongue out like a schoolgirl teased for having a crush on a boy in her maths class. 'Gross. He's not my type.'

'Why? Because he doesn't tick all the boxes on your list?' she joked.

'Exactly.'

'Well, you've got Rory, anyway.'

'Yes,' I said firmly, 'I've got Rory.'

And then, because talking about Ruby and Zach dating had made me feel strange, I asked Mia whether we needed strapless bras for our bridesmaids' dresses and she wanged on about her wedding for the rest of the evening.

*

'You picked one then?' Eugene asked the following morning when I arrived with the shoebox and my dress in a plastic cover.

'Yes, but shhhh,' I replied, putting a finger to my lips and hiding my outfit behind the till.

'Why?'

I pointed at the floorboards. 'Zach in?'

Eugene nodded.

'You know what he's like. He'll only start shouting about politics if I mention anything.'

Ironically, having missed Zach's chattiness all week, today I wanted to avoid him and banish all thoughts of his date with Ruby.

I escaped over lunch for a blow-dry and eyebrow shape at the Chelsea salon where Jaz worked. It was in a posh white townhouse a few minutes from the shop and owned by an exuberant Italian called Carlo. A haircut there normally cost as much as a small family car, but she'd promised to fit me in between appointments.

'And could I also have a quick pedicure?' I asked Carlo when I arrived. He was sitting behind the reception desk, his swirling floral shirt undone to his belly button.

He sighed as if I'd demanded world peace. 'Dalling, I do your eyebrows first, and then we'll come back upstairs for your hair and, if she has time, Skyla can do your toes.'

I waved at Jaz, who was standing behind a chair drying an old lady's hair, then followed Carlo down a flight of stairs into a windowless room which smelt of drains.

'Lie there,' he instructed bossily, pointing at the massage bed. 'And let me have a look.'

I held my breath as he leant over my face, before making a noise of utter disgust. 'These things!' he shrieked. 'They are monsters, Florence. I don't know why Jasmine has not sent you to me before.'

'Really? I thought just maybe a bit of a tid— ouuuuuuuuch!' I yelped, as the wax burned my skin before it was ripped off. Then the other brow. Then a strip of wax between my brows before Carlo hung over my face with a pair of tweezers. He'd recently eaten something that contained onions. Or maybe just an onion, crunched raw like an apple. The smell was rancid.

'It is much better now,' he said a few minutes later, standing back to admire his own handiwork. 'Gives your face more, how you say, definition? Here, take thees mirror, look.'

Yikes. They were different. The furry caterpillars had been replaced by neat lines. I waggled them in the mirror feeling like Betty Boop.

'Now, I pop some gel over them and we get your hair washed.'

He led me back upstairs and gestured at a seat in front of a basin and handed me a laminated blow-dry menu. 'Pick what you like and I go get Jasmine.'

I frowned at the pouty models in the pictures. The hairstyles had names like 'Fairytale Ending' and 'Gloss Like A Boss'. I sniggered at the thought of having hair like Norris.

Jaz appeared at the basin a few minutes later. 'Sorry, babe, it's mad in here today. How you doing? Brows look good.'

'Do you think?' I said, lifting my fingers to the red skin above my eyes.

'Don't touch it, the redness will go down. Now, what we doing with your hair?'

'I was thinking this one,' I said, pointing at a photo of a brunette model with shiny waves of hair that fell to below her shoulders and flicked up at the ends. 'Be the star of the show with this sleek and ultra-glamorous look,' it said ambitiously underneath the picture. The style was called 'Big 'n' bold, but I couldn't bring myself to say that out loud, even to Jaz.

'Big 'n' bold? Mmm.' She stood back and squinted at me. 'You trust me, right?'

'Yesssss,' I said slowly.

'Fine.'

'What are you going to do?' I asked with a note of panic.

'Nothing to worry about; just sit back while I wash it and tell you all about George.'

'Who's George?'

'The man from the shop that day, the day of the petition.'

'Oh my God,' I said, sitting up and turning round. 'You emailed him?'

'Lie back, please.'

I rested my head on the basin and Jaz turned on the shower head.

'Is that temperature all right?' she asked, as a jet of hot water scorched my scalp.

'Yup, fine,' I replied. Has anyone in the history of hairdressing replied otherwise to that question? 'But can you tell me what's happened?'

Jaz took a deep breath. 'So, I didn't email him that day because I thought it would be too keen, you know? I left it until Monday and then emailed and asked if he'd lost his pen.'

'He didn't leave a pen.'

'I know – head back a bit – it was just an excuse. I said someone had left their pen and was it his, and he said it wasn't.'

'Then what?'

'Then I said thank you again for signing the petition, and I hoped things were all right with him and Maya's mum.'

'You didn't!'

'What's wrong with that?' she screeched over the noise of the water. 'I was just being nice. And we had a few more emails and now we're going to take the kids to the playground.'

'When?'

'Next weekend, I think. He said he's a bit busy with work but he'd let me know.'

We fell silent as she scrubbed, rinsed, repeated, then wrapped my head in a turban and ushered me to yet another chair. She pinned my damp hair into sections, and handed me a plastic keyring of nail colours before snapping her fingers at the reception desk.

'Skyla, hun, can you get going on my friend's toes? It's not going to be a quick job.'

'Thanks,' I mumbled, looking down at the keyring. They

had moronic names too but Boudoir Nights, a cherry-coloured varnish, was the closest to my shoes.

Skyla was a small woman with a shaved head, who pulled up a stool and started hacking at my toenails, poor thing, while Jaz snipped around my face. I tried to avoid looking at myself in the mirror. Nobody ever looked worse than in the harsh light of a hairdressing mirror.

'You nervous about tonight?' she asked.

I was more nervous about the metal blades slashing around my ears but I didn't want to be unsupportive.

'Kind of. But I've got the dress and Mia's lent me some shoes.'

'Will you send me pics?'

'Course.'

Then the roar of the dryer put a stop to any talking and I sat flicking through a bad magazine, trying to concentrate on the story of a woman who claimed her dog was psychic.

'Ta-daaaaaa,' Jaz said finally, having flicked off the dryer.

I glanced up in the mirror and shook my head from side to side so my hair caught the light. It was like a L'Oréal advert; the frizzy dullness had gone and, running my fingers through it, my hair felt soft and smooth. She'd snipped away so my hair was layered towards the ends and it looked thicker. Together with my new eyebrows and cherry-coloured toes, I felt more like the sort of woman who could wear that red dress.

'Happy?' Jaz asked.

I nodded with a bashful grin. 'It's perfect, thank you.'

I tried to pay but both Jaz and Carlo refused. The only

problem was I didn't have any flip-flops, so I walked back to the shop in a pair of sticky, disposable orange flip-flops.

Eugene gasped and clapped both hands to his chest when I walked back in. 'It's like an episode of *Ugly Betty*!'

'Just the reaction I wanted.'

'Your hair!'

'Shhhhh. Can we not make it a big deal?'

'Why not? You look ravishing.'

Another bashful smile. 'Actually?' Nobody had ever described me as 'ravishing' before. Ruby was the hot one. Mia was the sophisticated one. I was the nerdy one.

'But what's going on with your feet?' he added, waving at the flip-flops.

'My nails need to dry, so do you mind if I stand behind here?' I said, gesturing at the counter.

'No, you stay, I'm going to go and have a go at Margaret Atwood's piles.'

Surreptitiously, when nobody was looking, I took a disgraceful number of selfies. Half of me wanted to send one to Rory, half of me wanted to keep it a surprise for later, until I'd got changed and put on my make-up as Mia had demonstrated. She'd even lent me a red lipstick that didn't make my teeth look yellow.

While waiting for the clock to drag round to six and everyone to leave, I allowed myself a brief daydream of my grand entrance: in my red dress and heels, with my new eyebrows and toenails, I'd arrive to gasps. Other guests would prod one another to look as Rory and I passed them, my arm linked through his. In the most glamorous outfit I'd ever worn, I wouldn't be the Florence who played Consequences or counted stairs. I'd be Florence Fairfax, elegant, sophisticated woman of mystery who definitely did not eat the same cheese sandwich every day. 'Oh, how simply fascinating, Prime Minister,' I'd say, 'you must tell me more about the situation in Brussels.'

Well, maybe some of that was overly optimistic. But it would be nice if Rory gasped at least.

When the shop closed, I locked myself in the bathroom, along with my dress, the shoebox and my make-up bag. I did my face first, listening to Mia's instructions in my head: moisturize properly, foundation, eyes, mascara. Oh no, shit, eyelash curler before mascara. Too late. Bit of powder on the nose and chin. Blusher where you smile. I grinned in the mirror and rubbed a light pink into my cheeks. Finally, the lipstick, applied with a shaky hand.

I pulled my work T-shirt over my head with extreme care, kicked off my trousers and dropped my bra on the floor. No bra required for this dress. I stepped in and wiggled it up my body to where th— Shit! The zip on the back. Mia had helped last night since I couldn't reach the top and fasten the little hook. Shit, shit, shit.

OK, Florence, no need to panic. Was going to Uber to the party in Battersea Park anyway. Could simply slide on duffel coat and ask Rory to do it up when I arrived. But what if he was talking to the Prime Minister? 'Hello, Prime Minister, nice to meet you. I do want to hear about the situation in Brussels but would you mind if my boyfriend did up my zip first?' No other option, I'd have to chance it.

I lowered the loo seat and sat to fasten the ludicrous shoes, then crouched to stuff the clothes littering the bathroom floor into my tote bag and throw a few make-up items into my clutch bag. Pinching the folds of the dress with my free hand, I waddled towards the stairs and hoped it didn't fall down.

The lights in the office were on, which meant Zach had forgotten to turn them off. Presumably he'd have left for his date with Ruby and they'd be in a bar or a pub somewhere already; Ruby flicking her hair like a dancing horse at the Olympics, Zach flexing his Greek tattoos.

This was why, when his head appeared from behind the office door, I dropped the clutch bag and empty shoebox and clapped my arms across my chest so my dress didn't slide to my ankles.

'Hi,' I squeaked.

Zach looked at me but didn't say anything.

'Actually, can you do my dress up? As you're there? It's the back, I just can't reach the top of the zip. If you wouldn't mind?'

He remained frozen; I carried on gabbling.

'Is it my lipstick? Do I look like I'm going on *Strictly*? I feel like I'm going on *Strictly*.'

He still didn't move.

'Or my shoes? I know they're mad. They're Mia's and I can hardly walk in them. I'm probably going to kill myself tonight. Or fall and break a few ribs, anyway.' I stopped. 'Zach, you all right?'

'Yeah, sorry,' he said, before a small cough into his fist. 'I mean yes, fine, but you look…'

I laughed at his confused expression. 'Is it weird to see me like this? I don't really feel like me. I feel like Cinderella off to the ball. Although I bet her glass slippers were more comfortable.'

He shook his head slowly. 'You look ridiculously beautiful. Truly. That's why I can hardly speak. You look… perfect.'

I blushed, obviously. 'Thanks.' Then I angled my shoulder at him. 'Actually, could you do me up?'

'Course.' The shop felt very quiet as he stepped around me and I flinched at the sensation of his fingers on my lower back.

'You all right?'

'Yep,' I squeaked, staring at an old tea stain on a patch of carpet in front of me. Concentrate on the tea stain, Florence, do not dwell on the fact you can feel Zach's breath on your neck.

'What's the occasion?' he asked, as he started tugging the zip upwards.

I twisted my head to answer.

'Stand still please, Cinders,' he said, nudging my shoulder forwards with his hand.

'Sorry. And don't laugh but it's a Conservative party.'

He didn't reply.

'Zach?'

'You said don't laugh so I am maintaining a diplomatic silence,' he said, as I felt his fingers reach the nape of my neck. 'There, you're done.'

'Thanks,' I said, turning round to smile at him, and then, because I couldn't help it, 'Why are you still here, anyway? Aren't you seeing Ruby?'

He looked surprised. 'Er, yeah. Yeah I am but not until seven, so I'm just finishing off a few bits and pieces.'

I nodded but felt embarrassed at having pried, so I picked up my skirt and made for the stairs.

'Florence,' he shouted, when I was halfway up and already cursing the shoes. I felt like a stilt man about to make his entrance at the circus.

'Mmm?' I said, pausing to glance back at him. It was just one word, my name, but he'd sounded strangely solemn.

'Have a good time. And I mean it. You look, no, I mean you *are* very beautiful. A modern-day Helen of Troy.'

I frowned. 'Which one was she?'

'The one they fought over, the Trojans and the Greeks, because she was supposedly the most beautiful woman in the world.'

'All right, let's not go overboard,' I said, rolling my eyes. 'But thanks. And you too. Have a good night, I mean.' Then I turned back and stomped up the stairs because this situation was awkward and I needed to get my Uber.

★

I played a quick round of Consequences while the Uber dawdled at a set of lights. If they went green in the next ten seconds, I wouldn't fall from my heels, say anything embarrassing in front of Rory's colleagues or go to the loo to see my lipstick had run down my chin and I looked like I'd had a bloody session at the dentist.

Two, four, six… The lights changed at eight seconds and I felt a sense of relief as the Uber moved again. I looked at my phone. Rory was waiting outside the marquee. The thought of him, my boyfriend, in black tie and taking me to a party like this made me shake my head in wonder. It sure beat my usual Friday night: a bowl of pasta on the sofa, Marmalade draped over my stomach like a draught excluder.

I spotted Rory before the car stopped. Light blazed out from the marquee entrance, illuminating him in the dark. His hair was slicked in a side parting, his jacket was perfectly cut across his shoulders and his shoes shone like soldier's boots. Standing there, nodding at people as they passed, he looked like Jay Gatsby welcoming people to his party.

I opened the car door and stepped out carefully. This was my grand entrance; I mustn't trip, stumble or drop my bag. Rory bounded forward as soon as he saw me and I bit my lip, hoping for that approving gasp.

'It's red!' he said, his eyes spherical with alarm.

'What?'

'Your dress, it's red.'

I looked down and smoothed the velvet over my stomach. 'Yes. Is that… bad?'

'Florence, it's called the Black and White Ball! Look!' He swung a hand around him as other couples walked past and I felt all my jittery excitement about the party turn to dust.

Every other woman was wearing black. Black sequins, black silk, black velvet, black fur coats in several cases. But no red.

'I didn't realize, I didn't think. Sorry, Rory, I just…'

'It's too late now. Let's go in,' he said, putting a hand underneath my elbow and pulling me towards the light. 'Come on, we need to meet everyone.'

'No kiss?' I asked, blinking quickly to discourage tears. He sounded so cold, so cross, and all I'd wanted to do was impress him.

Rory turned to face me and rotated his fingers around his mouth. 'You've got all that… stuff… on your lips. I don't want it to rub off.'

'OK,' I said, sinking my nails into my palm to stop my eyes from blurring. Don't cry, Florence. Can't cry. You've got too much eye make-up on. You'll look like a sad stilt man.

We walked along a short stretch of carpet – also black – and into the marquee. I tried to keep up with him but every step on my shoes felt like it could be my last and I lagged behind. While queuing to hand my coat and bag into the cloakroom, I counted the heads in front of us. Heads of silver, slicked-back hair. Heads of bouffant curls that smelled of Elnett if you got too close. Bald heads that shone like lightbulbs.

You could smell the money in that marquee. It was full of real-life *Vogue* mannequins and men in black tie. Eyes followed me as we pushed from the cloakroom deeper into the heart of the party. Rory stayed silent, his hand still gripping my elbow as he led me to a small circle of people, and my spirits drooped even further when I spotted a familiar blonde head: Octavia.

'Evening, all,' said Rory.

They spun to look at us.

'Lady in red!' said Octavia, with a squawk of laughter.

I grimaced. 'Yeah, Brainiac here didn't realize that being called the Black and White Ball meant you actually had to wear black and white.'

'I think you look marvellous,' said a tubby man whose shirt was buckling at every button. I wanted to fling my arms around him in gratitude but I worried it might cause a button to ricochet free and blind a partygoer on the other side of the marquee.

'Thank you,' I replied, smiling at him. I could still sense embarrassment wafting off Rory as he snatched two glasses of champagne from a waitress and handed one to me.

I'll get drunk, I decided. That would help. Ninety-three glasses of champagne would definitely help.

Rory introduced me to the others in the circle. I knew Octavia and Noddy. 'And you remember Lord and Lady Belmarsh?' he said, as I looked at an older couple – haughty as a pair of owls – and realized they were Octavia's parents who I'd met in Norfolk. 'And this is my boss, Clive, and Marigold, his wife,' he said, of the man with the alarming buttons and a rotund woman standing beside him.

'At least you haven't come as the Scottish widow like the rest of us,' said Marigold, which quite made me want to hug her, too.

We drank and made small talk about the cold weather and Clive and Marigold's new puppy, a Dalmatian called Stripey.

I reached for another champagne and ignored a tray of unappealing canapés that looked like baby's thumbs.

My feet started to ache and I shifted my weight from foot to foot as if I was standing on hot sand. The marquee was vast, held up by several large poles like a big top, with purple lights swirling across the canopy roof. At the other end, dozens of tables were decorated with cascading white flower arrangements, and there was a chequered dance floor with a stage behind it. I changed leg again as a man waddled on to it and announced dinner.

'We're on table seven, over there,' said Clive, pointing to the right of the dance floor. He led us and I caught half-sentences as we went. 'Oh helair!' people said to one another. 'Helair! I haven't seen you in yonks!'

Among them were faces I thought I recognized. There was whatshername, the Education Secretary. And wasn't that the footballer who won *I'm A Celebrity* last year? And in the distance, standing next to table one, I could just see the top of the Prime Minister's head, surrounded by a gaggle of disciples. That explained the men with necks as thick as elephant legs positioned around the edge of the marquee. Security.

'Florence, white or red?' asked Noddy, holding a bottle of wine in the air.

'Red, quite obviously,' said Octavia.

I did my fake laugh again. I was getting quite good at it. 'Red, please,' I replied, swallowing a huge swig as soon as it splashed into my glass.

Dinner was also black and white. A small mound of risotto

with flaked black truffle to start, followed by monkfish and blackcurrant pavlova for pudding. I managed four glasses of wine, which perked me up. Sitting next to Noddy, I realized, was just like sitting next to Hugo; you asked what his golf handicap was and off he went.

Every now and then, I stole a glance at Rory, sitting on my other side. He was in entertaining mode, charming Marigold or Lady Belmarsh with an anecdote, asking them about their children, about their next holiday, about where they were spending Christmas. Nobody else would have known he was embarrassed, but I knew because he didn't touch me once throughout dinner. I was momentarily distracted by the image of Zach and Ruby, heads bent together in a pub, but shook the thought away as an auctioneer leapt on stage and began selling off Verbier chalet holidays and safaris in Kenya. Clive bid for the chance to have Stripey painted by an 'eminent pet portraitist' and eventually won it for £12,250. I wondered if all the dignitaries gathered in this marquee had more money than brain cells.

When the auction had finished, Octavia leant towards me, a wide smile stretching her lips. If a snake slithered towards you in the wild, its face would look much the same.

'I gather you ambushed Rory about our little discussion in Norfolk,' she said.

I felt so many emotions at this that I wasn't sure which one should come first. Anger at Rory for telling Octavia this? Betrayal that he hadn't then told me he'd spoken to her? Embarrassment? Astonishment that Octavia would raise it again? But before I had a chance to reply, she'd carried on.

'Do forgive me for upsetting you. Nothing would thrill me more than you and he getting married.' As a performance, this was even less convincing than one of Eugene's, but I didn't have time to dwell on that because Marigold misheard her.

'Sweet! You pair of lovebirds. I didn't know you were engaged!' she said, looking from me to Rory and clapping her hands together.

'Is someone getting married?' piped up Lord Belmarsh.

'Nobody's getting married,' I replied, rallying myself and smiling back at Octavia. 'He's just very good in bed.'

It slipped out. I couldn't help it. I was that fatal combination of fairly pissed and fairly cross.

The table fell silent and Lord Belmarsh's face turned so puce I thought he might be having a heart attack.

Under the table, Rory's hand gripped my thigh. 'Florence, darling, let's try a glass of water.' He reached for a bottle and topped up my glass.

'Lucky Rory,' said Clive, winking at me.

'Clive!' reprimanded Marigold.

'Perfect timing,' muttered Rory, as a band started up on the stage. He stood and held a hand out for me. 'I think we should dance.'

I'm scared of dancing. At teenage parties, I used to watch the girls who could sway in time to Britney Spears with envy. There seemed to be a direct correlation between those who knew the steps to 'Oops!… I Did It Again' and those who had boyfriends. I didn't know the steps and never had a boyfriend. So, over the years, on the rare occasions I needed to dance, at a wedding or a birthday party, I'd developed tactics to avoid the dance floor. I needed another drink or I needed the loo. But here was Rory's outstretched hand, no avoiding it.

Without saying anything, he led me to the chequered floor as the band played a Sinatra and, to the backdrop of saxophones and a man at the microphone crooning 'That's Life', Rory spun me out and back into him again. I managed this and rolled back into his arms without skittering to the floor.

'I've been up and down and over and out and I know one thing...' crooned the singer, eyebrows waggling above the microphone.

Rory lifted his arm and I twirled underneath it, catching a glimpse of his thunderous face. I tried not to care. I just had to get through the rest of the party without anything else going wrong.

'Each time I find myself flat on my face, I pick myself up and get back in the race...' belted the singer, as Rory unravelled me from his chest again like a yoyo.

I felt it happening milliseconds before it actually did, as if the very moment that my right heel started sliding sent an alarm to the rest of my body to brace itself. My foot slipped from under me and then my knee, my hand and the rest of me came crashing to the floor like a chess piece knocked to its side.

Ah. Turns out something else *could* go wrong.

People around me stopped dancing and looked down and then Rory was crouched beside me, his hand digging into my underarm. I stood slowly, like a toddler who'd just learnt to walk, and tried my fake laugh again but it wouldn't come. Instead, the purple lights of the marquee went blurry.

'Right,' he said, 'let's go home.'

'I didn't mean to fall, I'm sorry,' I said, as he pulled me towards the entrance, pushing through people. 'What about my bag?' I added, with a thick voice.

'You sit here,' he instructed sternly, as we reached a line of black cabs. 'I'll collect everything.' He opened the door for me to climb in and then leant through the front window to speak to the driver, all polite again.

'I'm terribly sorry but could you hang about while I get our coats?' The driver nodded and Rory strode back towards the marquee. As I unbuckled my shoes, tears slid down my cheeks, making dark spots on the velvet of my dress. One dark spot, two dark spots, three dark spots; I counted them until they merged into one while the driver eyed me nervously in his mirror. Probably thought I was a vomit risk.

Rory came back minutes later with my coat and bags. He climbed in, gave the driver my address and sat back against the seat.

Neither of us said anything as the lights of Battersea round-about slid past the windows and my tears stopped, eclipsed by relief at having left that marquee. Marigold and Clive were all right but the rest of them could jump in the Thames. And Octavia was a witch in lipstick. If you pulled a strand of her blonde hair, I wondered whether it would slide off to reveal a bald scalp underneath. The thought made me smile and I turned from my window to glance at Rory.

'What on earth is funny about any of this?' he snapped.

I sighed and fluttered my lips. 'The whole evening? I'm

sorry, I know it meant a lot to you, but...' I sighed. 'Those people!'

'Those people are my colleagues,' he said, 'and friends. And you made a scene.'

Ah. 'A scene'. A scene was one of Patricia's biggest phobias too. 'Mustn't make a scene, darling,' she'd told me often when I was younger, out shopping when I wanted to count the coins in her purse or whenever I'd count the street lamps out loud.

'I didn't mean to fall over.'

'It wasn't just that,' he said, loosening the knot of his black tie while glaring at me, his eyes narrow with anger. 'It was what you said to Octavia, and that absurd dress. And I don't think the wine helped much either.'

For a moment, I was so winded I couldn't answer, stunned by the power of somebody I liked so much, who was normally so charming and sunny, to reveal another, cruel side of themselves. But emboldened by the wine, I fought back. 'Rory Dundee, don't be such a pompous wanker!'

The taxi driver's eyes peered nervously through his rear-view mirror again, but I carried on.

'I'm sorry that I wore the wrong colour, but nobody died because I wore red, did they? And do you know how nervous I was before that party? Do you know how loathsome Octavia is? Every time I see her she comes up with something poisonous. And I'm sorry about the fucking shoes but I practised wearing them for half an hour last night, up and down the kitchen, like some sort of amateur supermodel, although I was wearing tracksuit bottoms. And I hate dancing. I was never any good at it. But I only did it because you wanted to and then look what happened. All I wanted,' I said, almost hoarse by this point, 'was to make you proud.'

Speech delivered, I sat back against the seat and felt a renewed wave of tears spring. But Rory just laughed.

'What are you laughing at?' I said, sniffing.

'Did you actually practise in those bloody things?'

'Yes! For ages. Mia made me.'

'It didn't work.'

'I know!'

'You might as well have worn your work shoes.'

'I know!'

I turned my head from the window to look at him and we both smiled.

'I'm sorry,' I said again, as I shuffled along the seat towards him.

'That's all right,' he said, putting his arm around me. 'An easy mistake to make.'

I looked up at him. 'What was?'

'The dress.'

'Oh. Right,' I said, resting my cheek back against his jacket. 'But I meant for everything.'

'I know,' he said, kissing the top of my head. 'Tonight wasn't one of our better outings but do you know what?'

'No,' I mumbled into his shoulder, noticing that Rory hadn't apologized himself for being an arse yet.

'There'll be other parties. Tomorrow's another day and all that.'

That, at least, sounded more like him. More optimistic. More cheerful.

'We might just need to get you a different pair of shoes,' he added, with a wry laugh, before brushing his lips against my hair. 'You did look very beautiful.'

'Thanks.'

'You don't now. You look a wreck.'

'Oi!' I sat up and playfully hit his arm.

He smiled. The full Rory smile where dimples carved into his stubble, his eyes softened and my stomach responded with a backflip. And I was about to lean in towards him for a kiss but the cab stopped, making me lurch against the seat like a bag of shopping. We were home.

'Thank you very much,' Rory told the driver, retrieving a note from his wallet and passing it forward. I stuffed the shoes into my bag and stepped out barefoot.

Standing behind me as I unlocked the door, he whispered into my ear, 'I'm very much looking forward to taking this dress off you.' It made me shiver and smile at the same time, but, seconds later, this giddiness disappeared when I pushed open my bedroom door to a sour stink. I fumbled for the light switch and saw Marmalade stretched out on the carpet, a pool of sick beside him.

'Oh my God, Marmalade,' I said, dropping my bag and rushing to him.

'What is that ghastly smell?' asked Rory.

Normally when I came home late, Marmalade was asleep on my pillow. It was a reproach. He wasn't allowed to sleep on my bed when I was there. He had a basket at the foot of it. But if I didn't return at a time he deemed appropriate, he'd jump up and doze on it until I was back.

He was never on the floor and I'd only once known him to throw up, years ago, after he ate a frog in the garden. But I had a word with him about that and he never did it again. This was different. He didn't even raise his head as I stroked his stomach.

'Christ that stinks!' Rory added.

'I'll get some cleaning stuff,' I said, standing up.

'Don't you want to change?'

I looked down at my dress as if surprised to find that I was still wearing it. 'It's fine,' I said, making for the door. 'Will you watch him?'

Rory nodded as he stood over Marmalade with a wrinkled nose and shrugged off his jacket.

I raced downstairs, the folds of my dress in my fist, and rummaged under the sink for a bottle of bleach and a flannel. As the water ran warm, I squeezed a jet of bleach and Fairy Liquid into the washing-up bowl and filled it, before carrying the bowl upstairs as carefully as a Buckingham Palace footman. Couldn't trip twice in one night.

Marmalade hadn't moved. Rory was stretched out on my bed. Using several sheets of loo roll, I scraped the sick off the carpet, trying not to gag, and flushed the paper away.

'At least I'm not drunk any more,' I said to my cat, as I lowered him gently into his basket, then scrubbed at the stain with the flannel.

'Mmm?' murmured Rory.

As my hand scoured the spot back and forth, the stain disappeared under white suds and the smell of bleach over-powered the bile. I rinsed the flannel in the bathroom and gave the damp patch of carpet a final wipe before tipping the water down the plughole and, lazily, leaving the washing up bowl and flannel outside my bedroom door to carry down in the morning.

The door clicked shut and I turned to look at my bed. Rory was asleep on it, Marmalade was asleep at the end of it and I had a smear of sick on my dress, although at least it wasn't my own sick.

What a night.

*

I woke to find Rory's fingers slowly rubbing my nipple. But the thought of sex disappeared as soon as I remembered the previous night. Marmalade! Erect nipples weren't appropriate in this situation. I swung my legs to the carpet and squatted by his basket. I scratched his head, along his back and gently twisted his tail between my fingers and, although his ears twitched, his eyes barely opened. This wasn't like that time with the frog in the garden. I had to ring the vet.

'Come back to bed,' mumbled Rory, flapping open the duvet cover.

'I can't, Marmalade's sick,' I said, reaching for my phone from my bedside table. It was nearly eight, too early for it to be open, but they did an out-of-hours service. I searched for its name and rang the number. No answer.

'He'll be fine,' insisted Rory. But I couldn't possibly climb on top of Rory and listen to him shout 'Cowabunga!' as Marmalade lay poorly beneath us.

'I'm going to have a quick shower and then take him round the corner,' I said. 'You don't feel like coming with me, do you?'

Rory groaned and opened one eye. 'Sorry, darling, I would if I could but we've got a big meeting about European fishing policy today.'

'Don't worry,' I replied, before shutting myself in the bathroom and washing my face twice to try and remove the eyeliner smeared around my eyes.

He was still in bed, apparently asleep again, when I reappeared in a towel. I pulled on jeans and a hoody and decided to text Eugene when I got to the vet. Luckily, it was his week to open the shop early. I picked up Marmalade in his basket and carried him downstairs. Mia and Ruby's bedroom doors were both open. This wasn't unusual for Mia. She'd have gone to work. But where was Ruby? There was no chance she'd be up at this time. I paused in her doorway, realizing that she must have stayed with Zach after their date last night. But not even that could distract me. I was consumed with worry about Marmalade.

In the kitchen, I retrieved a clean tea towel from the drawer to serve as a duvet, tucked it over him and then set off for the vet with the silliest name in all London: Paws 'n' Claws.

I pushed open the door with my shoulder and stood second in the queue, behind a man wearing a trilby with a Labrador on a lead. The receptionist was muttering about her computer and my arms ached, so I lowered Marmalade's basket to a seat underneath a poster offering a free worming treatment, then resumed my place behind the Labrador.

'Good morning,' the man said to the receptionist when she finally looked up. 'I'm afraid my Labrador has eaten a pair of tights.'

She frowned. A veterinary receptionist presumably heard all sorts of stories involving guinea pigs and sick parrots but this seemed to perplex her.

'A pair of *your* tights, sir?'

'Good heavens no! They were my wife's tights that he took out of the laundry room. You're a very naughty chap, aren't you, Brutus?'

In his defence, Brutus did look quite contrite.

The receptionist sighed and asked him to take a seat. I stepped up.

'Morning,' I said, 'my cat was sick last night and doesn't seem to be very well today. He's not responding to much. I've brought him here before.'

'Name?' she said, in a bored voice.

'He's called Marmalade.'

'Your name.'

'Oh, sorry, Florence Fairfax.'

She tapped at her keyboard then glanced up at me again. 'When was he first sick?'

'Last night, when I got home.'

'And he hasn't been sick since?'

'Not that I know of, no. But he hasn't eaten anything either. Normally he'd have had his breakfast by now.' I glanced back at his basket.

'Take a seat and Dr Pennyworth will call you shortly.'

I sat and stroked Marmalade's back while the man in the trilby talked to Brutus. 'Such a silly, silly chap. What are we going to do with you, eh?'

Taking out my phone, I wrote a message to Eugene. *Marmalade sick so am at vet. Will text you when am leaving, sorry xxx.*

A few minutes later, a door to the right of the reception desk opened and a short, fifty-something man in a white coat said my name.

I looked from him to the man in the trilby, worried that I was queue-jumping, but stood and picked up the basket.

'I'm Dr Pennyworth. Come on through.'

He ushered me into a room which smelt of pine disinfectant and I laid Marmalade's basket down on a metal table.

Dr Pennyworth turned to his own computer in the corner and read from the screen without looking at me. 'He was sick last night, and isn't any better this morning, is that right?'

'Yes. But he was only sick once.' Suddenly, in this stark room of medical waste bins and boxes of disposable gloves, I felt the need to reassure him that it couldn't be that serious.

'And how old is he?'

'Seventeen,' I said as Dr Pennyworth snapped on a pair of

blue plastic gloves and gently opened Marmalade's mouth to feel inside.

'Lost a few teeth, haven't we, my friend.' He examined the rest of Marmalade's body before lifting him from his basket and on to a set of scales.

'He's on the light side. How's his eating?'

'All right. He has his biscuits and half a packet of Whiskas every morning.'

'And no change recently?'

I was about to shake my head but, actually, in the past couple of weeks, I'd found a small mound of biscuits left in his bowl every morning. I'd assumed he'd been filling up on snacks in the garden, and I'd been so distracted with the petition, and Rory, that I hadn't worried. 'He's been leaving more recently. Not a huge amount. Just a few biscuits.'

Dr Pennyworth frowned at Marmalade then lifted him back into his basket. 'I think the best way forward is a couple of tests.'

'What kind of tests?'

'Blood tests to check thyroid and liver function. It may be that he's just dehydrated. But he is thin. And, at his age, it depends on how far you're willing to go.'

'To go for what?' A note of panic had crept into my voice.

Dr Pennyworth pressed his lips together before answering. 'It tends to be a matter of cost at this age.'

'What do you mean?' My voice had become strangely shrill.

'Well, there's a cost to all this and at a certain stage, I advise people to try and weigh up the quality of life.'

'Can we do the blood tests?' I said, as the first tears slipped down my cheeks.

'Of course.'

'And can I wait?'

'Sure, it only takes a couple of minutes and then we should have the results back…' he paused and looked at his watch, 'probably after lunch.'

I nodded and wiped my cheeks with the back of my hand. 'Sorry.'

'Not at all. Here, have one of these.' Dr Pennyworth reached for a box of tissues next to his computer. I took a handful and blew my nose as he opened a cupboard behind him and pulled out an electric razor.

'If you could keep hold, I'm going to shave a small patch of fur. Got him?'

I nodded and he flicked the razor on. Marmalade barely flinched as the blades ran over his neck.

'Keep him there and I'll take his blood.' Dr Pennyworth opened a different cupboard and retrieved a syringe in a plastic packet. I stared at Marmalade's back. He tensed under my fingers but it only took a few seconds.

'There we go. All done,' said Dr Pennyworth, dropping the little tube into a silver dish.

'So will you call me or…' I trailed off.

'Alison will give you a ring when we have the results.'

I blew my nose again before stuffing the tissues into my pocket and scooping up his basket. 'Thank you' I said, as he opened the door for me. Brutus and his owner were still sitting there but I was beyond caring what I looked like and wailed the whole walk home, my tears dropping on to Marmalade's back. Poor cat. He hated the rain and refused to go out in it, but he didn't even seem to notice, which only made me cry harder. It had been a bad twenty-four hours.

★

At home, I poured a can of condensed milk into a ramekin and laid Marmalade's basket down next to it, but he wasn't interested. Then I texted Eugene saying I wouldn't be in and sent one line to Rory: *Vet taken some blood tests but not sure how hopeful he is xxx*. That was also the evening I was supposed to be seeing Gwendolyn for my last session, so I emailed her and asked to postpone it.

'So there's one good thing about all this,' I said to him, putting my phone down on the kitchen counter and staring at the basket, willing him to get up and snake his way around my legs or nose through the cat flap to menace the sparrows outside. He didn't, so I carried him to the living room where we sat on the sofa watching Eamonn Holmes interview a real-life ghostbuster.

I kept my phone on the cushion beside me, my eyes flicking to it every few seconds. Eugene replied with a string of heart emojis.

Is Zach in? I messaged back, curious about whether he was in the shop or lying somewhere with Ruby.

Yeah, downstairs, want me to tell him?

Could you?

Eugene sent back several thumbs up emojis.

There was no reply from Rory so I texted Jaz explaining the situation instead. She called instantly, the roar of a hairdryer in the background.

'You all right, love?' she bellowed down the phone.

'We're OK, sitting on the sofa watching TV.'

'Do you need me to bring anything? I've only got one perm… SKYLA, Mrs Gibbons has had long enough under that, can you sit her over there? Sorry, darl, Thursday morning means bedlam in here. All the wrinklies in for their discount colour.'

'No, no, we're good. Sorry to disturb you at work.'

'Don't you worry about that, treasure. But I'm worried about you. You on your own?'

'Yeah but I'm fin—'

'NOT THAT CHAIR, SKYLA, THE ONE NEXT TO IT. All right, babe, but shout if you need me and I'll come over. Leon's picking Dunc up today so once I'm through the purple-rinse brigade, I'm all yours.'

I hung up and Marmalade and I continued to watch morning TV. The ghostbuster had finished and had been replaced by a woman on the sofa claiming she wanted to be cryogenically frozen with her dog. After that, they tested high-street umbrellas by making Eamonn Holmes stand in a pop-up shower with each one. Marmalade dozed while I stared at the screen. Next, Lorraine Kelly interviewed Meghan Markle's make-up artist, followed by a phone-in debate about whether you could clean the loo brush in the dishwasher.

Paws 'n' Claws called back just after midday. I answered, expecting it to be the receptionist, but it was Dr Pennyworth.

'Florence, hello. We have the results back and it looks like it's a renal issue.' He was speaking in the tone of voice you'd use if you were telling someone their grandmother was terminal. 'It looks like it's kidney failure, I'm afraid.'

'What does that mean?'

He took a breath before answering. 'Well, we do have medication we can try, and we could do a round of fluids, but at this stage it's a question of prolonging things, a question of how far you're willing to go. It's normally a matter of weeks at this point, rather than months.'

'OK,' I said, more quietly, my hand on Marmalade's back.

'There is no wrong decision but it is a very personal one, so shall I leave you to think about it?'

'Yep,' I replied in a small voice. 'If I bring him in to, er, to go to sleep, can you do it today or do I wait or, how does it all work?'

'You can come in whenever you like,' he replied smoothly. 'Speak to Alison and we'll arrange everything.'

I hung up, dropped the phone on the sofa and sat immobilized, my hand still on his back. I knew what I should do. I knew the kindest thing for Marmalade was to go to the vet's: an injection and a long sleep. But the thought of coming home every day to an empty basket felt so cruel. I'd known him for seventeen years. He'd slept next to me for seventeen years. That was a marriage for many people. Better than a marriage, in fact, because he didn't fart in bed or demand I cook him dinner every night. All he wanted was his Whiskas. His only treat was condensed milk. It was the simplest, happiest relationship I'd ever known. Here, in this house, Mia and Ruby had always been a pair – yakking together in the kitchen or doing their nails together upstairs. But so long as I'd had Marmalade, it hadn't mattered. He was my other half, his back pushed up against my leg as I read on the sofa or his head on my feet as I wrote at the kitchen table. How could I sit here and make this decision with him lying so trustingly beside me? Some people would snigger at those who call their pets their best friend but I felt sorry for them. They've never known the devotion of a Marmalade.

I started crying again and picked up my phone to ring Rory.

He didn't reply so I tried Jaz.

No answer there either so I called Eugene.

'Hiya,' said a voice at the other end. But it wasn't Eugene. It was Zach.

I couldn't help it. I burbled down the phone making a noise that sounded like the cry of a humpback whale I saw once in a documentary. A high-pitched wail.

'Florence. Florence, are you OK? Florence? FLORENCE?'

I burbled further unintelligible sounds. 'Pnueeeeegh, vet, pneuuuuuuugh, Marmalade, pneuuuuuuugh.'

'OK, breathe,' he instructed. 'Stop making that weird noise. Breathe. That's it. No, not that noise. Another breath. In, out, in, out. That's it. In, out. OK?'

'Dank do,' I managed, between breaths.

'What's up? Tell me.'

Very slowly, between more instructions from Zach about breathing, I explained. 'And it feels so mean!' I cried. 'He's just lying here! He hasn't done anything wrong! How can I carry him back to that place knowing what I'm about to do?'

'OK, Florence. Florence? Florence, listen to me. Are you on your own?'

'No, I've got Marmalade with me,' I replied, 'but not for much longer.' Another wail. 'And what if he can hear me now? What if he can understand what I'm saying?'

'He can't understand you. When are you going to the vet?'

'I don't know! Later probably.' More wailing.

'Where's Rory?'

A sniff. 'He's busy sorting out the fish!'

'What fish? No, actually, never mind. What about your sisters?'

'Mia's at work and you probably know more about Ruby than I do.'

'What do you mean?'

Another sniff. 'I haven't seen her since last night. Where's Eugene?'

'Upstairs in travel so I'm behind the till. But if you can hang on… half an hour… I'll jump on my bike and come with you.'

I was so grateful I let out another whale noise. 'Would you?' I didn't care who was with me. I would have taken Patricia to the vet with me by that stage. I just couldn't face it on my own.

'Course. Text me your address and I'll be there.'

'Thank you,' I said again. I hung up and sent him the address, then curled myself around Marmalade's basket on the sofa, weeping into the cushions. The TV schedule had moved on to *Loose Women* and I could hear them all shouting about their pelvic floor muscles, but not even that could distract me.

It was only when the doorbell went half an hour later that I got up and glanced at myself in the hall mirror. My face was red and swollen, so I pressed the back of fingers to my cheeks to cool them before opening the door.

Zach grimaced, his helmet under one arm. 'I'm sorry,' he said, reaching out with his other one to pull me into a hug.

I let my face fall against his jacket before pulling back again and wiping the tears from the leather.

He laughed. 'Don't be daft. It's been through worse than this.'

'Come in,' I said, standing aside. 'Do you want a cup of tea or...' I trailed off, unsure what the alternative was. 'Do you want a cup of tea or should we go straight to the vet and murder my cat?' seemed too stark.

'Up to you,' he said, stepping in and closing the door.

'A tea,' I said, answering my own question. 'It might help me compose myself. I'm sorry to drag you away from the shop.' I gestured for him to follow me into the kitchen.

'It's fine. Don't worry. Eugene and Norris can manage.'

I flicked the kettle on and he put his helmet down on the table. 'Nice place.'

This mingling of my work life with my home felt strange.

I'd envisaged meeting Zach in my kitchen a few times recently, but never because it was me who'd invited him. As I reached into the cupboard for tea bags and pulled a milk carton from the fridge, I was grateful that I could stand with my back to him. Not because I looked so puffy, but because it meant I could ask the following question without my face betraying any sort of embarrassment or awkwardness.

'Anyway, how was last night?'

'Huh?'

I turned from the fridge.

'Last night with Ruby?'

'Oh.' He nodded. 'Yeah good, great, actually.'

'Cool,' I replied, turning back to pour milk into each mug. He sounded astonishingly relaxed about discussing his date with my sister.

'Yeah. I think she was pleased by the end. We got some good shots.'

'What?' I said, spinning round. 'What shots?'

'Headshots.'

'Headshots?'

'Yeah, you know, those little portraits that models need for their portfolio?'

'I know what they are. I just didn't realize that's what you guys were doing.'

'What else would we be doing?'

I scanned his face to see if he was teasing but he looked genuinely confused.

'Nothing, never mind.' I reached for the kettle.

'Wait a minute, did you think something was happening between us?'

I stared harder at the mugs. 'Er, maybe. She asked for your number and then said she was seeing you and didn't mention the headshots, so, yeah, I guess. What else was I supposed to think?'

Zach laughed. 'That explains it.'

'Explains what?'

'Why you asked about whether she'd texted me. And about seeing her. It all makes sense. Ha! I thought you were being weird last week.'

At this, I spun around. 'What? I wasn't the one being weird. You were.'

He laughed again. 'Only because I thought something was up with you. And I've been tired, I suppose, with everything at the shop.' He shook his head to himself. 'You see? This is why humans should communicate more. Dolphins are better at it than us. You still haven't sent me your caterpillar story, by the way.'

'I know, because you seemed less keen on the idea and all… silent. So I thought I should just leave it.'

'No way. I'm desperate to read about poor old Curtis. Send it to me.'

As I carried a mug over, I tried to smile, knowing that he was attempting to cheer me up.

'All Ruby told me was that she wanted new headshots,' he said, as he reached for the tea.

My fingertips stung from the heat so I rubbed them on my jeans. 'Maybe. But I think she kind of likes you as well.' I looked up and met his eye, then blushed.

One half of his mouth lifted in a lopsided grin. 'I'm very honoured but...' He stopped.

'What?' I said, heading back to the sink to pick up my own mug.

'She's your sister.'

'So?'

'I don't think that's... Well it's not going to happen, let's put it that way.'

'I wonder where she was this morning then,' I murmured.

Zach sipped at his tea. 'Audition for a washing powder advert,' he said, over the rim of his mug.

'Actually?'

He nodded and I nearly laughed, but then I remembered why Zach was here and my heart felt heavy again. 'Come on, he's through this way.'

He followed me into the sitting room, where Marmalade was still in his basket on the sofa. I sat down on one side of it, Zach on the other. 'Hey, big fella,' he said, running a hand down his back.

'You a cat or a dog person?'

'Dog,' he replied, not looking up from Marmalade. 'But I'm willing to make an exception for certain cats.'

Our discussion in the kitchen had briefly distracted me, but I felt a fresh wave of sadness at the thought of heading back to Paws 'n' Claws.

'It's the right thing,' said Zach, as if reading my thoughts. 'If he's in pain, it's a kindness.'

'I know. I just...' I stopped as another tear tipped out.

Zach lifted his hand from Marmalade to my shoulder and squeezed it. 'Making the call is the worst bit.'

I nodded and finished my tea before ringing Alison the receptionist and saying we'd be there in half an hour.

★

Zach offered to carry Marmalade but I couldn't bear to give him up. He kept up a steady stream of talk (Zach, not Marmalade) as we walked. About the shop's increased Instagram following, about his plan to make Norris dress up as Father Christmas for the Christmas party, about whether Norris would let him spray fake snow in the shop's windows. I stayed quiet, trying not to imagine making the return journey with an empty basket.

Alison looked at me more sympathetically this time. 'I'll let Dr Pennyworth know you're here,' she said, as soon as I stepped through the door.

The waiting room was busier. A woman wearing a fuchsia coat held a lead attached to a small dog with a cone round its neck. It looked embarrassed at this. Opposite me was a twenty-something man with a metal cage on his lap. I couldn't see any sign of movement inside the cage. A guinea pig? A hamster? A tarantula? I hugged Marmalade's basket closer to me as my phone vibrated in my pocket and I pulled it out to see a message from Rory. Finally, although it didn't say anything sympathetic about Marmalade. **Darling, nightmare day with all this fishing stuff. Might be here until late. Will ring when I get a chance X.**

I sighed and slid it back into my pocket as Dr Pennyworth

swung his door open. 'Florence, hello. Do you want to come in?'

I nodded and stuck my thumb out at Zach. 'Is it all right if my friend comes too?'

He smiled. 'Course.'

It was quick. I was grateful for that. After I signed a consent form, Dr Pennyworth shaved a small area of Marmalade's front leg. Then I gathered him in my arms and lowered my face to his head, nuzzling it with my cheek. 'Bye, sweetheart,' I whispered. My brain played a cruel trick as I did this, summoning up the memory of the first time I'd ever seen him. He'd arrived on my fifteenth birthday. It had been a relatively quiet birthday, because my counting was bad back then, so we'd celebrated with a family dinner at home. Dad had come back that evening with a box and called everyone to the sitting room before I could open it. He was so small I could hold him in my palm, and he'd slept in my room every night since.

'You ready, Florence?' said Dr Pennyworth, and because I couldn't bring myself to actually say yes, I just nodded.

He lifted the syringe and it was done. Seconds later, I felt him go.

I let out another whale noise as Dr Pennyworth took him and Zach wrapped me in a hug. Luckily, his shoulder absorbed a lot of the sound, otherwise those in the waiting room might have called the police. It was a hell of a racket but who are any of us to judge another when their heart breaks? Zach stood patiently and solid. He handed me tissues when I eventually pulled back and noticed a trail of snot stretching from my nose to his jacket. He helped me answer Dr Pennyworth's cremation questions. His arm remained around me while I paid at the reception desk, which was fortunate as otherwise I might have crumpled to the floor. He walked me home and offered to buy a bottle of wine, but all I wanted by that point was to get in the bath and weep by myself.

'It's all right, but thank you,' I said, hugging him again on my doorstep.

'Text me any time, OK?'

I nodded, let myself back into the house and let out another sob when I saw the untouched ramekin of condensed milk on the kitchen floor.

CHAPTER NINE

THE NEXT FEW DAYS felt heavy with sadness and getting through each one was like wading through quicksand. Rory was in Berlin. He'd finally called me, the evening after putting Marmalade down, to say he had to go to away again for work.

'Darling, I'll be back soon!' he said, assuming my tears were for him.

I explained that I was more upset because I'd had to put my cat down.

'I know, sweetheart, but at the end of the day you have to remember, he was just a cat.'

A huge bunch of cream roses arrived at the shop the following day as an apology.

Sorry about the cat. Can I sweep you out for
a special dinner on Friday? Rory X

Friday was my birthday, but the thought of that wasn't perking me up much either. There was too much pressure on adult birthdays. 'Did you have a nice birthday?' people ask and you have to reply positively to avoid disappointing them. 'Yeah, a great time, thanks, I got a book and a rude card about ageing from Scribbler!' Birthdays peak at around seven or eight, when you have a cake, balloons, mandatory presents from everybody at your party (otherwise why did you ask them?), and perhaps a magician. After that, it's downhill. Adult birthdays make you feel like a junkie who's clean but fondly remembers his first hit. Someone in the office uses petty cash to buy you a Colin the Caterpillar and you gather round the printer for a dutiful rendition of 'Happy Birthday', but it's nowhere near as thrilling as the princess cake you had when you turned seven.

As usual, I hadn't planned anything this year, figuring I'd just text a few people a couple of days in advance and see if anyone was up for a drink. This was my theory: if I didn't make a big spectacle out of my birthday, I couldn't be disappointed when I ended up counting beer mats in the pub. But I felt lifted by the idea of dinner with Rory, to make things feel more normal after the rockiness of the ball and to close a terrible week. So we made up via messages and he said he'd book an Italian restaurant that did 'sensational ossobuco'. I assumed this was a cheese but Google told me it was veal.

On Tuesday, I opened a box of deliveries in the shop to find Norris had ordered several copies of a new cartoon book called *How To Tell If Your Cat Is Plotting To Kill You*, which set me off again. The next afternoon, Mrs Delaney appeared while I was having another weep behind the till and asked if it was 'boyfriend trouble'. Eugene quickly escorted her to the gardening section.

He, Norris and Zach were all weirdly nice to me that week, like husbands who'd been caught shagging the nanny. Cups of tea kept appearing at the till. So much tea I had to ask them to stop in the end because that many cups meant multiple trips to the loo. Eugene cleaned the kitchen every day, Norris didn't shout and there were no Rory the Tory jibes. I also emailed him my Curtis the caterpillar story and, on Thursday, he appeared upstairs and suggested lunch in the square.

'I've brought my lunch.'

'I know, I know,' he said, surrendering his hands in the air. 'I wasn't for a second suggesting you try a different type of sandwich. But bring it with you. I want to chat about the Christmas party.'

Once on the bench outside, he revealed this had been a cover story. 'I do want to chat about the Christmas party, but I also wanted to check that you're OK.'

I smiled up at him. He was sitting on the wooden arm, his boots on the seat. 'Kind of. The house has been pretty weird this week. I get home and wait for the feeling of him around my ankles, but Ruby and Mia have been amazing.'

The previous night, they'd lined up in the kitchen, clearly holding something behind them.

'Why are you guys being so weird? What's going on?' I'd asked.

Mia had revealed a framed picture of Marmalade and me in the garden. Ruby had taken it from her bedroom window the previous summer; I was lying on my front reading, he was lying across a rectangle of sunshine on my back. It made me cry again, obviously, but it also made me more grateful for my half-sisters than I could remember. We'd got through two bottles of wine afterwards and I'd teased Ruby about Zach.

'How were the headshots, Rubes?'

She rolled her eyes. 'I tried. I gave him my best sex face but it didn't work so I guess that's that.'

Mia forced her to demonstrate her best sex face and Ruby had lowered her eyelids like a drunk and pouted her lips. We laughed so hard I'd almost choked.

'I think you're off the hook with Ruby,' I told Zach, as he ripped through his baguette.

He grinned, his cheeks stuffed with sandwich. 'Ah, she's great. But she's your sister. I couldn't. How's your fascist boyfriend, anyway?'

'All right. Been away this week but taking me out for my birthday tomorrow.'

Zach's eyes widened. 'Your birthday! You've kept that very quiet. What you doing?'

'Nothing, I hate it.'

He shook his head. 'You can't hate your own birthday. Even for you, that's tragic.'

'Thanks. And I know. But I do. So I'm having supper with Rory and that's it.'

'He'd better take you somewhere decent. I don't want to hear next week that you spent your birthday eating peri peri chicken in Nando's.'

'I don't think Rory knows what Nando's is,' I said, before catching Zach's eye and we both snorted with laughter. There was no way Rory would risk splashing hot sauce on any of his shirts.

'Hey, so what's happening with the Christmas party?' I asked, once we'd regained control of ourselves.

Zach brushed crumbs off his jeans. 'What do you think about carol singing?'

'Us?'

'No, Jesus, no! Can you sing? No, course you can't. I've heard you in the stockroom.'

'Watch it, I'm still sensitive.'

'You're all right. And I've been looking into it and the Chelsea Pensioners have a choir, so I thought we could try and get them in? A singalong, mulled wine and Norris in his Father Christmas costume. It's my last week in the shop so I want to make sure it's a proper knees-up.'

'Last week?'

'Yeah. I go to South America that weekend.'

'Oh, course.' I looked down at my sandwich and was almost overwhelmed by a wave of self-pity. My life felt small. I made the same sandwich every morning and double-wrapped it in clingfilm. That was pretty much the only element of risk I faced each day – arriving at work and checking the tomato pips hadn't leaked into my rucksack.

'Finally you'll be rid of me,' said Zach, gently punching my shoulder with his fist.

'About time,' I said, trying to grin up at him. 'Has Norris said yes to the carol singing?'

'No, but he will.'

The Chelsea Pensioners were army veterans who lived in a nearby retirement home and still pottered up and down the King's Road in red uniforms and black hats. I had no idea if their singing was any good but they were a local institution.

'How does the shop make any cash? Won't we need to pay them?'

'It's charitable,' he replied with a shrug. 'We pass a bucket around for the singers and stay open late for Christmas shopping. Offer free wrapping or something.'

'We already do free wrapping.'

'All right, Little Miss Pedantic, I'll think of something else. But do you think it's a good idea?'

I nodded. 'Yeah, well done, Superman.'

He raised his arm in front of him like Clark Kent flying through the air.

'Don't get too cocky. The landlord hasn't backed down yet.'

'He will,' said Zach, scrunching up his baguette wrapper, 'he will.'

★

Eugene offered to open up the following morning so I could have a 'birthday lie-in' but I still woke at seven. Lying in bed, I tried to gauge whether thirty-three felt any different to thirty-two. Looking at it from a purely mathematic basis, I'd gained a year and a boyfriend but lost a cat. Did they cancel one another out? Was I any wiser? Hard to tell.

I rolled on my side and looked at the photo taken twenty-nine years earlier of Mum crouched around me as I puffed my chubby red cheeks to blow out my candles. I frowned as if willing her back to life, wondering what she'd say to me today if she was still here.

'Get into the shower, probably,' I muttered, throwing back the duvet. My habit of talking to Marmalade in the morning hadn't stopped.

I dressed and walked to the shop but it was eerily silent. 'Hello?' I shouted. No answer. There was nobody behind the till, nobody on the shop floor and nobody downstairs. 'HELLO?' I shouted again, down the staircase at the office. Nothing. What the hell? I leave them for a morning and the place goes to sleep.

'Men,' I grumbled, pulling off my rucksack and very nearly dying from immediate cardiac arrest when Eugene, Norris and Zach leapt like salmon from behind the till. Well, Eugene and Zach leapt. Norris just stood up a bit faster than he would usually.

'HAPPY BIRTHDAY!' they shouted as I reached for a bookshelf to steady myself.

'Jesus!' I said, clutching the shelf. 'I wasn't expecting an aerobatic display.'

'I think my hip's gone,' said Norris. 'I need to sit down.'

'Hang on,' said Eugene, 'we have to give her the card.' He held out an envelope.

I opened it to find it was signed by all three of them plus, clearly, whoever had been into the shop that week. Rita the cleaner. Mrs Delaney. I squinted at one of the messages: *A VERY*

HAPPY BIRTHDAY AND I HOPE THE NEXT YEAR BRINGS YOU EVERYTHING YOU WISH FOR, BEST REGARDS, TERRENCE.

'Who's Terrence?'

Eugene looked embarrassed. 'He bought a book about bicycles yesterday while you were at lunch with Zach.'

'Thanks, guys.'

'There's something else in the envelope,' he added, nodding at it.

I pulled out a slip of paper: a voucher for a massage at a posh spa nearby.

'We thought you could do with it after, well, everything,' Zach added.

I grinned again. 'Thank you, I'm very touched.'

Norris limped downstairs and I kicked my bag under the till. I'd brought in the same black dress I'd worn on my first date with Rory and my trusty black heels, which I could actually walk in. I still wasn't sure where his Italian restaurant was. He'd texted me that morning saying I was to 'await further instructions'.

'What you doing later?' asked Eugene.

'Not sure, it's a surprise.'

'Remember what I said about Nando's,' said Zach, narrowing his eyes at me, 'if he even dares.'

'It's not going to be Nando's,' I said, reaching for my pocket as my phone vibrated against my hip.

Darling, the meeting's been delayed. Not sure what flight we'll get back but probably not much before 10pm at this rate. I have to stay until the minister's done. I'm so sorry, forgive me. Can we go out tomorrow night instead? Rx

'Oh,' I mumbled. 'It's not going to be anywhere.'

'What?' Zach and Eugene asked simultaneously.

'Rory's meeting has been delayed so he's not getting back until late.' I tried to smile at them. 'Want to come to Nando's for a birthday dinner?'

'No,' said Zach, shaking his head. 'We can do better than that. Eugene, you free tonight?'

Eugene nodded.

'Right, leave this one to me.'

'What d'you mean?'

'Never you mind, but Superman to the rescue. There will be no peri peri chicken and you will have a good time. Deal?'

'Deal,' I said, trying to sound less glum than I felt inside. Maybe a cat was better than a boyfriend after all.

★

When the shop closed that night, Eugene told me to put my coat on and Zach appeared from the office waving a blindfold. I almost told him about the time Rory pinched one of Mia's sleep masks and tied my wrists together, but I wasn't sure it was the right moment.

'What's this for?' I asked, standing in front of him while he fastened it around my head.

'You'll see. And drink this.' I felt Zach's hands over mine as he slipped a cold bottle into them. 'Beer. Dutch courage.'

'For what?'

'Wait and see,' he said. 'Eugene, is the Uber here?'

'Just pulled up.'

'I need my bag!'

'Eugene's got it. Don't worry,' said Zach.

As if carrying out a very civilized kidnapping where the hostage is given a drink before being bundled into the getaway car, Zach led me outside and gently pressed on my head so I could fold myself into it.

'Florence, can you put your fingers in your ears please?'

'What? Why?'

He sighed. 'If this was for real I'd have taken you back already, no ransom required. Just do it. I need to talk to the driver about where we're going.'

I propped the bottle between my legs and waggled my fingers in and out of my ears until I heard Zach shout that I could remove them.

'Can we have Magic?' Eugene asked from the front so the driver tapped at his radio and the speakers belted out Tina Turner's 'Simply the Best'. Eugene started singing along.

'Come on, birthday girl, you know the lyrics,' said Zach, before he joined in too.

'Give me a lifetime of promises and a world of dreeeeeeams,' they shouted.

I swallowed another mouthful of beer and pinched my lips together.

'Florence, I can't hear you,' said Zach.

'All right,' I said, opening my mouth and muttering a few words: 'Better than all the rest, better than anyone.'

'You sound like a virgin at choir practice, come on!' Zach urged, before bellowing another line.

'Zach, I had no idea you were such a fan,' said Eugene, pausing from his own harmony.

'Tina? Love her. Big fan of an Eighties ballad.'

Eugene tutted. 'I wish you were gay.'

'Sorry, buddy. But if I was, you'd be first on my list.'

I smiled into my bottle. This was crazy. Sitting in an Uber, blindfolded, singing Tina Turner while drinking a Peroni was crazy. But good crazy.

'Just here's great, mate, thanks,' I heard Zach say a few minutes later and the car stopped.

'Out we get, come on,' he said, taking my hand and pulling me across the seat. I felt his hand on my head again to protect it as I stood up.

I could hear the buzz of London traffic and the odd squeal of a child. Where were we?

'Ready?' said Zach, before untying the blindfold.

'SURPRISE!' came a unified shout.

I blinked at the fairy lights on the trees around us. We were outside the Natural History Museum and Ruby, Mia, Hugo, Jaz and Dunc were all standing in front of me.

'Happy birthday, doll,' said Jaz, stepping forward to give me a hug. 'Dunc, show Floz what you've got for her.'

He stepped forward and offered up a card with 'HAPPY BIRTHDAY' written in crayon. 'Made you this,' he said.

'Oh Dunc, thank you, is that me?' I said, pointing at the

drawing. It was either a woman or a blancmange wearing a wig.

He nodded.

'It's brilliant,' I said, crouching down to squeeze him. 'Thank you very much.'

After several 'Happy birthdays' and hugs from everyone else I turned back to Zach. 'So what are we doing?'

'We're going skating,' he said, pointing around the others to an ice rink at the side of the museum. That's where the squeals of children were coming from. Blue and pink neon lights flashed across the white surface as people skidded across it, circling a giant Christmas tree flashing in the middle. The sound of Justin Timberlake floated through a speaker.

'I can't skate!'

'Yes, you can,' he replied. 'Dunc, can you skate?'

He looked thoughtful for a moment. 'Yeah, but only if my mum holds my hand.'

'Exactly,' went on Zach. 'If Dunc can skate, so can you. Let's go, our time slot's up.'

He led us down a slope and into a marquee behind the rink. Shelves of blue plastic skates spanned one end of it.

'Size?' said a bored-looking man standing in front the shelves.

'Eight,' I whispered very quietly.

'Pardon?'

'Eight,' I said, slightly louder.

'EIGHT,' shouted Ruby, appearing beside me.

'Thanks, Rubes.'

We stomped outside like Transformers, unable to bend

our legs properly once the skates were strapped on. Hugo
muttered about whether the rink had the correct health and
safety insurance; Mia told him not to be a baby. Jaz said she'd
always wanted to be a skater when she was younger.

'Did you? Why?' I asked.

'I loved that Torvill and Jean.'

'Do you mean Dean?' said Zach.

'Yeah, her.'

She and Dunc slid out first. Then Mia and Hugo, followed
by Eugene, then Ruby, which left me and Zach.

'Come on,' he said, holding his hand out.

'I bet you're good at this, aren't you? That's why you've
picked it,' I said, as my fingers grasped his and I stepped on to
the ice like an old person.

He grinned. 'Maybe. I'll be Jean if you'll be my Torvill?'

I inched along the ice, praying not to fall immediately.
Small children slid around me like professionals. Ruby had
done several laps already, hair flying behind her. I laughed as
Hugo pulled himself along by the rail on the side of the rink
while Mia shouted beside him: 'Let go, don't be such a wimp.
Why am I marrying such a wimp?'

'I'm not a wimp, it's a long way down,' Hugo shot back in
a panicked, high-pitched voice.

'Go!' I said to Zach, who was tugging me along. 'This is
boring for you.'

He shook his head. 'It's funny. Look, concentrate, lean back.
You're bending like you're constipated.'

'Shut up!'

'Well, you are. That's it. And bend your knees a bit more. There we go. Use your arms for balance. Look, you're off!'

I was off. Sort of. There were still children outperforming me, but I sped up. I let go of Zach's hand and pushed one leg out behind the other, making a satisfying slicing sound with my boots.

'YOU'RE SIMPLY THE BEST,' shouted Eugene as he went past me, spinning in a little circle.

'Show off!' I yelled back.

Zach swooped up behind Dunc and took his hand.

Jaz let them go on ahead and skated over to me. 'The hero worship's strong in that one,' she said, nodding towards them. Zach was pulling Dunc along to gurgles of laughter.

'Cute.'

'It is,' said Jaz, looking from them to me. 'So where's Rory?'

'Stuck with work. Getting a late plane from Berlin.' I'd had increasingly apologetic messages that day and another bunch of flowers. Pink lilies this time, an even bigger bunch than the roses he'd sent earlier in the week. If you glanced through Frisbee's window, you might have thought it was a florist not a bookshop. Flowers seemed to be Rory's automatic way of apologizing. Send a big bouquet, all would be well.

'How are things with him?'

'All right.'

'Really?'

'Yeah,' I said, nodding. 'Really.' Then I sighed. 'It's just been a weird week.' She already knew about Marmalade but I explained about the Tory party, the dress, our row afterwards.

'Well,' she said, looking back out to the rink, 'either it's the first test of your relationship, and if you really like him then it's fine. Or...'

'Or what?'

She bit her lower lip.

'Go on, when have you ever been afraid to tell me something?'

'Just make sure you're not in a relationship for the sake of being in a relationship. There are others out there, you know. Look at me and George.'

'Me and George is it now?' I teased. 'So you've seen him?'

She smiled. 'Yeah, we went to the park at the weekend with the kids, and then he had a glass of wine at mine afterwards.'

'Snogged yet?'

She shook her head. 'Nah, I think it's going to be a slow burn, this one. He seems to have Maya most nights and I've got Dunc but, yeah, we've messaged every day. So all I'm saying is you never know when someone's just going to appear in your life.'

I nodded but, surprisingly, felt a flash of jealousy. Other women seemed to find boyfriends so easily, swinging seamlessly from one to the next like a monkey in the jungle. I'd waited years for just one and the thought of not having Rory made me feel panicked, as if I would be sliding backwards in life. I couldn't lose him this quickly. 'Jaz, I can't break up with Rory after one bad week.'

'I'm not saying you should. Just make sure you're in this for the right reasons. But enough chat, we can't stand here all night like a pair of pensioners.'

She pulled me away from the side and, as the opening chords of 'Livin' On A Prayer' twanged through the speaker, we skated around the Christmas tree, Jaz screaming Bon Jovi so loudly that parents pulled their children away from us. I fell over, a spectacular collapse to the ice as my legs slipped from underneath me and I found myself flat out, my jumper riding up and exposing my belly to the cold. This sparked a brief flashback to the dance floor of the Tory ball, except here nobody looked down their horsey noses at me. Instead, Jaz squatted to help, although unfortunately this meant she went over too and we lay, screaming with laughter, until one of the supervisors skated over and said we were obstructing the others.

Then came an announcement on the tannoy that our time slot was over, so we waddled back inside and swapped our boots for shoes.

'Drinks!' announced Eugene, pointing to a bar sign.

'I'm taking this one home,' Jaz said, inclining her head at Dunc. 'Happy birthday again, love,' she said, reaching her arms around me.

'Thanks for coming.'

'Have fun,' she said. 'Get pissed.'

'Will do,' I replied. And with hindsight, I blame Jaz for what happened next because I took her instructions very literally.

Upstairs, above the boot area, was a space which had been designed to look like an Alpine chalet: a wooden bar decorated with garlands of fir and fairy lights, long trestle tables and benches on which sat punters drinking glass steins of beer.

'Get a table,' Zach instructed, 'I'll get the drinks.'

We sat around a trestle table. Hugo said he needed to sit on the end of a bench so he could rub his sore shins. The boots had 'dug into them', apparently. Mia rolled her eyes and turned her back to him.

'When's the wedding?' Eugene asked.

'Three weeks tomorrow,' Mia replied in a tone which suggested genuine excitement. I glanced back at Hugo, wincing like a 4-year-old who'd fallen over in the playground and grazed his knee, and marvelled that she could seem so cheerful about it.

I checked my phone to see a missed call from Rory but ignored it as I spied Zach weaving through the crowd in the bar with a big tray.

'Dive in,' he said, putting it down. There was a jug of frothy beer, glasses and several packets of crisps. I went straight for the beer. Down one went, then another, then Hugo was sent back to the bar by Mia. Eugene did the next round and returned not only with vodka shots and more beer but also rubbery hot dogs. It was like chewing on salty tyre, but I'd swallowed mine in minutes and was back to the pints again. At some point, it was getting quite blurry by then, Zach appeared over the table, cupping the flame of a single candle in a muffin and there was a round of 'Happy Birthday'.

'Happy birthday, dear Florence,' sang our table.

'Happy birthday, dear so and so,' sang the rest of the bar.

'Happy birthday, dear meeeeeee,' I slurred.

'Love you guys,' I told them, grinning around the table afterwards. 'I love you,' I said, looking at Mia. 'And you,' I said to Ruby. 'And I have to love you since you're about to be my brother,' I told Hugo. 'I love you a lot,' I promised Eugene. 'And I didn't think I loved you but I do now,' I said, looking at Zach with droopy, half-lidded eyes.

'Relieved I made the cut,' he said, laughing.

'You're welcome,' I replied, before slumping on Eugene's shoulder.

'I think we might need to get the birthday girl home,' said Ruby.

'No!' I sat bolt upright again. 'Not home! More shots!' I hic-cupped and felt a mouthful of hot dog revisit the back of my throat. I swallowed quickly but it didn't escape Ruby's notice.

'Uh-oh, we're definitely going home,' she said. 'Mia, will you call an Uber?'

And then the weirdest thing happened: I tried to stand up but I couldn't. It was like my legs had turned to noodles. They couldn't push me up. I tried. I really tried to raise myself from the table but nothing happened. The next thing I knew, I was flying.

Sort of.

Zach had effortlessly swept me into the air, cradling me like a baby. As he walked downstairs, I exhaled over his shoulder so he wasn't asphyxiated by my breath. All the fairy lights had become one fairy light, other people's voices sounded as if they'd been put through a distorter to protect their identity and my hiccupping was becoming more violent.

He lowered me through a passenger door as if he was posting a parcel and I noticed the street lamps outside the car swaying like palm trees.

This is when I made my third major mistake of the evening. Another hiccup turned into another mouthful of hot dog and I scrabbled for my rucksack as a waterfall of beer and frankfurter poured out of me and into it.

I heard Mia apologizing to the driver while Ruby rubbed my back. 'Yup, OK, good, let's get it all out. Oh no, there's more. Good. Right, do you want a tissue? Oh no. Not done yet. That's it. Jesus, that is a lot of beer. We finished? OK, here you go.'

Ruby handed me a Pret napkin from her bag and I wiped my mouth. Then I wondered why we were in a gale; my hair was blowing around my face with individual strands sticking to my wet lips. Ruby later told me that the smell was so vile the driver insisted on winding down all four windows, even though it was near freezing that night. Also, when we finally got home, apparently Hugo tried to give me a fireman's lift upstairs but was too weak and had to sit down after one flight. Ruby and Mia took over: one at my feet, the other's hands under my armpits while I burbled another round of 'Happy Birthday' until they swung me into bed. Still, it had been a happy birthday in the end. Much happier than I expected. Less happy for Mia, though, since her Uber rating dropped two stars as a result.

★

'Bzzzzzzz,' went the giant bird. 'Bzzzzzz, bzzzzzzzzzz.' We were in thick green undergrowth and its giant beak was about to snap off my head. 'Bzzzzzzz, bzzzzzzzzzzzz.' I stumbled on a vine and waited to be engulfed. Oh no, this was it. Well, I'd had a good innings. Life hadn't been bad to me. There'd been friends, family, Marmalade, a job in a bookshop. The image of Dad's face briefly flashed before me as I felt the beak widen over my head and I felt bad that this would embarrass him in the papers: 'Ambassador's daughter eaten by giant bird.' But there were worse ways to go. 'Bzzzzzzz, bzzzzzzzzzz.' I braced for the end and... Ah.

The buzzing was the doorbell and the pain in my head was an ache so bad I wasn't sure I could move. Could I move? I flexed my fingers under the duvet, then tried my toes. They were all right. What about my arm? Nope, shifting my arm intensified the pain in my head. It was as if my brain was trying to burst free from my scalp. Water. Painkillers. I flapped at my bedside table and knocked my water glass to the carpet. Fuck.

Bzzzzzzz, bzzzzzzzzzz. The doorbell went again. Where was Mia? Where was Ruby? They were closer to the front door than me. I needed immediate medical attention. I opened the drawer of my bedside table and found a packet of Nurofen, staggered to the bathroom and lowered my mouth to the cold tap.

Bzzzzzzzzzzzzzzzzz. I stood up and swallowed the pills, then hit my head on the glass shelf attached to my mirror. Who was being such a dick this early on a Saturday morning? I reached for my dressing gown and knotted it as I went downstairs. If it was someone selling tea towels, fish or God, I would breathe on them as punishment.

Bzzzzzzzzzz, it went yet again as I reached the hall. Jesus, the hall stank. What was that?

My eye fell on my rucksack, lying under the coat stand, and I felt confused. I had the vague sensation that something bad had happened to that bag. Why was it down here and not upstairs in my bedroom? Where was my phone, come to think of it? But as I got closer to it, the smell intensified. I leant over it to open it and— oh Jesus no! No, no, no. Back away from the rucksack. Do not disturb the rucksack. The rucksack had turned evil overnight.

Bzzzzzzzzzzzzzzzzzzz!

'All right, all right, I'm coming,' I said, pulling the chain off the door. 'Zach!'

He was standing on the doormat with a cardboard box but threw his head back and barked with laughter when he saw me.

'Sorry,' he said, 'I was looking for Florence Fairfax but I seem to have come to the house of her elderly grandmother. Do you know where I might find her?'

'Don't make me laugh,' I said, putting my palms to the side of my head. 'It hurts. What are you doing?'

'Can I come in?'

'Er, yeah but I should warn you tha—'

'What is that smell?' he said, stepping past me into the hall.

'Never mind,' I said quickly. 'Coffee?'

'Yes, please,' he said, making for the kitchen. 'I've brought you some croissants.'

'How many croissants do we need?' I said, glancing back at his box. 'There must be hundreds in there.'

'This does not contain anything edible,' he said, placing the box gently down on the kitchen table.

'What is it then?'

'Have a look,' he said with a wide grin.

I narrowed my eyes at him and reached for the top.

'Careful,' he said, more seriously.

I lifted one flap, then the other and my hands flew back to my face. 'Oh my God, Zach.'

For in the box, no bigger than a teacup, was a ginger kitten.

'Are you kidding?' I said, looking up at him.

He shook his head, still grinning. 'No! Unless you don't want him?'

I reached into the box, picked him up and fell instantly in love. It reminded me of meeting Marmalade. Opening a box to find something so tiny peering up at you must be the closest you can come to having a gunky baby slapped on your chest after childbirth. Raising my hands to my face, I looked at him and he blinked back, quite still in my palms. 'Hi, pal,' I whispered, before kissing the top of his very small head. He replied with a very small mewl.

'Where did you get him?'

'From a cat lady in Neasden whose house smelt even worse than this one. He's been microchipped, by the way. I've got some paperwork in my bag.'

I held him to my chest, unable to put him down. There was a new felt bed in the box along with assorted toys: a mouse, a pink ball and a kitten with plastic eyes which was larger than the real one in my hand.

'I thought he might need a friend,' Zach explained.

'This is amazing. He is amazing. Thank you.'

'Do you want me to make the coffee?'

'Would you?' The mention of coffee reminded me that I was very ill, possibly close to death. I pulled out a chair and sat down.

Zach slung his rucksack on the floor and filled up the kettle. 'What you going to call him?'

'Coffee in the fridge, mugs in the cupboard next to the fridge, plunger on the side,' I said, as he opened various doors. 'And don't know. What d'you reckon?'

'Nothing too obvious.'

'Like Tigger, or Simba.'

'Or Garfield. Hmm. Harry?'

I frowned at him, unsure who he meant.

'Prince Harry, he's a ginger.'

'Harry,' I repeated. 'Can you have a cat called Harry? What do we think about animals with human names?'

'I like it. I think it's funny.'

'Rory's mother's cats are called after artists.'

Zach rolled his eyes. 'Course they are. Posh sorts always give their animals pretentious names. I heard someone shouting "Tybalt" at their spaniel in the park once.'

'Coming from the man with a Greek god on his arm?'

'I could take Harry back to Neasden?'

'Uh-uh, he's mine.' I looked down at him and felt a pang of guilt about Rory, remembering that I'd ignored his calls last night. But there wasn't much I could do. Presumably my phone was buried in that bag, covered in sick.

Zach put a mug down in front of me and coffee slopped over the rim. 'Sorry. Got any kitchen roll?'

'By the sink.'

'Plates?'

'In the cupboard next to the sink.'

He mopped the coffee puddle and found the plates, then reached into his rucksack and produced a paper bag. 'I wasn't sure what you'd feel like,' he said, tearing it open, 'so there's croissants, one pain au chocolat, a cinnamon roll and one with raisins in it.'

I lowered the kitten to my lap – Harry? Did Harry work? – and took a croissant.

'Thanks.'

'You're welcome.'

'Not just for this though,' I said, waving the croissant at him. 'For everything. For last night, and coming over now, and for him,' I said, looking down at the kitten, who'd wedged himself between my thighs.

'Hey, it was your birthday. And you didn't hate it, right?'

I shook my head. Thankfully the Nurofen was kicking in. 'I had a good time.'

'Any word from you-know-who?'

I grimaced as I ripped my croissant in half. 'Probably, but my phone is indisposed.'

He frowned at me.

'I was sick on it.'

'You weren't?'

I nodded slowly. 'In the cab on the way back. I didn't know where else to throw up so I used my bag.'

He smiled and shook his head. 'Florence Fairfax, usually so prim, I'm proud of you.'

'I'm not prim!'

Zach swallowed the last of his croissant.

'I'm not!' I protested. 'Am I?'

'Do you remember my first day?'

'When I thought you were a burglar?'

'Exactly, when you thought I was a burglar and you wanted to stab me with the Stanley knife for spilling my coffee?'

'OK, I was a bit prim. But I didn't know you!'

'And you do now?'

His frankness made me awkward, so I looked down at my lap and stroked the sleeping kitten. 'I know you can't be trusted with a coffee cup.'

'You always do that.'

'What?' I asked, raising my eyes to his.

'Make a joke when you're uncomfortable. It's called deflection.'

I didn't have time to make a joke about this because the door buzzer went again, making the kitten spring up on its paws.

Bzzzzzzzzzzzzzzzzz.

'Here you go,' I said, passing him to Zach.

As I trudged through the hall, I held my breath while passing my bag, only inhaling again once I'd opened the door.

It was Rory, also carrying a box. Although his was bright blue and had Smythson written across it.

'You're alive!' he replied, throwing a gloved hand in the air. 'But good lord, are you all right? You look like a ghost. And why aren't you answering your phone? I thought something terrible had happened.'

Before I could answer, I heard footsteps in the hall and glanced over my shoulder to see Zach and the kitten.

'What's he doing here?' added Rory. 'And what on earth is that smell?'

I sighed and stepped back to open the door properly. 'Do you want a coffee?'

He ignored my question and stalked past us both to the kitchen. I followed him, Zach after me.

'I'm jolly confused,' Rory went on, taking off his gloves and dropping them on his box, before draping his overcoat on the back of a kitchen chair. 'I've been ringing and ringing you all night but no answer. What is that frightful noise?'

He glanced at the kitchen ceiling as if there was a bat circling it.

'It's Harry.'

'Another stranger! Who's Harry?' Rory demanded.

'My new kitten,' I said, pointing to Zach, who was standing in the kitchen doorway, cradling the mewling kitten. 'Zach bought him for me.'

'Did he indeed?'

'I think I'd better get going, leave you guys to it,' said Zach, quickly. He lowered Harry into his box and picked up his rucksack. 'See you on Monday and, er, Rory, good to see you.'

Rory didn't reply. Instead, he looked at Zach in the same way that someone would inspect the contents of their hand-kerchief. I brushed past him to hug Zach. 'Thank you.'

'Don't mention it, and eat the rest of those,' he said, nodding at the bag of pastries. 'You'll feel better.'

I waited until the front door had closed and turned back to Rory.

'Florence, what is going on? I race back from Berlin and you don't answer your phone, and then I arrive this morning to find your house has become a menagerie.'

'What do you mean?'

'A kitten and a Neanderthal ape in the kitchen!'

I sighed and sat down. This morning was proving much more eventful than I'd anticipated.

'He's not an ape. He's my colleague. Last night he organized an impromptu birthday party for me and this morning he bought me Harry,' I said, reaching back into the box and picking him up.

Rory scowled with indignation. 'Sounds like he's got a crush on you.'

'He's just being nice.'

'Good,' he said, before crouching down in front of me. 'Because, darling, I realized something last night when I couldn't get hold of you, when I was having visions of you lying dead in a ditch.'

'Lying in a ditch? Rory, I live in south London. Where are the ditches?'

'Never mind the ditches. Listen. What I want to tell you is that I'm in love with you. I love you. That's what I realized on the plane last night. That's why I was so desperate to get home.'

'Oh.'

'Oh?' Rory's face remained inches from mine. He looked expectant.

'What's in the box?' I said, changing the subject. I needed to buy time.

He stood to slide it off the table and held it out.

'Can you take Harry?'

Rory frowned down at his navy trousers. 'What if he has an accident? These are a new pair.'

'He won't.'

As if handling a grenade, Rory took him and I pulled the box on to my lap and untied the ribbon. Under the lid, under a layer of tissue paper, was a black, crocodile-embossed handbag.

'Turn it round,' said Rory, so I lifted it from the box and found my initials stamped on the other side. FAF in gold capitals.

'I thought it was time you got rid of that revolting rucksack,' he said, 'so this is a proper handbag to say I love you. I love you, Florence Amélie Fairfax.'

'Wow,' I murmured, running my thumb over the initials. 'Thank you. This is crazy generous.'

Rory shook his head. 'No, it isn't. Not for the woman I love.'

He kept saying it and I wasn't sure what to reply. This was the moment I'd dreamt of. A handsome man, my boyfriend, was sitting in front of me saying that he loved me. In the films, this was the moment when violins started up, the camera zoomed in on the lovers' faces, the other person said it back and then they kissed, lips and noses pressed up against one another's faces so hard you wondered if they could breathe. And yet here I was, in the same situation, and all I could think was: is it too greedy if I have the cinnamon roll as well as the pain au chocolat?

'Thank you,' I said eventually, 'I'm honoured.'

Rory leant back in his chair. 'You're honoured? Is that all I'm getting?'

I winced. 'I'm sorry. It's just a lot to take in this morning and I don't want to be flippant about this. I want to say it when it's right. Not when I'm…' I gestured at my dressing gown, flecked with croissant flakes.

He nodded but looked so crestfallen I felt guilt pluck at my heart. 'I love this though,' I said, running my hand back over the bag, as if loving his present would make up for it.

'Do you really?' he said, looking more hopeful.

I nodded but I actually didn't. A crocodile-patterned bag was the sort of thing Patricia would like. I couldn't carry my cheese and tomato sandwich to work in this monstrosity. What if the pips leaked on the suede?

'Can we go upstairs?' he asked.

'Really? Now? Like this?' I said with a laugh, relieved to be off the topic of both love and handbags.

'Absolutely like that. I think it's the pinkness and the fluffiness of the dressing gown that's doing it for me.'

'But what about Harry? I can't leave him here, on his own.'

'He can't join in, sorry.'

In the end, I put Harry back into his box, on his new bed, and carried it upstairs. But I put the box in the bathroom because I didn't think Harry needed to see what we were about to do and I was still haunted by the memory of Marmalade's tail on my feet. I brushed my teeth – mindful that I hadn't since Mia and Ruby threw me into bed last night – and pulled the bathroom door almost closed behind me.

Rory was already lying on my bed. I climbed in next to him and laid my head on his shoulder, before he slid his hand underneath my chin and ran his thumb over my lips, parting them a fraction. 'I love you,' he said, before kissing me. I still didn't feel that chipper. My stomach was rolling like a battleship and the coffee had doubled my heart rate, but it's funny how sex can make you forget a hangover.

Or it would have been funny, if, at the exact moment that I started feeling a tingling in my feet, the heat spreading up my legs, I didn't imagine Zach's hand between my legs, instead of Rory's.

'Oh fuck,' I said, as the wave of heat continued to flood upwards.

'That's it, my darling,' whispered Rory, 'that's it. I've missed this.'

'Fuck, fuck, fuck,' I repeated. It was partly a response to the hot sense of release that I could feel growing as his finger pressed harder. But it was mostly the shock of seeing Zach in my head at that very critical moment.

What was he doing in there?

★

I was still feeling wobbly about this hallucination when I went for my final appointment with Gwendolyn that week.

Unfortunately, she now seemed to think we were such good friends that I deserved a hug. 'Florence darling, welcome!' she said, pressing my face to her chest so hard it was as if she was trying to take an imprint of it.

I mumbled 'hello' into her nipples. She was wearing a red mohair jersey tucked into a tulle skirt with purple tights and her green Crocs – she looked like a large child who'd got up that morning and ignored her wardrobe in favour of the fancy-dress box.

She released me and we sat.

'How are we? Is the relationship progressing?'

I nodded and answered cautiously, 'Yeah, I think so. He said that he loved me.'

She kicked her Crocs in the air and clapped at the same time. 'Ah, I'm so pleased!' Then she cocked her head. 'But why so glum, Florence poppet? You look like you've just swallowed a snake.'

I paused and pressed my lips together before answering. 'I'm not sure I love him back. How do I know? How do I work that out?'

'Ah, here we come to one of life's great questions,' she replied, settling back in her armchair. 'Almost everyone I see in here is trying to work that out. Whether they love someone, how much they love them, if they love them enough, if they can love them again, if they love someone else more.'

'What do you tell them?'

She smiled again. 'I can't answer that for them, my darling, just like I can't tell you. It's not that simple. We can't pour your feelings into a measuring jug and see where they come up to. Only you can work that out.'

'What if I can't?'

'Then that might be your answer.'

'But… but…' I floundered. 'He has all the things I wanted on my list! And my family like him!'

'Indeed. But perhaps the qualities you wrote on your list weren't the ones that really mattered?' she said, squinting at me. 'Maybe that's what this process has taught you. And of course your family's opinion counts, we're all swayed by our families. But ultimately it's your feelings that matter.'

I sighed. Falling in love wasn't this complicated in Disney cartoons. Then I steeled myself for my next question, opening my mouth before I replied, unsure how to phrase it.

'What does it mean if you're sleeping with someone but you see the face of someone else?' I blurted, as my cheeks turned the colour of Gwendolyn's jumper.

She frowned. 'Do you mean…' she dropped her voice to a whisper, 'in the act?'

I nodded. It had happened again that week. I'd stayed at Rory's on Wednesday and persuaded him to watch an old *Bake Off* rerun, but halfway through he'd hauled me on to his lap and we'd had sex on the sofa while Prue Leith talked about custard slices in the background. And as I was on top of him, his head bent to my chest, I closed my eyes and tried to imagine what it would be like if it was Zach's head there instead of Rory's. I had to shake my own head to get rid of the idea while ignoring Prue's voice at the same time. It hadn't been a relaxing session.

'But that's all right, isn't it?' I added. 'That happens in relationships sometimes, doesn't it? My friend Jaz says she sometimes sees Gordon Ramsay when she's having sex.'

'Whose face did you see?'

'It's a friend, someone I work with.' My entire body shriv-elled with shame. Saying this out loud made it real, even if I was only admitting it to the overgrown fairy in front of me. But what if someone else could hear? What if Zach had called me and my phone had picked up in my bag so he was overhearing this conversation? I'd have to emigrate to the moon. I leant down and groped in my rucksack to check. My phone screen was black. No accidental phone call.

'What's he like, this friend that you work with?'

'Lovely. But he's not my type. He's untidy and leaves mugs and his motorbike stuff all over the shop. He dresses like the lost member of Linkin Park. And doesn't even have a proper job.'

'I thought he worked with you?'

'It's only temporary.'

'But why does that matter? Why do any of these things matter?'

'Because...' I stopped and looked out of the window. Actually, I wasn't sure. I'd once read an article about evolution which explained that women were attracted to successful men because, when we were scrabbling around caves, the most successful men would have been the best hunters and provided hunks of woolly mammoth for us to ensure our survival, and the least successful men would have got picked off by a wild beast and left us to go hungry. But I didn't want to date someone like Hugo just because they had a company Mercedes and a pension.

'I don't know,' I said, looking back to Gwendolyn.

'I tell you what we need to do,' she said, one finger aloft in the air.

Here we go.

'And that's a little spell for clarity.'

Might have guessed.

'Lie down on the sofa and close your eyes. I'm going to do a short incantation.'

'Will this really help me decide?'

'It will,' she promised.

I lay down and listened to the sound of drawers opening and closing and a match being struck. Then she placed something cold on my forehead.

'What's that?'

'It's amethyst. I've put it on your third eye for clarity.'

'My third eye?'

'It's a site of mystical powers. Our sixth sense. And take this in your left hand. It's malachite to stimulate your aura and guard against any negative energies.'

I felt her press a hard, round object into my palm and closed my fingers over it.

'And this smoky quartz in your other hand to increase your focus.'

With a crystal in each hand, I lay very still so the amethyst didn't roll off my head, but the sudden stink of incense made me want to cough. It was like being in Camden Market. 'What's that smell?'

'It's cinnamon to raise the energy in the room. It's a very powerful tool, cinnamon.'

'Oh. I only have it on porridge.'

'Florence, quiet please. I'm not interested in your breakfast. I need to summon the goddess.'

I pinched my lips, frozen in position, hoping that nobody would knock and see me lying on Gwendolyn's pink sofa, clutching a couple of pebbles with a stone balancing on my face. I'd call the police if I stumbled into a scene like this.

'Repeat after me. I smell the power within.'

'I smell the power within.'

'I see the power within.' My nose twitched with an itch.

'I see the power within,' I said, trying to ignore the itch.

'I feel the power within.'

'I feel the power within.'

Then Gwendolyn read a short, very bad poem, but all I could think about was my nose. I didn't want to scratch it and earn a scolding so I just lay there contorting my face in an effort to quell the itch. I imagined her acting the poem out like Eugene, flinging her arms in the air, but I didn't dare open an eye to check.

'Worries be gone, she needs you no more, worries be gone, out of the door. Stresses and strains, worries and strife, leave now, depart, be gone from her life!'

On balance, I reckon 'The Owl and the Pussy-Cat' was better.

'Have you finished?' I asked, after she'd fallen silent.

'I have,' she said, removing the stone from my forehead and prising open my fingers for the ones in my palms. I sat up and scratched my nose.

'I believe this will help you see your path more clearly,' she said solemnly. 'You have a good soul, Florence. I know it will make the right decision in the end.'

As she clasped me to her nipples again in a goodbye hug, I wished I was as convinced.

CHAPTER TEN

'I SAID NO PENISES!' shouted Mia.

It was the Saturday before the wedding and twenty of us were sitting round a table in a Soho club. It was a new members' club just for women, Ruby had explained, and we were going to do a 'fun' activity before drinks and dinner.

She'd been very secretive about this activity. No wonder. It turned out to be a class called Milky Moments, which had nothing to do with milk. Instead, a man called Lewis was standing in front of us, explaining that we were about to enjoy a 'light-hearted' ninety-minute foreplay lesson. Lewis was a singer from Guildford who ran these classes to make extra cash, he confided to Ruby and me. Once everyone else had arrived, he'd handed out hot pink feather boas, novelty aprons with naked male and female torsos on them, and dildos. This is what had upset Mia: we each had a floppy, rubber dildo on the table in front of us.

'Keep calm and drink your Prosecco,' Ruby told her sister.

'I'm not sure I've ever seen one this big,' said Patricia, who'd finished her glass and was holding her dildo like a lightsaber.

'That's what they all say, madam,' Lewis told her with a wink. He'd draped a feather boa around his neck which clashed with his purple silk shirt.

'Less of the madam, please, and can I have a top-up?' replied Patricia, putting down the dildo and waving her glass at him.

Lewis went around the table refilling glasses and we began.

First came a warm-up exercise. 'Wiggle your fingers, ladies! We need to get those going. That's it, mother-of-the-bride, very good. And then we need to windmill our arms, watch the person next to you. There we go.' Lewis's pelvis rocked back and forwards towards us as he demonstrated, his arms sawing their way through the air like a swimming instructor.

There was a mixture of Mia's friends around that table. We'd all politely kissed and said hello at the start but I'd already forgotten the names. Some were fashiony sorts from her office. They were the most sombre. Dressed in velvet dresses or silk jumpsuits with blow-dried hair, they'd also looked at their dildos with grim horror.

Then there were the school friends. Less severe, more giggling, they were mostly all married with small children who they'd left at home for the day with Sloaney husbands called things like Biffer and JP.

Hugo's sisters – Holly and Henrietta – were sitting next to one another. I squinted at them and tried to remember what they did. One schooled show-jumping horses in Berkshire; the other was a teacher at a London prep school. Henrietta looked a bit like a horse herself – long nose, large forehead – so perhaps she was the show-jumper.

Plus Mia, Ruby, Patricia and me. Mia had been persuaded into a plastic tiara and a bride-to-be sash even though she'd protested that she was wearing Erdem and the props ruined her outfit.

After the warm-up, Lewis skipped round the table again handing out sheets of paper and pens and telling us we needed to pair up.

Henrietta guffawed – she was definitely the sort of woman who guffawed – and held the pen out in front of her. 'Look, even these have cocks on them!'

She was right. At the end of my pen was a very small plastic penis. I glanced at Mia. Her face had puckered with disgust.

Lewis's sheets were illustrated with a detailed diagram of a penis.

'You have to label all the bits,' he announced. 'And there's a prize for whoever gets the top mark.'

'Come on, darling,' said Patricia. Since I was sitting next to her, she was my partner. It was like being at school; pairing up with the least popular kid to burn a small strip of magnesium ribbon.

'That's obviously the shaft. And those are the testicles although they look very small to me. Your father has mu—'

'PATRICIA, I need to stop you there.'

'And look, that's the urethra,' she went on, unabashed. 'Chop chop, darling, write it down. How's Rory, by the way?'

'Fine,' I said, my head bent to the sheet. 'In Prague with Hugo.' They'd left for the stag the previous night and Rory had sent me a selfie of them on the plane holding up cans of

Heineken. Hugo was dressed as a woman, in a blonde wig with his chest hair poking from the top of a red dress.

'So nice that they're friends,' said Patricia, patting my knee. 'And I am glad he's coming to the wedding. As is your father.'

I ignored this and wrote 'foreskin' in very small letters on our sheet. Around us was high-pitched shrieking. 'It looks like a slug!' 'No, that's not the prostate, this is!' and so on.

Mia had partnered with one of her colleagues. Luckily, three Proseccos down, she was laughing.

'How we doing?' shouted Lewis. 'We all finished?'

'We have,' cried Patricia, snatching the sheet and waving it above her head.

We swapped sheets to mark them like school spelling tests.

'Which means in joint first place are Holly and Henrietta, and Patricia and Florence!' Lewis announced a few minutes later, before handing us our prize: a lollipop shaped like a penis.

'I will enjoy that,' said Patricia, sliding it into her handbag.

'Mum!' reprimanded Mia.

Then came the final part of the class: a foreplay lesson using the rubber dildos. Lewis handed out bottles of lube, threw a packet of wipes in the middle of the table and sauntered around us, offering helpful tips.

'No, Jessica, harder than that,' he told one of the fashion lot as she ran her manicured fingers up and down her dildo. 'That's it, Mia, perfect! Your husband's a lucky man. Well done, Patricia, that's excellent technique. But, Florence, oh dear! What's going on here?'

I looked up, my hand frozen. 'What?'

'You've got to grip it, not tickle it! Get your fingers right round it.'

I frowned at my dildo and held it more firmly. It was like being seven and back in gym class again when I couldn't do a cartwheel and everybody else could. Except worse, because ropey hand-job technique was much more shaming than not being able to do a cartwheel.

'There we go,' Lewis said approvingly. 'The penis is much more resilient than you think, ladies. You're not going to break it.'

'I wish I could break yours,' I muttered.

'What's that, darling?' said Patricia.

After the class, Lewis swept away with his box of props and we moved up a floor to a bar. The bottles of Prosecco continued and trays of canapés appeared.

'Can everybody get ready for the knicker game!' announced Ruby.

If you don't know what this is, consider yourself blessed. I'd only been to a couple of hen parties before. One for an Edinburgh friend, another for an old schoolmate. But we played the knicker game at both since it's become a hen party tradition. It will be mentioned in one of the 273 emails you receive before the event itself and the gist is that every hen has to buy a new pair of knickers for the bride to take on her honeymoon. At the party itself, they're all put into a bag and the bride pulls them out one by one, guessing who bought which pair. Some will be novelty thongs. Some will have Mrs 'So-and-So' stitched on their bottom. Others will be lacy, or leopard print, or huge elasticated pairs which could double as a tent. Ruby had mentioned this in an email several weeks earlier but I'd forgotten until she reminded me that morning. I'd raced back upstairs and scrabbled through the back of my drawer to retrieve the lacy thong that Mia had given me years before. In my defence, it was barely worn and the gusset looked fine.

We settled on bar stools and watched as Mia pulled out the first pair.

It was black lace with a red bow on the back. She squinted around the circle at us. 'Amy! It's got to be you. They're beautiful!'

They looked like the sort of pants that would ride right up your bottom, but Amy – one of the fashionables – nodded and smiled. 'Enjoy them, babe.'

Then came a pair with 'Just Married' written on them; an edible G-string made from sweets; a thong with the phrase 'Ain't going to lick itself!' on the front (from Ruby) and a frilly coral pair with the word 'wifey' on it. Mia squealed at this while I wondered which word was worse: *wifey* or *hubby*?

My pair were pulled from the bag last. 'They must be from Flo!' said Mia and I braced myself for a ticking off. 'How did you know I love this brand?' she said, holding them up in front of her. 'You're so clever, thank you.'

Phew.

Patricia left after this game and the rest of us returned to the table downstairs for dinner. Between the windows, Ruby had strung up home-made bunting made from photos of Mia and

Hugo. She'd also done a seating plan that put me at the end, next to Cressida from Mia's office.

Plates of salmon appeared but most people were too pissed to eat. The fashion sorts kept drifting to the window and back again to hang out of it and smoke, gazing down on the Soho street beneath as tourists and punters wandered between pubs.

'Are you the sister who's going out with Rory Dundee?' Cressida asked.

'Yeah, how come?'

She giggled and the smell of cigarette wafted from her mouth. 'How funny. My husband knows him.'

'Oh right. What does he do?'

'He's in politics.'

'With Rory?'

'In the Foreign Office, mmm.' She giggled again. 'I think they have quite a wild time on their travels.'

'Wild?'

She giggled again. 'Yes, sort of debauched. On that trip to Nigeria they did recently, Wilf said they were lucky not to have gotten arrested but Rory's so charming – he talked the policeman down. And there was that time in Brussels when Rory got in a fight with someone's husband. So funny! Naughty boys.'

At my silence, her giggles stopped.

'Debauched? Debauched like how?'

'No, sorry, I didn't mean... I think he's better behaved now. I mean, not better behaved. Oh gosh, this is all coming out wrong.'

I smiled at her, not wanting to give away that my heart was beating at double time under my dress. What did she know that I didn't?

Cressida waved a hand in the air. She had dark blue nails which matched her jumpsuit. 'Just drunken stuff. Forget I said anything. Wilf says he'll be prime minister one day,' she added, with a more sympathetic smile.

'He does want to be, yes,' I replied, the fake smile starting to make my cheeks ache.

'I'm going to have another fag,' Cressida said, clearly desperate to escape the situation she had placed us both in. She stood and hurried to the window with her clutch bag.

I leant back in my chair as an espresso martini was put down in front of me.

'I've ordered a round,' Ruby shouted at me from the other side of the table.

That was the moment Mia swayed to her feet and caught the room's attention – *ting, ting, ting* – by tapping her walnut-sized engagement ring against her empty wine glass.

'Ijustwanttosay,' she started. 'ThatIloveyouall. AndI'msogladyou'rehere.'

'SIDDOWN,' shouted Ruby, laughing at her sister.

Mia hiccupped and slumped back into her seat. There'd been talk of going on to a gay club round the corner where men danced on podiums but Cressida's revelation had winded me. Plus, I wasn't much of a podium person and was worried about Harry having been on his own for so long.

'Just going to the loo,' I mouthed at Ruby, before making for the door with my bag and taking the bus home. They wouldn't notice. Sneaking off was a skill I'd honed on university nights out, leaving when the party was in full swing so I could fall into bed with a book. This hadn't helped my romantic life, I knew, since people only started pairing off towards the end of the night. But I'd rather get into bed with Mr Rochester or Captain Wentworth than a dribbling student who'd drunk ten pints and wanted chips with curry sauce on the way home.

I let myself into the house, poured a pint of water in the kitchen and walked upstairs. Pushing open my bedroom door, I saw Harry curled under a corner of my pillow. I should have been cross. I was trying to persuade him to sleep in his basket on the floor, but he'd learnt to leap on to the corner of my duvet and claw his way up like a very small mountain climber.

I pulled my phone from my bag. Since the aeroplane selfie, I'd heard nothing from Rory, but Mia had told me that they were on a stag and 'as long as they didn't get arrested', it was better not to know what was going on.

I took a few photos of Harry and looked at the time. It was 11.43 p.m. Too late to message?

I opened up WhatsApp, scrolled to find Zach's name, and sent a picture of Harry to him anyway. *The baby's asleep xxx*, I wrote, hoping that it wasn't one of those messages I regretted in the morning.

*

For some extraordinary reason, Mia had decided that the Sunday after her hen party would be a good day for our final bridesmaid dress fitting. I didn't feel great but my hangover was nothing compared to Mia and Ruby. Sitting between them in an Uber to the dress shop the following morning (Mia had actually cried when I'd suggested taking the Tube) was like travelling with a couple of cadavers.

'This is all your fault,' Ruby said, slumped against the car door.

'I wasn't the one who ordered nine hundred martinis,' Mia replied, leaning against the other door.

'I need a coffee before we do anything else,' said Ruby.

Mia retched.

They climbed out of the car slowly, groaning as if they'd just finished a marathon.

'Morning, darlings!' trilled Patricia. She was standing on the shop's step wearing a beret and a pair of sunglasses.

Mia held a hand up in the air. 'Pat, not so loud.'

'Not that name, you know I don't like it. But oh dear, are we suffering?'

'Yes,' said Ruby. 'Aren't you?'

'No. I feel fine. Florence, how about you? You look wretched.'

I cleared my throat. 'I'm all right. Could do with a coffee.'

'We can ask them inside,' said Mia, pushing open the door.

We followed her in and the smell of expensive candles made me gag again. And it was too hot in here. Why did they keep it so hot? It was like stepping into a crispy pancake.

Hilda, the lady who'd helped with Mia's dress fittings, ushered us to a changing room and all three of us slid down on the sofa, as if our legs couldn't sustain us for another second. Dressing that morning had been an effort. The idea of peeling my clothes off to slide a silky peach gown over my head was deeply, deeply unpleasant.

'Can I get you ladies anything to drink?'

'Could I have a coffee? Black,' demanded Ruby. 'And a large glass of sparking water? And an orange juice?'

'A cappuccino for me,' said Patricia.

'I'd like a coffee with milk,' said Mia. 'And have you got any San Pellegrino?'

If Hilda was exasperated by the multiple beverage demands of my family, she didn't show it. She nodded and looked to me.

'A white coffee, please,' I said.

'How was the rest of last night?' asked Patricia.

'Mia ended up being smacked round the face by a penis in a nightclub,' said Ruby.

'What?' I said.

'WHAT?' demanded Patricia.

'Volume, please,' said Mia, leaning back on the sofa with her eyes closed. 'And she's exaggerating. We went to a club and I very briefly danced around a pole.'

'With a man who was wearing a sock shaped like an elephant on his cock,' added Ruby, just as Hilda reappeared in the room carrying the dresses. Her pencilled eyebrows leapt in alarm.

'Forgive my daughters, Hilda,' said Patricia. 'But these look wonderful. Don't they look wonderful?'

'This one is Ruby's,' said Hilda, inspecting a label attached to the hanger. 'And this one is for Florence.' They were exactly the same design – pale pink silk, floor-length, with thin shoulder straps and a deep V-neckline. But Ruby was shorter than me and had a more heaving bosom. She was going to look like a fairytale nymph in her dress while I'd look like a drag act.

Hilda looked at us expectantly on the sofa. Nobody moved.

'Come on, girls,' chivvied Patricia.

'I can't stand up until I've had my coffee,' said Ruby.

Embarrassed by my family and not wanting to annoy Hilda, I stood, pulled the curtain of the changing booth behind me and started undressing.

'Any word from the chaps in Prague?' Patricia asked loudly as I peeled down my jeans.

'No,' said Mia. 'Florence? You heard anything?'

'Nope,' I shouted back, while I scowled at myself in the mirror. Naked but for my knickers, bra and socks. Not a good look. The only messages on my phone that morning had been from Zach, a series of them sent at 1 a.m. in reply to my photo of Harry.

Hello, how come you're up so late?

Oh, Mia's hen. I remember now. Hope it was... fun?

Hey also, there's a new Quentin Blake exhibition on in Dulwich tomorrow which I thought I might check out if you feel up to it?

Curtis the counting caterpillar research?

But no worries if not.

I'd read them while lying in bed, staring at the screen for so long it kept going black, but I wasn't sure what to answer. The idea of going to an exhibition on the weekend with Zach made me feel uneasy. Rory was my boyfriend. Rory was the one who loved me. And I couldn't gallivant off to an exhibition, anyway, because I had to try on this unflattering dress. In the end, I sent one line back, using the dress fitting as an excuse, and said I'd see him in the shop the next day.

I unzipped the dress from its plastic sheath and held it over my head, letting the silk slide down my body.

'How's it going in there?' demanded Patricia.

I turned to look in the mirror again. The light bounced off my lumpiest bits – my hips and the curve of my belly. And my bottom looked enormous. I might as well slap a 'wide load' sticker on it and reverse out of the cubicle making a beeping sound.

Hilda whipped back the curtain and I turned to see them all frowning at me.

'Perhaps, with a better bra?' ventured Hilda.

'Turn round,' instructed Patricia, circling a finger in the air. I turned.

'Mmm,' Patricia went on, 'definitely a better bra.'

'And no knickers,' said Mia.

'What?' I shrieked. 'We can't wear no knickers.'

'Why not?'

'Because it's your wedding. We can't go down the aisle of Claridge's commando. What if there's leaking?'

'Oh, Florence, really,' said Patricia, wrinkling her nose.

'I don't mind,' said Ruby.

'I do!'

'Florence, do stop fussing,' said my stepmother, as Hilda stepped forward and adjusted my dress while the others watched over their coffee cups. She pinned it at the back and along the right side of my body to stop it gaping around my chest, but the silk still didn't look right because it was pulled more tightly across my stomach. Oh, too bad. On the day itself I'd be carrying a small posy of roses so I could always try and hide my belly behind that.

*

Hugo and Rory were supposed to come back to Kennington that night. Mia had said it would be fun, that we could order a takeaway and all have it on the sofa, united in our hangovers. But in the end Hugo arrived home by himself.

'You just got out of prison?' said Ruby, laughing at him from the sofa. She and I were watching *Grand Designs* while Mia plucked her eyebrows upstairs.

'No,' he said hoarsely, leaning against the doorframe. 'Why?'

'I've never seen you look worse. What did they do to you?'

Hugo flinched as if in physical pain. 'This and that. Where's the wife?'

I shuddered. He'd only started calling her that recently but it irritated me every time.

'In her room,' said Ruby.

Hugo trudged upstairs and she looked across at me. 'I thought Rory was coming back?'

'He was but he's got to work,' I said, staring at a message

on my phone. Darling, heading to mine as I need to do some work on this European summit before tomorrow. And I couldn't possibly see you like this. I need to wash Prague off me. Speak tomorrow? R

'Borrr-ring,' said Ruby. 'Hey, since you've got your phone out, do you wanna see what we want from Deliveroo?'

She embarked on a ten-minute soliloquy about whether she felt more like pizza or Chinese while I tried to decipher why Rory's message left me feeling so deflated. Because I wasn't seeing him? Because it was Sunday evening? Because I was still fretting about what Cressida had told me? Or because what I really wanted was to be with someone who'd come over to scoop me up and ask about my weekend even if he was presenting to the frigging UN the next day?

We had pizza in the end and I paid for it, obviously.

*

'GOOD NEWS!' said Zach, running upstairs in the shop the next morning and flinging his arms into the air like an evangelical priest.

I narrowed my eyes at him. 'You've cleaned out the fridge?'

Zach shook his head.

'Someone has emailed you saying you are the sole beneficiary of a fifty-three-million-pound will after everyone else died in mysterious circumstances?'

Another shake.

'They've discovered a new and entirely painless way to remove tattoos?'

'Very amusing. But no. The agent's interested in your Curtis story.'

'WHAT? You're kidding me. Zach, don't joke about this.'

'I'm not joking, I literally just got an email from her. She likes it and says could I put you guys in touch.'

I put my palms to my forehead. 'This is mad. I never thought... I didn't think... I—'

Zach was jumping from one foot to the other, grinning at me. 'So can I do it? Can I put you in touch?'

'Course,' I said, with a laugh. 'I mean, yes please, thank you.'

He reached his hand out to high-five me across the counter and our palms slapped just as Norris appeared, pinching a red furry jacket between his fingers and holding it out in front of him.

'Zachary, what is this and why was it addressed to me?'

Zach's face became more serious. 'Ah, yes. That's your outfit for Thursday evening. Part of it, anyway.'

'What am I expected to do with it?'

'Wear it, Uncle Norris. Where's the rest of it? There should be some trousers. And a belt. And a hat.'

Eugene sniggered from the history section.

'Funny, is it?' said Norris, spinning round and glaring at him.

'Ignore Eugene,' said Zach, 'he's got his own costume.'

'Excuse me,' said Eugene, hurrying over. 'I didn't know anything about this.'

Zach leant back against the shelves. 'It was going to be a surprise but seeing as we're all so uptight and anti-fun in this shop, I'll tell you. I've bought us all costumes for Thursday.'

'What am I?' Eugene asked warily.

'You are an elf.'

I snorted from behind the till.

Zach raised his eyebrows at me. 'Florence, I wouldn't get too cocky because you're a Christmas pudding.'

'Ha!' barked Eugene.

'And Norris is Father Christmas.'

Norris grunted.

'What about you?' I asked. 'You can't be the only one who gets away with it.'

'No, you're right,' said Zach. 'I will be attending the party as Mr Snowman.'

'How many kids are coming?'

'About fifty at the moment. So I thought you, Uncle Norris, could be stationed in a chair up here and hand out presents from your sack? Then a few carols with mulled wine and mince pies. If you guys don't mind being in charge of handing those out? They're being delivered on Thursday afternoon.'

'What sack?' said Norris.

'I've bought you one. And presents. Don't worry.'

'How much is all this costing me?'

'Very cheap. All made in China.'

'Zachary...' Norris growled again.

He held his hands in the air. 'I'm joking, I'm joking. Sort of. But come on, where's the community spirit? That's what we need. And Florence, I'm going to email this agent back right now and loop you in.'

He bounded back downstairs and I wondered whether my Christmas pudding costume might, in fact, be more flattering than my bridesmaid dress.

I walked to Rory's after work, happily weaving my way through the shoppers, untroubled by their lethargic pace. Zach had emailed the agent. Jacinta, she was called, and she'd emailed me straight back suggesting a coffee the following week. Just seeing her name and email signature in my inbox – Jacinta Ewing, Millward & Middleton Literary Agents Ltd – gave me a kick.

'Darling, how brilliant!' said Rory, when I'd explained the news. 'Although…'

'What?'

'It's just a meeting.'

'I know. But a meeting's more than I've ever had before.'

'Of course. I just don't want you to get your hopes up.'

I felt squashed but didn't want to let it sour the evening. I wanted one night where I didn't feel a spasm of insecurity about this relationship. One night where it felt like it had at the start.

'How was Prague?' I asked, laying my head on his shoulder. We were sitting on the sofa while Rory wrote emails on his laptop.

He mumbled under his breath as he typed.

'Rory, how was it? The stag?'

'Sorry, darling, so much to catch up on. And it was good. Not much to report. Beer, strippers, the usual.'

'Strippers?'

'Got you! No, no strippers. Just beer, and tequila, and some god-awful club I can hardly remember. But it was fun. He's not that bad, you know, your future brother-in-law.' He turned to kiss me on the cheek before looking back at his screen. 'Can you give me, five, maybe ten minutes to get through these and then I'm all yours.'

We had sex on his sofa as soon as he'd finished. Wordlessly, he placed his laptop on the floor and put his hand under my chin to tilt my face towards his. I was so hungry I almost protested to say could we eat and chat first, but then I felt my body respond to his touch. It was hunger of a different kind. Women are often accused of using sex as a weapon, a devious ploy, but Rory could do it too. He was like a sex wizard, I thought, which almost made me laugh into his mouth. But then his hand slipped under my T-shirt and I gasped instead. I just had to keep my eyes open throughout so Zach didn't appear in my head again. But that was all right, right? That was normal?

*

My Christmas pudding costume was absurd. I looked more like the turd emoji. The brown felt hung like a sack around me while on my head was a brown hat with a red felt berry stitched on top of it.

I stepped out of the way as the loo door opened and Eugene emerged in a green and red suit, with a pair of green booties that curled at the toe.

'Paaahahaha, you look ridiculous!' I said, reaching to jingle the bell on the top of his pointy hat.

'Stop it,' he said, batting me away. 'What am I supposed to do with these?' He held out a pair of large plastic ears.

'Put them on.'

He sighed and stepped in front of the mirror. 'Rory coming tonight?'

'Nope, he's got work.'

Eugene tutted. 'That's a pity.'

'Not really. Would you fancy this?'

He turned to look at me. 'No. Not even if you were the last Christmas pudding on earth.'

'Exactly. And also it's always weird between him and Zach. Easier if they stay apart.'

Eugene tutted again in the mirror as he fiddled with his ears. 'So stupid. It's just jealousy.'

'What's Rory got to be jealous of? Literally nothing.'

He caught my eye in the mirror.

'What? He hasn't! Zach is my boyfriend and Rory's my colleague. It couldn't be clearer.'

'You mean Rory's your boyfriend and Zach's your colleague?'

'Yes,' I snapped, 'obviously that's what I meant.'

'Knock, knock, can I come in?' said Zach from outside the bathroom.

'Course,' I replied, shooting a warning glance at Eugene.

He opened the door and both Eugene and I burst out laughing. If possible, Zach looked even sillier than us. His face and a couple of stray black curls poked out from a small hole in a white-felt costume that was too short for him. It covered his head and ran down his body, stopping just below his knees so his jeans and Doc Martens stuck out underneath. On his nose was a fake carrot.

'You guys look great! Hottest Christmas pudding I ever saw.'

'Thanks,' I said, blushing before flapping my arms. 'It's literally quite hot. Shall we go up?'

He nodded and we headed for the shop floor where the world's grumpiest Father Christmas was sitting in his chair, one leg over the other while his boot jiggled irritably in the air.

'Norris!' said Eugene, 'I've been a very good boy, can I have a present?'

Norris paused and glanced at us and I saw a smile twitch at the corners of his mouth before he erupted with a big belly laugh. 'Zachary, I don't know why I allowed you in this place. How's being dressed like the cast of a pantomime going to help anything?'

'Less of the defeatism, please, Santa.' Zach waddled around the shop, his legs restricted by the white felt, checking that everything was in order. Behind the till was an urn, warming the wine. Eugene had laid out glasses and two trays of Lidl mince pies on a table next to it.

'Sack ready?' Zach asked Norris. It was propped against his armchair. I'd spent all afternoon wrapping crap presents in tissue paper – small bouncy balls, novelty pencils, plastic yo-yos, dinosaur keyrings and neon putty that looked extremely poisonous.

'You need to be friendlier than that,' Zach said, still standing over his uncle. 'Try a smile.'

Norris raised his upper lip.

'Not that far. Dial it down a bit. Not so many teeth.'

Parents started arriving with their children and prodded them towards Norris. Eugene and I watched from behind the till, snorting disloyally.

'Merry Christmas!' he'd say stiffly to each one. 'Would you like a present from my sack?'

'He's got to stop saying that,' muttered Eugene. 'He'll be arrested.'

The small child looked terrified but, behind them, their pushy parent urged them on as if it was sports day: 'Come on, Orangina/ Archibald/Persimmon! Tell Santa what you want for Christmas!'

Little Orangina would perk up at this point and declare she wanted a real-life unicorn.

'I'm not sure I have one of those,' Norris replied, with a chuckle. 'But why don't you put your hand in here and see what you can find?'

'Seriously, I'm going to call the police in a minute,' hissed Eugene.

I hit him on the arm. 'Don't ruin it. This is nice.'

It was better than nice. It was magical. Zach had run white fairy-lights around the shelves and Nat King Cole was burbling from the speakers. The shop glowed through the windows, which encouraged more and more people inside, off the damp pavements.

Having texted me earlier in the week, asking if she could

bring 'a date', I spied Jaz arriving with Dunc, plus Maya and George. I grinned and waved at them across the crowd but had to stay put because there were so many punters queuing to buy books. I doled out the wine while Eugene put the sales through the till. I quite forgot that I was dressed like a pudding and he shook his head, making a little jingle every time a customer reached for their paper bag.

In another corner, underneath the gardening books, stood some of the NOMAD crew. Seamus had swapped his tatty old overcoat tied with string for a tweed jacket and looked like he'd brushed his hair, a Christmas miracle. Lenka and Mary were sipping nervously at their mulled wine and Elijah was frowning suspiciously at a mince pie. I'd never seen any of them outside our classroom before and felt a swell of pride that I'd brought them together here.

Although really this was all thanks to Mr Snowman. Every now and then I glanced up to see him taking pictures, his camera over his ludicrous plastic nose, and felt grateful. Not just for injecting energy back into the shop but for livening us all up. Even Norris seemed to be enjoying himself, smiling at Zach's camera less like a murderer.

'Carol singers are here,' said Eugene, elbowing me and pointing through the windows at a group of Chelsea Pensioners waiting outside.

'ZACH!' I shouted over the throng, before pointing at them.

He carved his way towards the door, his white head bobbing above the others. One by one he shook their hands, then turned back and stood in the doorway of the shop.

'EXCUSE ME, LADIES AND GENTLEMEN! Could everyone make way for our carol singers? No, not you, Father Christmas, stay right there. But if everyone else could make space, that would be grand.'

Shoppers, parents and children huddled together. Some sat on the stairs, others were pressed up against the bookshelves. I told a couple of people to lift their kids on the counter so they could see. It was as crammed as the Central Line at 8.01 on a Monday morning, just more festive.

I bent under the till to turn Nat off and poured myself a glass of wine as the Chelsea Pensioners shuffled themselves into a semicircle. One of them was holding a trumpet. There was a brief silence and then they were off, into a warbly rendition of 'God Rest Ye Merry Gentleman'.

Then the trumpeter picked up his weapon for a rendition of 'Hark! The Herald Angels Sing'. We joined in for the chorus, getting louder every time. And I don't know whether it was the wine, the music, the old soldiers singing in front of us or my hormones (a combination?), but I suddenly felt almost overwhelmed with emotion. I looked around the shop, from Jaz standing with Dunc on her hip, to the trumpeter parping his way through the last verse, and all my anxieties – about this place, about Rory, about counting and the colour of cars – seemed insignificant. For a brief moment, my head felt more spacious, empty of worry. I filled up my glass again and, looking across the shop, caught Zach's eye, grinning at him as the geriatrics launched into 'O Come, All Ye Faithful'.

They finished to loud cheers and calls for an encore. Zach

rattled a bucket for donations, which was passed round while they did a final number, 'Away in a Manger'.

'Cor, there are a few fifties in here,' said Eugene, peering into the bucket when it reached the till.

'It's for them, not us. Look, put that down and give them these.' I passed him a tray of glasses steaming with wine. The carollers' average age must have been ninety-four and I imagined they needed a sugar hit before one of them keeled over. It was a sweetly comical sight – Norris in his Father Christmas outfit drinking with old soldiers while a snowman shuffled around them taking photos.

I watched from the counter as Eugene handed out the drinks, and Zach lowered his camera and pushed his way back towards me.

'Not bad, huh?'

'The singing?'

He shook his head and smiled down at me. 'The whole party.'

I nudged his arm with my shoulder. 'Yes, OK, OK, well done. Good work.'

'Well done *all* of us,' he said emphatically, putting his arm around my shoulders and pulling me into him. 'Teamwork.'

I rested against his chest for a second but sprang back again at the sight of Jaz coming through the crowd, hand-in-hand with Dunc.

'Like your outfit, babe,' she said, a wide grin spreading across her face. 'Dunc, look, what's Auntie Florence wearing?'

He pointed at the berry on my head. 'Are you meant to be Rudolph?'

I laughed. 'No, not quite. I'm a Christmas pudding. But good guess. How are you guys doing?'

'Ace. We had a nice little sing, didn't we, Dunc?'

He nodded and then looked shyly up at Zach. 'But I like your snowman outfit best of all.'

Zach laughed. 'Thanks, buddy.'

'You want another drink?' I asked Jaz.

'Yes, please,' she said, waggling her empty glass at me.

I topped it up and nodded at George standing across the shop with Maya, talking to Norris. 'How's it going?'

Jaz's entire face erupted in a smile. 'Oh, Floz, he's such a sweetheart.'

I glanced at Dunc but he was distracted by Zach, who'd crouched down and was showing him animal pictures on his phone. 'Have you done it?' I whispered.

She shook her head. 'We were supposed to have a date this week but something came up in his office, so I think tonight might be the night. They're coming back to mine for a sleepover.'

'What's he do?'

She shrugged. 'Something with computers. Actually, talking of sleepovers, can I bring Dunc to the hotel on Saturday morning? I'll just sit him down with an iPad somewhere while I primp you.'

'Course. I'm sharing a room with Ruby but Mia's got the next one so there'll be loads of space.'

'Great.' She had a swig of wine. 'How's the mood ahead of the big day?'

'Mia hasn't eaten anything apart from apples all week, and Patricia's emailing us hourly weather updates and shrieking about the rain even though it's all inside, so, pretty much as expected.'

She lowered her glass. 'And where's Rory?'

'Work. He says he's got loads to do before this weekend and we've got the rehearsal tomorrow afternoon and then drinks, so I get it.'

Jaz raised an eyebrow at me and then caught Dunc's hand as it snuck towards the mince pie tray on the till. 'Hold it right there, my friend, that's enough.'

'What a GRINCH,' said Zach, scooping the small boy into the air. He tipped him upside down to loud squeals.

'Careful, you don't want sick all over that,' said Jaz, nodding at Zach's white costume.

Zach put him down again and Dunc tugged on Jaz's coat sleeve.

'Mum, Mum,' he said. 'Zach's showed me photos of his holiday. Can we go to...' He stopped, stuck on a word.

'Patagonia,' said Zach.

'Can we go there, Mum? Please? They have whales and dolphins and eagles.'

Jaz laughed. 'Maybe, although it sounds a bit expensive.' Then she looked at Zach. 'What holiday is this? You going for Christmas?'

'An extended holiday. Few months, probably, taking pictures.'

'Serious? I thought you meant a hotel and a pina colada kind of trip,' said Jaz, flicking her eyes from Zach to me.

'No, jetting off with my camera for an adventure at seven o'clock on Saturday.'

'Can we go, Mum?' Dunc pleaded.

'Maybe one day,' she said, before draining her glass, 'but right now, we need to go home.'

'For your sleepover?' I said, raising my eyebrows at her.

She picked up Dunc's little hand. 'Exactly. Come on, let's go get George and Maya.'

She and Dunc said goodbye to Zach, then she turned to me. 'See you Saturday morning.'

I nodded and watched as she made her way to George's side. She put a hand on his back and said something whereupon he nodded and shook hands with Norris, then waved at me.

'Thank you,' he mouthed across the shop. He prodded Maya to do the same and then they all left, the last of the punters to go. Jaz winked at me through the shop window as they walked down the street. She looked so happy.

At a shout from the front door – 'Ho, ho, ho!' – we all turned to look at Norris, who'd spun the open sign to closed and was grinning at us.

'Oh, hello, Father Christmas has perked up,' said Eugene.

'He has,' said Norris, pulling off his hat and rubbing his hair so the white tufts stuck up like meringue peaks. 'And do you know why?'

'You weren't arrested for indecency?'

Norris shook his head and clapped his hands together. 'That man. That man! He's just saved us.'

'What man?'

'That man,' said Norris, whose face had turned so puce I thought he might explode. I'd never seen him look so cheerful. 'George something who was here with Florence's friend.'

'Spencer?'

Norris nodded. 'Yes, that's it, George Spencer. He's an internet millionaire who founded some shopping site.'

'What shopping site?' I shrieked.

He flapped a hand in the air. 'Don't ask me. I don't know anything about these things, as you all know. But he's offered to pay our lease. Lives round the corner and thinks it's important that we stay open. Daughter's a big fan of reading, apparently.'

'You're kidding?' said Zach.

'He can't be a millionaire, he looks about eleven years old,' I added, thinking of George's smooth face and nerdy spectacles. 'Jaz just said he works in computers.'

'Exactly,' said Norris, still nodding furiously. 'Some shopping business that Google's just bought for a fortune and he wants to help us out. It was all thanks to the petition, apparently.' He bent over to pour himself another drink and raised his glass at me.

I shook my head in disbelief. Jaz was unknowingly dating a tech millionaire, and a modest tech millionaire at that.

We all glanced around one another in stunned silence, before Eugene leapt in the air and whooped, and we all followed suit, our arms over one another's shoulders. I winced as wine from various glasses spilled to the floorboards but told myself not to ruin the moment.

'So thank you all very much for all your efforts,' said Norris, once we'd calmed down. 'Because it's worked and I couldn't… I can't… I'm not sure I would ha—' He paused and blinked around at all of us.

'You all right, Norris?' asked Eugene.

'I'm fine,' he said, clapping himself on the chest and coughing. 'I'm just ever so grateful.'

'I can't get over this,' said Zach. 'We need to celebrate. Excuse me, elf,' he said, shuffling behind the till.

'What you doing?' asked Eugene.

Zach pulled his phone from his pocket, plugged it into the lead and the opening bars of Mariah Carey's 'All I Want for Christmas is You' tinkled over us.

We drank the urn dry of wine so Norris went downstairs to retrieve a dusty bottle of whiskey from his office. We drank that, too, even though I hated whiskey. I ate six mince pies while we danced around the hardback table to Wham! and Shakin' Stevens, then more Nat King Cole and Mariah Carey again because it was Eugene's favourite. If you'd passed the shop and seen a large snowman twirl a Christmas pudding under his arm while an elf moonwalked – very badly – back and forth against the floorboards you might have worried you were hallucinating. It was the perfect evening until I remembered Harry and started collecting up glasses, carrying them downstairs to wash up.

Zach dried while I washed and we hummed 'Hark! The Herald Angels Sing'.

'You packed?'

'Nah, I'll shove a couple of black T-shirts into my bag on Saturday morning.'

'We'll miss you,' I said as I handed him another glass. Declaring this collectively, on behalf of the shop, felt less intense than admitting it was me, personally, who'd miss him.

'Will you?' he said, wiping his hands on the tea towel.

'Course. Although I won't miss tidying up after you,' I added, and because I was tipsy and it seemed like a good idea, I scooped up a palm of bubbles and blew them at him.

Zach laughed, wiped them off his cheek and then we smiled at one another just long enough for it to feel weird. My cheeks went hot, and it was as if all the air in the small galley space had been sucked out of it.

'Come on, got to finish this lot,' I said, turning back to the washing-up bowl, embarrassed, feeling as if I had to look anywhere apart from at him.

'Why are you with him?' he said quietly.

'What?'

Zach didn't answer immediately. He just looked at me in the same way as before, the way which made me feel as if he could almost see inside me. 'With Rory. Why?'

'What do you mean? Because he's my boyfriend, that's why. Come on, dry this.' I handed him another wine glass.

He dried it in silence while I swished suds over a plate, trying not to feel awkward. From upstairs came the muffled shouts of Norris and Eugene belting out 'Joy to the World'.

'The guy is a selfish jerk.'

'Zach…'

'Where is he now?' he asked, spinning to face me. 'If he's so great, why wasn't he here tonight? Why is he never here for you?'

'Zach, I'm not a child that needs a minder. He's got work.'

He clenched his fists and growled. 'Jesus, Florence, you just deserve so much better. You're too good for him, and I wish you could see that.'

'Zach—'

But he ignored me, his voice getting louder. 'You think that he's everything you want because he dresses like an Edwardian and talks like a despotic medieval king. But he's going to squash you.'

'Zach, seriously, this is very dramatic,' I said, trying to lighten the atmosphere. I could sense my fear of any difficult, emotional conversation flex itself inside me.

'I'm going away on Saturday, I've got to be dramatic! Listen, when I first met you, I thought you were the weirdest, most uptight person I'd ever come across.'

'Thanks very much.'

'You're welcome. But then I got to know you, and I realized that underneath that weirdness and your genuinely astonishing obsession with mugs, you were also the kindest, sweetest, most loyal person I've ever met. And he's taking advantage of that.'

'Zach—'

'You don't love him, do you?'

I glanced at the lino floor, sticky with slopped coffee stains, and made a mental note to mop it on Monday. 'I... I'm not... I don't know.'

He shook his head. 'You don't, I know you don't.'

I felt a flare of anger. 'Why are you saying this all now?'

'Because I can't watch him eat away at you.'

'He won't, he doesn't. He's just busy. He's got a serious job instead of—'

'Instead of what? Taking pictures? Working for his uncle?'

'I wasn't going to say that, course I wasn't,' I mumbled, shamed by Zach's hurt expression.

We were interrupted by my phone vibrating in my pocket with a message. **Leaving office now and heading back to mine. Hope this evening was a veritable triumph. See you tomorrow my darling. R**

'I've got to go,' I said, suddenly desperate to get home to my own bed.

'Florence, please just think about *you*. And what *you* want for once.' He reached out and grabbed my arm, his fingers pressing into it.

'I've got to go,' I repeated, shaking his hand off.

'Fine,' he said, tersely. 'See you when I get back.'

I spun in the doorway, anguished at the idea that Zach and I could leave things like this, but also stuck, unsure what else I could do.

'Have a good trip,' I said, waving pathetically before running upstairs, saying goodbye to the others, who were slurring their way through 'Good King Wenceslas'.

Bursting out of the shop, I drew in large gulps of cold, December air. It was dark, nearly midnight, and the pavements were black with rain, but I walked the whole way home, rolling lines of the conversation around my head.

CHAPTER ELEVEN

ON SATURDAY MORNING, IN room number 432, I heard the hotel door click shut and Ruby climb into bed next to me, burrowing under the duvet covers like a wriggly child. It was still dark. There must be hours of night left. I closed my eyes again. No point in spending the night in Claridge's, in a bed as soft as candy floss with ninety-three pillows, only to be woken up early.

'Flo,' she hissed.

I ignored her.

'FLO!'

'Mmm.'

'You awake?'

'No.'

'I need to tell you something.'

I sighed and rolled over. 'What? Where have you been?'

'In Jeremy's room.'

Jeremy was one of Hugo's ushers, an American who looked like a young Arnold Schwarzenegger: big forehead, wide mouth. After last night's wedding rehearsal in the ballroom, the wedding party (my family, Hugo's family, plus select guests) had gathered in the bar for drinks. Hugo's family had left for dinner elsewhere while mine remained drinking. It wasn't a late night – we'd ordered bar snacks and decided to call it a night just after 10 p.m. All, that is, apart from Ruby, who was by that point sitting at a corner table with Jeremy, also staying in the hotel having flown in from New York.

I guessed that it was around 4 a.m. and didn't feel I needed to know the specifics of Ruby's escapades with Jeremy the usher right now. 'Can't it wait until morning?'

'It is morning.'

It couldn't be. It was as dark as a coal mine in that room. Ruby turned on a lamp. I clapped a hand over my eyes.

'Look,' she said, and I peered through my fingers to see her phone screen. It was 7.32 a.m. I glanced at the windows; the blackout blinds had tricked me.

'Listen,' she said, 'I need to tell you something.'

It was like sharing a room with a hyperactive 5-year-old. 'What?'

Ruby suddenly looked very solemn. 'I slept with Jeremy last night…'

'I guessed.'

'No, but that's not what I need to tell you.'

I frowned. 'What? You're freaking me out.'

She winced at me. 'He had a video on his phone.'

'O-K…'

'Of the stag. A video someone took in Prague.'

'Hugo's stag?'

She nodded.

'Of what?'

She winced again. 'Of this,' she said, offering me her phone.

I pressed play and heard rowdy male shouts and someone panting. The picture was blurry so I held the phone screen closer to my face, then grimaced and held it back out to her.

'Ruby, this is porn. Why are you showing me porn at seven thirty in the morning?'

'It's not porn, look!' She held up the phone to me and that was when I realized. It was Hugo, sitting in a chair, while a woman in a very small pair of red sequinned knickers rubbed her bottom against his groin.

'What's wrong with her nipples? Why's she got corn plasters on them? I can't watch this.' I tried to hand the phone back again.

'You have to!' instructed Ruby.

Reluctantly, I dragged my eyes back to the screen as the dancer turned to face Hugo and pushed one of her breasts in his face.

'What's she doing?'

'Watch it!' said Ruby, nodding at the phone.

I tutted as Hugo's hands reached around and clasped her bottom, pulling her towards him, then the dancer stepped back again to laddy cheers.

'They're marshmallows,' Ruby explained. 'On her nipples. Look, they're gone now. Hugo bit them off. But keep watching.'

'Do I have to? I need a coffee.' I looked around the room as if a waiter with a cafetière would spring up from behind a piece of furniture. This wasn't the wake-up call I'd envisaged.

'Yes, look.' Ruby nodded at the phone again as the woman in the spangly knickers dropped to her knees between Hugo's legs and unzipped his flies. She lowered her mouth and I flung the phone on the duvet as if it had scalded my hand. 'Rubes, I'm not watching that.'

From the end of the bed, as the video continued, I could still hear the laddy cheers floating towards us.

Ruby reached for the phone, pressed stop and we both sat frozen on the bed.

'Quite impressed Hugo had it in him, to be honest,' I said, after a few beats of silence. 'But does it… I mean… does he…?'

'Finish?' said Ruby, as if she was discussing a running race. 'Yes, he does. And then, well, sorry Flo, but it gets worse.'

'Worse? How can it get worse? How can there be anything worse than discovering a video of our almost brother-in-law getting blown off by a woman who looks like a lion tamer on the day he's getting married to our sister?'

'Shhhh,' she said, inclining her head at the adjoining door to the room where Mia was, hopefully, fast asleep. She held the phone up but I batted it down.

'I'm not watching any more.'

'OK, but…' she stopped.

'What?'

'Rory's in it too.'

'WHAT?'

'Shhhhh!' Then she tapped at her phone again and I saw a flash of the lion tamer grinding herself into Rory before I looked in the other direction.

'Rubes, I really can't… I just don't want to see.'

The room went quiet again.

'How does she get the marshmallows to stay on?' I mused.

'Seriously? That's your main question.'

'No, not my main one.' I glanced at her. 'I presume Rory, er, gets there too?'

She nodded. 'And you can hear him shout "Cowabunga!" Do you want to see?'

'No, I really don't,' I said, sighing and leaning back on the suede headboard. 'OK, a few questions. Firstly, how did you find out about this?'

'Jeremy was drunk and he thought it would be funny to show me.'

'What a comedian. But how have you got it on your phone?'

'From his phone this morning. He was passed out so I held his finger to the screen.'

'Top work, Agatha Christie. OK, and my second question is, do we show Mia?'

'Yes, obviously.'

'On her wedding day?'

'We've got to, haven't we? You'd want to know, right?'

I sighed again. 'Yeah, I guess.'

'Are you going to say anything to Rory?' she asked more gently. 'Are you all right?'

I pressed my lips together and thought for a moment. I was waiting for a wave of anger, of sadness at the knowledge that my boyfriend bit a sugary snack off another woman's breast before she gave him a blow job. But I didn't feel particularly angry. Instead, I just felt the tiniest twinge of relief. All the anxiety, all the obsession with keeping hold of him suddenly felt absurd. I'd done everything I could – seen a love coach, worn uncomfortable knickers, put on a blindfold, pretended that I'd enjoyed myself at his parents' house, gone to that awful ball, listened to him shout 'Cowabunga!' again and again but none of it was right. That was the very simple, very evident truth, and all it had taken was a naked woman wearing a pair of sequinned knickers for me to realize. The revelation made me snort with laughter.

'What's so funny?' said Ruby, frowning at me.

'You'll see,' I said, leaning across for my own phone, charging on the bedside table. I found Rory's name and hit the green button.

It rang a few times before he answered, groggily. 'Morning, my little *chou-fleur*, you're up early.'

'Please don't *chou-fleur* me,' I said coolly. 'What happened in Prague?'

I heard the sound of sheets rustling in the background and Rory coughed to clear his throat. 'What do you mean?'

'Did you or did you not get…' I paused, unable to say it aloud. What was the least bad expression? 'Oral sex from a stripper?'

'Florence, darling. How can you possibly think that I wou—'

'There's a video.'

His voice went up an octave. 'What video?'

'Hugo's friend Jeremy has it,' I replied, trying to stay calm. 'Of you and Hugo cavorting about like a pair of FUCKING TEENAGERS.'

The anger had started to hit; Rory's arrogance, the audacity to deny it and his feeble protestation all seemed so tawdry.

He paused at the end of the phone. I could almost hear his thoughts processing: how do I get out of this? How do I calm her down?

'Florence, I'm sorry,' he said eventually. 'It was a very foolish thing to do. Boys being boys. Can you forgive me?'

'I don't think so.'

His voice became more serious at this. 'Florence, it was a stag weekend. These things happen.'

'Oh, these things happen, do they? That's interesting. Because what I don't understand is how someone who's so desperate to be prime minister would allow himself to be filmed getting fellated by a stranger in novelty knickers?'

Beside me, Ruby punched the air with her fist.

Rory's voice went up another octave. 'Florence, please don't do anything silly. I mean it!'

'Is that a threat?'

'Just… just… just please can you delete that video? I'm sorry, it was a mistake. A silly, silly mistake. Hugo made me do it.'

'Oh, Hugo made you do it, did he?'

'Yes, yes! I didn't want to, honestly.'

'Rory Dundee,' I started, 'you are a spineless, self-obsessed, selfish *wanker.*'

'Florence…'

'I hate your poncey clothes.'

'Florence, please…'

'I hate your snobbery and your pretentious friends.'

'Florence, come on, I don't thi—'

'I think you're arrogant and smug and I would never vote for you to be prime minister. And I still don't even really understand what the home secretary does! Don't even think about coming to this wedding. COWABUNGA YOURSELF!'

I hung up and chucked my phone on the bed, my heart hammering under my T-shirt like a war drum.

Ruby whooped. 'Flo! I've never seen you like that. I'm proud of you.'

I laughed and put a hand to my chest to try and calm it. 'Yeah, I'm quite proud of myself. That felt good. *I* feel good.'

'So you should.'

'Right?' I paused, trying make sense of the thoughts racing through my head. 'I suppose everything I told him had been dawning on me for a while – he was pompous and selfish, and those stupid, stupid clothes – but I was too hooked on having someone.' I looked up from the bed to her face as if for guidance. 'I guess I was too hooked on having a boyfriend?'

She nodded and was about to reply when the double doors between our room and Mia's crashed open.

'What's all this shouting on my wedding day?' she said, stretching in the door, a Claridge's sleep mask pushed back on her head.

Ruby made a panicked face at me.

'It's my wedding day!' Mia said again, her arms still in the air, waiting for us to applaud her.

'Hurrah,' I bleated. Ruby stayed quiet.

Mia laughed and lowered her arms. 'Thanks for the

excitement, guys. Oh, I nearly forgot, hang on.' She turned back into her room and then skipped back towards us with two cellophane packets. Tucking one knee underneath her and sitting on the end of our bed, she held them out. 'I got you these.'

We opened them in silence. They were silky pink dressing gowns with 'sister-of-the-bride' embroidered on the back.

'You like?'

We both nodded.

'Good. But Jaz and the make-up artist are arriving in about an hour so if you want breakfast, order some now. I can't eat a thing but can someone order me a coffee?'

Ruby lowered her dressing gown. 'Mia, can we talk to you about something?'

'What?'

'I got talking to Jeremy last night.'

Mia clapped her hands together. 'Did you? I thought you'd like him. Apparently his apartment in New York is insane.'

'I'm sure, but ca—'

'I think he's sitting next to you at dinner, actually, I can't remember the exact seating plan but I think he might be.'

'Mia, forget the seating plan.'

'Or maybe I put you next to Dan. Did you meet Dan last night? He's the one who's got quite a big nose but I don't think you should be put off by that because apparently he's got the most enorm—'

'MIA! Can you listen?' shouted Ruby.

'What? Don't shout at me on my wedding day.'

Ruby took a deep breath. 'I got talking to Jeremy and he showed me a video.'

'What kind of video?'

'From the stag. From Hugo's stag.'

'Of what?'

Ruby glanced sideways at me as if for help.

'It's of a club,' I went on. 'At least I think it's a club. It's not that clear because the picture's fuzzy. It could be a bar. Or a restaurant. Or maybe it was in a hotel r—'

'Oh for God's sake,' interrupted Ruby. 'I'm just going to show it to you.'

She held out her phone and Mia watched the video in silence while I winced at the repetition of all those cheers.

'Mia…' started Ruby, when the video finished. But she held a hand up in the air.

'I don't want to hear it.'

'But wha—'

Mia held Ruby's phone back out to her and looked at her watch. 'Flo, you should get in the shower.'

'WHAT?' shouted Ruby. 'Aren't we going to discuss this?'

'I don't want to talk about it on my wedding day. Don't ruin it for me, Rubes. Flo, shower.'

Meekly, I stood up just as our door buzzed.

'I'll get it,' I said, grateful for a distraction. Any distraction.

'MORNING, DARLINGS!' said Patricia, pushing past me into our room. She was wearing a purple tracksuit and a turban. 'I can't believe one of my daughters is getting married. How are we all? Did you sleep well? Mia, sweetheart, you look pale. Have you had any breakfast?'

'No,' Mia replied, her voice flat. 'Could someone order me a coffee?'

'I will,' trilled Patricia. 'And shouldn't someone get in the shower? The hairdresser's arriving any second. Florence, don't just stand there. Why don't you go first?'

'I'm going,' I said, relishing the prospect of locking myself in the bathroom for a few minutes.

The shower knobs were more complicated than a spaceship but eventually I'd sorted out the temperature and stood under the hot water, my head reeling. A lot had happened in a matter of minutes. No more Rory. As I bent over to shave my legs, I tried to gauge whether I felt sad about this. Did I feel like crying? I scrunched up my eyes, testing myself. Nope, not a single tear. My main emotion seemed to be a sense of liberation. For weeks, I'd been trying to convince myself that I was in love when, really, it turned out having the wrong boyfriend was way more complicated than not having a boyfriend at all. I opened my mouth to laugh in the shower and choked as the water hit the back of my throat, but this only made me laugh harder. I leant against the tiles for support, hysterical with relief.

Then I thought of Mia. Poor Mia. Her situation was more complicated. But she wanted to get married so much. Maybe a grimy stag-do blow job wasn't a red line for her? She must love Hugo enough to overlook it, I reflected as I towel-dried my hair. It seemed strange but there's no accounting for taste, is there? Even Piers Morgan is married.

Back in our room, a waiter had arrived with a trolley of breakfast. Plus two pots of coffee and a bottle of champagne. Patricia waved a glass at me when I emerged from the bathroom, wrapped in a towel.

'Drink, Florence, darling? I thought we should.'

'Already?' I glanced at my watch; it was 8.02.

'It's a celebration. Here,' she said, pouring another glass. 'Just a little one.'

'Thanks,' I said, taking it with the hand I wasn't using to keep my towel up. 'What's with the turban?'

'Deep conditioning treatment. Oh, this is such a happy day. A happy, happy day. Ruby, you're very quiet. Are you all right?'

'I'm fine, Mum, stop fussing.'

'Where's Mia?' I asked.

'Having a bath with her coffee. Seems a bit nervous. Shall we put some music on? That might jolly everyone up.'

While Patricia fiddled with the television remote control, trying to find a radio station, I retrieved the seamless knickers I'd negotiated wearing with Mia, then knotted my pink dressing gown around my waist.

I threw myself back down on the bed next to Ruby. 'You mentioned anything?' I asked quietly while Patricia stood with her back to us. She'd knotted her pink dressing gown over the purple tracksuit. 'Mother-of-the-bride' was embroidered across it.

'No, obviously not,' Ruby muttered.

A few minutes later, there was another buzz on the door as Jaz, Dunc and Mel the make-up artist arrived.

Patricia opened the door. 'Morning,' she said, before pirou-
etting for them, her champagne glass in hand. 'I'm the mother
of the bride. Do come in.'

She stepped aside as Jaz and Mel wheeled in their suitcases
of work tools and Dunc traipsed behind them.

'Hiya, babe,' she said, as I jumped up to hug her. 'How we
doing?'

'All right, I think.'

'Bridal party ready?' she said, looking expectantly at each of
us as Mia appeared from her room after her bath. She looked
clean and pink-cheeked, not remotely like a bride who'd just
watched a video of her groom ejaculate into another woman's
mouth. I briefly closed my eyes at the thought.

'We're ready,' Mia said smoothly. 'Can I get either of you
a coffee? Or tea? Croissant? Champagne?'

'Better not get started on the bottle yet otherwise you'll
look very odd going down the aisle,' said Jaz. 'But I'd love
a coffee, thanks. Mel?'

She was laying out brushes and bottles of foundation on
a side table. 'Mmm, coffee, please.'

'I'll do that,' said Mia. 'Flo, why don't you get going with
your hair? Let's do make-up in here and hair next door.'

'Sure,' I said, leading Jaz through to Mia's room. 'Dunc, do
you want to come and watch cartoons next door?'

He nodded and ran after us, jumping on the bed.

'I don't think so. Shoes off please,' Jaz told him before turning
back to me. 'So, how's it all been?' she asked, before unzipping
her bag. Out of it came round brushes, straight brushes, combs,

hairdryers, tongs, straighteners, bottles, tubes and long cans of hairspray. I sat on Mia's bed and quietly explained that morning's revelations while she laid them out on the dressing table.

'Fuck me, it's like a wedding off *Corrie*,' she said, once I'd finished.

'Yeah. Little bit.'

She lowered her voice to a whisper. 'But Mia seems fine?'

I shrugged. 'The show must go on.'

'And you're all right?' she asked, unravelling a hairdryer cord.

'Yeah, weirdly I really am. It's like the thing I was most dreading isn't that bad at all. I feel quite free.'

Jaz squinted at me from the corners of her eyes. 'Really?'

I nodded. 'Promise. I keep waiting to feel sad, for it to hit me. But maybe it won't?'

'Well, hallelujah!' she said, reaching her arms into the air, the hairdryer cord dangling from one hand. 'Don't get me wrong, he was nice to look at. But he wasn't the one for you. Why did he dress like that? And speak like that?' Jaz looked down her nose and mimicked him with a snooty voice. 'Oh hello, my name's Rory and I'm much better than you. Don't you know I'm going to be prime minister one day?'

'How come you never told me this?' I said, laughing and throwing a pillow at her.

'Because you were so obsessed with him, and that list of yours.' She made a moving mouth with her hand, snapping her fingers down against her thumb. 'The list this and the list that.' She dropped her hand. 'I couldn't tell you before, could I? I had to wait for you to work it out.'

'Well I have now.'

'Not all of it, I'll bet.'

I frowned. 'What d'you mean?'

'Never mind. Sit here, we need to get cracking.' She nodded at a chair in front of her.

'Did Mia send you references?' I asked.

'Only about a million of them. We're doing it half pinned back, wavy, with a couple of roses tucked into it.'

'Exactly.'

Jaz got going with the dryer. I wondered how Harry was getting on with his babysitter. Eugene keeps a very tidy flat in Stockwell where you had to use a coaster if he made you a cup of tea, but I'd persuaded him to look after Harry for the weekend by asking him to be the kitten's 'godfather'.

Eugene's entire head had turned maroon at this.

'Me? Really?' he'd asked, placing a hand on his chest.

'Yes, you, absolutely. I know you'll do it brilliantly.'

I'd carried Harry over in his basket the previous evening and Eugene opened the door waggling a knitted fish toy that he'd bought from the pet shop. I hoped the novelty of a fluffy ginger godson hadn't worn off yet.

My thoughts slid to Zach and I looked at my watch – 8.48. He'd be in the air now, in an uncomfortable seat eating a frozen bread roll on his way to Buenos Aires. The idea of him travelling further and further away from London every second made me feel a pang of regret. We hadn't communicated since the Christmas party. No call, no message from either of us to say goodbye. And knowing that he was now gone, that I wouldn't see him on Monday or be able to shout at him for putting a mug on a book, made me feel bleak. I could ring him in Patagonia and apologize, say he'd been right about Rory, but perhaps that was too needy? I'd be all right on my own again. Always had been. Buck up, Florence Fairfax, moping after a man never helped anyone.

I was distracted from thoughts of Zach by the sharp pain of a rose stem stabbing my scalp.

'Sorry,' said Jaz, as I shrank my head into my shoulders. 'But that's you done. Will you send Ruby in?'

Ruby and I swapped places: she sat in front of Jaz, I held my face up to Mel in the other bedroom. Mia was having her photo taken by Pierre, the society photographer. Patricia was into her second bottle of champagne.

The average Briton takes forty-seven minutes to get ready in the morning, although I can be up and out of the door in my sensible shoes in fifteen. But oh, the long, torturous agony of a wedding morning. Nothing is done in a hurry. It took an hour for Mel to plaster my face with orange paint and coats of mascara so heavy that my eyelashes felt like butterfly wings.

Next up was Patricia. While Ruby and I lay on one bed watching *The World's Wildest Animals* with Dunc, she bossed Mel about for an hour, then Jaz.

Meanwhile, Pierre took snaps of our shoes, of our bouquets, of our dresses in their hangers, of Patricia in curlers. He even photographed a tray of smoked salmon sandwiches that arrived as an early lunch. I tried to imagine who would care about this. Would one of Mia's descendants look back on the salmon with interest? 'Look! Here are the sandwiches that your great-great grandmother ate on her wedding morning!' It seemed unlikely.

Several hours on, we slithered into our dresses, and helped Mia into hers while Patricia stood and shouted at us. She was wearing a pale blue dress and jacket from Catherine Walker because that was where her idol, Carole Middleton, had bought her mother-of-the-bride outfit.

'CAREFUL! You're going to get foundation on the neckline. Florence, pay more attention, help her with her arm. No, not that arm, the other one.'

'You all right, Mia?' asked Ruby, crouching at her feet as she fanned the folds of the dress out.

'I'm perfect,' she replied, smiling in the mirror. She wasn't being immodest; she looked exquisite. The dress was made from a floral lace, with a tight bodice that fell into a wide skirt and trailed behind her. Tiny silk buttons ran up her back and its long sleeves. Jaz's hands fluttered around her face as she made sure the veil, made from the same ivory lace, was secured. Mia stood quite still and continued to gaze at herself in the mirror while we fussed around her. This was the moment she'd been waiting for her whole life and clearly nothing, not even a dancer in a sparkly thong, was going to ruin it.

Patricia started weeping as Dad arrived.

He stood in our room and gazed at Mia for a moment then reached for both her hands. 'I am so enormously proud of you.'

'Thanks, Dad,' Mia replied. She sounded robotic but I presumed it was nerves.

'I don't believe I've seen a more beautiful bride,' said Patricia.

'Nor will I again, probably.' She let out another little sob and clutched her tissue to her face.

Dad glanced from Patricia's champagne glass to the empty bottles lined up on the bedside table. Four of them now. 'Patricia, darling, why don't you go downstairs with the girls and Mia and I will follow?'

She nodded tearfully and Mel powdered Patricia's face while Ruby and I gathered up our bouquets. They were cream roses, exactly like the ones poking into our heads, studded with red berries and wrapped with a piece of red ribbon.

'Ready?' Ruby said, looking from Patricia to me.

I nodded and Patricia sniffed.

'OK, let's go. See you down there, guys,' Ruby said over her shoulder to Mia and Dad.

*

They took the lift (I walked down, trying not to break a sweat into the silk armpits) and we met again to wait in the corridor that led to the ballroom. Over Patricia's sniffs I could hear the murmur of guests, plus the string quartet pumping out something classical.

'Mum, this is a wedding, not a funeral. Get it together,' ordered Ruby.

The corridor was decorated with tall vases of lilies and white altar candles. I imagined Dad escorting Mia along it and her train catching fire, so that she walked down the ballroom aisle with her dress in flames. That was all we needed.

The registrar, a round lady called Mary, hurried out to us

from the ballroom. 'Hello, hello, don't you look lovely? You could be sisters!'

This momentarily halted Patricia's snivelling. 'Oh Mary, you are funny,' she said, clearly delighted.

'Are the others on their way?' Mary asked.

'Hope so,' muttered Ruby.

'Great stuff. I'll wait by the door so give me a nod when we're ready.'

Mary waddled back to the ballroom door just as the lift behind us opened to reveal Mia on Dad's arm. Dad was in tears now too.

'Henry,' sobbed Patricia, 'here, have my tissue.'

'For God's sake,' sighed Ruby. 'Sis, you look sensational. Good to go?'

She smiled nervously and nodded. We waited for our parents to wipe their eyes. Patricia was going first, making an entrance all by herself. I was next, then Ruby, followed by Dad and Mia.

'Right,' said Patricia, with a deep breath. 'I'm ready.'

Ruby gestured at Mary by the door, who disappeared into the ballroom and suddenly the string quartet started playing 'Ave Maria'.

'Off you go, Pat,' chivvied Ruby.

Patricia started walking with such oversized steps it was like watching a dressage horse.

'Good luck,' I whispered to Mia, before following my cantering stepmother.

I counted the window panes at the top of the ballroom as

I walked down the aisle, trying not to feel intimidated by the eyes watching me. Stomach in, chin up. From the front, Hugo winked at me and I pretended to smile back but I fear it was more a grimace. Under the chandelier, his hair shone with oil.

Having reached the front row, Patricia, Ruby and I turned to watch as Dad and Mia came down after us. Even I welled up then, although I wasn't sure whether the tears were for Mia or me. Her face radiated a level of happiness I couldn't imagine reaching myself.

Beside me, Patricia was now openly bawling.

At the top, Mia flung her arms around Dad before they separated and he joined our row.

Mary looked out at the congregation with a wide smile. 'Welcome, everyone, friends and family of Mia and Hugo. And what a special day it is here in this very beautiful hotel as we gather to celebrate this special moment for the couple. A couple of quick housekeeping notices and then I'll get on with it because some of you look thirsty.'

Polite laughter rippled around the room.

'Firstly, the bride and groom have asked that there be no photos while they exchange their vows, just to keep that moment sacred. But you may take as many photos as you like, and please do upload them to social media. There is a hashtag and it's, hang on...' Mary paused to look down at her notes and cleared her throat, '#MiagotHugoed, and you're all encouraged to use that.

'Now,' she said, in a more sombre voice, 'the place in which we are all met has been duly sanctioned for the celebration of marriages. You are here today to witness the joining in matrimony of Mia and Hugo.'

Here, Mary paused and gestured at the bride and groom in case anyone wasn't sure which was which. 'If any person present knows of any lawful impediment to this marriage, he or she should declare it now.'

Mary paused and her eyes swept the ballroom.

She smiled. 'Marvellous. Now that's done I nee—'

'I do,' said Mia.

Mary's smile fell and she leant in towards Mia. 'Sorry?'

'I have an impediment.'

'You, the bride, have an objection?' said Mary, looking confused.

Beside me, Patricia had frozen in horror. 'Darling, are you feeling all right?' She leant towards her daughter and hissed more quietly: 'I think you might be having some last-minute nerves.'

'Shut up, Mum,' said Mia, before turning back to Hugo. He looked like he was about to soil himself.

'You bastard,' she shouted. 'You miserable BASTARD.' She started battering his chest with her bouquet. 'No stripper, you said. NO STRIPPER! And then I'm shown a FUCKING video of you waving your penis around like a FUCKING LOLLIPOP.'

There were gasps behind me as Mary looked from Mia to Hugo like an ineffective boxing referee, her mouth gaping wide.

'Mia, wait, I can explain,' he yelped. 'Ow! Mia, I'm sorry, listen to me.'

'I'm never listening to you again, you fucking MORON,' she carried on. There was another thud as the bouquet scored a direct hit on Hugo's chest.

'Henry, don't just stand there, do something!' said Patricia.

'You pathetic WANKER!' Cream petals floated to the carpet as Mia's veil slipped down the back of her head.

'Mia, darling, please listen to me. OW! That really hurts.'

'Henry!' Patricia snapped again at Dad, who was frowning at the unfolding drama as if trying to weigh up the most diplomatic way to solve it.

'Oh, for Christ's sake, come on, Flo,' said Ruby, pulling me forward and stepping in between the happy couple.

'Time's up!' she announced, trying to snatch Mia's roses from her. 'Mia, put those down. Stop it. Give them to me.' Ruby wrapped her arms around Mia's waist to pull her back from Hugo. 'Flo, get the flowers.'

'YOU TOTAL TOSSER!' Mia screamed, throwing her bouquet to the ground as Ruby dragged her away and I stood, like a bouncer, holding one hand out at Hugo.

'Let me GO, Rubes,' said Mia. 'It's fine. Let me go.'

Ruby relinquished her grip and Mia took one last look at Hugo before gathering her lace skirt up in one hand and sweeping out of the ballroom. Ruby followed. I hurried after them as the stunned silence among the guests broke and excited chatter started.

'Henry! Why didn't you do anything?' I heard Patricia wail, as the lift doors opened and I followed Mia and Ruby in. It wasn't the moment to be fussing about stairs.

Mia didn't say anything until the doors had closed, then she burst into tears and Ruby wrapped her in a hug. 'It's OK,' she kept saying. 'It's OK, it'll be OK.'

We made it along the corridor and back into our room where Ruby pointed at a bottle of champagne in an ice bucket. I nodded and filled up a glass.

'Here we go. Drink this,' said Ruby, pulling back and handing it to Mia.

'I want to go home,' she said. Her mascara had started to run and I watched a tear roll down her cheeks towards the dress.

'OK, we can go home. Drink this and I'll pack up,' said Ruby, just as the door buzzed.

I opened it to see Dad and Patricia. She pushed straight past me and stood facing Mia, manicured hands on her hips. 'Darling, this is all very silly. There's no point in ruining today over a little tiff.'

Mia shook her head in silence, her eyes narrowed with anger. 'It's not a tiff. He's a lying, cheating, and actually incredibly boring bastard.' She raised the champagne flute to her mouth.

'A little high-jinks on a stag do never killed anyone,' said Patricia, waving a hand in the air. 'Henry, back me up.'

Dad remained silent.

'Everybody's here, darling,' Patricia persisted. 'Everybody's watching. And your father's spent so much money. I'm not sure the champagne can go back.'

Mia drained the glass and lowered it. 'I'm sorry, Dad,' she said calmly, 'but I can't marry him.'

'That's quite all right, darl—'

'Henry!' screeched Patricia. 'It's not all right! Such a scene!'

'A SCENE?' shouted Mia. 'That's all you care about, isn't it? Not making a scene. Not being embarrassing. Doing the right thing. Well, sorry, Mum, but not today. *Fuck* the champagne.' She spun and stalked into her bedroom.

'Henry!' wailed Patricia as Ruby and I started quickly snatching up our belongings.

'Dad, why don't Flo and I take her home?' Ruby suggested, as she slid a couple of unopened bottles of champagne into her bag.

'You go,' he said. 'Quite right. Don't worry. Your mother and I will sort everything out here.' Then he sighed. 'I never liked him much, actually. Never trust a man who wears that much hair gel.'

★

We left the hotel via a side exit, avoiding all guests, and jumped straight into a black cab. None of us had changed so we sat, in our dresses, passing the champagne bottle between us.

'I thought you were being weirdly quiet but I put it down to nerves,' said Ruby. 'Did you know you were going to do that this morning?'

Mia wiped her lips with the back of her hand. She'd already taken off her engagement ring. 'Not straight away. I lay in the bath like Dr Evil, plotting the most humiliating revenge I could think of.' She frowned at me. 'You said anything to Rory?'

I nodded. 'Mmm, I just took the more traditional route of calling him and ending it down the phone.'

Mia sniggered, then I laughed, then Ruby started too until we were all shaking on the back seat of the cab. As we slid through Mayfair, the driver cast anxious glances in his rear-view mirror.

'I'm sorry,' Mia said between breaths. 'I'm sorry, Flo, I'm not laughing at you. It's the whole thing. I've been planning this fucking wedding for months, and now look at me. At us!'

If you'd been strolling along the pavement and peered into our cab, it would have made a confusing sight. A runaway bride with running eye make-up and smeared lipstick flanked by two women in silky nighties, all cackling with laughter.

'But are you all right?' I asked.

She sighed and laid her head back against the seat. 'I don't know. No. Yes. Maybe.' She sighed again. 'I'll be fine.'

'There's an upside to all this, you know,' said Ruby, looking from Mia to me.

'What?' we chorused.

'You no longer have to listen to him grunting "Who's a hungry girl then?" in your ear.'

'True.'

'And the rest of us don't have to listen to Rory shouting "Cowabunga!",' she said, turning to me.

My hands flew to my cheeks. 'You could hear?'

'Sometimes,' she said with a shrug. 'I just used to put my earplugs in.'

This set us all off again.

Ruby, perhaps for the first time ever, offered to pay for the cab when we got back so Mia could hurry into the house.

I layered the various bag straps over my shoulder and trudged up the path like a packhorse.

As Mia opened the door and bent over to pick up the post, I felt sorry for her. Coming home in your wedding dress, accompanied by your sisters and having to scrape up that day's pizza leaflets and flyers offering gutter cleaning is no bride's dream. Right about now, I figured, looking at my watch, we should have been nailing the prawn tempura and lobster tacos.

'Flo, delivery,' said Mia, holding out a thick brown envelope.

I dropped the bags in the doorway and took it. There was no address, just my name, so it must have been delivered by hand. I slid my finger under the flap and tipped the envelope up into my other hand. A memory stick and several black and white photos fell out, plus a card which fluttered to my feet.

I ignored the card and concentrated on the photos. They were all of me: me standing behind the shop counter with a pile of hardbacks, me laughing as I served a customer, me standing in front of the window display and gazing out at the street, me standing on tiptoes as I reached to slide a cookery book into its shelf, me sitting on stage next to Fumi. Finally, a close-up of me at last week's Christmas party, grinning in my pudding costume.

I bent over to pick up the card. *I DIDN'T WANT TO LEAVE IT AS WE DID ON THURSDAY EVENING. I HOPE THESE AREN'T CREEPY BUT IF YOU'RE GOING TO BE A BESTSELLING AUTHOR YOU'LL NEED A FEW PUBLICITY SHOTS, SO HERE ARE A FEW I TOOK WHEN YOU WEREN'T LOOKING. SEE YOU IN A FEW MONTHS. ZX*

'Oh my God,' I murmured. People often say it's like being hit by lightning but that's not true. Standing there, holding Zach's photographs, the realization of how strongly I felt about him felt more like a memory, familiar and safe. The feeling made sense. I liked Zach. I liked him so much I wanted to burst out laughing at how slow I'd been. Zach, the kindest, most thoughtful, emotionally astute and supportive person had been by my side for months while I'd been obsessing about Rory and that stupid, *stupid* list. I felt like one of those people who turned their house over to find their keys, only to realize they were in their pocket the whole time. This was just a slightly more romantic version.

'What are those?' said Ruby, standing on the doorstep behind me.

'Photos,' I said, handing them to her.

She leafed through them. 'Flo, these are insanely beautiful. Look at you! Look at your expression in this one.' She held out the picture of me staring through the shop window. 'And this one in the hat!'

I laughed. 'Rubes, I look deranged.'

She shook her head. 'He's got you completely. Goofy and self-conscious at the same time.'

'Oh, thanks very much.'

'They're from Zach, right?'

'Yeah,' I said, staring back down at the card.

'What's he say?'

I read the card aloud and she raised her eyebrows.

'What?'

'I don't know what you're still doing standing here in that negligee, that's what. If Zach had sent me these before flying to the moon, I'd rent a rocket and go after him.'

'Rubes, be serious. I can't go after him. I've got a job. And Harry. It's not practical.'

'PRACTICAL! Flo, our sister just walked out of a very expensive wedding which may or may not cause our mother to have some sort of stroke, and you're banging on about the relatively minor practicalities of booking a flight to Panama.'

'Patagonia.'

'Whatever. The point is the guy's in love with you.'

'Do you think?' Suddenly, having realized how I felt, the answer to this felt crucial.

'Oh please! He spent that whole evening he took my head-shots talking about you and how much you did for the shop. I can't tell you how unerotic it is to try and seduce a man while all he does is talk about your sister. Florence Fairfax, seriously, for once in your life can you do something spontaneous?'

'What's going on?' said Mia, reappearing at the top of the stairs. 'There's been a lot of shouting today, even for this family.'

'Zach is in love with Florence, that's what, and she's refusing to go after him.'

'Zach from the shop?'

'Yes, exactly, Zach from the shop. He's delivered these photos and he's obviously mad about her, but she won't do anything about it.'

'Why not?' Mia said, frowning down at me. 'Please, Flo, we might as well have one happy ending today.'

'Except there's not much I can do. He's on his flight to South America. I'll just have to text him.' It seemed a feeble response but I had no other option.

'Oh, a text. Be still my beating heart,' said Ruby, sarcastically. 'Well, your loss. He'll probably pick up an absolute babe in South America.'

'There's nothing I can do,' I repeated over my shoulder, trudging upstairs with the bags. 'Here, this is yours.' I handed Mia hers and continued upstairs to my room.

Lying on my bed, I texted Eugene first to say there'd been a change of plan and I could go round to pick up Harry that afternoon. Then I spent about half an hour trying to strike the right tone in a message to Zach so he'd have something from me when he landed.

Welcome down! Thanks for my photos, you pervert. And thank you for, well, everything really. Email me? I'll send you pictures of Harry. Big wedding drama here but I'll tell you another time. Safe travels xxx

I clicked send and flopped back on my bed. Then I heard Dad and Patricia arrive from the hotel and her shrieks penetrate the floor. I wasn't sure how long I could hide up here.

My phone vibrated on my stomach. It would be Eugene. At least I had collecting Harry as an excuse to escape.

But it wasn't Eugene. It was Zach.

I fly tonight! Just on my way to Heathrow. And you're welcome. Drama? Hope everyone OK. X

I thought you flew at 7am? I typed.

7pm!

Ruby's cry echoed in my head: 'Do something spontaneous.'

I ran back downstairs where everyone was sitting in the TV room glaring at one another.

'Ah, Florence, there you are,' said Patricia. 'I gather you've ended your relationship with Rory too? I don't know what's got into you girls today, going around the place and breaking up with perfectly good boyfriends willy-nilly.'

I ignored her and turned to Dad. 'How long would it take to drive to Heathrow?'

'Now?'

I nodded.

He looked at his watch and puffed out his cheeks. 'An hour, depending on the traffic.'

'OK, will you take me?'

'What, *now*?' he said again.

'Yes. You're the only sober one.'

'Florence darling, have you gone mad?' said Patricia.

'We haven't got time to discuss it,' I shouted, heading for the hall where my work shoes were under the table. I was still wearing my bridesmaid dress so it wasn't an ideal look but too bad. 'I'll explain in the car.' I grabbed an old fleece from the coat stand and poked my head back into the TV room to gesture at Dad.

'Is this Zach?' said Ruby.

I nodded.

'Whoooooop!' She punched the air. 'In that case I'm coming too.'

'And me,' said Mia, getting up from the sofa. 'I could do with a distraction.'

'Well I don't know what's going on but I'm not being left behind,' said Patricia, putting down her glass and standing up.

'Come on!' I urged, waving my arms towards the front door in an attempt to inject urgency into the situation. This was mad. Totally mad. Madder than Gwendolyn and all her spells put together. But I had to get to the airport in time.

It took several minutes but eventually my family were bundled into the car: Dad in the driving seat, Patricia next to him, Ruby, Mia and me strung along the back like small children.

'Heathrow, please, driver,' I said. 'Top speed.'

'Can somebody please explain what's happening?' demanded Patricia as Dad reversed into the road.

'I'll do it,' Ruby said, before leaning into the gap between the front seats. 'OK, parents, listen up. Florence was going out with Rory, right?'

'The one who works for the Foreign Office?' said Dad.

'Yes.'

'I do like him.'

'No, we don't like him any more.'

'Oh. Why not?'

'Because he was with Hugo on the stag and he also, er, became very good friends with that poor stripper.'

'Ruby, please,' said Patricia, puckering her mouth in disgust.

'Well he did,' went on Ruby, 'so Rory's out of the picture. But do you remember me talking about Zach, who worked with Florence in the bookshop?'

'Wasn't he the one you took a fancy to?' asked Patricia. 'The communist?'

'Give me strength,' muttered Ruby. 'Yes, I briefly had a teeny-tiny crush on him but it turns out he was actually in love with Florence. And now he's flying off to Patagonia and she needs to tell him she loves him too.'

'Hang on,' I said, 'I'm not sure that I actually lo—'

'Flo, quiet!' said Ruby, holding her palm in the air at me. 'You'll only confuse them.'

'I remember now!' said Dad, tapping his fingers on the steering wheel. 'He's not a communist, he's the photographer. I met him that day when you were doing your petition?'

I nodded at him in the rear-view mirror.

'But we hardly know anything about this Zach,' sniffed Patricia. 'Where did he go to school?'

'PAT, FOR GOD'S SAKE GET A GRIP!' shouted Ruby. 'It doesn't matter. This whole drama was created by you in the first place. If you hadn't sent Florence to see that mad love coach—'

'She wasn't mad. She was in *Posh!* magazine.'

'Whatever. If you hadn't sent Florence to see her, and if she hadn't made Florence write that crazy list, then none of this would have happened in the first place.'

'But without Rory she might not have realized she loves Zach,' added Mia.

'True,' said Ruby, then she turned to me. 'What time's his flight?'

'Seven,' I said, looking at my phone. 'He said he was on his way there twenty minutes ago. But what if we miss him and he goes through security?'

She shook her head. 'Not going to happen, don't you worry.' Then she leant forward again. 'Dad, can you pull some strings? Get him held back or something?'

'I'm not sure that's a good idea, darling.'

'Oh, come on, Dad. This is your daughter's entire happiness we're talking about. Surely you can do something?'

Dad met my eye again in the mirror. 'Which airline is he flying with, sweetheart, do you know?'

'British Airways to Buenos Aires.'

'Right. Patricia, can you take this,' said Dad, reaching inside his suit jacket for his phone, 'and look up Garry Stevens.'

'Who's he?' she snapped.

'VIP liaison at British Airways,' said Dad, winking at me before glancing across at Patricia. 'Found him?'

She nodded and hit the green button.

After a few rings a man's voice rang out across the car's speaker system. 'Hello?'

'Garry? Hello. It's Henry Fairfax here.'

'Henry! Good to hear from you. How are things?'

'They're fine but I wonder if you might do me a favour?'

'Anything. Ask away.'

'I believe you have a passenger called Zach, er...'

'Taylor,' I shouted.

'A passenger called Zach Taylor travelling on the 7 p.m. flight out to BA tonight. But I need to give him something before he goes. Official business, you understand. So I'm on my way but do you mind calling him to the information desk in the departures hall?'

'Not at all. I'll get one of my team to do it now.'

'Much obliged.'

'Consider it done.'

Dad thanked him and Patricia hung up. Ruby whooped again. 'Dad, that's so badass.'

'Is that a good thing?'

She nodded. 'It's a very good thing.'

As we pulled on to the motorway and the traffic slowed, I heard a siren start up behind us.

I didn't look. I was trying to work out what kind of siren it was. If it was a police car, I told myself, then I'd get to Heathrow in time. But if it was an ambulance, this would be a disaster and I was about to experience the greatest humiliation since I'd gone onstage with Percy the pug.

Ruby glanced back and tutted. 'An ambulance, that's all we need.'

I took a deep breath.

'Rubes?' I said, as we slowed to a crawl.

'Mmm.'

'What do South American women look like?'

'Smoking,' she said. 'Think Salma Hayek.'

'She's actually Mexican,' said Mia, from her other side.

'Oh all right. Shakira, then.'

I stared glumly at the red lights stretched in front of us, thinking about Shakira's bottom and checking the time on my watch every other minute, wondering what I was going to say when I got there. *If* we got there.

★

'EXCUSE ME,' I shouted at a man with a clipboard standing just inside the doors of Terminal 5. Dad had pulled up outside and Ruby had quite literally pushed me out of the car.

'Yes, madam, how can I help?' he said, casting a surprised glance at my dress. And my fleece. And my shoes. My hair was presumably pretty wild by this point too.

'Where's the information desk? The British Airways information desk?'

'Can I help you at all, madam?'

'NO!' I shouted, before lowering my voice. 'Sorry, no, it's just that I'm meeting someone at the desk, quite urgently.'

'Oh I see, that's quite all right. In that case it's over there,' he said, turning to point towards the corner of the building, 'just to the right of Area G, beside the First Cla—'

'Florence!'

I turned to see Dad hurrying around the car.

'Dad? What?'

He stopped in front of me.

'I just wanted to say…' then he paused.

He looked so serious that I didn't want to scream that he had to hurry up but also, he did need to hurry up. 'Dad, what is it?'

'I just wanted to say that I'm sorry that I haven't been around much for you in recent years. And all this…' He waved a hand around him at the car and the departures area. I glanced at the man with the clipboard; he'd been straining to hear us but suddenly busied himself with a trolley.

'All this has made me realize how little I've known what's going on in your life.'

'That's all right, Dad,' I said quickly, not wanting to ruin this moment by looking at my watch but, equally, feeling every second tick away.

He shook his head. 'It's not all right. It's unforgiveable and I am going to be better in the future.'

'OK, Dad, thank you, but I should go an—'

'I want to be more involved, in all your lives,' he said, looking back to the car where Ruby was hanging out the window and manically tapping at her watch.

'Pick your moment, Dad,' she shouted. 'Go, Flo, quick.'

'Sorry,' Dad said, squeezing my hand. 'But I love you very much. Now go and find that communist.'

I reached forward and hugged him, and then ran for the door, shouting 'he's not a communist,' over my shoulder. I had to clutch one arm around me to stop the fleece from flapping open and any accidental flashing of breast. Didn't have time to be arrested right now. 'Sorry, excuse me, sorry,' I shouted as I slid past trolleys, families and avoided a small child dragging a suitcase that looked like a tiger.

I saw him leaning on the desk with his rucksack at his feet, and my heart turned over. It was Zach. Just Zach. The same old Zach in his usual mourning outfit of black. But suddenly he meant so much more. This wasn't just like seeing him in the shop every morning. This was bigger. So much bigger. This was everything, and as if on cue, I felt myself start to sweat. Sweat patches would definitely show up in this dress.

'Zach!' I said, tightening my fleece around me.

He looked up and stared for a few seconds before laughing and shaking his head. 'What are you doing here?'

'I needed to make sure you'd had all your injections,' I said, grinning back.

'Actually?'

'No! Obviously not. I wanted to come and s—'

'What on earth are you wearing?'

I looked down at the hideous shoes and smoothed my dress with one hand. 'Can you overlook this? Didn't have much time.'

'For what?'

I inhaled before the words tumbled out. 'To get here to say I'm sorry. I'm so sorry, Zach. You were right. You were right about everything and Rory's a wanker and I didn't realize, I just got so caught up with everything because I so wanted it. I so wanted it to be something that I didn't realize it was the wrong thing, completely wrong.'

He frowned. 'Hang on, slow down. What's happened with you and Rory?'

'Long story involving a stripper and, er, some marshmallows but basically he's gone.'

His face briefly clouded. 'So you've run straight here to me as the alternative?'

'Yes! But no, I know that sounds bad. It's not just because of him. It's because it made me realize how I feel about you. That I feel more than I realized, much more, which is why I'm here now. Because I was worried that if I didn't catch you and say all this before you left then you might end up with Shakira.'

'Wha—'

'Not necessarily her because she's married, isn't she? But someone who resembles her. And I think I would mind that a bit because, well, I like you quite a lot, I've realized.'

He dropped his head and shook it again while I stood and watched, paralysed with suspense. If he thought I was crazy, that was all right. I'd go home again, fetch Harry from Eugene's and forget the past few months ever happened. I'd be sad and cry but, after a period of mourning, I'd cheer up again and devote the rest of my life to cats and books. No more boyfriends. No more trying to fall in love. It was, as I'd always suspected, too much trouble.

I totted up the floor tiles in front of the British Airways desk as I waited for Zach to answer, but was distracted by a smiley, middle-aged woman sitting behind it. She was waving her fingers at me. They were crossed.

I tried to smile back as Zach lifted his head.

'You're mad, you know?'

'I do know.'

'And demented.'

'Yup, that too.'

'And I will probably regret thi—'

'Regret what?'

'FLORENCE! Can you just listen to me?'

I nodded.

'Come with me. Come with me to South America.'

'What, now? Like this?'

'Well, not exactly like that. I don't imagine you've got your passport with you?'

I shook my head.

'But come with me tomorrow, or the next day, or the day after that. Just come with me.'

'What about the shop?'

'The shop's fine. Norris and Eugene will be fine.'

'OK, but what about Harry?'

'He will also be fine. Ruby can take charge.'

I wasn't sure I liked that idea but I didn't want to get too hung up on it. 'OK, but what about Curtis? I've got the meeting next week with Jacinta and I don't want to miss it.'

'So go to the meeting and then come out. They have email in South America,' said Zach, 'and they probably even have cheese and tomato sandwiches. Which means you're out of excuses.'

He stepped forward and reached for my hands, which was awkward because they were shrouded in fleece so I had to release them from the sleeves before he could take hold of my fingers. 'Listen, you lunatic, why not just do it? London's not going anywhere. What's to lose?'

And I opened my mouth to protest again but he was right. I was out of excuses and there was nothing to lose but plenty, maybe everything, to gain. I could do something impulsive, something adventurous, and the result didn't have to be disastrous. This trip to the airport had already proved that.

'OK,' I said, smiling shyly. 'OK, I'll come.'

'Seriously?' he said, his fingers tight around mine.

I nodded but my face fell again. 'Although…'

'Oh Jesus, what now?'

'What injections do I need for South America?'

★

Three months later…

'How many steps?' Zach shouted, smiling from the top of the terrace.

'Not sure,' I said, racing to catch up. The thought of counting them hadn't occurred to me.

'Come on, sun's nearly gone,' he said, extending a hand to pull me up the last couple.

I looked out across the open rooftop. He was right. A scrap of yellow was sinking behind the city's domes and a pink blanket had thrown itself across the sky. Beneath us, a busker's guitar chords floated from the streets. I wanted a cold beer. After the dry cold of the south, the air in Buenos Aires was hot and damp, turning my skin sticky.

A waiter led us to a table in the corner.

'We're early,' said Zach, glancing at his watch.

'You're nervous,' I teased, flipping open the drinks list.

'No, I'm not.'

But he'd replied too quickly, too defensively. 'You are! I can't believe it. You're nervous.'

He'd grown a beard while we'd been on the road but I saw his mouth twitch underneath it. 'All right,' he said, his smile broadening, 'maybe. But it's your dad. And I know how much this means to you so…'

He trailed off and I frowned at him.

'So it means a lot to me.'

I smiled as he ordered from the waiter. *Dos birras.*

It had taken a couple of weeks to extricate myself from London. First, I'd told Norris that I was leaving. 'But temporarily, just for a few months, if you'll have me back?' I'd asked. We'd been sitting in his office and he'd immediately thumped his desk with his fist, sending several ketchup sachets into the air, and shouted that it was very bad timing. I replied that he was talking nonsense, the lease was sorted and that I wanted to go travelling with Zach. This had radically altered the matter. I thought Norris might cry. His face went red, he clasped me in a hug and told me to take as long as I liked.

Upstairs, Eugene agreed to take in Harry (and he'd sent me so many pictures of him since I'd had to mute his messages).

I met Jacinta, the literary agent, who told me she liked Curtis the counting caterpillar very much and, with my approval, wanted to start the hunt for an illustrator.

I went to a final NOMAD meeting and told the group I was going to South America for an extended holiday. They had various worries about this (Mary wanted to know how bad the malaria was; Lenka fretted that I'd be forced into a drug gang; Elijah warned that I'd have to eat guinea pig. Jaz had told them all to pipe down, given me a huge goodbye hug and promised to keep me updated on the George situation. Her most recent email had said she was 'as happy as Barry').

Mia and Ruby had helped me pack. Kind of. Mia stuffed several pairs of tiny knickers in my bag, the ones she'd been given on her hen party. 'They're all clean,' she insisted, 'sniff them if you don't believe me.' I'd declined this offer and taken them out, insisting that Zach had told me to pack light.

The reason for packing light became clear when we arrived in Santiago and Zach picked up a motorbike, an old Honda that looked like it had served in the war. It had been our first tense moment. How could I spend the next two months on that, clinging to Zach's back like a baby possum? He'd promised it would be all right. And it had been. Apart from an alarming few seconds in a forest when Zach swerved to avoid an armadillo, they had been the most electrifying, affirming, worry-free months of my life.

From Santiago, we'd headed south along the Pacific coast, roaring past lakes and jewel-coloured houses. We stopped for the night wherever we felt like it. Sometimes camping, sometimes staying in a cabana when I insisted that I wanted to sleep on a proper mattress (have you ever tried to have quiet sex in a tent? It's even less relaxing than having sex while Prue Leith's talking on the telly).

Zach gave me surfing lessons over a few days in a small town where we bought *ceviche* from the fishermen every morning. He took me hiking, he took me kayaking, he made us get up early several times, promising 'the best sunrise' I'd ever see. They usually were. Right down in the toe of Argentina, we saw his black and white dolphins as well as a humpback whale fling himself in the air like an acrobat, not far from our boat. This made me cry.

Most nights we sat up late, the blaze of campfire on our faces, drinking red wine from paper cups while talking. We talked a lot in the evenings because during the day we spent so long riding on the bike, watching the landscape change around us. But I was grateful for this time because it allowed me to think and, gradually, to fall in love with him. It wasn't like with Rory. There was no rush and I wasn't worried that Zach would vanish. There were no doubts, no anxiety about my own behaviour or that I'd say something wrong. He was here in front of me, my arms around his jacket.

I felt safer on the back of that bike than anywhere I'd ever been before. Turns out, you can't write a prescription to help you find that person, your person. You might think you want blond hair and blue eyes but it doesn't work like that, fortunately. There's magic in life that remains beyond our control. I thought I'd known exactly what I wanted but been proven wrong. Zach was what I needed and I felt grateful every day that I realized this before it was too late.

As the waiter put down the bottles in front of us, the last flash of sun dropped away and I looked back to him.

'What?' he asked, squinting at me sideways. He'd become used to a constant barrage of questions in the past two months, most often 'What are we having for lunch?'. In Patagonia, my devotion to cheese and tomato sandwiches had been superseded by one for Argentinian hot chocolate, as thick as golden syrup. I was drinking one a day and the waist of my jeans now cut into me when I sat behind him. Well, it was either the hot chocolate or I was pregnant. Patricia would be appalled if I had a baby without being married. Apparently she was still in mourning about Mia's wedding and, from the sound of Ruby's emails, there was little danger of another family wedding for some time; she and Mia were out partying almost every night and the house was chock-a-block with Jeremys again.

'Nothing,' I replied, shaking my head and reaching for my beer. 'Just happy.'

He smiled before his glance slid past me and his eyes widened in recognition. 'He's here,' he said, pushing his chair back to stand and lift his hand in a wave.

I glanced over my shoulder and saw Dad approaching, and then stood with him. 'You'll be fine.'

'Course,' he said, his hand dropping and reaching for mine. 'I've got you.'

ACKNOWLEDGEMENTS

Stupidly, I can't remember the name of the person I have to thank most of all for this book. The idea came about when my friend Jackie invited me to a 'sex tech' dinner she was hosting in London. Jackie works for a trendy tech start-up which had recently launched a range of 'pretty' and 'elegant' pastel-coloured vibrators, the sort of sculptural object that wouldn't look out of place on a mantelpiece. Everyone going to the dinner would get given a vibrator, said Jackie. Free food *and* a free sex toy? I RSVP'ed immediately.

At this dinner, I sat next to a woman who told me a story which made me quite forget the vibrators. Some years before, she'd become pregnant with her boyfriend who'd upped and left halfway through her pregnancy. She was devastated: left alone, soon to have a baby and heartbroken. As a coping mechanism, she decided to write a list of what she was look-ing for in a man. It was a very specific list detailing physical attributes as well as character traits and his hopes for life. 'And then I met him,' she told me, with a shy smile. According to this woman whose name I cannot remember, a man with all the qualities on her list subsequently came into her life, took her small son on as his own and she was now grateful that her previous relationship had broken down.

Well, call me an old softie but I loved the romance of this and decided to write a story which included some sort of list. This book is the result and I am hugely grateful to both Jackie and the anonymous woman for sparking the idea.

After them, I am most thankful to the team who helped pull this book together. My agent, Becky Ritchie, continues to provide enormous support and terrific therapy. Emily Kitchin, my editor, is not only a very talented, unflappable and stupendously encouraging person, she is also incredibly cheerful on Twitter and I am a big fan of that. The whole team at HQ remain the dream to work with. On the editorial side, special thanks to Lisa Milton, Joe Thomas, Katrina Smedley, Mel Hayes and Jo Rose, who quite literally never seem to stop working. I'd also like to salute the production skills of Angie Dobbs, Halema Begum and Tom Keane and the colourful genius of Charlotte Phillips, who designed the cover *does actual salute from behind laptop*. Writing this against the backdrop of the news, as the coronavirus crisis deepens, I am in awe of the lengths everyone is going to in order that books continue to be published. Thank you.

I wrote much of this book while living in Norfolk, in a house I borrowed from the exceptionally kind de Stacpoole family. Every morning, I got up and wrote for several hours before striding out across the marsh and beaches of the North Norfolk coast thinking about Florence, Rory and Zach. I also visited Sandringham three times while up there, so I'd like to thank the Queen for that distraction as well as for the excellent shortbread sold in the Sandringham gift shop. Well worth a trip for that alone.

Family and friends, to say 'I'd be lost without you' is such a cliché. It's also not true. I'd actually be nothing without you. Particularly at low moments, on bad days and during the weeks when life can feel heavy, you are everything to me and, although I often grumble about the WhatsApp groups, I'd much rather have them than not. Thank you all.

Loved *The Wish List*? Make sure you pre-order the new laugh-out-loud romantic comedy from Sophia Money-Coutts

High-powered lawyer Nell Mason cast off her romantic ideals long ago. She's absolutely fine living with her sweet, if slightly dull, boyfriend Gus in their London flat, where they have very sensible sex once (ok, sometimes twice) a week. She's definitely not stuck in a rut.

But when Nell is forced to return home, she bumps into childhood friend and first love Arthur Drummond, who broke her heart fifteen years ago. After seeing Arthur again, the seemingly perfect life she's worked so hard for starts to feel, well, less perfect. Maybe Nell's been kidding herself all these years. Can she ever get over her first love?

Make sure you've read Sophia Money-Coutts' funny and feel-good debut

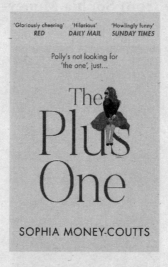

'Gloriously cheering'
RED

'Hilarious'
DAILY MAIL

'Howlingly funny'
SUNDAY TIMES

Polly's not looking for
'the one', just...

The
Plus
One

SOPHIA MONEY-COUTTS

Polly's is *fine*. She's single, having sex (well, only twice last year), and stuck in a job writing about royal babies. So the chances of her finding a plus one to her best friend's summer wedding are looking worryingly slim.

But it's a New Year, a new leaf and all that, and Polly's given herself 365 days to get her sh★★t together. Her latest piece is on the infamous Jasper, Marquess of Milton, the last man she'd consider a plus one or 'the one'. After all, she's heard the stories, there's no way she'll succumb to his charms…

Turn the page for an exclusive extract from the hilarious rom-com *What Happens Now?*

After eight years together, Lil thought she'd found 'the one' – until she finds herself dumped. So she does what any self-respecting singleton would do, swipes right, puts on her best bra and lands herself a date with a handsome mountaineer called Max. What could go wrong?

Well, a number of things. First Max ghosts her, and then she discovers she's pregnant. Single, thirty-one and living in a thimble-sized flat in London, it's hardly the happily-ever-after she was looking for.

Lil's ready to the baby-thing on her own, but first she should tell Max – if she can track him down. Surely he can't be *the* Max currently trekking up a mountain in South Asia? Oh, maybe he wasn't ignoring Lil after all…

PROLOGUE

I WASN'T SURE I had enough wee for the stick. I pressed my bladder through my jeans with my fingertips, holding the pregnancy test in the other hand. Not bursting but it would have to do. I peeled off the top of the foil packet, balanced the stick on the top of the loo roll and unzipped my flies. I sat down and reached back for the stick.

Looking down at my thighs, I realized I was sitting too far forward on the loo seat, so I shuffled my bottom backwards and widened my knees until there was enough space to reach my hand underneath me, trying to avoid grazing the loo bowl with my knuckles. Christ, this was unsanitary. There must be better ways.

I narrowed my eyes at the bath in front of me and wondered if it would be easier to step into that, crouch down and wee on the stick in the bath, letting it trickle out down the plughole. No worse than weeing in the shower, right?

I shook my head. I was in my parents' bathroom. Couldn't do a pregnancy test by pissing on a stick in my mum's bath. She loved that bath. She spent hours in it wearing her frilly bath hat, shouting at Radio Norfolk.

I frowned down into the dark space between my legs again

where the stick was poised in mid-air, ready for action. What a simple bit of plastic to deliver such potentially life-changing news. It was the shape of the vape my friend Clem carried round with him everywhere, loaded with lemon sherbet-flavoured liquid.

'Why lemon sherbet?' I'd asked him once. He'd shrugged and said he just liked sweets.

I shook my head again as if to try and physically dispel thoughts of Clem and lemon sherbet. Concentrate, Lil. The stick. Wee on the stick. Get on with it. But I couldn't. At this, the most important moment of my bladder's life so far, it had stage fright. Funny how, when you really concentrate on weeing, you can't. And yet normally, when you sit yourself down what, six, seven, eight times a day, out it comes, no trouble.

I sighed. The other problem was I wasn't sure where to hold the stick in order to catch maximum wee. I shifted my hand slightly towards the front. Was that a good place? Maybe. But if it came out as more of a trickle than a jet it would need to be in the middle.

'Oi,' came Jess's voice from outside the bathroom door. I'd locked it because I knew she'd come in otherwise. 'Have you done it yet?'

'Shhhh,' I hissed back. 'No. I haven't. And pressure from you won't help.'

Jess went quiet for a few seconds, then I heard her whistling from outside the door.

'Why are you whistling?'

She stopped. 'It makes horses pee when you're riding them.'

'I'm not a horse.' Although it gave me an idea. With my left hand, I reached across for the bathroom sink and twisted the hot tap, then held my hand underneath the warm water.

It worked instantly. I started weeing and moved the stick into prime position, sort of between the front and the middle. Please could I not be pregnant, I thought, my eyes fixated on the stick as I felt warm wetness on my fingers. Brilliant, I'd weed on my own hand. Please, please, please could this not be positive. I was thirty-one, single, barely able to afford my rent. I had a life plan. Well, a vague life plan. This was not it.

I finished and jiggled up and down on the loo seat, trying not to drop the stick. Then I turned off the hot tap with my left hand and tugged off a few sheets of loo roll. I retrieved the stick, resisted the urge to tap it on the section of loo seat in front of me like a teaspoon on the side of a teacup – ting, ting, ting! – and wiped myself.

I looked at the test in my right hand, feeling as if I'd swallowed a jar of butterflies, before gently dropping it on a pile of Mum's *History Today* magazines and pulling up my jeans. I picked up the stick without looking at it and unlocked the bathroom door.

Jess was standing there, picking at her cuticles like a nervous father outside the delivery room.

'Show me,' she said instantly, holding her hand out for the test. 'What's it say?'

Come on, Lil, I told myself, stomach still churning, look down. Get it over and done with and then you can go to the pub with Jess and have a drink to celebrate. After that, no more sex. Never again. Not worth it. Not worth the hassle and the drama and this panic attack over the infinitesimally small chance you might be pregnant. I'd take a vow of celibacy and get a cat. I'd become a priest. I'd move to somewhere in the Far East, become a Buddhist and renounce all physical desires. I'd convert to asexualism. Just please, please, please, God, if there is one, if you are there, I know I'm always asking you things and swearing I'll never ask again, but this time I really mean it. I promise I'll never ask anything trivial again if you grant me this one tiny wish: please can I not be pregnant.

I looked down at the stick.

'Fuccccccccck,' I said, looking at it, holding it out for Jess. No question about it, there were two little purple lines. 'I'm pregnant.'

CHAPTER ONE

I'D RATHER HAVE EATEN my own foot than go on a date that night. The whole thing was Jess's idea. She said I needed to 'get back in the saddle'. Hateful expression. I didn't feel like doing any sort of riding, thank you very much. But she'd insisted I download a dating app called Kindling, which is why I was now sitting on the bus, so nervous it felt like even my earlobes were sweating, on the way to some pub in Vauxhall to meet someone called Max. We hadn't been messaging for very long so I knew almost nothing about him. Only that he was thirty-four, had dark curly hair and seemed less alarming than some of the other creatures I'd scrolled through – no, no, no, maybe, no, no, definitely not, you're the sort of pervert who'd have a foot fetish, no, no, YES. Hello, handsome, stubbly man who looks like a cross between a Jane Austen hero and Jack Sparrow the pirate. That was Max.

He'd asked me out a couple of days after matching, saying he didn't believe in 'beating around the bush'. I liked his straightforwardness. No messing about. No dick pics. Just, 'Fancy a drink?' I figured it was better to meet and see whether you got on with someone rather than message for several weeks and paint a madly romantic picture of them in your head, then meet up and realize you'd got it wrong and in real life they were a psychopath.

So, even though Max's question made me want to throw up with nerves, I'd agreed. A tiny, minuscule part of me knew Jess was right, knew that I had to make an effort. Otherwise I'd never get over Jake, the one I used to think was The One before he broke my heart into seventy thousand pieces and turned me into a cynic who had bitter and self-pitying thoughts whenever I saw a couple holding hands on the Tube.

Jake and I had split six months earlier. He split up with me, I should say, if we're being totally accurate. It was after eight years together, having met at uni. Various friends had started getting engaged and, all right, I'd very occasionally allowed myself to think about what shape diamond Jake might buy for an engagement ring. But only once or twice, tops. Maybe three times. Tragic, I know, but in the absence of a ring I was happy with Jake. I just wanted us – married or not. And I thought he did too. We used to fall asleep making sure we were touching one another every night. My arm over his chest or our feet touching. Or holding hands. And if one of us woke in the night and we'd moved apart, we'd reach out for the other one so we could feel them there again. It was real. I knew it.

Well, some clairvoyant I was. Six months ago, Jake came home from his office to our flat in Angel and told me he that he felt 'too settled'. That he wanted more excitement. And as I sat at the kitchen table, crying, wondering whether I should offer to dress up as a sexy nun or be more enthusiastic about anal sex, he told me he was moving out to go and live with his friend Dave. It felt so sudden that I could only sit at the kitchen table weeping while Jake packed and left ten minutes later with the overnight bag I'd bought him from John Lewis for his last birthday. With hindsight, not the sexiest purchase. But he'd said he loved it. It had a separate compartment for his wash bag. Practical, no?

The Dave thing turned out to be a front for the fact that Jake had been shagging a 24-year-old called India from his office. Jess and I had devoted hours (whole days, probably), to stalking her on all forms of social media. On Instagram, she was a blonde party girl who never seemed to wear a bra; on LinkedIn, her profile picture showed a more serious India, smiling in a collared shirt, blonde hair tied back in a smooth ponytail. It was also via LinkedIn that Jess and I discovered she'd only been working at Jake's law firm for two months before he left me.

'Quick work,' I'd slurred, pissed, lying belly down on the floor of Jess's bedroom where we were stalking her on my laptop one evening.

The next day, I'd got an email from Jake.

Lil, you can see who's been looking at your profile on LinkedIn. I'm not sure this is healthy. Please leave Indy out of it.

Indy indeed. I'd thrown my phone on the floor in a rage and smashed the screen. But my fury was helpful. Anger was more motivational than sadness. Sadness sat in my stomach like a stone and made me cry; anger made me want to get up and do something. I decided I needed to move out of the flat I'd shared with Jake and find another room somewhere. I'd start again. Optimistically, I bought a book about Buddhism and tried a meditation I found on Spotify, half-hoping to wake up cured the following day.

I didn't wake up cured. But I knew I had to give it time. The oldest cliché there was and the most irritating, depressing thing anyone can say to you when you're in the depths of a break-up, staring at your phone, longing to message them. Or for them to message you. But the time thing was true. Annoyingly.

Six months later, I was living in a flat in Brixton on a street just behind McDonald's. My flatmates were an Aussie couple called Riley and Grace – he was a personal trainer, she was a yoga teacher – who made genuinely extraordinary noises when they had sex. I'd joked to Jess that Attenborough should study them ('And now the male climbs on top of the female'), but they were lovely when they had all their clothes on, and my room was cheap. Plus, India had made her Instagram profile private which meant I couldn't stalk her any more. Probably better for all of us that way.

So, here I was, on the bus chugging towards Vauxhall for this date with Mystery Max, sweat patches blossoming in the armpits of my new Zara shirt. I'd gone shopping earlier that day for an outfit because my wardrobe was full of sensible work dresses and it felt like the last time I went on a first date women wore bonnets and floor-length gowns. And although the shops seemed to be full of clothes designed for thin hippies

– sequinned flares in a size 8, anyone? – I'd eventually found a pair of black jeans that made my legs look less like chicken drumsticks, and a silky black shirt which gave me exactly the right amount of cleavage. Not too Simon Cowell. Just a hint, so long as I was wearing my old padded bra which hoiked my small to average-sized breasts up so high I could practically lick my own nipples.

While showering, I'd had a brief moral battle with myself about whether to shave my legs or not. I didn't want to go on this date feeling like a rugby player, but there would be no sex because the thought of sleeping with someone other than Jake still terrified me, so what was the point? Plus, I hadn't bothered for so long my razor was rusty. Can you get tetanus from using a rusty razor? My Google search history was littered with such quandaries: 'sharp stabbing pain under ribs cancer?' Or 'walk 20,000 steps a day lose weight?'

In the end, I'd used Grace's nice new pink razor and shaved because I thought it was sloppy preparation not to. Like going into battle without armour. I felt a twinge of guilt at blunting her razor on my legs – it was like scything through a jungle with a machete – but I figured certain household items like this could be co-opted in an emergency. I'd told myself the same that morning when I stole the batteries from the flat's Sky remote for my vibrator. This was an emergency, I decided as I'd sat on my bed, solemnly removing the triple AAAs from one device and sliding them into the other. But I'd also realized this was a new low and that I should probably go out and at least flirt with a human being again. I couldn't rely on my vibrator all the time. What if I got so used to it that no man could ever make me come again? That happens. I read about it once in a magazine.

I felt my stomach spasm again as we pulled into Vauxhall bus station. It was mostly nerves, I hoped, but Jess's twin brother Clem, a haphazard cook, had made us curry the night before at their place and I'd spent much of that morning on the loo, trying to ignore the grunting coming from Grace and Riley's bedroom. I reached into my bag to check I'd brought my Imodium with me. I'd taken one just before leaving the flat but figured I should bring the packet. Just in case. Got to be prepared. The packet was there, safely zipped from sight in my bag's side pocket. Then I looked at my phone. Missed call from Mum which could 100 pc wait. A message from Max asking what I wanted to drink.

Vodka and tonic please! I texted him back, annoyed at myself for using an exclamation mark – so perky! – but worried I sounded too demanding otherwise.

The bus doors hissed as they opened and my heart sped up at the anxiety. Jesus, come on, Lil. It's a date, not an induction into a cult. You can do this. Literally thousands of people go on first dates every day. And they weren't all total disasters. They couldn't be. Otherwise the human race would die out. It was going to be fine. One or two drinks in the pub with a man, like a normal person. Or at least as much like a normal person as I could manage. I wiped my clammy palms on my jeans as I stepped down from the bus into the sticky evening air.

I continued chiding myself as I walked towards the pub.

You're going to be fine. What did that Spotify meditation say? Breathe. Smile. Imagine your higher self, whatever that was. Ignore your stomach, the Imodium will kick in soon. I pushed open the pub door and was immediately hit by noise from clusters of people ordering at the bar and others laughing at tables. For the billionth time that day I wondered if there was anything worse than a first date. Waterboarding?

Then I saw him wave from a table by the window. Max.

Oh.

My.

Days.

Was this a joke? Some kind of set-up?

He was so good-looking, so obviously, absurdly handsome, that I felt instantly more nervous. I'd always been someone who'd appreciated classically good-looking men from a distance. Sure, that man at the bar, or the party, or the wedding might be so hot he was almost beautiful – Superman jaw, wide shoulders, big smile – but he was never going to go for me, so I wasn't going to consider him. It was self-defence – I had mousy hair that fell to my shoulders and frizzed out at the ends, and a nose with a weird bobble. I often squinted at women I saw on Instagram – perfect fringes, matt skin, flicky eyeliner – and wondered if I could ever be one of them. But whenever I tried to do flicky eyeliner, my hand wobbled and the line went all watery.

Jess once told me my best attribute was my height since I was only a couple of inches off six foot. But ask a man what he looks for in a woman and none of them reply 'a giantess with a nose like a bicycle horn'. The handsome ones were out of reach, I'd long known, and yet here was a man so mesmerizing I could barely look at him without blushing. He was trying to mouth something at me from the table. What was it? I squinted at him to try and guess what he was saying, then regretted it. Don't squint at the handsome man, Lil.

'Hi!' I mouthed back at him. Maybe he was short, I thought, as I pushed my way through other people. Maybe that was the problem. That was why he was single. Face like a gladiator, legs like a hobbit. That had to be it.

He stood as I approached. Not short. He was several inches taller than me. Well over six foot, for sure. In jeans and a dark blue shirt which was undone to reveal a perfect triangle of chest. Not hanging loose to his navel like a dancer from *Strictly*. Not buttoned to the top, which was too East End hipster. Couldn't see his shoes. And shoes were crucial. But so far, so excellent.

'Lil, hello,' he said, leaning forward over the table to kiss me on the cheek. He smelt good. Course he did. Woody. I pulled back but he went in for a kiss on the other cheek. A two-kisser. We brushed cheeks on the other side and then both laughed awkwardly.

'I got you a vodka,' he said, nodding at two glasses on the table. He sounded posh, a low drawl like James Bond.

'Thanks,' I said, trying to slip off my leather jacket in a manner which didn't reveal my sweaty underarms.

'Good to meet you,' he said, once I'd sat down, lifting his glass towards mine.

'You too,' I replied, raising my glass slowly, still trying to keep my right arm clamped. I grinned shyly at him and my mind went blank. Suddenly, it was as if I'd lost the power of speech. I'd gone mute while all around us people laughed and talked normally.

'This is an all right location for you because you're in Brixton, right?' he said.

I had a sip of my vodka and nodded. What can I ask him? *Come on, Lil, think of something otherwise you might die of awkwardness.*

'Where are you again?' I asked.

'Hampstead?' he replied, as if it was a question.

I nodded again.

'Cool,' I said, having another sip of my drink. Quite a big sip. 'You been there long?'

'Yeah,' he replied, 'a few years. I love it. Got the park. Can get out of London easily. It's great.' He had a sip of his drink. 'You?'

I frowned at him. 'Huh?'

'Have you been in Brixton long?'

'Oh right, sorry, er, no. Not really. Like, six months.'

'Where were you before?'

'Angel?'

He nodded.

We both had another mouthful of our drinks.

'And you said you were a teacher?'

'Mmm,' I replied. '5-year-olds. I love them most days, want to kill them on others.' *Why are you threatening child murder on a date, Lil?*

He smiled. He had good teeth. White. And the vibe of a man who owned and, crucially, used dental floss. 'You must be unbelievably patient,' he went on. 'I have a couple of godchildren who I love, but I get to hand them back again after a couple of hours.'

I laughed. People always said that about teachers, that we must be 'patient'. But children were easier to handle and less complicated than most adults I knew.

'What about you though?' I asked him. 'How come you're always jet-setting? Are you a spy?' *Well done, a joke! That's more like it, this sounds more like an actual conversation two human beings would have.*

Max laughed. 'No, I'd make a terrible spy. Very bad at keeping secrets. But I travel a lot because I'm a climber.'

I frowned. 'A climber? Like… of mountains?'

'Exactly. Mostly mountains. Walls when I'm in London. Not many mountains in the city.'

'Wow,' I said. 'Cool. I didn't know it could be a job.'

He laughed. 'I carry rich Americans up Swiss mountains to pay the bills, then go off and climb elsewhere for myself.'

'Like where?'

He shrugged. 'Wherever. Europe. America. Himalayas. I'm about to go to Pakistan to try and climb a mountain there.'

'Pakistan? Wow, amazing,' I said. I worried I sounded vacuous. But I didn't know much about climbing. And if you handed me a map and asked me to stick a pin in Pakistan I wasn't absolutely sure I could. I taught my 5-year-olds basic reading and writing skills. Not geography.

My phone lit up on the table. A message from Jess.

'Sorry,' I said, sliding it into my bag, feeling quite grateful that the screen hadn't flashed up again with 'Mum calling'.

Max shook his head. 'No problem.'

'Just a mate checking up on me,' I said, rolling my eyes at him.

'That you're not on a date with a crazy?' he teased. His tanned forehead had lines running across it and smaller lines at the corners of his eyes which crinkled when he smiled. A modern-day Robinson Crusoe who'd clearly spent more time outside than cooped up in an office.

'Something like that.'

He nodded and ran a hand through his hair. Then he grimaced at me. 'I'm sorry. First dates are awkward, aren't they?'

I grinned sheepishly. 'I thought it was just me. But… yeah, they are. You do many of them?' Then I cursed myself for letting that slip out. I didn't want to sound like I was trying to suss his intentions so early.

He shrugged, unfazed. 'Not millions. I'm away a lot. Don't do much dating in the mountains. You?'

I shook my head. 'Nope. Not a huge… dater.' I could feel the vodka loosening my hang-ups. 'This is my first date since a break-up, actually, so I may… er… I may be a bit rusty.'

I looked down, fingers encircling my sweating glass on the table during the awkward silence that followed. It was dumb to mention Jake, so I wondered how long it would take me to get to Jess's from the pub. If I jumped on the Tube to Hammersmith I could probably be there in forty minutes.

Buy a bottle of wine from Nisa on the walk to the house, order a Deliveroo. Perfect. It wouldn't be a wasted night. And I could take this bra off and let my breasts settle back down at their usual altitude.

I looked up again at Max across the table, his mouth in a lopsided smile.

'What?' I asked, narrowing my eyes at him.

'Then we're in the same boat, you and me.'

'What do you mean?'

'I broke up with someone not very long ago.' His smile fell and he looked suddenly serious. 'Although, to be fair, it was more a mutual decision in the end.'

'Ohhhhh,' I said slowly. 'Brutal, huh?'

He shrugged. 'All part of life's rich tapestry.'

'Why d'you break up?'

He shrugged again. 'I wasn't around much. She wanted to settle down. Get married, children, that sort of thing.'

'And you… didn't?' I said it carefully. Again, I didn't want him to think I was trying to work out his potential as a baby-daddy. For him to think I was on some sort of husband-hunt myself.

'No. Well, not no. Just… not yet. Things to do. Places to see.'

'Mountains to climb?'

'Something like that,' he said, smiling and leaning towards me. 'What about you?'

I frowned. 'What do you mean?'

'Well, if we're having a joint Jeremy Kyle session, how come you broke up?'

'Oh.' I grimaced at him. 'We'd been going out for eight years. Living together. I thought it was going one way, he… didn't. So that was that.'

I picked up my glass and was raising it to my mouth when Max laughed.

'What?' I said, defensively. I still found it hard to articulate my feelings about the break-up. I went over it in my head all the time. Over and over again. Over things I could have done differently. Over moments that I realized should have given me a clue. Over Jake's increasing reluctance to hang out with my friends. Over his late nights in the office. But I felt like even Jess had heard enough now so I kept quiet about it unless prompted.

Max shook his head and waved a hand at my expression. 'I'm not laughing at you. I'm laughing at us. Sitting here, nursing our drinks like we're at a wake. Come on, let's have another drink and cheer up.'

I laughed back. 'OK, but my round.'

Max shook his head again as he stood up. 'No. Absolutely not. Same again?'

'Yep, please.'

'Grand. And when I get back, no more talk about break-ups. This is supposed to be a date, not a counselling session. Deal?'

'Deal.'

I watched him push his way back to the bar and touched my right cheek with the back of my fingers. It was warm. We were one drink in, the point at which I'd envisaged one of us making excuses – 'Good to meet you,' awkward kiss

goodbye, never message one another again – but I didn't
want to escape to Jess's house. I wanted to stay here talking
to Max. Initial awkwardness over, I could sense that I liked
him. Sitting here, chatting, I could feel a spark of excitement
at exploring someone new, at finding out all those first things
about someone. I hadn't felt that for a long time. Years, if I
was honest. The excitement of finding out about one another
dissipated early with Jake and lapsed into something more
comfortable. This Saturday night already felt more exciting
than most of our relationship. Or maybe that was the vodka.

'I took the liberty of buying some crisps,' Max said, returning to the table a few minutes later with a drink in each hand
and two packets in the crook of his arm. 'And also, here's a
menu.' He put the drinks down, dropped the crisps (one ready
salted, one salt and vinegar – promising taste in crisps), pulled
two menus out from underneath his elbow and handed me
one. 'You hungry?'

I'd been too nervous to eat much all day. Too adrenalin-y
at the thought of the date. Plus there was my dodgy stomach
issue. All of which probably accounted for why I felt a bit
pissed already.

'Yep,' I replied.

'Great,' he said, sitting down. 'Me too. Although I warn
you, I'm greedy. It's all freeze-dried food on expeditions. So
if I'm out, I go a bit mad.'

With hindsight, the second bottle of wine was probably
what did it. We'd ordered food – actual steak for him, tuna
steak for me, then shared cheese – and stayed at the pub until

closing. One bottle of red wine, then another. Conversation had meandered more easily from travels to where we grew up. When I told him about being raised by two eccentric academics in Norfolk, he laughed.

'No way!' he said, grinning at me. 'Mine live just over the border in Suffolk. I'll drive up and we can go for a walk along the beach.'

'Which beach?' I asked, trying to stay outwardly cool while all my internal organs were cheering. A walk on the beach meant there had to be at least one more date. I envisaged us strolling along Brancaster, my hair blowing in the wind in a manner which left me looking tousled and sexy rather than a woman who'd recently escaped the local asylum. Perhaps we'd hold hands. Perhaps we'd have sex in the sand dunes! Calm down, Lil, I told myself, this is a hypothetical situation.

'I don't know the beaches of Norfolk,' went on Max, doing his lopsided smile again. 'You'll have to show me.'

My stomach flipped so hard this time I was nearly sick on the table, but I managed to claw it back. 'Sure,' I said, trying to keep my voice steady. 'Do you go home much then?'

Max puffed out his cheeks as he exhaled. 'Not as much as I'd like, but then I'm away a lot. You?'

I nodded. 'Yeah, quite a bit. It's home. And I went back for a while after, er, the break-up and everything.'

Max took one of my hands from my lap in his and shook his head, looking at me with a mock-serious expression. 'Nope, I told you, no exes. We're having a good time. Let's not ruin it.'

'OK, deal,' I said, feeling his fingers curled over mine, hoping that my palms didn't start sweating again.

And it was nice. More than nice. It was wonderful, actually, sitting, gently flirting with one another. It was the kind of date you never wanted to end, and I tried to bottle every minute in my head (after the first half hour was over), so I could go over it again and again the next day. To luxuriate in the pleasure at having met someone who made me feel this giddy. I'd always inwardly cursed any of my girlfriends when they talked excitedly about meeting someone new and having 'a spark'. I often wanted to suggest they save it for a soppy card and not subject the rest of us to their Hallmark ideas of romance. But there was… something here. I felt it.

'Can I kiss you?' Max said, shortly afterwards, having shifted closer to me when the waitress took our plates away. I nodded, even though I was worried that I had red wine teeth and a tongue that tasted of cheese. He gently reached out and put his hand behind my head, pulling me to him. His beard tickled my chin. It was softer than I'd expected. And you know that kiss in *The Notebook*? On that boat jetty in the rain? In my head, the kiss with Max looked a bit like *The Notebook* kiss. A proper, steamy, full-on-the-mouth snog. In reality, it probably looked a good deal less romantic, given all the vodka and wine. But I didn't care. Look at me! I was out on a Saturday night kissing a man like a normal person instead of crying on my sofa! I pulled back after a few moments, though, aware that we were in a public space and people might be trying to enjoy their dinner around us.

'You want to get out of here?' he said, his hand still on the back of my head.

'Sure. To where?'

'My place?'

I didn't hesitate, even though this was a man I'd known for less than five hours. I just had a sense that it would be all right. Murderers have eyes that are too close together and matted hair. Or no hair. Max had thick hair that I wanted to run my hands through, and a collared shirt. Murderers didn't wear collared shirts.

'Cool,' I replied.

As we stood on the pavement outside the pub minutes later, I felt less confident, as if I was about to lose my virginity again. I could just about remember which bit went where. But what if Max was into something weird? What if he wanted me to talk dirty? I couldn't do that first time. I didn't even know his surname. Or, what if he wanted me to put my finger in his bottom? I wasn't into that.

'Lil?' Max was standing by a black cab, holding the door open for me.

'Oh great, sorry, was just… thinking,' I said, jumping in the taxi.

'Hampstead, please,' Max said to the driver. 'East Heath Road.'

The cabbie pulled out and I fell back against the seat as Max put a hand on my leg. It made my stomach flip again. I don't want to say 'I felt something inside me stir,' because that would be embarrassing. But I did feel something I hadn't for several months, or longer, if I was honest with myself, as happiness unfurled itself underneath my ribcage. I put my hand over Max's and gently ran my fingers over it. Then he drew me in for another kiss, more urgent than the last, his mouth pressing hard against mine as he ran his hand up my thigh.

'I'm glad I messaged you,' he said, pulling back, but remaining inches from my face.

'Me too,' I said back. I nearly added 'Just please don't murder me,' but I decided it would kill the vibe.